Basikasingo

John Matthews is a young British writer. He has
worked as a journalist and in the diamond
business, but now writes full-time. He is
presently at work on his second novel.

Basikasingo

John Matthews

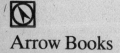

Arrow Books

Arrow Books Limited
17–19 Conway Street, London W1P 5HL

An imprint of the Hutchinson Publishing Group

London Melbourne Sydney Auckland
Johannesburg and agencies
throughout the world

First published 1982

Set in Linoterm Times by
Book Economy Services, Cuckfield, Sussex

Made and printed in Great Britain by
The Anchor Press Ltd, Tiptree, Essex

ISBN 0 09 927570 8

For Marilyn; through both innocence and understanding.

O Conspiracy,
Sham'st thou to show thy dangerous brow
by night,
When evils are most free.

– William Shakespeare

Contents

PROLOGUE

The grey canister was loaded deep into the base of its chamber. A powerful spring hurtled it high into the air, and for a moment, at its peak, everything seemed to be suspended. When it landed and exploded, reality returned – a heavy mass of black people reeled away from the sudden, billowing white clouds of tear-gas. Some on the edge of the group were already running from the advancing police, glancing back at intervals and breaking their frantic stride only to judge the fate of those behind them. The air was filled with screams of anguish, frustration, hate and rebellion. But above all, coming at intervals and more profound in their delivery, were screams of fear and pain. The harsh yet calm voices that broke through the wild cacophony were those of the police; ordering, directing and amassing their forces into one collectively strategic body to either quell or crush the people before them.

The street was wide, a stretch of dark tarmac separating broad expanses of paving stone – white slabbing merging into towering office blocks of matching concrete, broken only by parallel sections of steel and glass. Already strewn across the tarmac and pavement that the sprawling mass had left behind was the debris of conflict, the remnants of political dissatisfaction.

Moving slowly, something appeared to be breaking the mass at its front lines. The crowd parted in two unequal groups and then spread outwards. The break in the line spread downwards towards the police, and then those in the distance appeared to be forming back together in one solid running block. The grey top of a police Land Rover was now clearly visible, and as the last thin band of people split up in its path, it trailed quickly away from the mob.

It slowed down approaching the police ranks and then, making its way through a gap left by them, speeded up again. The vehicle attracted no more than cursory attention from the security forces, for it obviously had a purpose and a destination. During the riots, that was not unusual. Each police group had its specific instructions and small mobile forces were being used to deal with looting.

The Land Rover picked its way through the bricks and broken glass and stopped outside a fourteen-storey office building. The last batches of riot police were over a quarter of a mile away and rapidly becoming more distant as the frantic mob picked up pace. Some minutes later only sporadic bursts of rifle fire and distant shouts and screams remained to signal their presence.

Out of the back of the Land Rover came six uniformed men. Unlike their riot-police colleagues, they carried automatic rifles: Armalite AR-18 military issue. The driver and front passenger carried automatic handguns. In his other hand the driver carried a large black leather bag.

All eight men, the two from the front taking the lead, walked swiftly towards the main entrance of the office building. One, appearing to know his way, led them through the swing doors and across a broad expanse of dark marble until they approached a security guard standing by a door to one side of the foyer. He stood puzzled and alone, one employee not allowed to vacate the premises during rioting.

He forced a smile of acknowledgement as the eight uniformed figures came closer, and then suddenly his expression changed. There was something wrong and that unexpected realization froze him momentarily, the instinct of five years' security training suddenly at work. He had never visualized it to be this way, but suddenly it was, and he was reaching for his gun because that's what the manual told him to do. Never in his wildest imagination had he dreamt this would be the way it would happen. And then automatically his mind was slipping back into gear and his gun was out from its holster. There was only one surprise left for him.

The third man in the approaching group stepped to one side, and with his rifle held waist high, eased the trigger. Bursts of gunfire came like an avalanche of boulders on a corrugated iron roof, a spread of them picking up the security guard by his stomach, smashing him helplessly back into the wall.

As the echoes died down the man at the front leant over the body. He tugged at a set of keys attached by a chain to the guard's pocket and, snapping the steel loops, bundled the chain and the keys into the palm of his well-manicured right hand.

He stood up thoughtfully, pulling the peak of his police cap sharply down on to the bridge of his nose, then turned his attention to the small door to one side of the corpse. Insignificant enough, it appeared to be the door to a broom cupboard. He selected a key and opened the door. The room was no more than eight feet long and four feet wide, and there were boxes and crates stacked to one side, confirming the image of a storage area. Halfway up on the side wall was a small metal box. He moved towards it.

He already had a small key, picked out from the bunch, which he inserted into the lock on the front panel of the box, opening the metal flap. Exposed was a unit resembling a calculator, but with a much larger opaque glass display screen and push-button area. The digits ran only from one to nine and the red plastic numbers were as large as those on a push-button telephone. The second man, still clutching his black bag, was beckoned into the room.

Using his left hand, the man at the front punched in a series of seven digits. He constantly referred to a small booklet held in front of him by the second man. There were few words spoken. The completion of the keyed-in digits was signalled by a faint buzzing from the metal box and, as the sound died, he purposefully pressed the four fingertips of his right hand on to the opaque glass area.

There was another buzzing sound and then the wall at the

back began to move. Slowly and silently it slid across. Through the opening a six-foot-square platform could be seen with a staircase leading directly down from it at a right angle. Six of the men made their way through on to the platform, and the third man, turning from the group, pressed a large red button on the wall to one side of the gap. The wall section slid back into place, insulating them from the small room and the marble foyer.

Beyond the stairwell was an oblong area leading into a much longer corridor which ran off at a sharp tangent. At the end of that forty-foot expanse stood two guards. They had heard the shooting above, but then there *was* a riot going on and shooting had been expected. With the noise muffled by the connecting doors it had been hard to judge its direction, and their diminishing conversation centred on just how long the riot would actually last. The electronic door they guarded led to a large office occupying an area directly beneath the central section of the building's foyer. Beyond that, and protected by another electronic door, was a slightly smaller room, dwarfed only by comparison with the large vault on its far wall.

In the large office adjoining sat the vault's chief examiner, marking off items on a long list as one of his assistants in the vault called each one out. The connecting door between the two rooms was open. At first, he heard only faint, muffled sounds coming from the steel door leading to the corridor. Then, in sudden contrast, the door opened and a hail of bullets propelled the guard across the width of the room. Through the gap of the door he could just make out the corpse of another guard on the other side.

In his scholarly way he stood up to object to the intrusion. He pressed the button which sealed the vault door and then the alarm in virtually the same motion. He saw the first man approaching raise a revolver, and he heard the shots only faintly above the constant whining of the alarm. But the two jolts to his body had come earlier; one to his stomach and then another to his shoulder as he fell backwards and down. Then everything went dark. . . .

Some time later, he was aware of footsteps at his side, and some voices. He wasn't sure exactly how long had passed, only that the door to the vault was closed again, its control panel smashed from the wall. One of the last men to pass kicked him, and then he felt some warm spittle strike him on one cheek.

The six men made their way swiftly along the corridor and back up the stairwell. The last door was opened and its control box smashed, as with the other. The last two men were collected, and the eight, walking hurriedly, made their way back across the foyer.

Uncharacteristically, the first man lagged behind. Of all the men, he knew there was no haste; there would be no more problems. Pacing the cool marble, back through the glass doors and across the wide pavement towards the Land Rover, he smiled. Then he peeled off what appeared to be a surgical glove from his right hand, taking special care with the four fingertips.

And he thought of Leon. And Joachim.

All sounds, however faint, had disappeared, and at last it seemed safe to move. With what felt like his last effort, the old examiner wiped the spittle from his cheek. He realized the futility of his action – with a smashed shoulder and stomach it was perhaps not so important. Those of his type had never got used to degradation. The bullet wounds were acceptable, but someone else's spittle was out of the question. But there were other things to be done, he thought. For the moment all pride must be forgotten.

He lifted his cheek hesitantly from the carpet, unsure of what sensations of pain the movement would bring. He felt a deep churning from inside. For the third time his stomach tried to reject the ragged shell lodged in its sensitive lining. He raised himself up on to one elbow. From his position, he could just see the straggled corpse of the security guard at the far end of the room. He glanced at the steel block leading to the vault. There was no other choice. He would have to do it; there was nobody else. He only prayed that he could reach the telephone on his desk. His vision blurred, not focusing on his hand stretching for the cradle. Curiously, there was little feeling in his arm, or sense of direction.

There wasn't much time, but there were other things equally as important on his mind: that the first man, who appeared in charge, spoke in an unrecognizable foreign language; that the second man carried a black leather bag into which the vault's contents were probably emptied; that the third man was abnormally large, and that the fourth was wounded – probably by one of the guards on entry. He scanned his memory for any other relevant details, and then his last thought warned him that all was rapidly sinking into oblivion. He jabbed again at the receiver. With an ungainly movement, he pulled the entire phone off the desk. After some tapping he got a line.

He started dialling.

The telephone rang in a large room adorned with expensive and tasteful antiques. A black servant in a starched white uniform turned from his polishing and, crossing the thick Persian carpet, picked up the receiver. His customary greeting was a rich and polished Oxford English.

He nodded, informed the caller that they should wait one moment, and placed the receiver down at the telephone's side. He stood, puzzled and undecided for a moment, turned to the door behind him, and paused in doubt before opening it. A decision made, the door led him into a wide Regency-style hallway. He headed straight across it towards a set of wide marble steps on the far side. At the top of the four steps, the contrast was absolute. The room was a large and modern glass enclosure. At its centre was a Roman-style swimming pool, and dotted around the edge of the glass framework was a wide variety of luxuriant tropical foliage. The furniture, to a large extent, was white wicker.

The man seated in the wide chaise-longue was not particularly tall; his hair was thinning slightly and he was fighting off late middle-age. The quiet power and dominance he exuded was evident by the way in which the rapidly approaching black servant addressed him. Some initial concern was shown, his expression quickly relaxed, and then he lifted the white phone at his side as the servant made his exit.

A moment later an insignificant click told him that the receiver on the connecting extension had been replaced. He made his introduction, but there was no response. He waited a moment, adjusting to the silence at the other end, and spoke again. Again there was no answer. There was a faint sound, but just as quickly it was gone. Only some interference remained. He made to place the receiver back. There was a sound through the earpiece that could have been a crackle. Something told him it sounded more like a cough. Bringing the receiver back, he repeated the name of the man he expected to hear at the other end.

There was no answer, but now there was certainly an apparent sound. Finally he recognized a faint and barely discernible noise.

It was the sound of somebody breathing.

Part One

Basikasingo

1

Thursday 19 August 1976 continued the saga of the hottest English summer ever recorded, the doggedly persistent sunshine parching the normally rich pastures of southern England to a fading, corn-coloured landscape.

Richard 'Moby' Cleary steered around another of the characteristically long and gradual curves which meandered from the coast. He was on a slight hill now and could see down into a small valley, a lazy panorama of fields with the gently undulating Sussex hills like dumplings in the distance beyond.

To those who knew them, Moby and Sue sometimes appeared an unlikely couple. He was rotund, almost obese; she was slim and blonde, and in a poor light looked quite youthful, a tinge of silver-grey hair and a few sun-worn lines being the only testament to approaching middle-age.

Moby's lips were dry with the heat and he lightly moistened them with his tongue, as if to ease the passage of the thick American drawl which sprang from the back of his throat.

'Jesus,' he muttered. 'Whatever happened to the green, green grass of home?'

Sue appeared curiously unmoved, although through the past years she had become used to such comments; invariably, no answer was required. Now, with the tension of the last few hours, silence seemed appropriate.

It was the same tension that spurred the opposite reaction in Moby, some forced distraction from his most pressing thoughts, however inconsequential. He lifted his arm in a deliberate motion.

'Great, there's plenty of time,' he affirmed. 'London by

two-thirty, three.' He remembered as a vague afterthought that their schedule before boarding had seemed a lot tighter. 'What do you make it, Sue?'

They were passing beneath a long line of trees which overshadowed the road, and the intermittent flashing of sunlight picked out the sheen of her hair as she looked down.

'Just one forty-five,' she offered, turning back pointedly.

'Are you sure?' he asked, allowing the first edge of concern in his voice.

Sue looked again at her watch. 'It was okay by the clock on the boat.'

'Shit! That means the damn thing's stopped,' Moby exclaimed, spitting the words into the windscreen.

'What have you got then?' Sue enquired.

'Oh, it doesn't matter.'

Moby shook his wrist. His watch was a square-faced digital model with a constant quartz display and the numbers stayed in position as if in defiance.

'Would you believe it, the fucking thing's jammed. You buy a Japanese watch 'cause you hear the bastards are working hard and turning out some good stuff, and then you get this shit.'

Moby rattled his wrist more violently, but still in vain. 'You know, if it wasn't for us after the war, the Japanese wouldn't even know how to wipe their own asses. We taught 'em everything, and then they go and swing the goddam thing around on us by serving up crap.'

Sue returned to her silence. It was one of his more familiar traits: he always made a scene about something small going wrong, but when it came to a real crisis he was usually speechless. In fact, it was the big crises that really perplexed him, but he couldn't deal with them verbally, so he would let them build up inside and then would let off steam over something small, or at least not quite so important. If confronted with that diagnosis, he would claim that he wasn't really upset, but things like that just 'bugged' him, although Sue had never quite managed to work out the subtle different between the two. She felt that now he looked even more perplexed than usual, even taking into account the worries and frustrations of the past weeks. Sweat beads massed on his forehead, and large wet patches were obvious under his armpits and in the centre of the open-neck shirt which covered his large frame and hung loosely over his trouser waistband.

All the car windows were open and the cool-air blaster whirred away at full pelt, but somehow it still wasn't cool enough. Sue would have thought that Moby's profuse perspiration was caused by the heat, but as she looked across at him, it was something else that showed in his face; a look of confused worry, almost fear. His eyes never left the road except for furtive, hurried glances into the rear-view mirror; an obsession that seemed to be growing with the passing miles.

'What's wrong?' she queried.

'Nothing's wrong for God's sake.'

This time she looked more intently at him. 'You definitely look upset over something.'

'It's just the timing, Sue. That watch has thrown me right off track. I wanted to get you booked into a hotel when we got to London and have a quick freshen-up before my meeting at four.' He glanced again at his broken watch, as if in confirmation.

'We've got plenty of time to make it,' Sue remarked.

'I know that we'll make it, Sue, but it means that I've got to be rushing my ass off.'

For a brief moment afterwards, he was aware of the sudden edge in his voice, and something else – the mention of *speed* bringing back an earlier concern, his eyes flickering nervously towards the rear-view mirror. He could see it clearer now: a black Granada, too distant to make out the occupants, but staying with them steadily, just within vision on a long stretch. He eased down on the pedal and gained a bit more distance, satisfying himself after a moment that they were sufficiently out of view, then settling back again.

He suddenly became conscious that he had been tapping

impatiently at the wheel and stopped the motion abruptly, wondering, at the same time, exactly how long it had been now: Angola in March '75, South Africa in July '76, and then Paris just a few days beforehand to pick up the final lead. God, for almost two years they had been 'out in the field', as Langley liked to phrase it.

There had been a change of directors in that period, he reflected: William E. Colby to George Bush, and if it hadn't been for Bush's decision to leave a 'sleeper' in Angola after the Russian-backed MPLA takeover, he'd have been out of there long beforehand. Even then, he suspected that the decision to pull him out of Angola had been more because of the urgency of the South African situation – and a question of available staff – than anything else. And now, in the final analysis, there was a piece of paper, a *small* piece of paper with a single African word on it.

'What's so interesting in the mirror?' Sue looked over at him.

'Just a car,' he said. 'We left it behind for a while, but it's back with us again now.'

'How long have you noticed it for?'

'About the last ten, fifteen minutes.'

'Come on, don't be so stupid,' Sue said sharply. 'This is a main road, and you're worried because a car is behind us for ten minutes or so. Calm down, for God's sake.'

'I don't know. I don't know,' he muttered. 'There's two men in the front, I can just make 'em out now. But it's probably nothing.'

'I just don't think that every damn carload of people heading for London is automatically going to be following *us*.'

'I told you, I don't know for Chrissakes,' Moby snapped, and glared at her. 'Why don't you concern yourself more with your end of things. We'll have to file in for another set of papers soon.'

It was an uncomfortable reminder, and Sue stared out blankly across the undulating hills to one side. How long could they live as Langley's marionettes, she thought. In Angola, it had been Mr and Mrs Bailey, in South Africa the Claydons; from there to Paris the identities had been lost, reverting back to their real names. It seemed ironic, she considered, that Langley saw fit to present them to the world as husband and wife, and yet in real life the closest they could lay claim to was common-law. And through it all – the changes of name, the constant living out of suitcases, the small wars of tension – there were memories, although somehow *one* always appeared more prominent than all the rest: Moby's final return from a 'delayed' assignment with Ken Holden, Istanbul station chief, and the cold, empty feeling when she'd touched the strange, almost sunken scars on his abdomen that same night, as she lay in bed beside him.

It was shortly afterwards that the agency had started sending him on quieter missions, and her own papers had been upgraded. Admittedly, she thought, Moby's subtlety of thought had increased with age, and in that way he was more suited to diplomacy. But at the same time, she knew that some small part of his inner nerve had been weakened by that one incident and it was that factor, above all else, that had worried her most about South Africa. It had started with all the earmarks of a fact-finding mission but more and more, practically by the day, events had become more tense, building one upon the other.

And now what? she thought, clenching a fist to one side: a one-hour meeting in London and the whole thing became just another file, along with all the other files that the last nine years represented.

The next thing that Sue became aware of was the sudden surge of acceleration, and her thoughts were broken abruptly.

'What is it?' she quizzed.

'The same car. But I can't tell yet,' Moby mumbled hesitantly, wiping his forehead with a shirt-sleeve. 'Somethin's not kosher, that's for sure.'

Moby kept his eyes fixed to the rear-view mirror as he

pressed down harder on the accelerator. Eighty yards ahead he could see the road widening out to a long, flat stretch, and he checked their speed: fifty, sixty, seventy; they were picking up steadily.

Moby flicked another glance in the mirror and then, with a look of disbelief on his face, continued to check the mirror intermittently, fighting to measure distance. Involuntarily, he felt the muscles tighten at his temple. Shit, they were still the same distance behind, he cursed to himself.

The two men in the front were much clearer now. Both were wearing suits, one grey, one dark; and the driver, who was wearing the grey suit, sported a dark moustache. There was also a figure in the back, he could just make out now, but it was too shadowed to pick out any detail. They were closing on him.

'Jesus,' Moby hissed under his breath as he looked down at his speedometer just topping seventy.

There *was* something to it, his mind raced, and he started checking for possible angles of fire; the left-hand passenger side and the back were both equally as likely.

Sue saw Moby's fevered expression, and swung round to see the Granada hanging on their tail.

'Get down!' Moby screamed.

Sue brought her head down and hunched by the dashboard.

Suddenly, the Granada swung out from behind them.

'For God's sake,' Moby stammered aimlessly, and he felt a shiver rise from the base of his spine as the Granada edged up closer, the 'rush' of its engine flooding in through the open windows.

For a moment, everything appeared suspended. He could see Sue flipping open the glove compartment, and the matt-grey butt of the ·38 standard-issue revolver nestled inside. The Granada was almost parallel with them and he could see clearly inside, the front passenger looking over at them with mild curiosity.

In the same instant, the back passenger was startlingly

apparent, and Moby felt the cold rise still further: it was an old lady, wearing a small dark pill-box hat with a black veil. Sue had thrust the gun into his hand, but he held it loosely, aware of his palm sweating on the grip as he remained transfixed: the old lady's mottled and wrinkled skin appeared so close that for a moment he felt he could almost reach out and touch her.

Just as quickly they were past.

Moby swallowed hard and eased back on the pedal. He lowered the gun slowly, finally resting it by the handbrake on the centre partition.

'Did you see that?' he muttered uncertainly; he tried to ease the sickness in his stomach, slowly forcing a more positive tone into his voice. 'There was an old lady in the back.'

'I'm sorry,' Sue retorted, 'I missed that from where I was sitting. What was she holding – a machine-gun or a cannon?'

'You must admit, for a moment it looked unusual.'

Sue straightened up in her seat, and immediately she was annoyed at herself for having made the comment; there was a growing intensity to Moby's expression that suddenly clouded all else.

'Yes, I know. Anyway, no harm done,' she placated him warmly, and she leant over and kissed him lightly on one cheek.

Moby mellowed after a moment. 'All the same, you should have seen the look on that old lady's face, honey. It was a picture. I think she just caught sight of the gun as they went past.'

'Maybe you could wave it at the next old lady that passes,' she said. 'Just for my benefit.'

'The gun, you mean?'

'What else?' Sue lowered her eyelids in mock coyness, enjoying the sudden change in mood.

The Granada was far ahead now, only just visible on a long stretch.

As far back as she could remember, there had always been a constant yet subdued fear, punctuated by humour, or anger, or sorrow, or whatever emotions they could cling to for some balance; an ever-elusive normality.

It was at times like this that she felt most protective towards Moby. At heart he was still the Mid-Western farmboy, 'with all the inherent hang-ups and prejudices that could possibly be dumped on any *nouveau* middle-class American', she recalled from Ken Holden, in one of their many heated debates on racial equality. She was the city girl from Baltimore, tough-skinned and street-wise, and in Moby's eyes, 'far too opinionated for a woman.'

Still, she thought, whatever the imbalances, there was at last a compensation in sight. Moby was coming up for a 'C' transfer within the year, and would be able to secure a desk job either in Langley or Washington. There had been no place for children in their globe-trotting life so far, and she blamed their postponement of marriage mostly on that factor. But soon it would all be different. Of late, it was the one thing that had increased her concern. They had something to live for now, something to look forward to.

The Second *Arrondissement* in Paris is one of the darkest quarters of that city at night. In the daytime it is a fast-paced, vibrant business district. But at night shutters are drawn and the only lights are those of the main thorough-fares and a few of the large office towers signifying a spark of residual life that would re-awaken at 8 a.m. the next morning.

The small network of avenues interlacing the Palais de la Bourse – the French Stock Exchange – and the Place des Victoires is the darkest of all. Streetlamps are sparse, and in many of the streets shop-fronts and offices are buried deep under archways built during the reign of Louis XVI, and now preserved as much as the new purpose of the area allows. The archways are cream-coloured and, in places, crumbling, but in shallow light they appear grey, sometimes black. Now, in the deepest part of the night, they seemed somehow foreboding, cavernous, silent.

Malusi Ugbaja kept as close to the buildings as possible,

merging with the heaviest shadows along the long line of archways. His skin was ebony black and the heavy shades of his suit, shirt and tie completed his submergence into the darkness. He was a very large man, his features full-blown and heavy. In his right hand he carried an attaché case, further enhancing his appearance as an office employee kept late, or one of the shift-work computer personnel of the area. As with them, the case contained the tools of his profession.

The Wagon-Lit agency was half-way down the small street, and Ugbaja eased his pace as he came close to the doorway. He set the case down carefully, and then stood still for a moment, listening to the sounds of the street. There was a dog barking somewhere in the distance, and some faint traffic noises, but nothing more.

Ugbaja brought his eyes back to the door. It was as he'd thought: a 'tumbler' and two mortice locks. Although he'd dealt with the same type before, he was no expert; it would take some time. He snapped the attaché case open.

Inside were only two items: a 9mm Luger automatic with a silencer and a set of cloth-bound tools. Ugbaja snuggled the gun into his trouser waistband and set to work quickly with the tools.

His appearance at the agency earlier in the day had passed unnoticed. He seemed just another of Europe's large population of Westernized Africans. In many ways he considered himself very much an 'international' man, but his original heritage was far away, buried along with that of many other Ovambo tribesmen, deep in the heart of South-west Africa. Now, in the stillness of the Paris night, there was only one thing that still connected him with that heritage: a short iron-bladed hatchet fitted snugly into a leather pouch under his jacket. It was a souvenir from the many 'faction fights' of his youth, and the carved wooden handle depicted an ancient Ovambo village scene.

It was a heritage that Ugbaja knew had now been almost totally corrupted and perverted, and primarily he blamed European whites: first the Germans, and then their Dutch and English counterparts. A hundred years of all but constant subjugation. Now he would play in their world, the most final game they knew.

The last latch clicked free, and Ugbaja concentrated sharply on both locks, alternating from one to the other. After a moment, he could just discern a faint glimmer in the door crevice a few feet from the ground, and his earlier assessment was confirmed; there was a contact alarm fitted just above one of the mortice locks. He took out a copper strip, bent it double, and inserted it between the metal joints. As he eased the door open a fraction, the copper strip sprang outwards, keeping the connection. Then he took a length of copper wire from his pocket, squeezed a small amount of liquid solder on each end, and applied it to the two contacts. Within a minute it had dried, and he opened the door slowly, stepped over the wire, and closed it firmly behind him.

It took a moment for his eyes to become adjusted to the room. Then the previous familiarity of the layout became apparent: there was a long, counter-like desk facing him, forming an L-shape, and to the right a bank of shelving containing holiday brochures. But it was the two cupboards set in a small alcove at the back of the room that took his attention immediately, and he moved towards them. He found the electricity meters in the top cupboard and promptly switched off the main power supply. There were probably no other alarms, he decided, but best to play safe.

Ugbaja went to work quickly on the filing cabinets to one side, leafing through the letters of the alphabet. He stopped first at C: nothing there; he flicked onwards hastily, stopping again at H. At that instant he paused. There were some footsteps from further up the road; but he had almost found it now, he spurred himself, aware of the footsteps getting ever closer . . . Harquot, Havre . . . it was there, under Helmcken: Susan Helmcken and Richard Cleary. He made a quick mental note of the file details, edging down below the counter top as the footsteps became more ominous, pressing.

They were still a good ten yards away or so, but the echoes from the archway made them seem more imminent. As the sounds approached the shop-front, they slowed slightly, and then there was a faint shuffling.

Ugbaja heard a mumbled, 'Alors,' followed by something indiscernible. Below the desk-counter to one side was a small gap, and Ugbaja eased down further, looking out from underneath. He could just make out dark blue trousers over black shoes, and he cursed himself for being so clumsy; the copper strip was still lying on the ground outside and a part of the copper wire was probably just visible. The figure was crouching, pushing the door open, and there was no longer any doubt; the flat, cross-lined gendarme cap was clearly discernible. A penlight flickered on the ground as the door gap widened then advanced quickly to the back wall, effecting a hasty semi-circle in each direction.

Ugbaja jerked his head back sharply, but he could still tell that the gendarme was coming in closer by the growing intensity of the light beam on the far wall. The beam moved across and stopped for a moment on the open filing cabinet then swung around, taking in the other cabinets and the safe, and returned to the same point. The circle of light grew stronger on the grey metal of the cabinet, and Ugbaja stole his hand inside his jacket, tentatively gripping the carved wooden handle of his hatchet. No doubt the gendarme would be armed, but silence would also be a factor: another local gendarme patrol or a vigilant local citizen, both were potential dangers. For a moment he hoped the gendarme would turn back, it would save possible complications; but by then he could sense the movements coming close to the partition at one side.

The commitment was made, all hesitation forgotten.

Ugbaja tensed himself sharply, coming up from behind the gendarme in one motion, a faint scything of the air the only warning.

The blow came to the side of the gendarme's head as he started to turn, splitting his flat cap and his skull in one, and

31

he fell to his knees, the penlight slipping slowly from his grip. A second blow came quickly to the side of his neck and he was laid out full length, staring up into the darkness. Ugbaja laid his hand softly over the gendarme's mouth, muting whatever faint sounds remained.

In that moment the gendarme saw his attacker for the first time: a dark and florid countenance, the eyes bulging and distended.

Ugbaja brought the hatchet down for a third time, severing the gendarme's neck totally. For a few seconds afterwards he settled back, allowing the adrenalin to subside. Then he wiped the hatchet blade on the thick blue serge of the gendarme's uniform.

Within minutes, he had slipped back into the night.

A heat haze hung low in the dip of the road ahead, and Moby adjusted his eyes to the shimmering air. The marker cones appeared first, a neat row of orange dots between tall evergreens two hundred yards away, sectioning off one lane as it swung into a narrow curve.

Slowing gradually, Moby noticed a large red stop sign heralding the start of the roadworks turned in his direction and he pressed down on the brake.

'Did you see that, honey?'

'What?' Sue responded blandly.

'That guy sees me coming, and then turns the sign our way. Of course, I'm supposin' he knows one end of that damn thing from the other.'

Moby had drawn to a halt now. He looked at the workman standing by the stop sign, who had his shirt off and was turned sideways, looking back up the road ahead of them, his body glistening with sweat in the intense sunlight. He could see another three men clustered together, talking feverishly to each other. As far as he could make out they'd sectioned off about three hundred yards of the road ahead.

Moby was bristling. 'Would you believe it, not one damn car coming, and we're sittin' here like a couple of baked potatoes.'

32

Moby looked again at the man holding the stop sign, who this time had turned to face them. Then he looked closer, focusing with renewed intent on the man's right shoulder. Just below the collar-bone was a ragged yet rounded scar; it wasn't exactly the same as the three in his stomach but close enough not to be mistaken. Moby's brain raced; a workman with a bullet wound? He looked feverishly at the two men further up the road; they weren't working. He could see a shovel there, but where was the digging? There were plenty of marker cones but no roadworks. Moby stared back at the man by the stop sign. How much longer? he asked himself, tapping his fingers impatiently on the steering wheel. Still no traffic had come the other way.

It was then that he saw the Granada again, just within view in his mirror; the same black Granada that had passed them earlier, edging closer rapidly. Moby's eyes flashed nervously to the man by the stop sign, then back to the mirror. There was the question of the old lady in the back, but then again he'd seen too many professional face masks to be fooled. And, he recalled, the dark veiling would have further shielded the cosmetician's handiwork. . . . *How convenient!* There had been a couple of turn-offs and a garage since they had passed him, but then the coincidences were too many: marker cones and no roadworks. Men not working, and a man with a bullet wound holding a stop sign! . . . *And now the Granada again!* The messages were clear.

With a quick jerk of the wheel, Moby swung the car out from in front of the stop sign and jammed down hard on the pedal. The bonnet lifted sharply as he picked up speed past the marker cones.

Sue screamed at him. 'What the hell?'

'It's a. . . . '

Moby was about to say 'trap', when the staccato, machine-gun hammering deafened him, pouring suddenly through the open window. Moby instinctively ducked slightly, and then his eyes started scanning the car. . . . *The bullet marks. . . . Where the hell?* He looked quickly in the

33

rear-view mirror. The fading image of a pneumatic drill crashed into his mind, and in that split-second he questioned his reasoning; but his rational thinking was disarranged, fractured. He checked his speedo: the needle flickered around sixty. It was then that he noticed the three men waving their arms, almost thirty yards ahead of him. They weren't waving at Moby though; it was something to his left but directly ahead, behind the roadside trees. By now he was totally confused. Who are these people? .... Who the hell are they waving at?

The back end of the answer was only ten yards ahead when it roared out of the trees and on to the road in a cloud of dust. The giant caterpillar was only five yards away by the time that its huge carcass had shifted sufficiently to block the road. In that short space, Moby had miraculously cut their speed from sixty to forty-five.

He heard Sue screaming at the last moment as the large yellow frame of the caterpillar filled the windshield. The noise of Sue's screaming was intermingled with shouts from the three men by the roadside, who by now were holding their arms up in horror. As a last split-second effort, Moby jerked the wheel to the right.

The collision caught the bonnet of the car on the left-hand side, the heavy caterpillar chain jamming under the lid and forcing it back into a crooked vee. At the point of impact, Moby's body assumed the force of a two-ton weight. His heavy frame was flung helplessly forward like a rag doll, his head smashing a hole in the windscreen before coming to rest with his shoulders and chest on the bonnet of the car. Moby's skull was smashed and his neck broken. He died instantaneously.

Sue had kept her seat belt on. She would often remind Moby about wearing a belt, but his size invariably made it difficult. The belt had saved Sue from hitting the wind-screen, but the whiplash had broken her neck. Half of the engine and gearbox had smashed through her legs, breaking them off at the knee. Her body was still alive but her brain had died. For a full two minutes after Sue's brain had lapsed into a coma, her heart pumped blood through her veins and her lungs forced air through her mouth.

The three workmen were still holding their arms up after the collision. A bit of flying glass had reached them, but it was a full minute before they realized the full horror of what had just happened. One of them, stepping from the group, moved towards the wreckage and looked into the car for signs of life. Sue's breathing was so shallow it was barely perceptible.

'I think they're both dead,' said the man by the car.

'Whatever you do, don't move them,' replied the second man.

The third man started running for the phone box. It was hot, and the nearest phone was over a mile away, but he was already over fifty yards from the wreckage before he really thought of how far he had to go.

It was three-forty in the afternoon when Jeffrey Steel passed East Grinstead, weaving his way swiftly along the tree-lined B road towards the accident.

Investigation of the accident had been handled first by the local Sussex Constabulary. From there, all procedure had become, in local police terms, 'un-routine'. Richard Cleary was not classified as a CIA employee, even on his own papers; instead, they identified him as a staff member of the US Defense Department, which warranted notification of the British Defence Intelligence Staff (DIS); a direct information service operated between the two trans-Atlantic counterparts. Susan Helmcken was identified as his secretary, of the same department.

The Sussex Constabulary were obliged to use Scotland Yard as an intermediary, and when the appropriate US Defense Department numbers were fed into the DIS computer, it read: *refer to section 5*. Section 5 was 'Management and Support of Intelligence (Admin.)', who in turn were referred by their file to SIS; and, in a more pertinent sub-section, to MI6. It was then that the details were passed to Jeffrey Steel . . . through Stannard, through Kenton, Steel

35

mused whimsically . . . *proper channels!* The whole process, however elaborate, had taken less than forty minutes.

Steel had expected to see Cleary at 4 p.m., but not under these circumstances. There had been the call from Paris just the day beforehand; something about 'Heathrow, within a week's time'. He tried to recall the exact wording, but couldn't. So much had been left until the meeting: thoughts, facts, assumptions, clues, interpretations. Whatever they could possibly cling to.

As Commander Stannard had said, 'experience will tell', and Steel wondered if that had referred to his own experience in Section A4: South Africa, Botswana, South-west Africa, Rhodesia and Mozambique. It had been only a six-month posting, shortly after transfer from DIS; surely, he thought, the other five 'contact' agents involved hadn't, in turn, been selected because of similar experience. If they had he guessed that to a large extent their 'diamond knowledge', like his, was limited; and yet that's what the postings had entailed, acting as watchdogs in respective world diamond markets: New York, Antwerp, Amsterdam, Tel Aviv and Rio de Janiero. Now, he cursed to himself, whatever progress had been made would probably have been lost. Nonetheless he hoped for something: the name of a contact, an address, or even something more substantial that might have been committed to paper.

In the distance now, Steel could see a group of diversion signs, sectioning off one lane to re-route traffic off the road straight ahead. This is it, he recalled from his earlier instruction. Almost a mile they'd said. Steel strained his eyes for any signs of the accident. The first objects came into view after only a few hundred yards. Even in the intense sunlight, the flashing lights of the police and emergency vehicles could be seen through the heat haze.

The fire-engine was the first in sight, with an emergency vehicle tucked directly in behind, cutting equipment lying forgotten at its side. Beyond them were three police cars, strung out in a line, and then Steel could see the wreckage, sprawled out almost sixty yards ahead, blocking the road.

36

Steel decided to park behind the fire-engine and walk the remaining distance. As he approached, he could see where the marker cones had been moved to allow the emergency vehicles closer access. Steel looked up as he passed the fire-engine. Two men sat high in the cab engrossed in feverish conversation. Two men also sat in the cab of the salvage vehicle, their shirts unbuttoned at the neck and their uniform jackets hanging loosely. One of them peered down as Steel passed, perspiration dripping from his face.

Steel's first thought was that it was all over, and he scanned the length of the road for confirmation. Two unmarked cars came into vision beyond the chain of police cars. Probably plain-clothes or forensic, he considered. Policemen were dotted along the roadside past the wreckage, mostly engaged in interviews with the workmen.

Steel's eyes focused sharply on the wreckage. To one side of the sharply angled bonnet, he could make out the shattered windscreen still in place, except for a football-sized hole on the driver's side. From the same angle he could also see a gaping hole in the passenger side where the emergency cutting equipment had forced its ragged passage.

The full horror of the figures inside took a moment to register, the first image to imprint itself on his mind being that of the woman in the passenger seat. He could see her head flung back at an impossible angle, her face grey and eyes wide open. There was something peculiar about the eyes. Steel concentrated his gaze. There were no pupils in sight, the shock of impact having jolted them back high into their sockets.

His concentration was broken.

'Mr Steel?'

The man confronting him was small – most certainly close to the police requirement's minimum, Steel judged – and he was almost totally bald. His dress appeared unusual for the weather: a heavy tweed suit, a woollen tie over a crisp white shirt, and brogues. Whether because of his heavy dress or not, his face bore a distinctly ruddy complexion.

'Inspector Mallinder,' he smiled, advancing a few more

paces. 'Special duties, Sussex Constabulary.'

Steel rarely wore sunglasses, but the sunlight of late had been intense, and he had finally settled for a gold-rimmed tinted pair. Aware that now they might give him an unintentionally mysterious air, he removed them and slipped them into his shirt pocket. 'So you're the chap they've taken from Gatwick for this little one, are you?'

For a moment they indulged in the trite formalities of duties and protocols, then Steel produced a small card from his side pocket: a series of eight numbers on the card had been quoted to Mallinder immediately before, as part of the normal SIS identity confirmation process.

'That seems to be in order,' Mallinder said at length. 'We might as well get started. There'll obviously be a fair few details to cover.'

They turned and walked closer to the wreckage. Steel had pushed the image away before, but now it was hard to ignore: where the passenger's legs had been a mass of matted flesh and blood spread like a thick skin between the seat and the carpet, the bones beneath bared in parts. Steel felt a sour bile rising at the back of his throat and tore himself away.

'How long have you been here, Inspector?'

'About half an hour, sir.'

'I see that they've already taken the car door off. Has everything been taken out as instructed?'

'Yes, sir. There were three suitcases in the boot of the car. Two contained items of clothing, and the third case, which was much smaller, contained a variety of shaving articles, cosmetics and a few bottles of spirits and wine.'

'Has an inventory been made as yet?'

'One of the lads has just completed it, I understand. I'll check with him.'

'There was also a request that you search all clothing found in the car for any loose articles there might be in the pockets. Has that been done also?'

'All loose articles found in the car apart from clothes, cosmetics, toiletries and alcohol have been placed in bag

"A" over there, sir.' Mallinder nodded to one side, towards the line of police cars. 'As for the inside compartment of the car, all loose articles from there have been placed in bag "B".'

Steel walked across, following Mallinder's indication. Both polythene bags rested against the wheel of the first police car. He picked up bag 'A' first.

'Could you pass me some gloves please, Inspector?'

Steel raised the bag slightly and looked through the polythene: assorted pens, holiday pamphlets, cards and a box of ammunition were immediately obvious. Then he used the gloves which Mallinder produced from one of the police cars to rummage at the bottom: receipts, tickets, and a button, but nothing of great interest. He decided as an afterthought that some of the pamphlets and cards might at least give some clues to places that Cleary had visited while in South Africa.

'I'll take this bag if I may Inspector.'

'Certainly,' Mallinder complied. 'There's nothing there we'll be needing.'

'Have your men taken statements from all the workmen here?'

'They're doing that right now, sir. They should be finished quite shortly.'

'Were there any other witnesses?'

Mallinder's expression clouded faintly. 'Yes, some people on their way to a family bereavement. We couldn't hold them up for long, so we took their statement first. Apparently they'd overtaken your man further up the road, and said that he was behaving rather oddly. Said that he'd speeded up as they'd tried to pass. Two men and an old lady, it was. Very odd.'

'I see.' Steel studied the disarranged roadworks slowly, shielding his eyes with one hand. He turned back after a moment. 'As far as the statements are concerned, I'd like them in my hands before midday tomorrow, if possible. So if you can have them typewritten and sent by express courier, I'd be much obliged.'

'Of course there are certain procedures to be observed,' Mallinder retorted sharply, and for a second his face appeared more ruddy.

There was an officiousness about Mallinder that Steel found irritating, but for the moment he let it pass.

'Just you do your best.' He forced a grin, then turned away again. 'Tell me, Inspector, apart from loose articles that you've taken from the inside of the car, has anything else been moved?'

'Yes, sir. The man's body was moved so that his wallet could be extracted for the purpose of identification.'

'Was anything else disturbed?'

'No, that was it. As soon as the man's identity was discovered, we proceeded through the normal channels, following which we only carried out instructions received from *your* department.'

Steel looked back towards the wreckage. 'I see. Would you mind showing me the original position of the body, please, Inspector?'

Steel followed Mallinder around to the far side of the wrecked car. At close quarters, Cleary's face appeared dark, somehow ominous, and Steel studied it closer: the hair was matted with blood, which spread in a thick layer down his face and had now coagulated to form a dark maroon mask from his head almost to his shirt collar; the dried blood was cracked in places where the intense heat of the sun had accelerated the drying process.

The stench of the bodies mixed with leaking petrol fumes was now overpowering. Steel stepped back a pace, turning in the opposite direction, trying desperately to let some fresh air into his lungs to quell his rising nausea.

Mallinder was pointing towards the shattered windscreen. 'If you look over here, sir, this was the original position we found the body in.'

Steel looked across, and Mallinder outlined the position more distinctly.

'The body was found with the head and shoulders protruding through this hole in the windscreen. Apparently it was very heavy, and it was quite a job to move back into a sitting position.'

Steel walked away from the car, surveying the length of the road thoughtfully. 'Is there anything you've found, Inspector, that would suggest this was anything other than an accident?'

'No, sir, nothing at all.'

'Was there anything suspicious about the roadworks here?' Steel asked, indicating the re-arranged marker cones.

'No. We checked them out with the Sussex County Council. Everything was as it should have been.'

'Have you checked the car yet?'

'Yes. There were absolutely no signs that the car had been tampered with. I had the mechanic check it over just before you arrived.'

'Could you arrange for a written mechanic's report to be sent to me also, Inspector?' Steel glanced back at the two bodies in the wreckage. 'How about forensic. Have they done their stuff yet?'

'No, I was about to get them cracking when you arrived.'

Steel walked back to the first police car. Mallinder followed. Steel crouched down by the front wheel.

'I hope this one's a bit more exciting than the first.'

Steel picked up the second polythene bag and looked inside. Cleary's gun was the most conspicuous object, lying among various papers, and he fished it out first. He opened the chamber and sniffed. From sight, it was fully loaded and from smell hadn't been fired recently. He snapped the chamber shut and turned his attention back to the polythene bag: road maps, pens, mints, more receipts, a silk scarf, and a diary. Steel picked it out and started flicking through the pages, concentrating on the address section at the back. There were no African addresses at all, and only one English address was apparent, a Master Sergeant at the United States Air Force base in Lakenheath, Suffolk; probably a relation or friend in the services. Steel skipped through the Uncle Harrys, Aunt Mabels and Cecilias in

Washington and Philadelphia, and turned back to the diary section.

June onwards. Damn it, from June the pages were blank, nothing having been listed for the total six-week period in South Africa; the diary itself had probably been sent ahead to Paris along with other personal and agency effects that might have betrayed identity. Steel turned the pages slowly. Entries started appearing from 14 August, but all were the sort of information that could be found in any man's diary: arrangements for the boat trip from Dieppe and times and payments for picking up a car from a Paris garage. Nothing significant at all.

He turned two more pages, and there written in near the top of today's page was the four o'clock appointment that Cleary would never make. Ironically, it had two stars either side of it. Not unusual, Steel thought, that he would make a special note of such an appointment. There was no address, no names or details in the entry, only the time and the word 'London'. Only the stars either side gave it any form of significance.

There was a piece of paper resting against the page opposite the entry, its facing side slightly soiled and obviously well-thumbed. Steel had assumed it to be another receipt or a ticket of some kind, but now, out of mild curiosity, he turned it over. What he saw increased his curiosity. There was only one word on the paper, very long and written in large, bold capitals with a black pen or biro: '*BASIKASINGO*'. What was it? A place? A name? Obviously African, but had it been written down while Cleary was in Africa or on his return to Paris? If it was important, then why write it down at all? Why slip it in this page of all pages? But then the safest place for anything incriminating was in the memory. *Why, for God's sake, why?* Perhaps too unusual to memorize, was that possible?

Steel closed his eyes and, keeping them closed, tried to remember the exact spelling. It was difficult. Steel opened his eyes and looked again. He'd put in a 'b' instead of the 'ng' near the end. He placed the scrap of paper carefully back in its original position and slipped the diary back inside the polythene bag. He rifled through a few final items in the bag with little interest, and then lifted his head.

'Found anything, sir?' Mallinder asked.

'Obviously, if there's anything your department should be made aware of, you'll be informed in due course.' Steel smiled politely and handed Mallinder's gloves back.

He picked up the other polythene bag and turned away, heading back towards his car. Before getting in, he looked back towards Mallinder, who was still standing in the same position, looking faintly exasperated.

'Oh, and don't forget those reports and statement, Inspector. After tomorrow, they will have lost a lot of their validity.'

2

'Pat' Hinchley had been in Scotland Yard's Flying Squad for almost eleven years. He'd started off as a Detective-Constable transferred from the Metropolitan CID, and had worked his way through the ranks to Detective-Inspector. His first assignment in Hatton Garden had been over five years ago now, when a carrier named 'Old Willy' had been coshed and the goods he was carrying on behalf of four or five merchants stolen. 'Old Willy', it transpired, had walked the short street for the last twenty years, with anything from fifty thousand to five hundred thousand pounds' worth of diamonds tucked loosely inside the many folds of his old brown coat, without incident. They were mainly cut gems, although sometimes the main bourse would use him, and Hinchley had only been surprised that the robbery hadn't been committed before; there couldn't possibly be an easier target than an old, unarmed man, and the haul that day had been close to three hundred thousand pounds.

At the time, Hinchley had gained a working knowledge

of the 'Garden', and since then had been called in on other similar cases. Over the years, his 'working knowledge' had become almost incomparable.

It was for these reasons that in late June he had been contacted regarding a 'watchdog' operation in Hatton Garden: Jeffrey Steel of the SIS would co-ordinate, assess and direct; Hinchley and his boys would be the 'leg' men and, from their previous case experience, would advise where necessary.

When the phone rang that morning in Hinchley's Putney flat, he was not surprised to find Jeffrey Steel at the other end.

'There's been a bit of a complication.' Steel paused. 'The information we expected hasn't come through, it seems – but we'll know a lot more tomorrow.'

'What about the meeting?'

'This afternoon now, yesterday was postponed. Even then, it doesn't really give us enough time to sort it all out.'

Hinchley was thoughtful. 'Lost your chap, have you?'

'We never *lose* them. They just get retired – one way or another.'

It was as far as Steel could go, Hinchley sensed, but he appreciated even that small gesture; the few 'security' men he'd worked with previously had been almost completely stonewall.

'Okay, I suppose we'll just have to wait. I'll check with you tomorrow sometime,' he said, and then rang off.

Steel placed the receiver back slowly and sat in silence for a moment, the muted sounds of Park Lane traffic filtering up to his eighth-floor window the only disturbance.

Six weeks, he considered, but then surely their work in Hatton Garden wouldn't be wasted totally. Even at first sight, it had appeared an unusually tight-knit world. Hinchley had told him the story abut the diamond merchant who wouldn't give evidence in a case which involved not only the robbery of his diamond store, but the murder of his own brother, because of a mistrust of *all* outsiders, including the police. And then Steel had seen it for himself, in the long weeks that followed: the blind leading the blind.

Through necessity they had been dealing in vague terms: several million pounds' worth of cut diamonds, ranging from approximately one carat to forty carats; although not only the package but also the individual diamonds could have been split, giving a range of infinite variables. Source: South Africa; but then again, they may have been 'washed' through another market, thereby appearing from an alternative source.

Steel had sensed the protective mist wherever they'd probed. It wasn't a protection of anything concrete or tangible, but mainly ideas and principles that had been built up through the years, as if the merchants considered their integrity itself was under question. 'In the "Garden",' Hinchley had explained, 'integrity is very important. Millions of pounds' worth of diamonds change hands every day on nothing more than a handshake and a promise.' But still, questions were answered with more questions, responses were short and guarded, quickly followed by a 'who wishes to know?', or 'what purpose will such information serve?'

Steel looked thoughtfully across the room. To one side some large french windows led out on to a small balcony; the heavy drapes to each side pulled open, allowing a wide beam of sunlight to break in, highlighting a long dressing-table and a small desk. On one side of the desk were the two polythene bags from Cleary's car. It had been too late to process their contents on returning to London the evening before, and now Steel began to time things out: an examination of Cleary's effects in the morning, the reports and statements by midday, and then the re-convened meeting at 3 p.m. It didn't leave much time for preparation.

There would be Kenton's disapproval to contend with; that sour approach, as if humour had no place in their business; no real humour, simply pleasantries, just as the 'norm' has to be preserved in a mental asylum, where that same constrained, taut atmosphere can be observed.

At one time he'd had a theory about the closed-up atmosphere: the schools were Eton and Harrow; clubs, the Garrick, St James's and the White Elephant; universities, predominantly Oxford, with the accent on St Anthony's; and transfers were almost exclusively from the Foreign Office and Military Intelligence. A snowballing form of sectarianism, the circles growing ever tighter within themselves, something Steel had never considered himself totally a part of. His own contemporaries – those few that had entrenched themselves successfully – were a product of Sir John Rennie's reorganization in the late sixties. True, he belonged to the White Elephant Club, and his background was Naval Intelligence – from a Lieutenant on Polaris, through the ranks with DIS Sections 1 and 5 to Lieutenant-Commander – but there the similarity ended. His school was Judd Grammar, Tonbridge; university, King's College, London.

The traffic noises outside seemed to have built up slightly, and Steel stepped across to the window. From the eighth floor figures milling back and forth were easily discernible; faces were more difficut. Traffic was quite heavy now, and cars shunted spasmodically in both four-lane carriageways, although those heading towards Hyde Park Corner were noticeably slower, almost at a standstill. Beyond the wide, tree-split road, the view stretched out across the rambling green acres of Hyde Park.

Steel had always liked Park Lane. He much preferred the country outlook of his home in Abinger, but if it was a case of 'staking it out' in London hotel rooms, Park Lane was a welcome compensation. He stayed in the same position for a moment, and then decided on a short bout of exercises and a shower.

It was a ritual that he had observed since his navy days. Something, he considered, that had maintained his physique very much as it was then; even now, twelve years later, edging just over forty.

The exercises were in stages – leg-bends, trunk-curls, squat-thrusts and press-ups – taking fifteen minutes in all. And then Steel allowed his breathing to come back to normal as the shower ran, standing once again by the french window, gazing aimlessly at the forecourt below. There was a momentary flash of a bald head as it disappeared into the back of a Rolls Royce, a group of Middle Eastern businessmen deep in excited conversation, three women in evening dress, and an assortment of people entering or leaving the main lobby. Nothing of any consequence registered. From the eighth floor nothing appeared unusual about the man who glanced with mild interest at the sign above the hotel's main entrance.

It was going to be another hot day. Steel picked up his robe and headed for the bathroom.

Malusi Ugbaja confirmed his arrival at the correct hotel, paid his taxi, then headed under the large concrete portico.

There was part of a Nigerian delegation in the lobby that morning – mostly filling the semi-circular seating areas at the heart of the open-plan expanse – and nobody paid much attention to the large black African who made his way swiftly through to the bank of lifts at the back of the room. He stabbed at one of the 'Up' buttons impatiently.

After a moment a lift to his left announced its arrival, a faint ring coinciding with an illuminated arrow pointing skywards. Ugbaja ambled in. It was empty. He pressed button eight.

As the lift doors started to close, a small man in shirt-sleeves darted in quickly and, turning to face the blank wall that the lift doors now presented, pressed button five.

Ugbaja scanned the man's swarthy complexion and neatly cropped dark hair for a moment, placing his origin somewhere between southern Europe and the Middle East. The difference in size between the two men was almost comical, the small man's head reaching only a fraction above the top button of Ugbaja's jacket. Ugbaja settled back, watching the progress of the lighted indicator with mild interest.

On the fifth floor the bell rang and the small man stepped out; no other people got on, and the lift remained empty up

to the eighth. There, the corridor seemed curiously empty –
quiet, except for the faint hum of the air-conditioning.

The corridor was lushly carpeted, and Ugbaja padded
silently along. He had walked its length and turned into
another, shorter corridor when he caught sight of what he
was looking for: a red-uniformed valet coming out from a
room near the end. Ugbaja forced a smile as he approached
the valet.

'Excuse me, I wonder if you could help me?'

The valet busied himself with putting the last cup and
plate on a small trolley to one side. 'Yes, sir?'

'I wondered if I could have an extra towel? There's only
one in my room right now.'

'Which room are you in, sir?' The valet looked up for the
first time.

Ugbaja smiled again. 'While I'm here, I might as well
pick it up myself.'

The valet faltered for a second, and then led the way
towards the end of the corridor. 'If you'd like to follow me,
sir,' he said, and jangled some keys in his pocket as they
came around to the shorter extension.

'There was one other thing you could perhaps help me
with,' Ugbaja mentioned as he watched the valet open a
small cupboard and start to rummage through the towelling
and linen inside.

'What was that, sir?' The valet handed a white towel
across and shut the cupboard door.

'I have some friends staying in room eight-o-six, and I did
say that I would call in on them early in the morning. But I
didn't want to disturb them while they're having breakfast,
so I wondered whether you'd know if you had served them
yet or not.'

'Certainly.' The valet produced a black note-pad from
his back pocket and started running a finger down the
columns. 'Here it is, room eight-o-six, continental breakfast
for one for eight o'clock.' He tilted his arm to look at his
watch. 'About ten minutes, sir. If you check with them in
forty minutes or so, it should be all cleared away by then.'

Ugbaja tried not to let his surprise show at the mention of 'one'. He forced a 'Thank you', but his large eyes suddenly bore an expression of cold wariness.

The valet half-turned to re-lock the cupboard door, and the motion appeared only as a faint flicker in the side of his vision.

Ugbaja brought the hard edge of one hand down on the base of the valet's neck, the jolt thrusting him sharply forwards into the door. A part of his nose split on impact, his body slumping slowly and awkwardly to the floor.

Ugbaja leant over the prone body and rocked the head back and forth until totally satisfied that unconsciousness had taken control. Then he opened the laundry-room door, took two tea-towels from the top shelf, and thrust the limp figure inside. Pulling the valet's arms tight behind his back, he tied them securely with one towel. With the other he tied a thick band around the valet's head, thrusting the centre of the band deep into his mouth. Satisfied that the figure was secure, Ugbaja locked the door behind him and, still with the keys in his hand, set off down the corridor ahead.

Sweat was massed on his forehead now. Ugbaja liked killing in hotels. There were a number of factors that made it so much easier than most other locations. Not only were the rooms easy to obtain access to, but layouts were very much standard throughout the world, in particular in modern chain hotels; size didn't vary much, there were only a few positions in which the bathroom could be located, and usually no hidden corners. It was ideal, one of many scenarios Ugbaja had perfected over the years: get there early and pose as the breakfast waiter. If breakfast had already been served, say you wanted to clear away the cutlery. If the cutlery had been cleared away, the room cleaner might be expected next. The possibilities were endless.

Ugbaja thought back: the exact location they'd given him the night before had been the most important factor, but there were other details taken from the earlier tape: a large, fat, Caucasian man, early fifties; a younger Caucasian woman, thirty-five, forty. It had been almost three weeks since his first meeting with the young American negro in Accra, but the tape had been with him throughout, and at times he had wondered about the deep cultured voice he'd never had the benefit of matching a face to. Still, the information was precise, delivered by a man of seemingly obvious conviction. There was the reminder of *one* breakfast, but he pushed it away, the numbers were already in view: eight-o-eight . . . eight-o-six.

Ugbaja stood still for a moment, allowing his thoughts to collect. Then he gripped the Luger in his trouser waistband and raised his other hand to knock on the door.

Inside the room, Steel had finished his shower, and stood with a towel around his waist, shaving carefully. He used a new twin-bladed razor, although the washbag on the shelf in front of him contained an assortment of relics: a cut-throat from his navy days, and three older-style safety razors.

The door between the bathroom and bedroom was closed just behind him, and Steel barely heard the knock on the outer door when it came.

'Yes,' he shouted.

'Breakfast, sir.'

Steel noted nothing unusual about the voice that strained through the outside door. 'Okay, bring it in.'

Ugbaja's Luger was the first thing to make its entrance, the barrel following his vision in a semi-circular sweep, swiftly encompassing the room. Satisfied that the room was empty, Ugbaja turned his attention to the bathroom door to his left. He was almost sure now that the voice he'd heard had come from behind the door. He had to be completely sure.

'Where shall I put it, sir?' he asked.

For a moment, Ugbaja was uncertain whether the bathroom occupant would actually come out, and he kept his Luger trained on the door as he waited for a response. He cast his eyes to each side again; there was certainly nobody

50

else in the room, unless they were also in the bathroom. The sounds of running water and slight movement became more obvious.

'If you could just leave it on the coffee table, please,' Steel replied, lifting his chin in an effort to complete his shaving and get to his morning coffee before it went cold.

Ugbaja moved closer to the door, straining to pinpoint Steel's position inside. He confirmed the sound of running water as the trickling of a tap directly ahead, and from the slight movement of Steel's body, guessed his position as no more than a few feet the other side. There was probably nobody else inside. He tucked the Luger back into his trouser waistband and gripped the handle of his hatchet, slipping the shining blade out slowly. With the adjoining rooms so close, silence would be vital, and with only one target it would be that much easier. *Perhaps no more than one pace the other side.* . . . The opening of the door and the hatchet movement would be virtually one. It was ideal. Ugbaja felt a surge of adrenalin course through his body, and he let its pitch dictate the right moment. He raised the hatchet slightly above his head and reached for the bathroom door handle.

Steel halted the progress of the blade on his chin and stared into the mirror ahead. It had been almost a full minute since the breakfast boy had arrived, and he hadn't heard him go out yet. If he was still there, where was the normal clanking of cutlery and china that announced their entrance? *Where were the sounds of movement?*

Steel's eyes widened, taking in the full force of the reflected figure that loomed suddenly behind him. He caught the glint of an iron blade high above his head as the bathroom door smashed into the wall beside him. In a split second Steel saw a flicker of surprise on Ugbaja's face that he felt should have belonged solely to him. Steel threw himself on to the tiled floor, his chin cut by his razor from the sudden movement. Ugbaja was already in motion, too forceful to halt in mid-track, his hatchet blade completing an arc above Steel's head and crashing relentlessly into the door beside them.

The first thing that Steel thought was whether there was a weapon to hand; then he remembered the cut-throat, and reached his arm out, sweeping the washbag from the sink shelf to the corner of the room in one action. He started moving towards it.

Ugbaja brought the hatchet *down* this time; an image caught in vision, yet its inevitability not fully accepted. Steel scuttled frantically across the bathroom floor. His body had shifted sufficiently, but the blade caught the back of one of his calves as it trailed across, scything off a thick layer of skin.

Steel took refuge at the far end of the room, pulling the cut-throat razor from the washbag. He flicked out the blade to its full extent.

Ugbaja's sudden downward motion had brought the gun loose from his waistband, and it clattered to the floor as Steel straightened up. For a moment they were frozen, both glancing hesitantly at the gun, both realizing that the time taken to stoop and grab the butt would probably make them too vulnerable.

It was the first time that Steel had studied his attacker: a large, fat man, surprisingly fast for his size. His features were heavy and full-blown, now heavily bathed in sweat, and he had seen similar eyes before in rural Africa: distended and bloodshot, as if with some virus. A set of thick, stubby fingers were gripped tight around the hatchet handle, and on the blade there was some blood. Steel looked down at the tiled floor and at the thin towel around his waist. All were smeared with his own blood. He felt nausea rising, and yanked at a towel on the rail at one side, picturing himself suddenly as a gladiator in a blood soaked arena.

Ugbaja was annoyed now; not only by the fact that he hadn't yet killed Steel, but by his initial hesitation. A medium height, fat man, they'd said. . . . *And where was the girl?* But it really didn't matter anymore, he was committed; perhaps an exchange or another contact, he spurred himself on, what the hell. . . .

Steel made his move. As Ugbaja came in, he darted forward quickly and slashed out with his razor at the fat man's throat. He retreated back from reach with equal speed. Ugbaja had tucked his head in and tried to swerve from the open blade, the tip of the razor slashing across his cheek as he leant forward. Steel knew that he had connected with flesh, and now with his back again to the far wall, he observed a strip of skin on the fat man's cheek paling in colour; it remained so for a second, and then a band of maroon welled forwards, droplets falling rapidly and in quick succession to his jacket lapel.

Disbelieving, Steel thought that for a moment he saw the fat man smiling. The perversity of the grimace froze him momentarily as the fat man loomed suddenly forward.

The blow was aimed at the centre of Steel's skull, and he had moved slightly, but not quite enough; at the last second he parried Ugbaja's arm as the blade sank into his shoulder. He felt some blood spurt up to the side of his face, and nausea and shock swept through his body rapidly, the leering black face shifting from a vision back to reality. In desperation he kept a grip on the arm that had swung the hatchet.

Ugbaja brought his other hand to Steel's throat, pinning him back still further against the wall. Steel felt his nervous system collapsing as the pressure increased, his legs and abdomen beginning to shake uncontrollably.

Very soon it would be too late, a fading message told him, and he lashed out again with the razor, a forceful, sideways blow to the fat man's arm.

The blade cut through the thick cloth of his jacket and into flesh beneath. Ugbaja eased his grip almost instantly, groaning audibly in a mixture of pain and fury. In the same motion, he ripped the hatchet blade free and up again, high above his head.

Steel saw his opportunity.

As the hatchet reached the top of its arc, he brought one foot up sharply, pushing hard at the centre of the fat man's chest, the wall behind maintaining his balance.

Ugbaja gasped as the full force of the kick flung him the length of the room and he crashed into the far wall, his arm still raised high above his head in a striking position.

In that moment, Steel fought back unconsciousness. The adrenalin was there. As Ugbaja hit the far wall, his head was flung back viciously, exposing a wide area of his neck. Steel leapt forward, drawing the blade of his razor deftly across the fat man's throat. He stepped back. Ugbaja's throat opened up, blood pouring down his shirt-front.

Steel saw the hatchet blade still suspended above the fat man's head, poised to strike, and he raced for the open door before it came down, dragging his mangled body as far from the bathroom as possible.

Ugbaja sank to his knees, the hatchet falling forgotten to the floor. Reaching one hand out as far as he could, he curled his fingertips around the gun that lay on the tiling and made one last frantic effort to finish the job he had come for. The Luger firmly in his grip, he pointed the barrel at the vague figure running from the bathroom, and squeezed twice; his last action before toppling over.

At first, Steel hadn't heard the shots, or at least didn't associate the two dull thuds with gunfire. He saw a momentary explosion of plaster on the far wall, but nothing else, aware only that he had fallen headlong, his face suddenly flat on the carpet. His thoughts were clouding rapidly. There was some blood flowing on to the hand pinned beneath his chest, and everything in the room seemed to be smaller, more distant. Then he remembered the Luger.

Steel struggled to look back towards the bathroom; if the fat man was still alive, he intended to ask him what the hell was going on.

Part Two

The Consortium

3

The Union Buildings in Pretoria are among the South African capital's most impressive. They were constructed in 1910, but the architecture employed was mock Classical, with wide columns supporting its concave centre and two domed towers at each end. On one side is an impressive garden, split into neat rows by jacaranda trees and Mediterranean firs. On the other, passing through the central archway and amphitheatre, is the crest of Meintjeskop, a hillside which dominates the city and looks out almost directly on to the opposing promontory of Muckleneuk Hill, on which stands the University of South Africa campus.

At the heart of the Union Buildings is a large conference room, used mainly for government debates when Cape Town is 'out of session', and capable of holding more than sixty people around its oval mahogany table in comfort. It was in one of the small antechambers, though, that the eight men sat in conference. The size of the room suited both the nature and tone of their discussion.

A set of large shutters had been drawn at the end of the room, allowing only thin pencil-lines of light to filter through; the only sound was the faint whir of a cine-projector.

The men were silhouetted by the light of the projector. At the head of the table, John Vorster, South African Prime Minister; to his right, Defence Minister Piet Botha, Justice Minister Jimmy Kruger, and Finance Minister Horwood. On the opposite side, as though there should be a deliberate separation, General Geldenhuys and Captain Calbeck of the South African Security Police, and General Van den Bergh, head of BOSS, the 'external' security equivalent; and on that same side, at the far end, Sir Philip Oppenheimer, Chairman of the Central Selling Organization and a Director on the board of De Beers.

A square of light flickered and then centred itself on the screen a few feet from the end of the table; feeble, straggling trails of smoke from a freshly lit cigarette drifted lazily through its beam. A picture slid into the frame and some abrupt focusing brought forward the image of a mass of people. Most of them were black, and in the background were several office blocks. In the foreground, with backs and part-profiles visible were groups of Security Police. Some had drawn batons, others carried rifles and tear-gas guns, and the majority were protected by almost body-length plastic riot shields.

Colonel Jan Ostermeir of BOSS stood to one side of the table conducting the presentation. He pointed towards the centre of the screen with a short baton.

'Some of you have already seen the slides I am about to show, but I will be recapitulating for the benefit of all present.' Ostermeir paused and looked around the table, then quickly back to the screen. 'The main scene for this affair was set by the Soweto riots which started on June 15th, building rapidly and attracting public attention by the 16th and 17th, when most of the main conflicts in fact took place. However, the date we're interested in is the 19th. On that particular day, riots also broke out in the centre of Johannesburg, concentrated between Market and Marshall Streets.' Ostermeir picked out a particular point on the screen. 'At the same time, a group of men in a police Land Rover broke through the crowds and stopped here. And it was in *this* building that a robbery of the South African Diamond Consortium was effected.

'These pictures were taken later in the day, not long after the robbery. What we have to realize here is that the 19th was the *only* day that the riots spread to this particular area.'

'You suspect some form of collaboration?' broke in Defence Minister Botha.

'I'm afraid it isn't for me to draw conclusions,' replied Ostermeir. 'Only to present the information.'

'It's rather early to tell yet,' General Van den Bergh commented supportively.

Ostermeir resumed. 'There are a number of things of which we are still uncertain, but from varying eye-witness reports two things seem quite clear: all the men were armed and dressed in Security Police uniforms. Four men were identified positively as such by people inside the Consortium, and reports from the police involved in the riot around the time of the robbery support this. In addition, all the men were wearing masks with white skin-colouring and from the evidence of one of the Consortium employees who was particularly close at one point, we can assume that at least three of the men were blacks. The *total* number of men involved isn't known, and we can only come close to determining this from a study of the robbery itself.'

Ostermeir pressed a button at the side of the projector and the next frame slid into position. It showed a large foyer, half of it marble-floored, the other half in front of a bank of lifts, carpeted. To one side was a small door marked with an 'X' on the transparency itself. Around the door were several small craters circled in navy-blue chalk, but this time the markings were clearly on the wall and not the transparency. At the foot of the door was the white-chalked outline of a body. Ostermeir explained the appearance of the room beyond the small door, and how entrance had been gained to it; he further demonstrated its insignificance to the casual observer with the next slide, which showed the confines of the room itself.

Ostermeir worked through a series of slides, emphasizing the importance of each one as he came to it. He showed the way in which each fingerprint-sensitive control panel had been operated to open the series of steel doors. The slides combined with Ostermeir's narrative followed an imaginary path through doors, down stairs, and finally along corridors deep below the foyer shown on the first slide.

The fifth slide showed the office of the diamond vault's

chief examiner, Dr Hinrich Rosenkrands. Ostermeir illustrated the respective positions in which a guard covering the office door and Rosenkrands had been shot. In particular he emphasized the importance of the telephone on Rosenkrand's desk, its final position, and the receiver gripped in the doctor's hand.

'A call,' he concluded, 'that was never completed.'

Ostermeir pressed the button and the last slide appeared.

'Finally, this is the main examination room and vault,' he said, with more emphasis than for anything he had previously described.

Ostermeir went on to explain that the five occupants of the room, four examiners and one guard, were not harmed. He drew comparison between the way the combination locks of the vaults and the fingerprint-controlled door panels were operated. He also explained the purpose of the series of work benches spread the length of the room, for sorting and evaluating large quantities of diamonds that would, eventually, be placed in the vault itself. The vault, a shining wall of steel almost eight feet high, dominated the room and the picture.

Ostermeir left the same picture in place as he spent a few more minutes detailing a final few actions and some finer points that the slides might not have made totally clear. When he had finished, he switched off the projector and opened the blinds at the back of the room.

Prime Minister John Vorster scanned the length of the table, his jowls, neck and the pouches under his eyes appearing suddenly more pronounced in the stark sunlight. It was a countenance that had gained him the nickname 'The bulldog of Africa'. He was not fat, but had settled into those more comfortable and generous proportions of middle weight, the loose flesh of his face and neck being the only testament to past obesity. The general effect was one which conveyed profound seriousness, even when he was in a mildly jovial mood.

He turned to Colonel Ostermeir.

'How serious is this robbery?'

'Even taken on its own, Prime Minister, it's a very sizable theft,' Ostermeir answered. 'But of course there are much more serious implications.'

'Of course.' Vorster became impatient. 'You know to which area I refer. Does it pose a threat to national security?'

'It depends on which level we take it.'

General Van den Bergh could sense Vorster's building impatience, and cut in. 'Perhaps I could throw some light on this, Prime Minister. You see, we really have two areas at stake here. First, we are obviously dealing with a well-organized force. It may be that they wish to purchase arms, or in some way become more organized. Because of the high value of the diamonds stolen, we have a threat on that score.' Van den Bergh peered over the frame of his steel-rimmed spectacles.

'Secondly, because of the nature of the organization the diamonds were stolen from, we have a threat both to South African and international diamond markets. On that score, there are several possible repercussions.'

'By "organization", you're referring to this Consortium,' confirmed Vorster.'

'Yes.'

A silence settled slowly around the room.

'It seems from the disguises used that we're also facing a breach of police security here,' commented Kruger after a moment.

'If there *has* been, it would be the first case of such a serious kind that I can immediately call to mind,' said General Geldenhuys.

'Are you forgetting Loginov,' Botha rebuked.

'Loginov was a totally different affair,' defended Geldenhuys. 'More a matter of *government* security than a specific breach of *police* security.'

'Gentlemen, past affairs aren't important here,' Vorster interrupted. 'Colonel Ostermeir, what do we know of this from the investigation so far?'

Ostermeir took a seat at the far end, by Senator Horwood.

'We are almost certainly dealing with a breach of police

security; that's why we've used solely BOSS men so far and, of course, outside assistance.' Ostermeir looked down at the table.

'Unfortunately, though, we've had a set-back in that area. A CIA agent transferred from Angola picked up our main lead, confirming it finally with an export agent in Paris.' Ostermeir paused. 'He died in a road accident yesterday, before the lead could come to fruition.'

'What happens now?' asked Vorster.

'They're having a meeting in London to cover details of the accident – possible suspicious causes, et cetera. SIS Commander Stannard is aware of some of the details from our end of it, but only enough to secure their involvement at the outset. I understand that these will also be discussed. I'm expected there in two days' time to make a full presentation.' Ostermeir looked down the length of the table. 'At present, there's really nothing more we can do. We asked for outside assistance, not only because our own men were hamstrung due to possible internal security breaches, but also for reasons of manpower – and the respective positioning of that manpower. It would be impossible for us to cover international diamond markets, and yet those are the *prime* areas in which this package would be likely to show up. However, having said that, we've only been able to secure their assistance by emphasizing the possibility of an international diamond market threat – and that's *all* they know. But we can't keep them working in the dark *ad infinitum*; at some time we have to come up with the goods: why, where, when, who, and what for?'

'What exactly *are* the international implications?' asked Vorster, and for a moment there was no answer.

Sir Philip Oppenheimer lifted his pen up. 'Perhaps this would be an apt time for me to talk about the Consortium itself.'

Oppenheimer's voice seemed somehow out of place; unlike the others', his English was Oxford, without the raw Afrikaaner's edge.

'You see, what we're talking about are varying degrees

of market security and control.'

Oppenheimer passed some files around the table and sat back again.

'The only copies of these files are held by the CSO and Senator Horwood's department,' he said, and then allowed a few moments for everyone to read the contents.

'As you can see, the Consortium offers a unique form of protection to the world diamond market,' Oppenheimer said at length. 'Unlike gold, platinum or other comparable commodities, diamonds are the only *falsely* protected commodity, in so far as large quantities are withheld from the market so as to maintain a good supply-demand situation. In this respect the CSO can only go so far, and this is where the Consortium comes in. However, both the public and more especially the traders would not take kindly to another 'buffer' organization, and it is in this area that the fundamental difference between the CSO and Consortium may be found. The Consortium is a *secret* organization, the CSO is not. The chairman of the Consortium and key staff are members of the South African mining establishment, but their identities are known only to me, a few of my CSO associates and now, due to these investigations, General Van den Bergh and Colonel Ostermeir.'

Oppenheimer looked slowly around the table. 'Without making a meal of it, gentlemen, possible offloading of this parcel and subsequent public knowledge of the Consortium would be disastrous. It would create a run on world diamond markets the like of which has never been seen before.'

'I think it also has to be said that we are probably dealing with a breach of the Consortium's security,' Ostermeir added. 'Or certainly, a person or persons who are extremely close to their activities. The operation of the fingerprint control panels, the safe, et cetera, all point to this.'

Vorster's expression clouded over faintly. 'Do we have *any* idea who is responsible?'

'We do have some strong leads at least.' General Van den Bergh took a file from his case. 'Most of these are with

63

student and rebel organizations we believe are connected in some way with the riots: the ANC, the outlawed PAC, Umkomto we Sizwe, the 'Black Consciousness' movement – names that are all familiar to you.'

'And what progress?' enquired Vorster.

'We'll know more in a few weeks. I'll be passing on the file to General Geldenhuys, and he's agreed to detail Captain Calbeck and a force from Port Elizabeth Department to search for the rebels. They should be free of possible security infiltrations down there. Captain Calbeck will report directly to General Geldenhuys and Colonel Ostermeir, who will in turn pass the findings on to me.'

'On their own, surely these rebels pose little danger to internal security,' quizzed Botha. 'I mean, as we're all aware, we've never in the past been dealing with an *organized* force.'

General Van den Bergh adjusted his spectacles slightly. 'As I mentioned earlier, the key word *is* "organized", gentlemen. Because this force is most certainly that; and they are, by all accounts, well-armed. The danger is one of increasing armament, which a haul like this could very easily provide.'

'But if arms were the only aim,' Kruger pointed out. 'The Russians are ready, willing and able to supply any crackpot rebel force anywhere near South Africa. We know that from experience.'

'The Russians will send arms to a trained force, or their own men with arms – nothing in between. However, the show of a more organized rebel force within South Africa would be a different matter. Then, yes, the situation would be ripe for the Russians.' Van den Bergh paused heavily. 'If that happens, apart from the threats we've already talked of, we would almost certainly be facing closure of many of our mineral resources mines. The show of a strong rebel force would be like a siren call to black labour throughout the Republic. And that, gentlemen, represents over sixty per cent of our total labour force.

'Of course, having said this, we could be dealing with an

outside force – SWAPO, MPLA, ZAPU – but it's all arbitrary. If any external forces of this kind gained a foot-hold in South Africa, there would be rapid support from within – the effects would eventually be the same.'

'On both fronts, internal and external, recovery of the diamonds appears as the only immediate solution,' Ostermeir said. 'And our main chance for that lies with the international security forces: the CIA and SIS.'

'From what I've judged, their continued co-operation seems to depend strongly on you building up the *inter-national* threat,' commented Finance Minister Horwood.

'They shouldn't need much more convincing than the facts already laid down,' Vorster told him sharply. 'I've warned them often enough. If South Africa falls into communist hands, apart from the loss of abundant mineral resources, the Cape route would almost certainly be affec-ted. If Suez is blocked again, the West would be totally cut off from oil supplies from the Middle East.'

There was a heavy silence around the table. In many quarters there was dissent to Vorster's 'Cape route' theory, a disbelief that any shipping lane over two hundred miles wide could be blocked effectively.

Van den Bergh was the only one to show his support. Through the years, on various campaigns, he had become familiar with Vorster's dogmatic reliance upon *kragda-digheid* – a dictate of 'law and order' at all costs.

'Anyway, that is as may be,' Vorster said at length. 'Colonel Ostermeir, when you go to London, you *will* emphasize the international threat to the security agencies present.' Vorster looked slowly around the table, and for a moment his 'bulldog' expression held a look of almost total desperation. 'I don't think there remains any doubt that the security of South Africa is threatened in the most profound manner. And I'm buggered if I'm going to let a load of Kaffirs tag this Republic Azania without putting up one hell of a fight.' Vorster studied Ostermeir intensely for a moment, adding with exaggerated finality. 'So learn your lines well.'

The remainder of the meeting was spent in a re-examination of some of the points already established; and then the various infra-levels of contact were confirmed. By midday they were concluded.

Ostermeir stopped Calbeck in the corridor outside. He knew Calbeck from the East Cape division of the Security Police, before his own transfer to Kimberley: a hard-nosed, head-breaking bastard, if he remembered correctly.

'You'll be out there with a load of flatfoots, Calbeck,' he said. 'So don't fuck it up. Report to me as early as possible on your progress.'

Calbeck smiled thinly and saluted, then made his way down the long corridor towards the security compound.

Ostermeir appeared pleased with himself; that was the sort of language the Calbecks of this world understood, he thought.

Within two days he was aboard a South African Airways 747SP bound for London. And he had learnt his lines well.

A group of Malinke women were pounding millet when the Land Rover first became visible on the east of the village, crossing the path of the early morning sun as it came out of the closely encroaching jungle.

The sound of its engine brought out several young children from the tightly huddled *soukhala* huts, followed by the older people, who observed with more subdued curiosity. Mud was thick on the Land Rover's wheels from the recent heavy rains, and some of the children prodded playfully at them with short sticks as the vehicle finally came to rest.

The last to emerge were the men of the village, some from the huts, but most from the close recesses of jungle foliage. Their dress was a curious mixture of their normal tribal *bante* and ex-army clothing: camouflage jackets, trousers, or sometimes only a hat. Some carried rifles, others simple knives and spears.

There were four men in the Land Rover: a white driver, who stayed in the vehicle, and three negroes, who alighted quickly.

The first negro was middle-aged and distinguished in appearance, his hair greying at the sides of the closely matted curls. He was known to the people of the village from many past medical trips as Dr Magonde, and had come to be regarded as a patriarch. The other two were both a good ten years younger, one abnormally large and known simply to them as Karfi; the other an American named, as were all foreigners to their village, Bature.

A man in a full-length robe and headdress stepped forward to greet them, and Magonde spoke in Hausa, addressing him in tribal terms.

'How goes it, *sarki?*' he enquired.

'Very well, my doctor friend. We are blessed – the season's rains have not been as heavy as usual.'

They walked through a gap that had opened in the assembled mass of village people.

'Have you enough medicine and supplies?'

'Yes, yes. Ample.'

'And illnesses – have you also been free in this respect, since my last visit?'

'Nothing that could not be put to rest by the *sama likita*,' the old chief nodded solemnly.

'You must show me your crops,' Magonde urged after a moment, and they walked out towards the edge of the village, from where the largest clearing could be viewed.

'Sorghum, millet, and now some yams and cassava.' The chief picked out the neatly separated fields. 'Very soon, though, we will be clearing deeper. The moisture in the dip is just right for fruit – perhaps some papaya and banana. The only orchard we have now is a small one, on the other side of the village.'

'Yes, I remember. You have progressed far, and still with yet more admirable improvements to look forward to – affairs look good.'

They talked of other, less important developments at some length, and then turned back towards the village. Magonde's expression dulled faintly.

'There was one other matter, *sarki*. If I could assemble the men for a moment.' Magonde paused. He noted the chief's hesitation, and added softly, 'It is the matter of which I spoke to you on my last visit.'

The chief remained subdued, but showed his under-standing with a faint nod, and summoned the men of the village to a central clearing among the *soukhalas*.

'I have good news, my brothers,' Magonde addressed them from a raised mound of earth. 'Our cause is ever closer. Soon the fight will be over, and from there my friends. . . .' He raised his arms heavenwards dramatically. The crowd were spellbound by his words and actions, and he revelled in his increasing power over them.

And then suddenly his mood changed, becoming irate, vehement. He spoke of deceit and treachery to the 'cause'. 'When it is from within, from your own *brothers*, it is that much harder to accept.' Magonde eyed the crowd slowly. 'These men will be punished. . . .'

At that moment, three men broke away from the main crowd, running towards the closest jungle fringe. Karfi pounded after them.

The actions seemed pre-arranged: Magonde shot the furthest man with a quickly produced revolver, and Karfi brought the other two to the ground within fifty yards of the first trees. He grappled with them for a while, and then to save himself some trouble, rendered one unconscious with a flat-handed blow to the back of the head, crushing the man's skull.

Karfi then dragged the two men back to the centre of the village, and with the help of one of the tribesmen, staked them flat to the ground with spear-shanks and rope.

Magonde confronted the two men solemnly, his placid veneer suddenly returned. 'You will die as a lesson to others,' he said simply.

There were twelve shots remaining in Magonde's auto-matic, and he fired until it was empty, the two figures becoming quickly unrecognizable, small swarms of mosquitoes and other scavenger insects settling within minutes among the carnage.

Bature walked back to the Land Rover.

'How did you know it was them?' he asked as Magonde returned.

'I didn't. I knew there was a leak of some kind – nothing more. Their own guilt singled them out.'

Bature turned away. It was the warm, soft-spoken side of Magonde that had first attracted him to the cause when they had met in Ghana. 'A unique and unwavering Pan-African view', as fellow Berkeley specialists had reported – there was a sense of clear direction in Magonde's sincerity and singular devotion. But now such displays of unpredict-ability were becoming harder to comprehend.

'Is something wrong?' asked Magonde.

'Just the heat – and the blood, perhaps,' Bature lied easily.

'I see: the blood,' Magonde agreed sarcastically. 'Drive on.'

Within three hours they had crossed the Ghanaian border, keeping close to the ragged path of the Volta at the lowest levels of its basin. By midnight they were in Accra.

4

Arthur Kenton walked from the small news-stand outside Holborn Underground station heavily engrossed in the front page of the *Daily Telegraph*. He remained so, breaking off only momentarily to open his car door and seat himself back behind the wheel.

He looked further down the page, now using the steering wheel as a lectern. An article covering the release of ninety Arabs held hostage aboard a Cairo-Luxor-bound 737 by six Egyptian paratroopers briefly caught his interest. He looked at the bordering articles and then at the 'Stop Press' before flicking over the page. He scanned downwards quickly, picking out headlines and leaders only: forest blazes in Hampshire, a 7·3 Richter-scale earthquake in China, and a man killed by South African police during a Soweto riot: the 253rd since mid-June. Nothing there. He scanned and turned, giving pages three, four and five an increasingly rapid appraisal; son re-united with mother after escape from Foreign Legion, Richard Burton marries Susan Hunt, more Prince Bernhardt and Lockheed scandals and assorted trivia.

The remainder of the paper was similarly dealt with. It was a simple task. There were only a few projected headline possibilities in Kenton's mind; none of them had appeared. Folding the paper on the passenger seat, he turned the ignition and filtered into a small gap in the heavy build-up of traffic streaming down Kingsway. He negotiated the circle that harboured Australia House and headed down the Strand towards Trafalgar Square.

Stannard was right. The 'D'-notice had probably proved effective. That was at least one advantage. Perhaps the only one so far.

There was something else in the newspaper that had stirred a grain of Kenton's curiosity, but now he couldn't think why or which particular article; nor could he determine by mentally cross-referencing current concerns which article it was likely to have been. The traffic moved.

He decided to look again after the meeting. Just in case.

The response to the light tapping sounded curiously distant behind the thick oak door.

'Come in.'

Kenton walked in on the middle of a telephone conversation. Commander Stannard sat at the far end of his small office, behind a large and resplendent oak desk.

'Yes, sir, I know.' Stannard's grey-haired head nodded. 'Well, we've got the co-operation of the hotel. They seem just as eager as us not to have any publicity.'

Stannard lifted his eyes to Kenton for a moment and made an abstract motion towards the thick leather chair just opposite. Kenton sat down.

'When the possibility of no publicity was first mentioned to the manager he jumped at the opportunity straight away, sir.'

Stannard listened intently for a second. 'No, sir,' he responded. 'I don't think there's anything unusual about that. It isn't the first time for something of this nature, and this was a particularly messy affair. As an international hotel group, I can quite easily see their interests would lie in keeping something like this under the covers.' He shook his head from side to side this time.

'No possibility, I would say. They were found by one of the hotel's most trusted and longest-serving employees. Apparently the manager has already had a satisfactory conversation with him on the subject.'

There was a longer break this time. 'Well, of course, sir. The police were notified immediately, but there's no problem there either. Everything was handled through Section R at Scotland Yard.'

Stannard allowed for the obvious question. 'No, sir,' he added quickly. 'They took care of everything from their end.'

He paused.

'I know, but that's the way the procedure stands at present.'

Stannard appeared worried for a moment, and then for the first time his expression lightened.

'No sir, certainly not. I don't think we've got anything to worry about in that direction, but I'll obviously keep you informed of any new developments.'

He nodded, impatiently now. 'Of course, sir. Yes, I understand.'

Stannard placed the receiver back in its cradle and looked up, visually appraising Kenton; after the conversation just past, it was a reaffirmation of their respective positions. The 'kicking line' routine, thought Kenton.

'I suppose it's to be expected.' Stannard glanced back wearily towards the telephone. 'He's coming up for a

GCMG soon.'

As Kenton well knew, the reference was to the head of MI6, known simply as 'C', as were all the successors of Sir Mansfield Cumming, who'd originated the post in 1910. The GCMG was the hightest rank of the Knight Commanders of the order of St Michael and St George: CMG, Call Me God; KCMG, Keep Calling Me God; GCMG, God Calls Me God – Kenton recalled the irreverent sub-department references.

'Any indication of the 'D'-notice response?' Stannard enquired.

'I think it was favourable,' said Kenton. 'I checked the *Daily Telegraph* – if it wasn't there, I doubt if anyone else would have the story.'

'No, I suppose not. Still, it wouldn't harm to put a few of the "search pool" chaps on to it for a while. If you could prepare a list of relevant editorials.'

Kenton mumbled an agreement and made a note in a small black book from his side pocket. 'D'-notices were invariably effective in restricting the press from publication of 'information normally protected by the Official Secrets Act, the release of which could endanger National Security', as the first paragraph of the notice proclaimed. On occasion though, most especially in 'fringe' publications, there had been some non-observances.

'I presume that Miss Harrigan has already introduced you to Colonel Ostermeir.' Stannard turned a hand towards the outer office.

'Yes.'

'I see, jolly good.' Stannard fumbled in a top drawer and took out a file. 'Ostermeir will just be sitting-in this morning.' He looked up. 'Will there be anything else beforehand?'

'No sir, I've already arranged Miss Harrigan for the minutes.'

Stannard looked at his watch. 'Well, we might as well be going in.'

*   *   *

The main conference room was large and lit dimly by circular lights suspended on long cords from the high ceiling, one over each seat. Those over the positions occupied, eleven in all, cast pools of light over the assembly: Steinberg, Davis and Randall of the CIA; Lohnes, Ryland and Merrick of SIS; and at the far end, Colonel Ostermeir and Dr Terence Hobbs, resident electronics expert. Miss Harrigan took a seat next to Stannard at the head of the table and Kenton flanked his other side.

At each position was a file slashed by a rich, red OHMS confidentiality band. Under Stannard's direction, the files were opened around the table, then Stannard looked towards the far end of the room, as if to encompass all present.

'The first issue at hand is that of CIA agent Cleary and the women, Susan Helmcken and, of course, that of Lieutenant-Commander Steel.' Stannard spent a few moments covering respective duties, and then by way of the details explained why the meeting had already been post-poned on two occasions, and the final decision to combine their own briefing with Colonel Ostermeir's. He concluded by emphasizing the 'watchdog' duties of those present.

'We had hoped that information received from Cleary would pinpoint exactly which market the diamonds were likely to appear on. Unfortunately, with the advent of his death, we have very little to work on. However, what we have received tends to indicate London as a likely desti-nation.'

Stannard looked up purposefully, holding his place in the report with his right index finger. 'Lieutenant-Commander Steel telephoned me shortly after visiting the scene of Cleary's accident. He said that in a call that Cleary had made from Paris the day before, there was a mention of some form of activity at Heathrow. There was no elabora-tion. Steel also mentioned an African word which he had discovered in a key page of Cleary's diary, on the basis of which we've made as full an analysis of the word as possible – you'll find that on page seven of the report. But I'll be coming on to that later.' The commander looked back at the report.

'There was no further information gained from Agent Cleary. So, gentlemen, if we can resume with the details surrounding his automobile accident . . . the rest of this page and the next two summarize information from the autopsies of Richard Cleary and Susan Helmcken, the mechanic's report and police observations. . . .'

The monologue that followed was largely a chain of Latin words and medical terms which Stannard fought his way through along with the file details. The main facts quickly became evident; there were no injuries or medical irregularities that could not conceivably have been caused by the accident itself. There were no signs of drug ingestion. From the mechanic's report, the car was in perfect running order apart from one defective tyre which would have caused some mild discomfort, but certainly no more than that. Nor were there any signs of tampering or excessive mechanical adjustment. There were, however, two irregularities in the police report, items which in printed form seemed to bear little or no relation to the accident itself. One detailed a watch stopped over two hours before the accident. The other was the question of a road worker with an old bullet-wound scar. No explanation was offered in the report, just the facts.

'. . . From the remaining police roadside interviews and their files, it appears that two of the labourers had past records,' Stannard continued, pausing as much for effect as to regain his breath. 'One was for petty theft only six months previously – the other a case of common assault over two years ago. Hardly preliminaries for international crime.' Stannard lifted his head momentarily.

'Another workman at the scene would have fitted the bill quite well. He was most likely the first labourer that Cleary saw as he approached the roadworks, and he was boasting a four-year-old scar from a ·22 rifle shell just below his right shoulder.'

Stannard surveyed the length of the table. 'The operative

words, gentlemen, are 'would have'. He perhaps *would have* fitted the bill if his wound had been gained during a shoot-out with Interpol, or during some form of armed robbery. However, it was nothing so extreme. During the police interview, he explained in lucid detail how he had been caught as an innocent bystander during crossfire between the Provos and the armed forces on one not-so-out-of-the-ordinary day in Ulster. In addition, he was rather eager to add that on extraction in hospital, it transpired to be a British Army regular issue shell. The dates he gave were pre-rubber bullet. From the unit concerned, the Belfast Royal Infirmary and the local Ulster Constabulary, his story checks out right down to the last detail.'

The commander raised a faintly cynical eyebrow. 'Unless somebody has some suggestions that might connect a somewhat unfortunate Irishman to a South African diamond theft, I think, gentlemen, we would be best served to accept the facts as they appear in the report.'

'Was there anything to indicate Cleary's current position in this case?' Randall enquired. 'How near or how far he might have been from discovering something concrete?'

Stannard looked back at the file. 'The last point in the section on Cleary falls into this category. We have, of course, the African word that Cleary wrote down and was subsequently picked up by Steel, but on its own it really doesn't tell us a lot. Having said that, the fact of Cleary's stopped watch only serves as an indirect indication – the possible threat that he posed at that time.'

The commander looked around the table for a moment. 'I know the thought probably going through all your minds right now,' he said. 'That is why we've entered it last in Cleary's report. Apart from the pure weight of technical data involved, as you'll soon discover, there is more than a natural progressive connection between Cleary's death and the Steel incident. There's an abridged version of the technical report continuing on to the next page, followed by full details of *that* particular incident, which I will be coming on to next.'

Stannard gestured to one side. 'But first I'll be calling upon our electronics expert, Dr Terence Hobbs, to elaborate on the technical information which you can follow in the text.'

Stannard sat down unceremoniously, leaving the floor to the shabbily dressed Hobbs.

Hobbs held up a plastic bag containing a bullet.

'You'd be right in saying that this is a ·38 calibre shell, unfired,' he said. 'There is, however, something slightly different about this particular shell. Something that you probably wouldn't discover unless you attempted to fire it.'

Absently, Hobbs raised one hand and scratched the crown of his head. 'The reason being that, instead of gunpowder, there is, contained within this shell, a number of micro-circuits integrated to produce high frequency radio waves, following a source-gate-drain principle. This is, in effect, what is known as an FET – a field-effect transmitter.

'As you can see by the report, the field-effect transmitter is a high-resistance device, and is less prone to distortion than a conventional bipolar transmitter, particularly over short distances. Conversely, the bipolar transmitter is a low-resistance device and, while its signal is subject to quite high distortion levels, it is always effective to some extent over long distances. What we have, gentlemen, with the FET, is an extremely effective, accurate and distortion-free radio transmitter over short distances. Probably the most effective within a five to ten miles radius that could be chosen.' Hobbs faltered for a second, adding as an afterthought, 'As usual, this is dependent on the prevailing tropospheric conditions.' He looked back towards the polythene bag, raising it slightly again.

'This *particular* FET transmits a form of pulse signal. To locate the source of the signal, an operator would merely employ the use of a signal tracking device, similar to those used by radio licensing authorities. In this case, I would suspect one of the more compact models available.' Hobbs lowered the bag. 'By measuring the strength and regularity of the signal, the FET may be located extremely accurately,

sometimes to the extent of only a few yards in any direction.'
Hobbs looked down at the page and back again in a manner
that suggested the action bore little importance, and then
looked towards the far end of the table.

'The question that you are probably asking yourselves is
what has a miniature radio transmitter to do with a stopped
watch and the incidents surrounding Cleary, Helmcken
and Steel.' Hobbs paused, inhaling audibly. 'I for my part
can only explain the technicalities involved in this. The
answer lies in the scientific properties of radio waves. They
are, as some of you may be aware, nothing more than
electromagnetic waves; certainly not strong when dissipated
in the troposphere or lower atmosphere – although at
extremely close ranges, we have a totally different picture.
In all transmitters, these electromagnetic waves take the
form of a series of oscillations, better known as megahertz.
Anywhere within 100mm of a sensitive object their effectual
power is extreme. These oscillations vary, depending on
the wavelength on which one might wish to broadcast. On
the FET transmitter in question, the megahertz concerned
were 400·05.

'The liquid quartz watch taken from Agent Cleary's car
also depends on a series of oscillations for an accurate
digital count. The oscillations in this particular case were
tuned at 16·39 megahertz. Such a watch placed in
extremely close or direct contact with an FET would
produce one of two effects: first, for the time it was in
contact, the transmitted oscillations would override that of
the watch, causing it to operate at twenty-five times its
normal speed. Secondly, and more likely, the watch's
internal mechanisms, in resisting such an operation, would
stop completely.' Hobbs surveyed the length of the table.
However obvious already, the *coup de grâce* of his briefing
had, he felt, to be delivered after at least a few seconds'
silence. He rested his hands back on the table melodra-
matically.

'On examination, it appeared that Agent Cleary's watch
had chosen the second of these two options,' he said simply.

Hobbs stayed in his position momentarily, observing reactions, and then turned to Stannard. 'Thank you, Commander.' He seated himself, tucking the small polythene bag back into his side pocket as if it were now a used Kleenex.

'Thank *you*, Dr Hobbs.' Stannard emphasized his return appreciation as more pertinent, and then resumed his stance at the head of the table.

'The transmitter was discovered among the effects that Steel had collected from Cleary's car. It was contained in a box of ammunition, which Inspector Mallinder, the presiding accident officer, informs us was removed by some of his men from the boot of Agent Cleary's car. It was placed at the bottom of the box, thereby minimizing the possibility of discovery, assuming that Cleary loaded his gun using the top cartridges of the box first. From the time that his watch had stopped, we believe that he must, for some reason, have loaded his gun towards the end of his boat passage to Newhaven. We assume his watch came close enough to the transmitter about that time.' Stannard looked up.

'There are a number of other assumptions involved here. First, that the transmitter was planted while Cleary was still in South Africa – it was unlikely to have been planted while he was in Paris, or during the boat trip. Secondly, that those who planted it were aware of his intended return to London; the fact that they employed a receiver in London and tracked the signal down, obviously makes that rather likely. Thirdly, that there was a purpose behind them planting the receiver outside of an intended assassination.

'In terms of size, some extremely powerful explosive and gas devices now available are equally as compact as the transmitter found. If murder was the only aim, it would have served their purpose better to employ one of these. It would have been speedier, more efficient, there would have been nothing left to chance, and it would have saved them a great deal of unnecessary trouble and expense. No!' Stannard stressed, clenching one hand on the desk top. 'We must assume an ulterior motive. It is more likely that the transmitter was planted quite early during Cleary's investigations in South Africa. His movements were probably watched closely during his entire visit, and at some time or other it was decided he should be killed. Whether this was as a result of something he had discovered, we can only guess. For some reason it must have also seemed inappropriate to kill him while he was still in South Africa. The only possible clue to this was the mention of a *final* lead in Paris – passed on to Colonel Ostermeir just prior to departure. When the export agency concerned was checked, all possible trace had long disappeared; obviously it had been formed for the purpose of only *one* transaction. As a matter of course, we also checked the agency name with Heathrow – but with no joy.'

Stannard glanced to a shuttered window at the far side of the room. Heat and traffic noises became more obvious to him. For a moment, a peculiar silence settled over the boardroom table and its immediate surroundings.

'Lastly,' Stannard exclaimed, forcing his attention back, 'although this is a much safer assumption – our assassin appears not to have had any previous visual identification of Cleary.' Stannard paused. 'The rest, gentlemen, is now history. Identification seems to have been based purely on the transmitter's location. Subsequently, Steel, in collecting Cleary's effects, became a mistaken target.'

Davis heralded his question by lifting his pen. 'Have any similar radio transmitters been discovered previously that might indicate some connection with this case?'

Stannard scanned down the report and then turned the page. 'A compendium at the back of the report will show you that. The events are listed in chronological order, and the asterisk and footnote on page five will tell you which section to look in. As far as I can remember, there were two incidents involving Russian agents – one in Turkey, one in East Germany – and another case involving Cuban insurgents in Jamaica. You might like to verify that, Davis.' He looked up briefly. 'From our own files, there have been no previous recordings of this form of device anywhere in

South Africa. Would that also be safe to say from BOSS experiences, Colonel Ostermeir?'

'Nothing that I've ever been made aware of,' Ostermeir said, as though with some slight reservation.

'This might be an appropriate time to bring in the information BOSS has assisted us with regarding Steel's assailant, Malusi Ugbaja – that is, as much as was available.'

Ostermeir mumbled his agreement, and Stannard flicked over to the page in question.

'Ugbaja was, to all intents and purposes, a professional assassin. We have two reported incidents just last year in Angola, on behalf of the MPLA, just before the final takeover. There are two further reports of assignments in South Africa on behalf of Mozambique, one for Cuba in the Congo; a series of assignments, reportedly Russian-backed, all again in Africa – Kenya, South-West Africa, Rhodesia; the list is endless. There's only one assignment that we are aware of, backed by Chinese communists, and only two occasions on which Ugbaja was contracted outside Africa – once in Munich on behalf of SWAPO, and once in Houston, Texas, on behalf of Libya. There are,' he stressed, lifting his head from the report, 'two very obvious and consistent correlations – Africa and communism. All the assignments were backed by communist countries or left-wing factions, and were in Africa, barring two, which were again backed by African groups of the same persuasion. There are no doubt a number of incidents of which we are unaware. As you know, reports are based on a study of the murder itself and a series of interviews conducted in the vicinity of any political, key civilian or agency assassination. Passport officials, hotel receptionists, car-hire firms – any points of probable contact. A list of "likely" professionals is prepared, and where possible, photographs and lists of known aliases are employed. Only one case in five can we safely connect to any one particular individual, and out of those, much of the evidence compiled is circumstantial and non-admissible in a court of law.'

Stannard gripped his hands on the edge of the table.

'Whilst what evidence we do have doesn't indicate connection with any *one* particular group it does, however, indicate that Ugbaja was contracted by a group with left-wing sympathies, probably based in South or Central African regions.'

For the first time, murmurs of conjecture rose around the table. Opinions seemed to be forming.

Stannard raised one hand. 'However, we are still in the midst of speculation. We can only use the information as a guide, not a dictate.

'Finally.' Stannard referred back to the report. 'The autopsy shows the cause of Ugbaja's death to have been laceration of the jugular vein and trachea. As for Lieutenant-Commander Steel – just before dying, Ugbaja fired two shots: the first buried itself into the ceiling a few paces from the bathroom, the second just missed Steel, passing so close to his head that it affected the balance of his inner ear, rendering him unconscious almost immediately. Steel's wounds were to a large extent superficial. The most serious was a blow to his shoulder, which caused a hairline fracture of the scapula, and his present hospitalization is mainly due to loss of blood. A full medical report can be found in sub-section nine, for those interested.'

Stannard faltered for a second, as though he had run ahead of himself. He leafed forwards a few pages in the file, and then back again.

'. . . Which brings me to the African word mentioned earlier,' he stated in a fresh tone. 'If you would all like to study the definition entered at the top of page seven.'

There was a faint rustle of paper around the table. Stannard remained silent. One word stood out in bold capitals in the margin: *BASIKASINGO*. It was followed by a short definition:

Small African tribe from the north-western shores of Lake Tanganyika. Date of tribal origin unknown, although certainly pre-colonial. At present its settlements neighbour the much larger Balega tribe in what is now known as Zaire.

There had been almost a full minute's silence around the table. All had finished reading the definition, but some were backtracking, analysing it.

Stannard resumed. 'Most of you are probably wondering what connection a small tribe in Central Africa has with a theft of diamonds in South Africa. Unfortunately, there are only a few possible but rather unhelpful answers to that question, a handicap that could very easily lead us away from believing in any connection between this word and the case in hand. The fact that this one word was discovered in a key page of Cleary's diary points us back to it.

'The first possible connection is that an ex-member of this tribe is associated with the diamond theft in some way. As Colonel Ostermeir's first report indicated, it has become increasingly common for native black Africans to leave their tribal homelands to work in the more industrialized regions – the gold and diamond mines of South Africa, in particular, now import tribal labour from a number of neighbouring states. Even assuming that such a person was not already in South Africa, tribal Africans have shown themselves as being strongly susceptible to outside political "mouldings" – particularly those of the communists. It is possible that the theft was planned by an outside group. Alternatively, we can assume that instead of the connection of one or a few individuals, it is the tribe itself and its location that is important; that the tribal village is where the diamonds are located now, or is at least a transit point before they are shipped to world diamond markets. The French have got the best men for those parts, so we've passed it on to SDECE R4 unit. We expect a report back from them quite soon.'

The heat was building; Stannard was aware that the room's two circular fans, set at each end, did not appear as effective as they had done earlier. He poured a glass of water from one of four symmetrically placed jugs, took a sip, then started summarizing his presentation.

Within fifteen minutes, he had finished. He mentioned that Rober Stockman, an examiner from the CSO's London headquarters, and Colonel Ostermeir would be covering most of the afternoon agenda, then looked at his watch: 12:24 p.m.

He suggested lunch.

The man occupying the penthouse suite of Claridges Hotel had very much the same thought in mind. However, there was just one thing he sensed he must do before he'd feel completely comfortable in eating.

Middle-aged, blond hair greying slightly in wisps swept back over his ears, and dressed comfortably for the warm weather in a lightweight grey suit, he fitted well into the mould of men that Claridges liked to see occupying their penthouse suites.

He walked down the wide sweep of stairs that ran above the 'Causerie' restaurant to a telephone alcove by the main lobby that he felt, after the last few days, was becoming familiar to him. He picked up the receiver on the farthest booth and dialled out a series of numbers that were equally familiar. He waited patiently.

The voice that finally answered carried a mixture of accents, but the laboured vowels and consonants of an East European were predominant. It asked curtly who was calling.

The man in the grey suit also had an accent, but the vowels and consonants were sharper.

'Joseph,' he announced. 'It's Franz. I have some news.'

'Tell me.'

'It's all set – two days from now.'

'And the exact time?'

'Eleven a.m. Everything's arranged. We're meeting in the same place as before.'

'That's good,' the voice agreed. 'You'll be safe there.' Then his tone changed, sounding mildly concerned. 'And how was Magonde?'

'As unpredictable as ever,' the man in the grey suit commented. 'But he seemed confident – almost smug.'

'Where are you now?' the voice demanded.

'In the hotel.'

'Was there anything else?'

'No.'

'Take care, Franz,' the voice said softly. 'Keep in touch.'

'I will, I will.'

There was a short and significant silence, and then the man in the grey suit said questioningly, 'Joseph?'

'Yes,' returned the voice, after a second.

'I'll contact you again the morning of the meeting. If you don't hear from me then, you'll know something is wrong.'

'As now, Franz. When you've met with them – call.'

'And if something does happen?'

'One call to Switzerland and they'll be finished. And they know it. Don't worry.'

The man in the grey suit wasn't worried, but he had learnt to be cautious. And precise. He said 'Goodbye' distractedly, his mind already turning to other matters. There was nothing to worry about, nor any plans or precautions yet to be introduced, he reminded himself. Everything had 'been arranged' and 'taken care of'. But there were two days to kill. He moved away from the booth.

It had been quite a while since he had done absolutely nothing, and he sensed that the inactivity would make him feel awkward, that sitting and waiting would make him think of things that were best not thought of at that time. Then he remembered that through several years and equally as many opportunities, he had never taken in the sights of London.

When, five hours later, he hailed his eighth taxi, heading back towards the hotel, he was glad of the decision he had made. It reminded him that sometimes even the most important problems were best forgotten. Sometimes.

5

For the meeting that day, Colonel Ostermeir had chosen a navy-blue pin-striped suit, wishing to merge in as much as possible with the mood of the London boardroom.

In every respect, Ostermeir had appeared the ideal choice: he had experience with the South African Diamond Security Police attached to Kimberley, and had been with the normal SASPs and BOSS; increasingly, because of his past diamond experience, he was called in on most 'external' matters requiring such expertise. Even so, to compile the great depth of information now in the file before him, he had required the assistance of Sir Philip Oppenheimer and other key CSO board members.

Ostermeir spent the first hour after lunch in much the same way that he had done in the Pretoria meeting: showing the six slides, conducting a descriptive monologue – with special emphasis on the likelihood of 'inside' contacts – and answering relevant questions.

'Exactly how much was involved?' came the last from Lohnes, as the blinds were re-opened. 'So far we've only had approximations.'

'One hundred and twenty-eight million dollars in cut and polished collection pieces* – at trade prices.' Ostermeir paused significantly. 'First of all, yes, the amount is in itself large enough to have possibly serious economic implications, but there are many other factors involved, and while you're considering things in monetary terms, perhaps it would be wise for me to pass on another figure – one hundred and fifty billion dollars.'

Ostermeir studied everyone coldly. 'In the final analysis,

* Jewellers' term for diamonds in a perfect or near-perfect condition.

that, gentlemen, is what's at stake. However, having said that, the figure on its own doesn't have much relevance – nor can the natural connection between the two figures be demonstrated, without a knowledge of the Consortium's operations and the particular type of diamonds stolen. Those two factors are paramount.'

Ostermeir directed everyone to sub-section four in their files, and then started reading himself, purely to judge time; the text was a modified version of the report that Oppenheimer had produced for the Pretoria meeting:

DIAMOND CONSORTIUM.

Founded on 25 April 1965, to represent the interests of major diamond mining companies within the Union of South Africa, and of those same mining companies with significant holdings in South-West Africa (Namibia). Affiliated by a series of covenants and trading agreements to the Central Selling Organization (CSO), based in London. Offices are not registered, although under one of the same convenants, two addresses are shown: Johannesburg and Kimberley, respectively. The Johannesburg address is recognized as the headquarters and operational offices of the Consortium. The Kimberley address is used as a transition point for the bulk of diamonds, which come from mining concerns with headquarters in that area. Covenants between the CSO and Consortium also cover the exclusion of official company registration, blueprints from local planning authorities, and all recorded essential service plans: gas, electricity, water, etc. Security arrangements are exhaustive. As with the CSO, the Consortium acts as a protective 'filter' between the diamond mines and major diamond markets in the free world, thereby maintaining a proper balance between supply and demand, and ensuring a pre-determined degree of 'rarity' in diamonds necessary to a steadily rising market value of the same. The prime differences between these two organizations are as follows:

1. (a) The Consortium handles only cut and polished diamonds of a high grade. It maintains its own cutting and polishing staff, and those diamonds that do not reach a specified grade are placed immediately back into circulation. (b) The CSO handles rough diamonds of all grades.

2. (a) The Consortium eventually passes the majority of its stock on to dealers in Africa and Europe. These are mostly described as 'packages resulting from the mining companies experimentation of

optimum and perfective cutting techniques with selected quantities of high-quality diamonds'. (b) The CSO passes its stock directly on to major cutting centres worldwide.

3. (a) The Consortium is protected by a complete security blanket. It publishes no report, and only key members of the Consortium, the CSO and the South African Diamond Security Police have access to any form of statistical information. (b) The CSO is publicly known and publishes an annual report detailing stocks held, total trading, profits, expenditure, etc.

4. (a) The Consortium represents interests only in South and South-West Africa. (b) The CSO represents interests worldwide (approximately 80% of the overall market), excepting Russia and certain independent, state-controlled markets, e.g. Ghana, Ivory Coast, Angola.

Apart from these fundamental differences, the policies of the Diamond Consortium and the CSO are closely entwined, each dependent on the other's continuing stability for its own, and each serving separate purposes towards the same collective and enduring goal – the total protection of the Free World Diamond Market as we know it.

Ostermeir allowed a few minutes beyond his own reading time, which he felt would be sufficient for all present to have absorbed the same information. He commented on an item at the beginning of the report.

'The founding of the Consortium in 1965 was strategic for a number of reasons. In the late fifties and sixties two things happened within the diamond industry.' Ostermeir referred back to the text briefly. 'First and foremost, the world demand for diamonds increased, but mostly for industrial use, whereas the demand for gem diamonds remained roughly the same. Secondly, a number of mines in Africa were producing higher quantities of gem stones than previously experienced – notably a number of mines in South and South-West Africa which already dominated a large proportion of overall world production. Now the diamond producers were faced with a dilemma. It was the same dilemma that had led to the CSO's formation in 1934, following the great depression – how to balance supply against demand?'

Ostermeir paced to one side of his chair, stroking his chin thoughtfully. 'This time though, it presented an extra problem. Before the 1930s there was no organization to protect world diamond prices. It was considered that such an organization would not only help stabilize overall world prices, but would also be welcomed by the industry as a whole. It was forecast that demand would increase after the depression, and that the large stocks built up could then be offloaded on to the market. As it was, many mines had to close down during that period. However, the forecast proved right, and the CSO was there to take care of any similar lulls in demand.

'In the 1960s everything suddenly appeared in a different light. The largest mines were presenting the market with quantities of high-grade diamonds that wouldn't foreseeably be absorbed by demand, not for a number of years at least. The only hope was that the supply would decrease and the demand increase. That didn't happen. Production stayed the same, as did demand. The mining companies, as they'd done in the thirties, withheld diamonds from the market, but again there's a limit to the period of time for which this can be done effectively. Passing the diamonds on to the CSO would have also proved ineffective. The CSO is required to publish its figures annually. A build-up of diamonds in any one category over one or two years would be accepted, but a constant and continuing backlog over a number of years would not. By 1964 the situation had reached crisis level.' Ostermeir waved his arm as if throwing invisible dice the length of the table.

'The very same class of gems that the diamond industry had revered for decades was now threatening its downfall.' Ostermeir studied expressions around the table. 'It seems almost ironic,' he added, 'but by this time it had been ascertained that by a change in marketing policies, an increased demand for many of the smaller and slightly imperfect gems could be created – promotional campaigns for engagement, wedding, anniversary rings, et cetera; you've probably seen the type of thing. Now there remained only one problem: the larger and near-perfect gems – the cream of a crop of high-grade diamonds.'

Ostermeir introduced a fresh tone to his voice. 'The importance of these particular diamonds should not be underestimated. Although only twenty-five per cent of the world's production is of gem stones, this is measured in carat volume and, when sold, the situation is reversed. That same twenty-five per cent makes up seventy per cent of the total monetary value, leaving the industrials with the remainder. And of that, the higher-grade diamonds, to a large extent, set the pace for those that follow.

'For example – and I'm going to use terms here with which you should all be at least vaguely familiar after the past few weeks – first of all, you take an internally flawless, fine-white, one-carat diamond and set the price at, say, eight thousand dollars – a figure that reflects its rarity at the time. And then the next thing you know, because of an over-abundance of diamonds of that grade, the most that could realistically be asked is six thousand dollars. Well, there's nothing wrong in that. You could wait for the over-flow to die down and pick up the price again – but then you discover that there aren't any signs of the overflow dying down, and there's another small problem: the six thousand slot is occupied by the next grade down – a one carat, fine-white with very, very small inclusions; so that has to be lowered accordingly, because you can't have a VVS one carat going at the same price as an internally flawless one. And then you discover that the VVS is going at the same price as the VS, and so on down the line. Then you start trying to fix a price on the colour gradings . . . before you know it, in order to balance the price you began with, you've tumbled prices in every category as surely as pushing that first domino.' Ostermeir bunched a fist on the table in mock emphasis. 'And believe me, gentlemen, top-grade diamonds are always the first and most dangerous dominoes in that line.'

A heavy silence filled the room, and Ostermeir responded to the gravity of its atmosphere. 'By late 1964 the diamond industry was faced with an explosive situation: a backlog of high-grade gems, so great and so strategic in overall diamond pricing that the very fabric of the industry itself was threatened. But we have to analyse that threat a little closer, because it wasn't just a matter of keeping those particular diamonds off the market, it was a matter of knowledge – knowledge that the diamonds might sometime come on to the market, and knowledge of their existence; both would have exactly the same effect. So, in the end, we have a question of relative secrecy.'

Ostermeir sought quick confirmation from the text. 'So finally, in February 1965, representatives of the major mining concerns, the South African Diamond Security Police and the CSO convened in Johannesburg, and the groundwork was laid for the formation of the South African Diamond Consortium. A series of covenants and trading agreements were prepared, tying the mining companies, the CSO and the Consortium. Among other things, these ensured absolute secrecy and a firm control on the flow of diamonds in and out of the Consortium. As with De Beers and the CSO, top Consortium officials were selected from directors of the major mining concerns. By having an interchange of directors between each boardroom, a great deal of control could be effected over – what was to them – a strong common interest; although, as before, overall knowledge and discretion were important factors in these decisions. The final choice of a Johannesburg headquarters, as opposed to the more natural choice, Kimberley, was mainly due to the size and closeness of the Kimberley community – once again, a question of relative secrecy.'

Ostermeir went on to explain the 'extra' security precautions of the current Consortium president at some length, and then looked up with an air of conclusion. 'And so in every respect, from its formation up until the present period, the Consortium has appeared competently structured to handle the problems that had ensued prior to 1965.'

Ostermeir paced back and forth behind his chair for a

moment. He thought again of Vorster's words in Pretoria – emphasize the 'international' threat. Certainly much had been said that morning regarding the possibility of communist involvement – it would be wise not to labour the South African viewpoint of that factor, when it could so easily be considered biased. Ostermeir abruptly stopped pacing and faced the meeting.

'The theft of diamonds from the Consortium nine weeks ago revived those problems. Only this time the situation is magnified: the Consortium has been in operation for thirteen years, and its diamond stocks are much larger than in 1965. We also have the possible threat of organized communist infiltration, although you are no doubt well aware of that factor, and its possible repercussions. Right now, the main issue is a world-financial one – a question of whether an industry worth a hundred and fifty billion dollars survives or not.'

Ostermeir rested his hands resolutely on the table-top. 'The financial details are important,' he stressed, 'but they don't have a lot of relevance without a complete understanding of the type of diamonds involved. That's first and foremost.' Ostermeir went on to explain that Rober Stockman would be covering that portion of the briefing. He looked at his watch, and then confirmed with Stannard the time of Stockman's arrival.

Kenton had been making notes throughout the day, but now his thoughts were wandering; the general build-up of comments regarding Africa turning his mind back to the newspaper item that had snared his subconscious that morning: it was a small article detailing the formation of rebel forces in the African state of Amgawi. On its own it wasn't unusual, but its position in the newspaper, bordering the article on the riots in Johannesburg, had given that page an ominous tone: one of rapid, violent and momentous change within Africa. It was the general feeling it had created and not the article that Kenton, in retrospect, finally decided was the most significant.

Only in time would he choose to alter that conclusion.

*   *   *

For a while everything seemed vague yet warm to Steel, even those parts that were still numb. Through the long hours, there had been thoughts of other warmths: the nurse at the bedside when he had first awoken, a stewardess whose face appeared so clearly, although he could never quite remember her name. As with so many others, it had seemed distant and fleeting: pleasant faces, smiles, a few forgotten promises, but nothing permanent. Uncomplicated but enjoyable. And then, of course, there was Christine.

Before that was the memory of a mother who once kept him warm but now treated him only as a friend and occasional companion. Who on his rare but important visits to her cottage in Edenbridge would never delve into his work, but on his departure would eagerly tell her friends of how her boy who had now grown into a man and had an important job in the government had paid her a visit. Further back there was a father, a vague and bitter remembrance of someone who, when he was thirteen, had left him with the responsibilities of manhood.

But through it all, scanning back over a life that he suddenly felt curiously grateful for, Steel wondered exactly *why* he had been attacked. Kenton had called earlier the previous day and mentioned something about an 'identity error', but now the meeting would be in progress and he would have to wait till afterwards to see an official report. 'I'll bring you a copy,' Kenton had confirmed. It was a tedious and infuriating delay, waiting to see the analysis of a past event, as if an explanation of the 'cause' would somehow stem his indignation. Already he felt a mood of revenge mixed with his morbid curiosity to discover who was behind the attack, but he pushed that element back, keeping to professionalism; he had already mildly agreed with Kenton that it would be awkward to put someone on the London end at this stage. Still, the medical report of the next couple of days would determine the final outcome.

Shortly after he had come round, he had glanced in the

mirror by the bedside to try and discern the more subtle scars; a trace of fear perhaps in his eyes, a nervous facial reaction that hadn't been there before. But all he could tell was that his features were more gaunt, sallow, his eyes deeper set.

One of the nurses had mellowed the passing hours with her deft and sly humour, making a comment about 'you navy boys' as she'd changed the dressing on his shoulder. For a moment he had faltered, and then remembered what would be under 'profession' on the entry form – at times, he thought, the 'cover' carried its own irony and humour. Since his period with Naval Intelligence, the files had been carried over, and to all intents and purposes – outside of a select few – he still worked for DIS, Section I. It was a less obvious cover than a 'department of the Foreign Office', and to a large extent, being an extension of the old War Ministry, people respected that secrets were involved and didn't ask awkward questions. At other times, though, the façade created a certain distance, especially with those with whom he wished he could share 'all' – particularly his mother and Christine. It was one of those things he could never quite be reconciled to.

Steel dragged his thoughts away and looked towards his watch on the bedside table: 12:44. In another four hours Kenton would arrive, and then, perhaps, everything would be much clearer.

Paul Ensor walked through a set of familiar doors that he knew he would not see again for the next few weeks. For that alone, he smiled appreciatively. The doors, as with the windows and part of the building's interior, had recently been modernized, although the thick brown stained brick-work told of another industrial age, of cotton mills, work-houses and consumption.

A ring of factory chimneys fencing off the central Manchester skyline would usually fuel a blanket of heavy grey clouds that would hang low overhead. For the past month, though, the clouds – with miraculous regularity –

failed to appear, and the tall brick obelisks begrudgingly settled for a thin, straggling trail of grey mist that would turn pinky-red in the evening sunset. Paul Ensor fumbled for a set of keys in his right-hand pocket.

'Goodnight, Jack,' he shouted to one side without looking. Jack had left only seconds beforehand, and he had no problem identifying the footsteps he heard in the loose gravel of the car park.

'Have a good time,' Jack replied. 'Don't forget to send a postcard.'

'I won't,' Paul said reassuringly. He watched Jack drive out of the car park as he locked the building's double glass doors. He waved briefly and then made his way to his own car. Within minutes he had turned out of the industrial maze of small streets and on to the Oldham Road towards Failsworth.

Rows of dirt-brown terraced houses were strung in an almost unbroken line either side of the road but tomorrow, Paul Ensor reminded himself, he would be away from all of this. He relaxed in his seat. In another half an hour he would be home in his comfortable detached house with Deborah, and Schweitzer – their black cat, named by Deborah in an impish mood. It was at times like this that Paul Ensor drew some satisfaction from his manufacturing chemist's business. Not the job itself, but what it provided – the moments away, the lifestyle, and not least the home life he relished so completely; something he considered fully separate from his work.

At this moment Paul Ensor was sublimely happy. To-morrow he was going on holiday, and nothing, but nothing could interfere with that.

Rober Stockman stood at the end of the table next to Jan Ostermeir, a pair of pince-nez glasses perched precariously on the end of his nose. Heavy waves of grey hair swept like bird wings either side of his head, and on top there was a small bald patch that on Saturdays his skull cap would conveniently cover. With his scholarly stoop, he appeared only slightly taller standing than most people at the table did seated. Jan Ostermeir had introduced him formally, and the small man surveyed the table as if assessing his audience. He had already prompted everyone to turn to page fourteen, one of only two pages that lay before his position at the table.

'You will notice that there are no less than fifty-four entries on this and the following page. This represents the eighteen trays of diamonds which were stolen, each one split into three sections to signify varying weights, colours and clarities. There are, in all, a total of eighteen thousand, eight hundred and forty-two carats, with diamonds ranging from point eight-six of one carat to the largest at twenty-nine point two-four carats.'

The small man lifted his head briefly. 'There are a few expressions on this page I would like to explain to you, although I also understand that a number of these may already be mildly familiar.' He glanced at Ostermeir and then adjusted his glasses. 'Next to the margin you will find the expressions "blue-white", "fine-white" and "white", which obviously refer to colour. You will notice that the blue-white is extremely rare, and there are no large quantities of these until we reach the smaller gems in the list. By comparison, the fine-white diamonds are not so rare and can be seen throughout the list, whilst the ordinary white are almost common except that they only appear among the larger exceptionally clear gems.'

Stockman adjusted his spectacles again. 'This brings me to the expressions IF, VVS and VS. These are abbreviations relating to clarity, and mean, respectively, internally flawless, very-very small inclusions, and very small inclusions. They are applied to varying degrees of flaws observed and judged by an accredited examiner using ten-times magnification. As with the colours, you will notice that the expression IF occurs mostly among the smaller gems, whereas the terms VVS and VS are seen only among the larger diamonds or where the colour concerned is blue-white or fine-white. So, as you can see, there are three main factors that contribute towards rarity: size, colour and clarity. If the diamond is large, then the other two factors are not so important. Alternatively, if the colour and clarity are good, the diamond need not necessarily be large to be classed as rare. The more that these qualities are applied the rarer the diamond will become, assuming a steep upward curve if measured on a graph.' Stockman lifted one hand to indicate the steepness of gradient such a line might follow.

'All the diamonds stolen were of a standard brilliant cut containing no less than fifty-eight facets. This particular cut is popular for its light-reflection qualities. It is generally considered that, under a bright light, even a poor quality diamond will reflect the spectrum radiantly if cut this way.

'Finally, we come to the size of the individual diamonds and the total package that was taken. The smallest gems were approximately ninety cubic millimetres, and they range upwards to the largest which were roughly three point two-five cubic centimetres.'

Stockman paused, sensing that very often precise mathematics did very little towards creating an accurate mental image. 'To put this in more graphic terms, the smallest diamond would be no larger than the normal shirt button, and the largest perhaps only slightly bigger than a cherry. The entire parcel would weigh just over eight pounds and could be contained in something no larger than a shoe box.'

Stockman illustrated the size of a possible container on the table top before him. 'Any questions?' he offered.

There were a number of questions, most of them revolving around the same point: that such a large and vitally important batch of diamonds could be held in such a small container.

Stockman's answers were carefully measured and precise, very often punctuated by momentary adjustments of his spectacles; unknowingly, as he concluded, he had introduced a topic that would lead Ostermeir into his final points more effectively than he would have ever believed possible earlier.

'The fact that the diamonds could be concealed in such a small container is highly significant,' Ostermeir resumed. 'In particular, the initial impression would be that a package so small, that geographically could be practically anywhere in the world, would be extremely difficult to locate. And you wouldn't be far wrong. But then you would be forgetting the probable intent of those who have the diamonds right now – monetary gain. Even if we are dealing with political gain, the same point of contact has to be made. At some time the diamonds will have to be exposed to people in recognized diamond markets. There aren't any fences that could touch anything approaching this size, and even the largest markets would have problems absorbing them – in a spread form or not. That's why,' he asserted, 'for the past few weeks you've all been directed to watch recognized diamond markets.' Ostermeir pointed back to the report.

'The fact that the diamonds are of a particularly high grade gives two factors in our favour. First, because diamonds of such a calibre do not appear everyday, it increases the likelihood of anyone noticing them. Secondly, and as a consequence of that first factor, it heightens the curiosity as to their origin; in short, it wouldn't be too long before somebody in the diamond business attached a special significance to the diamonds. So the race is on,' Ostermeir illustrated, waving his hands forward in unison. 'And all we are left with is the hope that we can recover the diamonds before anybody else is able to draw that conclusion. Because *that*, gentlemen, is when we return to the consequences detailed earlier.'

Ostermeir studied the table slowly. 'Last year, the sales of rough diamonds worldwide by the CSO were one billion dollars. To get the figure for cut gems, you'd have to multiply that figure two or three times. Thus, in the parcel stolen from the Consortium we have something that repre sents between five and seven per cent of the world's total diamond production for one year. That might seem insigni- ficant, until I tell you that it is equivalent to about seven months' rise in diamond prices, and that the market is strongly dependent on constantly increasing values. So, you'd assume, they could take a loss for seven months and then continue as they'd done before. That would be okay, only we aren't dealing with *any* five or seven per cent – it just happens to be, in this case, the most important percentage – the top-grade diamonds. Also, when there's a drop in prices, people tend to sell rather than buy. Based on that information alone, the CSO forecasts at least a twenty per cent fall in world diamond trading prices: approximately ten per cent would be absorbed in a freezing of projected prices over the next twelve to eighteen months, another ten per cent in an immediate fall in current values. That's the least that could happen.'

Ostermeir gazed round the table. 'The most that could happen is unfortunately nothing so mundane. Speculation as to the diamonds' origin would not inspire investor confidence. Subsequent suspicion or any form of knowledge regarding the Consortium's existence and actions over the past years would be disastrous. Unfortunately, the scales balancing diamond prices don't have to tip much to topple completely. Heavy selling creates more selling and so on and so on. The only possible end to such a run would be total collapse. And that, gentlemen, is where we return to the one hundred and fifty billion dollars I mentioned earlier today.'

Ostermeir paused, observing the expressions around the table. 'I suspect that many of you have been wondering about that figure. I know that I did, the first time it was presented to me. Interestingly enough, that figure is an estimated compilation of the values of gem stones held in the public domain and retail trade, industrial diamonds in business, stocks and shares in diamond mining companies and their affiliates, diamond reserves held by the same, and all diamond sales over the next ten years, both trade and retail. And all of this calculated worldwide and taking annual inflation into account. The exact figure, as provided by the CSO computer, was in fact closer to one hundred and fifty-five billion. Quite a complete and accurate calculation of the overall consequences, you would think.'

Ostermeir stopped suddenly. For the first time that day, his calm, precise manner had disappeared, a total and desperate seriousness taking its place. 'Only you'd be wrong, *quite* wrong. South Africa also happens to produce over 70% of the free world's gold, not to mention abundancies of uranium, platinum, copper, iron ore, manganese . . . the list goes on and on.' Ostermeir rested his hands heavily on one end of the boardroom table. 'In short, gentlemen, South Africa is by far the world's largest precious minerals producer. Speculation as to the stability of the diamond market would almost certainly – at least in the financial sense – turn attention to these other markets. . . .' Ostermeir was suddenly aware that it was unnecessary to say any more, and paused. 'Now you know what's at stake, gentlemen, in *every* sense of the word – and the consequences that *must* be avoided.'

Ostermeir started concluding matters, and Kenton brought his attention back to his earlier notes, aware of the monologue fading slowly into the background. Unlike Ostermeir's summing-up, which served purely as a refresher course of selected details, the notes formed a straggling trail of unrelated questions, each with its own related expansion:

Cleary's death: Convenient or inconvenient – planned? *Radio transmitter:* Technical advancement. Other devices? *Malusi Ugbaja:* Death suspected – independant hired to bury any possible links? *Communists:* Political or monetary? *Basikasingo:* Anthropological connections? *South Africa:* Mineral wealth, political opinion, or both? *Soweto:* How much rebel power? Chicken and egg situation – riots staged for robbery or vice versa? *Inside information:* A communist in a capitalist stronghold? *Rosenkrands:* Who would he try and call in his final moments? *Diamonds:* A market strongly dependent on controls – possible collapse – who would benefit most? *Consortium:* Power and control. Worth more in operation than not – awareness, conspiracy? *Shoe box:*

Size important, or just a distraction from total magnitude? *150 billion dollars:* If so, where would most of the loss fall?

Kenton studied each point carefully, using his pen as a marker. By the time he had finished, Ostermeir and Stannard had conferred and officially closed the meeting. He slipped the notes inside the front page of the meeting's report, wrote 'Jeffrey Steel' at the top and, with the file under his arm, followed the others out of the boardroom.

The house was hidden in a small jungle clearing in the Bimbila district of Ghana, close to the border. The nearest road – a mud track – was over a mile away, and approach could be made only by foot, for those few that knew of its existence.

It appeared to be a game-hunter's residence, but was in fact a remodelled version of a traditional *soukhala*, the dried mud walls replaced by thick mortar; beneath the straw roof, heavy beams supported layers of corrugated iron.

Inside the house the main room was adorned with native spears, masks and shields, and at intervals, seeming an incongruous mix, some English University diplomas. The furniture was heavy mahogany, the floor mostly bare, except for two zebra-skin rugs at each end.

Amwre Magonde addressed the man opposite with obvious respect. The man was older, but in almost every other way they were contemporaries. They were both well-versed in Du Bois, Padmore, Cesaire and Garvey, and more recently, King, Baldwin and Malcolm X – their Pan-African views were exchanged and developed with each new meeting.

It was late; they had talked well into the night. Magonde's host strode to the far side of the room, smoothing the bright towelling wrap across one shoulder of his white cloth robe.

'How long has it been now?' he enquired.

'Almost eleven years.'

'And Leon, is he prepared to enact the final part of the plan, if the occasion should arise?'

100

'Yes,' Magonde affirmed. 'As with the others, everything is set.'

The old man settled back down in a large chair opposite and stretched out his legs. 'So, you are in the final stages, my brother. I salute you. When is it you go to London?'

'We'll be there by tomorrow night.'

'Are there any other arrangements to be made in that respect?'

'No, Bature has gone ahead of us. Whatever small matters there are will be resolved before our arrival.'

'Then I wish you well,' the old man acceded after a moment. 'The blessings of the *sarakhunas*, you might say.'

They concluded their business, and then shook hands in the traditional manner of interlocking forearms. The old man seemed reluctant to part, keeping grip a moment longer than usual. And for a while afterwards, making the final preparations, Magonde would wonder exactly why.

6

This was Lawrence Wilson's big day. Of all the things that had happened during his thirty-five years of life, nothing would quite equal the events that lay ahead of him now. He thought of his years of poverty in the West Indies and his continued promises to his wife, Martha, of how he would make it one day. That day had finally come, he thought, smiling inwardly as he felt the warmth of realized ambitions overwhelm him.

The roar of a jet overhead disturbed his thoughts, and he glanced upwards, resting back against the main doors of the bonded warehouse that extended over four hundred yards behind him. The doors had been opened to their full extent to reveal a mass of racking and packages trailing back into the darkness of the interior. Straight ahead, the main Heathrow Airport terminals just over half a mile away shimmered through the intense heat. The reflected light gave the runway which separated the warehouse from the terminals the impression of containing scores of small puddles and rivulets of water, the dark grey tarmac a canvas to receive the sun's painted mirage.

He remembered his first day, almost a year ago now, looking at that same view, and how proud he'd been to get the job as a workman in the bonded warehouse. Above all, he recalled the lengthy explanations to Martha, in an effort to make her understand the importance of his new position and how much better it was than working on the railways. It wasn't only the money, but also the trust and responsibility that made it that much better, he'd told her at the time. That same reverence had remained unshaken until a man who referred to him as 'brother' had come along and talked to him about *other* values. Since then, he'd turned the figure around in his mind as many ways as possible – a new house, a new car and perhaps a visit home as well. Whichever way he looked at it, thirty thousand pounds was the sort of money he'd never before thought of in real terms.

And for it to be so easy, he thought, looking at the thermos flask in his hand with mild disbelief. As on the railways, he had brought the same flask into work along with his packed lunch, and had poured a variety of Martha's thick soups into its bright blue cup. During the last few months of unusually hot summer weather, he'd switched to cool drinks, but today the flask was empty.

The lunch hour had finished and Wilson drained the last few drops of invisible liquid before screwing the cap back on. From the outside it looked the same as any other flask, its sky-blue colour matching exactly his normal daily thermos. But the standard shiny interior had gone, a deep and warm darkness taking its place. Only a torch or bright light shone into the neck of the flask would reveal the interior: a rich and continuous layer of cushioned black velvet.

Despite thoughts of what would be in the flask later that afternoon, Wilson remained calm. Although more frequent of late, spot checks were rare, and in all his ten months there he'd never seen a thermos checked.

There were footsteps behind him, and Wilson turned to see the works supervisor, Peter Bryden.

'There's a load back 'ere on urgent, Laurie,' Bryden indicated with his thumb. 'The boys want to have a look as soon as poss'.'

'Okay, Pete, I'm right with yer,' Wilson answered.

By 'boys', Wilson knew that Bryden was referring to three of six customs inspectors who worked the first dual shift.

'Shouldn't take long,' Bryden remarked, leading Wilson towards the far corner of the warehouse. 'Then we can get stuck into that electronics consignment.'

He turned down the fourth aisle from the end and stopped just over halfway down. Wilson placed his thermos on a shelf two racks in and then followed.

'Mind yer balls, Laurie,' Bryden quipped, positioning himself behind a large cardboard carton. 'It could be heavy, yer know.'

'Don't worry, I dun lost 'em a long time back.'

'Is that right?'

'That's right,' Wilson confirmed, letting out his breath with the first strain of the lift. ' 'Twas part o' me tribal rites, didn't yer know?'

Bryden laughed, enjoying the light self-mocking. As far as he was concerned, too many blacks nowadays were uptight. They took themselves and everything else too seriously. In his books, Wilson was 'all right'. Together they moved down the central aisle formed by high rows of racking each side, and placed the carton on the long inspection bench at the end. To the right of the bench and higher up was a glass-fronted office, a short flight of stone steps leading to its dull green door.

Looking through the glass, Wilson could see the three customs inspectors. Only one of them still had his jacket on, and all of them had their ties loosened at the neck and their caps off. They were laughing and joking with each other as they drained the last dregs of tea from their paper cups. One of them inadvertently looked over at Bryden and Wilson, and then at the carton on the inspection counter. He gestured to his colleagues and the three put on their full uniforms and then made their way down towards the store men, appearing suddenly formal.

Wilson had always wondered about the magic of the peaked cap. He had never seen any of the inspectors smile while wearing them, of that he was sure. The first inspector, approaching, personified that humourless attitude.

'Is this the lot from BA 2107 we asked for?' he demanded, glancing at a clipboard in one hand.

'Yes, sir,' Bryden replied.

'It says here, twenty-two items of porcelain. Open her up, will you, please.' As always, his tone made it unnecessarily clear that it was an order, not a request.

Bryden took a Stanley knife from his overalls and cut a neat line through the seal and the thick brown tape beneath. He opened the flaps and stepped back.

The procedure that followed was, to Bryden and Wilson, predictably standard: one inspector took the porcelain figures from their foam wrappings. Another matched them to descriptions on the import sheet, ticking each one off as he went. The last inspector would then weigh each item on one of two sets of scales at the end of the bench, matching readings to those given in a neat column alongside the descriptions. Finally, in the case of porcelain figures, all three conferred on artistic value before deciding an applicable duty.

The rules were quite clear: the contents of any bonded container could be removed only by a government-appointed inspector, a privilege which, if compromised by a cargo-handler, constituted a breach of Customs and Excise regulations. Those same contents, once inspected, were effectually un-bonded and could be handled by regular warehouse employees. Bryden and Wilson re-packed the carton and then it was weighed again, and overall comparisons made.

It reminded Wilson that it was the weight he was most concerned about. He remembered the assurance that once he'd emptied the diamonds into his flask, not only would the weight of that single item be similar to the other thirty-five items in the crate but, as with the total package, would check exactly with the weight entered on the import sheet. It was only if the diamonds were not removed that problems would occur. Still it wasn't enought to allay his fears. One milligram either way and the package would be bound over for a much fuller inspection. It could be a single diamond stuck in the bottom, a faulty scale at the export warehouse, a damp package, anything. He had seen it happen so many times before. *And then what*, he thought, taking a handkerchief from his overall pocket and mopping his brow lightly.

One of the inspectors was looking over at him curiously. 'Okay,' he prompted. 'Let's get into this big one that came in this morning, shall we.' He flicked over a couple of pages on his clipboard. 'ATZ 5283 is the first package, I believe.'

Wilson helped Bryden carry the re-packed carton to the unbonded section. The walk, a full one hundred feet crossing the main body of the warehouse, allowed him to take fresh stock of the situation. He could see a figure towards the end of the bonded section, but couldn't make out who it was. Jim Walsh and Fred Hazler, he remembered, were still off at lunch, having left early. That left one person, depending on who it was he could see already. He caught glimpses between gaps in the racking, but the man's back was towards him and still over sixty feet away.

'Yer lost something, mate?' asked Bryden.

'Jus' wonderin' where I left me thermos, tha's all,' he answered cannily. He knew that in the next work lull he might well want to excuse himself to look for it.

If he was making his move, it would have to be soon, he reflected. The electronics consignment would take perhaps an hour, an hour and a half at the most, he'd estimated. After that it would be too late. The African consignment was one of three they could possibly choose for the inspection following. To leave it till then would be an unthinkable risk. No, it had to be done during the electronics inspection, he decided: the earlier, the better.

Time passed swiftly. Wilson was aware of other people's positions and movements, but not his own. He followed Bryden blindly. He could feel his palms moistening and a persistent film of sweat returning to his forehead. He wiped it impatiently with his cuff, silently cursing the heat.

Bryden, he could see, was pointing to a large carton to their side. Lifting it, he was aware that his hands had been trembling, but the weight quickly dulled the sensation, transferring it higher up his arms, although, at first, it was surprise he felt more than annoyance. He had always thought that when the moment came, he would be super-cool. Okay, he admitted, there were a number of small concerns and worries and perhaps, under the circumstances, a bit of sweat and an unsteady hand were normal. But somehow it didn't seem right. He had always been 'laid-back' by nature. And now he felt uncomfortable in his new role. Soon it would be over, he told himself. Then he could be cool again: thirty thousand pounds cool. The reminder of money brought him quickly back to cold planning – observing positions, movements, judging the weight of the carton in his grip. Consignments with lengthy import sheets usually weighed more, he remembered. At the end of the main aisle he could see the first inspector indicating that he wanted the package to one side of the bench.

'Let's have this one near the scales, shall we,' he directed; adding as they got closer, mostly for the benefit of his colleagues, 'From the list, we appear to be dealing with quite a large number of small items.'

The other two inspectors nodded their approval on his choice of position. Bryden cut into the top of the box and opened it up.

On top was a layer of small, equal-sized boxes, each roughly six inches square. The inspectors took the first few out, revealing the next layer, which was split into two uneven sections. In one section the boxes appeared in miniature, certainly less than playing-card size, but filling the much smaller section. The larger one was packed with slightly longer oblong boxes.

It was a mixed batch, Wilson considered, but one that would take as long as any he was likely to get that afternoon; each item would have to be checked by weight. There could be others with longer import sheets, but then on the other hand each could easily contain only a handful of items. It was arbitrary. Transfer time, he remembered, was four minutes at the most, even allowing for complications. The package on the inspection, he judged, would take at least fifteen minutes to examine. He made his decision quickly.

'Jus' goin' to check where I left me thermos,' he said casually to Bryden. 'Won't be a minute.'

He turned and made his way up the centre aisle. *An image of the figure came into his mind.* Knowing that it was the third corridor in which he'd left his flask, he took the second, walking its length. More time to reflect on positioning, he thought. *It was a life-size photograph that he could see clearly – a tall, slim figure; a spade-shaped jaw, teeth gritted, praying; features almost alive, animated.* He turned down the third aisle. *There was the distinctive phallus, legs cut off at the thigh, long arms, the bulging eyes tightly closed; an unearthly expression.*

And there was the thermos. He could see it clearly, towards the end of the third corridor where he'd left it. He walked a bit faster. *It was another photograph now: a carton, oblong, a single Johannesburg stamp, a seal to match the one in his pocket.* He picked up the thermos and walked back the way he had come.

There was a sudden sound. He stopped. He could hear it distinctly now – a faint rustling coming from the end of the warehouse where he had seen someone just a few minutes earlier. There would be a guard outside, he remembered, and Walsh and Hazler were still out at lunch. That left one cargo-worker. He stayed still a moment more and listened carefully. There was no movement in the close vicinity. He moved on, walking up the end aisle and taking the sixth corridor in. The carton would be about halfway down, he recalled.

It was a voice this time – ordering, directing, warning. And the face of a messenger; a slim-featured negro, excitable, his countenance taut, deadset – conveying a purpose that words were unable to. He could see the package now. The Johannesburg stamp and customs seal were there, just as in the photograph. *The words of warning returned.* He paused for another second, listening to the sounds around him. Muffled conversation from towards the bench told him that the inspection was still in progress. Everything else was as it should have been a moment earlier. *The voice directed him.* He took a knife from his pocket and cut into the top of the carton. A surface layer of nine oddly shaped carved wooden figures was there before him. He could hear his own heart-beat, a mass of body sounds he had never heard before. *Only the voice broke through them. It was reassuring but exacting. He followed it carefully.*

He could see the figure easily, positioned at the end, as it should have been. It stood out, somehow more unusual, more demonic than the others. He picked it up. *The tone of the voice was strong, affirmative, a smooth flow of instructions forming.* He could hear nothing else. His palm sweated. The three anti-clockwise turns of the obscene, extended phallus. Then there would be a small click. The head could then be unscrewed, again anti-clockwise. *The voice rose to a crescendo.* The open neck of the figure would be exposed, and the diamonds could be poured from its hollow neck.

It was so easy.

At first it was only a whisper of a sound that merged with the others from within. As he carefully turned the wooden phallus once anti-clockwise, it built up, breaking through the haze of Wilson's nervous concentration, and he looked up abruptly.

It took several seconds for the image of the relief duty customs inspector to fully implant itself in Wilson's mind.

He stood wide-eyed and motionless, his fingers delicately entwined around the figure's wooden phallus like a praying mantis about to partake of food. Then it hit him like a tidal wave. He kept a tight grip on the wooden figure with one hand, but his legs started moving involuntarily backwards, commanded by some detached portion of his mind. He picked up speed away from the advancing customs inspector, turning and half-stumbling over a mound of packages at the end of the narrow passage.

As the last few boxes tumbled to the ground, he was back solidly on his feet and heading towards the large block of light that was the main warehouse entrance. A rapidly diminishing shouting from the customs inspector barely forced itself through the hammering intensity of sound in his head. He could feel his pulse at his temples. His heart, too, drummed a rapid tattoo. By the time Wilson had exited into the intense sunlight outside the warehouse, he had broken into full pace, heading in a straight line from the main doors.

A security guard stood idle but alert to one side. His duty was to prevent unwelcome visitors from *entering* the warehouse, and his momentary confusion was broken only by another frantic shout from the pursuing customs inspector. In that time, Wilson had gained a full fifty yards. Quickly recognizing that safety gap, Wilson slowed his speed, trying to determine the best route of escape.

To each side there were large warehouses at regular intervals, bordering the narrow perimeter road. Many of them were fenced off but all, without exception, carried their own security guards. He eliminated the option immediately. The extra guards could be alerted too easily, and already the angle of a clear route had been narrowed by the pursuing guard and inspector. He turned his attention straight ahead.

Shimmering in the heat haze over half a mile away was terminal 3, a mass of passenger tunnels stretching out from it like prostrate tentacles. There would be people, a lot of people, Wilson reminded himself – passengers, baggage-workers, maintenance staff, airline officials and very few guards. A milieu that he could very easily be lost in. He picked up pace. It was hot and he could feel his pulse increase as if the blood was boiling in his brain. In his eyes, the jolting image of a main runway was directly ahead, and he remembered from his airport geography that he would have to cross the turning circles of another two taxiways to reach the terminal. But it was flat and there were no obstacles. That was all he thought of.

Wilson heard the noise before he knew where it had come from, a distant high-pitched sound of rushing air. But there was something else – a low rumble, alternating to a roar with each change in the wind. And then he could see it: a silver glint with tinges of blue, slowly becoming larger, more threatening. It was a large plane, and seemed to be fighting its way through a surrounding aura of hot vapours.

Wilson felt his heart pounding like a hammer at the inside wall of his chest. A decision had to be made. He slowed to a mild jog, and looked back. The security guard and customs inspector were less than forty yards behind. When the noise from the aircraft swirled away from him, he was sure he could hear the sound of their footsteps and heavy breathing. *And then the voice was back again; talking swiftly but surely of agreements, of consequences.* It was a simple matter, he decided. He couldn't be caught. But he knew that if he waited for the plane to pass, that would be the result. And then there would be *consequences*, he reminded himself.

There was no decision anymore. He was running blindly now. And then suddenly the edge of the runway was looming closer and he knew that he could make it. He would have to run a bit faster, but there wasn't any further doubt in his mind. He was sure of it.

Ten full paces brought him solidly on to the smooth tarmac. He pumped his legs hard in a frantic bid for the far side. It somehow seemed hotter on the tarmac. He could feel his breath burning in his lungs and exhaling in dry repeated bursts through his parched throat.

The distant roar was building steadily. The plane was advancing faster than he'd first anticipated. The runway, too, now seemed much wider. There was another heat now; a burning, toxic vapour that nauseated him. His lips were dry and cracked on the outside, and were stuck together on the inside by a thick film of congealed saliva. The roar was mixed with an ear-splitting whine, rapidly coming closer, bursting at his eardrums, smothering all thought from his mind. Then, as if catapulted, the plane swept irresistibly towards him, its wing-tips seeming to fill the runway and his vision. His legs stretched out in an incessant and swift stride. He could make it, he told himself. There would be *consequences*. . . .

The plane bore down on him like a giant bird of prey, a deafening roar and rush of wind rising to a crescendo, a tumultuous vortex that started to envelop his body. Suddenly, he wasn't so sure.

In the cockpit of the 747, the pilot had jammed the forward thrust full down and was rolling furiously towards take-off at over 150 mph. The image was low and entered the side of his semi-circular glass vision about three hundred yards ahead.

'The dumb bastard,' he spat, about to turn back the thrust and jam the brake in the reflex action. But it was too late.

His co-pilot shouted, 'VI,' to signify the point of no return in their frantic bid for lift-off speed. Simultaneously, the burst of a voice through their radio announced the appearance of an object on the control tower's ground radar. The pilot knew that a human body sucked into the jet intakes would probably knock out an engine, and yet the noise during take-off would deny him knowledge of whether he'd made contact or not.

'I've got aggro on the runway, Berny,' he hissed to his co-pilot. 'I might have to take her up on three.'

Any deviations now, he knew, would endanger the lives of everyone on board. The figure flashed quickly below the bottom line of his cockpit vision.

'VR,' the co-pilot shouted, a slight strain in his voice as the only sign that he had heard his captain's last comment. They had lift-off speed.

'Okay, rotating,' the pilot responded, pulling back on the stick. They were up.

He decided to check his instrument panel when he had cleared five thousand feet.

Wilson lay flat, spread-eagled on the tarmac as the shadow of the plane fell over him. He held his body firm, but tightest of all was his grip on the wooden figure in his right hand.

At first, it was the profound thunder of the jet engines that seemed all-consuming. But then, his ear close to the ground, an ominous rumble took over. Three sets of wheels, eight feet high and carrying over two hundred tons, rolled by. A strong rush of wind dragged at his overalls, finally lifting his body from the ground and shifting it over four feet forwards. As the plane tilted, two jet exhausts enveloped his body with a furnace-like heat, scorching the back of his hands and neck. The crescendo of sound was now shattering. Wilson closed his eyes and uttered a heavenwards plea that he was never able to hear. And then, just as suddenly, it was gone, an unusual quiet, by comparison, taking its place.

Wilson was up quickly. The inspector and guard had been slowed up by the passing plane. They looked hesitantly down the length of the runway before setting foot on its smooth black tarmac.

Wilson had, by then, cleared the far side, and was rapidly striding it out on the bordering expanse of dry, baked turf. A quarter of a mile to go, he thought, trying to spur some extra adrenalin. At that moment, three distant figures emerged from the main cluster of buildings behind the taxiways to his left. They were airport security guards, alerted by the control tower's ground radar. Wilson could see their uniforms quite clearly now. They seemed to be heading to a point almost equidistant between him and the buildings in his direct running line. He veered slightly to his right to widen the angle.

In his path now was one of several concrete and glass protrusions radiating from Terminal 3. He estimated that he would clear its apex at least a hundred yards ahead of the three guards. The inspector and warehouse guard were losing ground by the minute. They would probably be no problem, he thought. But the new guards presented a different picture. They were fresh and would eventually gain on him – then there would be other guards and customs inspectors, fresher and most likely closer than those chasing him now. There would be baggage workers, hailing or shouting at him, attracting more pursuers. It was time for some realism, he concluded. He would probably be caught. That much he reluctantly conceded. For a moment he reflected upon the *consequences* of that. One thing, above all else, became compellingly certain – he must not be found with the figure. It must be hidden. But where? His thoughts were clouding. There was too much pain now for him to think clearly. There were sharp, stabbing pains in his abdomen, and his chest ached as if an anvil had been dropped into the chasm of his lungs. But in his mind he felt nothing. There were thoughts there, but no decisions. There was impulse, but no clear direction. His finer senses were dulled, a crude but necessary protection against the ravages of fear and pain. Only instinct remained, as a hunted rabbit knows, by instinct, which way to run and where to hide. And then, suddenly, he could see it. The nose of a 707 jutting out from behind a concrete and glass building. A glimmer of possible opportunity started to form in his mind. He couldn't be sure yet though. Not until he could see it clearly.

The rest of the plane, the long, sharply angled wings, the cigar-shaped body, slowly became visible. There was a clear gap between the far side of the building and the plane. Wilson headed for it. He fought to gain more distance from his pursuers; and time. He would need time to hide the figure. Time, if he were ever to escape.

Behind the building he could now see three large warehouse-type buildings, and a tall wire fence at the far end, separating the terminal approach road from the baggage-loading areas. The three security guards were a good hundred and fifty yards away, Wilson judged as he disappeared fully into the gap. As he'd thought, they were certainly fresh, but it was hot and their heavy uniforms appeared to be making exertion difficult.

Wilson raced on. Sweat bathed his hands, threatening to loosen his grip on the figure. It was streaming into his eyes, too, but he could still judge shapes and directions. He wiped his eyes to clear the blurred image. He could just make it out now. The gates to some of the warehouses were open, but then the nearest would be too obvious. He chose the second one.

Getting closer, he slowed, approaching cautiously. There was nobody within the pool of daylight at the entrance. He moved inside.

He became increasingly aware of a loud, continuous churning sound. It was coming from the centre of the warehouse, where a large conveyor belt angled down to a shallow rubberized platform. On its far side two baggage-workers loaded suitcases, as they hit the platform, on to a large wire trolley beside them. Wilson sank back into the shadows to keep out of their view.

And then he could see them; he'd thought it a possibility when he'd first seen the 707 – consignments of unsupervised baggage awaiting loading. There were two trolleys; the closest just in distant view of the two baggage-workers, the furthest concealed behind a high bank of locker-style shelving. Both were piled over six feet high with luggage.

Wilson studied the figure in his grasp, measuring it, calculating. It would certainly fit in most of the cases. He thought quickly of options. There was an exit on the far side of the warehouse, but he might be stopped by the baggage-workers. The third warehouse he couldn't be sure was open and the wire fence was both too high and too dangerous. He heard a sudden patter of distant running and a frantic, lone shout. This was not time for indecision. He looked back to the cases. Each would be clearly labelled, he remembered. They would all be leaving the airport and could be easily traced, the figure recovered. It was ideal, he concluded. He moved towards the second trolley.

The footsteps grew closer, more menacing. He yanked the top suitcase from the trolley. It was locked. He hurled it to the floor disgustedly, taking another.

Activity was building outside, another voice now.

The second case was heavily strapped and too full. 'Jesus, man,' Wilson cursed to himself. He became frantic.

The footsteps had died, but the voices had come together, conferring.

He took down more cases, shaking each one for apparent movement. The third felt and sounded right. He tried the catch. It was open.

A security guard flashed by the open entrance, running towards the third warehouse.

Wilson thrust the figure quickly into the case, closing it firmly in one motion.

The second guard stood in the oblong of light at the entrance.

Wilson was reading the label on the case, forcing it into his mind, memorizing it scrupulously.

The guard stepped inside a pace, adjusting to the light.

Wilson saw him in a break in concentration and straightened up sharply. For a moment, both men were frozen. Then, in a fluid motion, Wilson brought his weight against the far side of the trolley, tumbling a mass of suitcases from its open end to the ground.

The guard lunged towards him with one frantic, hopeful shout.

Wilson got behind the trolley, ramming it sharply into the advancing guard; the upright bar caught him squarely in the chest, hammering air from his lungs and throwing him to the ground. Wilson turned and ran.

The second guard had swung round at the shout. He was the heavier of the two, and had built up a steady momentum as he approached the entrance, closing in quickly as Wilson headed deeper inside. Wilson was faster, but at that moment, he had barely started to get into his pace.

Twelve heavy strides in, the guard's shoulder hit the centre of Wilson's back with the force of a coasting locomotive, and they tumbled to the ground in one. Wilson felt all the fight leave his body in one sudden exhalation of air, a wave of total physical and nervous exhaustion sweeping into its place. He felt peculiarly subdued, drained.

The other two guards had come over and were looking down at him. They were joined only seconds later by the customs inspector and bonded warehouse guard. The inspector appeared to be trying to control his breath in order to speak.

The baggage-workers, disturbed by the commotion, started reloading the upset trolley in a hasty effort to keep on schedule for the next flight out. Only one person paid any attention to their actions, his eyes flickering nervously, catching every motion, his mind oblivious to the demanding questions fired at him by the customs inspector.

He was thinking that perhaps, just perhaps, it might be his big day after all.

Bradley Vansen walked down a palatial sweep of steps, away from the tinted-glass monument to skyscraper architecture that he owned. The Johannesburg winter air was slightly crisp but, as usual, clear. Responding to it, Vansen walked briskly.

Ahead of him in a courtyard was the statue of a bare-chested negro miner, bearing the torturing weight of an operative air drill. The sculpted bronze gave an effect of sweat that would glisten brighter as the sun rose; the same sweat that Bradley Vansen liked to think his organization was built upon.

There were no bold letters announcing the building's ownership, no flashy signs. A simple brass plaque by the

entrance, bearing the inscription 'VANSEN CONSOLI-
DATED MINES INC.', was enough and always would be,
the chairman had said. Nobody would ever hazard to argue
with that or any other dictate. The company name was later
shortened to 'VANSENCO' by stock traders and financial
journalists – an action not entirely approved of by the chairman at the time. As it gradually became popularized, he
revised his opinion, deciding that the label had a good 'ring'
to it. Especially for PR.

Vansen strode across the courtyard towards a dove-grey
Rolls Royce waiting on its far side. An ebony countenance
looked out expectantly from behind the driver's wheel.
Vansen slid into the back.

'Just get me out of here, Mik,' he said with a defeated
sigh.

As the car started to move, he glanced through the
window to his side, but for all his expression conveyed the
outside world might not have been there. The streets
seemed emptier than usual, some of the buildings bearing
the mark of unrest: boarded windows, bullet-chipped stone
and concrete. He looked away. The whole business sickened
him; 1965, he remembered all too well, had provided a
similar lesson. Admittedly, people like Mik were different
to the 'street blacks', but then he had always considered
himself able to control all blacks, to command respect from
them, manipulate them. It was an ability he prided himself
on, that he felt had helped him through the 'tough' years.
Succeeding where others failed. Some men would never
have the ability to control blacks, he would often conclude.
They so often let their prejudice take command. And now
these problems, he thought, gazing blankly at the passing
streets.

The board meeting had gone well, he reflected. Under
the circumstances it might have been worse. For a while it
had been touch and go, but then he'd sensed a gradual
acceptance replacing any doubt. But for how long, he
mused. And was the acceptance total? There were clever,
intuitive men on the board. He had surrounded himself

with their support for just those reasons. He was sure that some of them would now be speculating, asking themselves what the aura of concern behind the chairman's outward expression might be. Mik knew. But they were different. Whatever happened over the next few weeks, Bradley Vansen knew that he would not be able to share that one secret with them. It would be a cold day in hell before that would ever be a possibility.

When he arrived back at his Houghton residence, there was a message waiting for him from Sir Philip Oppenheimer.

It was the morning of Steel's release from hospital when Kenton's call came through.

'What did you think of the report?' Kenton enquired after some brief preamble.

Steel felt somehow cheated on learning that his own attack had been purely a mistake but he didn't want to give Kenton the satisfaction of showing it. 'Well, we waited long enough for it – what exactly did you expect?'

'Something fitting and hopefully poignant, perhaps.'

'Try the Foreign Office, they go in for that sort of thing.'

'Talking about *foreign*,' Kenton picked up, 'as you know, if this package does show up in London, you'll be back on it – we just don't have the time to put someone else in. Hinchley is still doing his bit in Hatton Garden, so it'll probably just be co-ordination; nothing more than that. We'll push the medical through for now, then balance up with a couple of extra weeks' leave when all is clear.' Kenton paused. 'A "safe" house has already been arranged.'

'Where?'

'A flat by Regent's Park. Hotels are out of favour right now.'

'No need to ask why?'

'It's no joke, Steel,' Kenton rebuked flatly. 'Apart from the obvious, with such a prominent hotel the 'D'-notice procedure was pure hell.'

'Well, I would have asked him outside, but he just didn't seem the approachable type,' Steel jibed.

'In fact, we could have done with him left alive. Information, if you see what I mean.'

There was no winning with Kenton.

7

The row of terraced houses in London's Notting Hill lay in the darkness that fell late during the warm summer nights. Only an hour beforehand, children had been playing on the streets in the fading evening light, the noise of their shouts and laughter mixing with strains of reggae music that had poured from an open window halfway down the row. Streetlamps along the length of the road made a succession of evenly spaced shadows seem more prominent as darkness became intense. The shabby houses were pressed tightly together, closely bordering the pavements on either side, the only relief to their dull exteriors being the vividly painted pastel colours that covered doors, window-frames and the occasional brick-facing along the continuous line. The street lay only spitting distance from the route that the West Indian Carnival took each year; this summer it had erupted into mass violence as animosity between the large black community and the police reached boiling point.

Lawrence Wilson hated the street and the area but now, as he paced slowly homeward along the shadowed pavement, a mixture of emotions jumbled in his mind. There had, earlier that day, been a hope that he would soon be able to leave that shabby environment for a better life for his family. But now he was unsure. There would be a date set for the trial soon, he reminded himself. The charges, after a six-hour detention, were read out almost perfunctorily: 'Contravention of Her Majesty's Customs and Excise Act, 1957, and two counts of assault and battery'. He'd been lucky on that score, he reflected. It would be a minor case – six months' imprisonment or a five hundred pound fine at the most.

At first, there had been some doubt regarding his story. Then, he recalled, there had been some form of verification and then a sudden, final acceptance. He had wondered what that verification might have been, but now it didn't seem to matter anymore. What mattered now, he thought, looking anxiously at his watch, was that he had missed a 6 p.m. rendezvous by over two hours. It was to have been on a deserted portion of the Perimeter Road, landmarked by a derelict stone cottage. He remembered wryly the many times he had visualized the meeting taking place, the money changing hands. And now for it not to have taken place at all. 'Huh,' he grunted dejectedly towards the pavement. There would still be his payment, he hoped; perhaps at the most, a heavy deduction for inconvenience caused, but still a healthy sum. There were other alternatives, other *consequences*, he remembered. He tried, as best he could, not to consider them. He continued briskly, lifting his contemplative stare from the paving slabs.

And then suddenly he faltered. His step remained the same, but a visible shock seemed to pass through his body. It was further down the road, on the same side as him, he could just make out. At first he wasn't sure about the shape or colour. Moving closer, walking faster, he tried to define it clearly from among the surrounding shadows. When he was near enough, he wasn't sure anymore whether walking faster had been the right thing to do. At least, not in that same direction. He controlled his apprehension and walked on. But more slowly. It was even clearer now, a shiny black Mercedes saloon. He could see the polished chrome of its bumpers and hub caps; its distinctive tri-point emblem. It appeared triumphantly ostentatious, wedged between rust-torn relics either side, a few neighbours paying homage to that rare occurrence through quickly parted curtains. It was parked directly in front of his home, Wilson could now tell. It would be too late now for any thoughts of retreat – already he could make out a head turning in the back seat of the car, sighting him, its outline appearing vaguely familiar.

There had been moments of fear throughout the day, but now he felt unusually empty, devoid of feeling. It would be all right, he assured himself weakly. He was closer now. A few paces away, he saw the back door opening. A man in a light-green suit stepped on to the pavement, confronting him. It was the same man, he remembered, more certain now of his previous supposition. He had never been told a name. He knew him only as his 'contact'.

'You is a bit overdue in bringing the goodies back to the roost,' the man exclaimed; then, coming closer: 'I told you not to fuck with us, man.'

Wilson stared back impassively. The man half opened his jacket. Wilson could see a gun, a large steel frame enclosed in a shoulder holster. It was not necessary for it to be produced.

'Get into the car,' the contact directed. He hustled Wilson into the back seat.

From the faint glow of the interior light, Wilson could discern the silhouettes of another three people inside the car. They were all negroes, except the chauffeur.

'Hey, what's this ol 'bout, man?' Wilson muttered.

Nobody answered. The silence seemed forced, pro-longed. Bature slid into the back seat, closing the door, wedging Wilson against the negro on his other side. It was the first time that he really noticed the man on that side. He became aware of immense size: the man's hands, legs, everything. A set of broad shoulders rose majestically to a strong, bull neck, and on his head, making him seem even taller, was a snakeskin-banded trilby hat. The man in the front passenger seat made a small motion with something in his right hand. The car started to move. Wilson studied the object closer: it was a delicately carved short stick with a series of leather thongs at one end. He recognized it as an African-style fly-swatter from an old newsreel about Jomo Kenyatta. The man wielding it was particularly distin-guished, Wilson noted, tightly knit black curls greying into sideburns; sharp-chiselled, finely proportioned features. The man turned slightly.

'Where are my diamonds?' he enquired in a matter-of-fact tone.

Wilson faltered. It was the voice, he reflected. He had always heared it on taped messages from his contact – ordering, directing, warning of *consequences*. Now it was before him. There was no doubt. He tried not to let his surprise show.

'I can explain,' he muttered, at the same time thinking desperately of how he might start. A spontaneous and jumbled mass of the day's events appeared as the only coherent mental image. 'I gone an' had some problems today,' he continued after a second, conveying his thoughts sporadically. 'I di'n' have no choice in the matter.'

'I am a patient man, Mr Wilson,' Magonde prompted. 'But don't test me. What of these problems?'

The events of the day started to unravel in Wilson's mind. There was a constriction in his throat, a tightening fear that he felt preventing his speech. He cleared it hastily, mustering some words that he hoped would relate his thoughts accurately. He began by explaining the predicament that had led to the unfortunate chain of circumstances. That, for some reason, a relief customs inspector had been called on duty earlier than usual. He continued fluently, describing his frantic escape from pursuit by both customs inspectors and guards, and his frighteningly narrow encounter with a 747.

The distinguished head nodded indulgently, as might a priest in the confessional. Wilson explained how, as escape became unlikely, concealing the figure had become his prime intention.

He detailed the final stages of his run, his placing of the figure in a suitcase out of view of the pursuing guards, and his careful memorization of the address on the suitcase's destination label.

The head remained unnaturally still now. The short wooden stick was lifted slightly, a silent but powerfully obvious signal. Wilson stopped talking. The stick was placed down and a gold pen and manila folder produced from the front glove compartment.

'Mr Wilson,' Magonde instructed casually, 'read me that address slowly and carefully.'

Wilson spelled it out letter by letter. It was a long and awkwardly spelt address. One that had been difficult to remember. Wilson found it easier to recall the lettering than try and wrap his tongue around some of the words. When he had finished, the manila folder was held up directly before him.

'Tell me, Mr Wilson,' Magonde enquired. 'Is this exactly what you saw today?'

Wilson scanned the lettering, quickly nodding a confirmation.

'Yes,' he muttered.

The manila folder was put away, as was the gold pen. Wilson sat back for a second. He noticed that they had already driven some miles heading west. The city lights were now sparser.

'There's only one thing that remains unexplained,' came the voice from the front seat, an insistent tone apparent. 'And that is why you are here now?' Magonde turned again. 'I would be most interested in knowing why the airport security people let you go. What reason did you give for taking the figure?'

'I told 'em I was collectin' wooden carvin's.'

'And they believed you?'

'Not at first,' Wilson replied fervently, sensing the faint doubt. 'But I been describin' a couple o' figures me uncle gettin' from Jamaica a few years back. They goin' out o' the detention room for a while. When they gettin' back, they acceptin' this, no trouble, all of a sudden.'

There was a heavy, overpowering silence. The distinguished head remained prone for a second and then turned away, facing the road directly ahead.

'And what of the figure's disappearance?' he enquired, almost uninterestedly.

'I told 'em it flew from me 'ands as the plane goin' overhead,' Wilson retorted without hesitation. And then he realized how ridiculous it sounded; almost as much as it had earlier that day, although then it had been delivered in an audience with at least some technical expertise.

'And?' prompted Magonde, failing to see the relevance of such a statement.

Wilson felt particularly clever at that moment. He related the explanation given him by Peter Bryden, the day they had both viewed half a flock of sparrows disappear in the path of a steadily rising DC-10 to be destroyed by the tremendous suction of jet-engine air-intakes during take-off and the combined effect of both rotor-blades and engine-heat. He finished by stating how the customs inspectors and guards would not be surprised at finding no trace of the figure if it had been sucked into one of the engines.

Magonde remained unnaturally still, eyes downward towards an inanimate object, pensive.

There had been no airing of an explanation earlier that day, although the more Wilson considered it, the more he felt sure that it had been that same technical acceptability that had finally made his story seem plausible. That acceptance was more important to him now. He watched the man in front immovably. There appeared to be a decision forming. The short stick was lifted again, leather thongs wafted slowly back and forth. The silence became uncomfortably intense. Wilson remembered earlier warnings of *consequences*, but there was no mention of them now. He relaxed at that thought. His explanation, he knew, had been good. But for some reason, the man ahead appeared unmoved, as if any decision bore no relation to that explanation. He became more aware, also, of the men sitting staunchly on either side of him. There was a richly mingled smell of leather, expensive cologne and cigar tobacco, but above it all, he could smell his own fear.

The inside of the car was much darker now. They had driven over five miles, he guessed. They were turning into a long, flat stretch of darkened road, an intermittent orange light flickering on the steadfast ebony countenance of the negro to his right. He could see the man's bull-like head turned slightly away from him, staring nonchalantly out of the side-window. As Wilson looked past him, there seemed, for a moment, to be something familiar about the house on the corner of the junction. The car turned into the road. Then he recognized it: the old stone cottage where they had originally planned to rendezvous. He looked forwards again. Ahead was a long, deserted stretch of the Perimeter Road. His mind was peculiarly blank, numbed. There was a significance there, he knew. He had visualized being there that evening, but the circumstances, in his mind, had been different. It all seemed so wrong now.

The man in the front was speaking again, and he felt relieved at the sound of a voice breaking the tension. He leant slightly forwards to understand the words; then quickly realized it was a foreign language being spoken, one that he could neither comprehend nor identify. It seemed to be directed towards the negro to his right.

For a moment he wondered what had been said; and then, as though in answer, he saw a large hand come across and grip the neck of his overalls. It was a slow, purposeful motion, but at that instant a paralysis of fear and surprise overwhelmed him. His body wanted to move, but a part of his mind stayed put, watching in a form of detached fascination. He felt the coarse cotton of his overalls dragging, his body shifting with it in a sideways motion.

'What's ol this, man ?' he protested weakly.

A blank silence returned. Everything seemed already to have been decided. He felt himself dragged further, lying almost prone now, looking back at the slim negro on his other side; a surrealistic image above a steadily advancing thick steel gun barrel.

There was a thrust of rapid acceleration. The inside light flickered on without warning, causing him to squint. Simultaneously, there was a sudden, billowing sound of rushing air from behind his head. Then there was a heavier-set, more determined face above him, glowering in the downward beam. He had been dragged still further back, he realized. He could feel the loose, cooling sensation of rushing wind around the upper half of his body. Through the corner of his eye, he could now see the open door.

He started clutching at the seats, the negro, anything. Thrashing wildly, he spluttered a frantic chain of obscenities. But it was no use. The giant negro was using both hands now. Wilson felt his whole body sliding backwards resolutely towards the open gap. He could feel the tremendous strength of the negro's grip, a raw power that induced nothing but inert weakness and fear in his own body. He was being moved like a puppet now, his head and shoulders thrust easily through the gap, a vision of rushing ground gaping suddenly below him. There were no obscenities anymore. Just faint surprise, and a weak, muted scream, as if a form of final surrender.

In a last bid, Wilson clutched on to the metal door-rim above him. He left two fingernails there, but the rest of his body kept on moving, a stretch of spinning, dark roadway rushing suddenly towards him, striking him in the face. He felt the flesh stripping from his cheek and, lower down, a sudden burning as the rough asphalt tore through his thick cotton overalls. It took a full ten yards for Wilson's flailing body to finally come to rest, just over the white line in the oncoming lane.

The large negro peered backwards, briefly satisfying himself with Wilson's position. He closed the car door, returning the interior to its previous quiet. And then his expression changed. His favourite hat had gone; the realization that it had probably flown from the car in the preceding struggle annoyed him almost as much as his sudden cranial nakedness.

Lawrence Wilson stayed in the same position for almost two minutes. The main impact of his fall had broken three of his ribs, one of them pushing its way through his lungs to start internal bleeding. He tried desperately to take stock of the situation. Everything seemed hazy, distorted, his mind verging away from the brink of delirium and then back again. He made an effort to move. In certain positions a wave of pain enveloped him, a sense of muscle torn and wrenched. Other muscles felt numbed, painless but unable to respond. He stayed prone a moment longer, his cheek pressed flat against the cool asphalt.

At first it appeared slowly. A gradually advancing distant light breaking the total darkness. A glimmer of hope entered his mind. If he stayed long on the road he might not live, a faint sense began to warn him; he would need medical help, hospitalization. He stirred fractionally. It was a car, he could now tell, straining his ears to catch the whir of its distant engine. The people in it could call for help, he told himself. He lifted his head slightly. It was clearly visible, a more distinct brightness at the end of a tube-like black void. He fought to raise the upper half of his body from the road.

The car was closer now, a brightness that was almost upon him. He made a last-ditch effort, finally pushing one arm rigid, supporting his upper torso; he waved his other arm weakly in the air.

The light hit him.

Sure now that the advancing driver would see him, he waved more frantically. It would be all right soon, he thought. He would be home soon, an abstract consolation that warmed him inside.

And then he could see it. The distinctive tri-point emblem, a shadow of faces and figures. For a second he remained transfixed. An inner instinct fought to lower his body again.

The twin headlamps bored down like two dazzling spheres, bathing him in light. He thought of Martha, of Steven; and then he was a boy again, running barefoot through the streets of Kingston, Jamaica. But it was much duller than he remembered. He felt confused. Outside it was all so bright.

The chrome bumper caught Wilson on the side of his jaw, whip-lashing his head back violently, his skull opening on to the asphalt like an overripe watermelon. The car screeched to a halt a second after impact, finally coming to rest a full twelve yards past. In the surrounding quiet, the back door opened. The large negro stepped out and started walking back. He headed towards the grass verge at the side of the road, stopping abruptly just before it. Bending down, he picked up the distinctive trilby hat tucked in amongst the kerb-side shadows and perched it back over his shiny ebony baldness.

Walking back to the car, he ignored the corpse that lay only a few yards away.

8

The White Elephant Club in Curzon Street is one of London's most prestigious private restaurant clubs. It is one of three favoured strongly by the upper echelon of the SIS, government ministries and the Foreign Office – the private rooms in its raised section at the back are ideal for private meetings; serious business is somehow mellowed by the neutral ground, the ambience and the first-class cuisine. Of late, the club has also become popular with film and music celebrities, and the private rooms are now used equally as an escape from the garish intrusion.

For the past hour, Jeffrey Steel had been closeted in one of the back sections close to the main body of the restaurant, in the throes of a private meeting with Jan Ostermeir. In a way, he was struck by Ostermeir's emphasis – if not over-emphasis –on the *international* implications; although his original intention, as arranged through Kenton, had been to discuss any small details from the earlier meeting that the official report might not have fully covered.

It was lunchtime and the club was crowded, and Ostermeir appeared momentarily distracted by the attentions of the waiter as they touched on the topic of a possible 'inside' connection.

'In some ways that's probably the strangest element of all.' Ostermeir raised one eyebrow.

'Why's that?'

Ostermeir took a sip of wine and gazed more intently across the table. 'A security question more than anything else. All the Consortium employees have been checked – they're clean. The president keeps a duplicate batch of "fingerprint" transparencies in a private safe as an added protection against internal fraud.'

'Fingerprint?' Steel picked out the single phrase.

'Yes, it's a trade term – an almost foolproof method of keeping a stock-check at any given time.' Ostermeir looked down and picked at the last of his Lobster Neuburg. 'But that isn't the only thing that the president holds privately – there are also blueprints for the Consortium building itself, codes, combinations, print patterns, et cetera. In short, even an inside connection appears somewhat unlikely.' Ostermeir paused heavily. 'But then again, what else are we left with . . . we can but try to discover how the impossible, on this occasion, became possible.'

For a moment they remained silent, each of them with his own thoughts, although to a large extent, Steel's were still forming, tying the new information into that of the earlier report. He recalled his impressions from A4: the vibrancy and innocence of Africa, yet its strong and vehement yearning to rid itself of every last remnant of white dominance, to the exclusion of other, more tangible threats from within its own black power structures. Little had been mentioned in the report or by Ostermeir regarding South Africa's enemies *within* Africa.

'Anyway, the Consortium's breach of security won't be so much of a concern from your end of things,' Ostermeir added at length. 'I suppose you *will* be continuing much as before?'

Steel looked down to one side, as if in acknowledgement; the strapping on his shoulder served only to raise one side of his jacket a fraction, and the faltering on his leg when he walked was so slight as to go almost unnoticed. 'Too late to change horses now, I'm afraid,' Steel grinned wryly. 'Training, briefing, case history – you know the score.

They'll push the medical files through until this one's over.'

For a moment Ostermeir appeared faintly uncomfortable at the mention of SIS internal intricacies, then slowly responded to Steel's wry grin. 'I thought as much from your chap Kenton. Otherwise we'd be wasting our time here, wouldn't we?'

It was a self-evident comment and Steel didn't reply. They ordered coffee and Armagnac.

'Of course, this "inside" connection isn't the only unusual thing about it all,' Ostermeir commented, and then, as if regretting the remark, continued with a straightforward summary of the main points of their discussion of the past hour – the initial robbery, the manner in which the print patterns were employed, the value of the gems and their more strategic, overall significance – coming finally to respective procedures and protocols. 'I'll co-ordinate everything as well as I can from Johannesburg. Obviously, as far as you're concerned, my direct lines of contact will be with Kenton and your Commander Stannard.'

Steel acknowledged the remark blankly. To a large extent they had merely covered the details already in the report, he considered, and now Ostermeir was recapping yet again. Much had been said about the 'international' threat, but what of South Africa? Exactly where did their viewpoint lie? Or was it so totally in accord with the international viewpoint that it hardly merited a mention? And even then, what little additional information he had gleaned had been used to support that same initial premise. Ostermeir was looking pointedly at his watch.

'Well, I think that just about covers everything,' Ostermeir remarked. 'I have another appointment this afternoon, so if you'll excuse me?'

They made their goodbyes curtly and Ostermeir threw back the last of his Armagnac, commenting as though it was an afterthought, 'My flight back to Johannesburg leaves quite early tomorrow morning. But if you should want to get hold of me beforehand I'll either be at the embassy or my hotel.'

'Right, thank you,' Steel replied, and he watched Ostermeir turn and make his way back through the main body of the restaurant: the closely grouped tables, the jostling white-coated waiters, the subtle Victorian blend of rich red velvet, ornate mirrors and polished rosewood.

The last time that he had visited the restaurant had been with Christine, he remembered, and suddenly he could visualize *her* walking between the tables, appearing as she had done on that day: her long auburn hair as she'd untied her headscarf, her easy, carefree air of confidence, and her smile, her *smile*. . . . But there were too many complications now, he thought, too much to explain away – his own injuries and their time apart, not least of all. And again he found himself cursing the charades, that same distance. . . . In that instant he began to wonder exactly *when* he would see Christine again.

Fifteen minutes later, driving back along Piccadilly towards St James's, the alert from Heathrow came through on his car telephone.

Paul Ensor sat next to the window halfway down the row aboard the 747. Through the small glass square to his left he could seen the broad sands of the Saudi Arabian land-mass over thirty thousand feet below. It was a predictable, monotonous landscape, sporadic relief provided only by sharp, rocky outcrops and plateaus which shaded small crevices from the rising desert sunlight. They had just left Dubai airport after a time-consuming refuelling and hectic duty-free excursion which he could well have done without. He had hoped that they would make up some of the two hours lost at Heathrow. Little chance now, he thought, studying the flight magazine for the third time since take-off. He followed the yellow dotted line in the centrefold map. Another five hours south to Singapore, he reflected, and then the short haul north up the Gulf of Siam to their final destination. He flicked the page, scanning pertinent details from a spread of alluring descriptions: 'Bangkok – lively, vibrant, colourful, historic; Venice of the East.

Pattaya – palm-fringed, restful, picturesque; just right for that 'away from it all' feeling.'

He rested back in his seat, glancing languidly towards Deborah. She was still asleep, he noted, faintly surprised that she had remained undisturbed during the renewed activity.

There was a twelve-year gap between them, and at times Paul was reminded of her youth. He remembered their first meeting; Deborah was as light-hearted as any nineteen-year-old in the late sixties could possibly be; he was slightly worn around the edges after his divorce from his first wife. There was a flippancy about many of her own age group that she found hard to come to terms with; paradoxically, he was attracted by her *joie de vivre* – something which had gradually lightened his own attitudes. Whatever gaps could not be reconciled, the years had mellowed.

The crackle of the intercom disturbed his thoughts. The captain announced their current flight position, and Paul looked back through the window. The captain described their path over the Gulf of Oman, which Ensor could now discern as a blue haze on the horizon, and their approach towards the south-western shores of India. More window-shutters started rising to receive the increasingly bright morning light. Paul felt a stirring beside him.

'Okay?' he questioned, turning to his side. 'Another six hours, the captain estimates.'

Deborah looked up slowly, blue eyes flickering hazily from between an uneven surround of auburn hair.

'Don't worry, I'll survive,' she muttered dreamily.

'It could be hectic when we get there. You might need all the energy you can muster.'

'Don't remind me.'

'Looking forward to it?' he asked her affectionately.

'Yes,' she nodded. He had asked the same question so many times before she found it was all she could do to agree weakly with a smile. But then she knew how much it meant to him. As if it was a form of appeasement for what would probably follow. Paul, she knew, wanted to start a family

132

soon. God, she thought, they had talked about it enough. Mostly Paul though, warning her with a chain of related stories about the dullness of pregnancy, dirty nappies, tied to the home, et cetera; she could almost hear him now – 'This might be our last chance to get away for quite a while, darling,' he would finish. If it was just up to her, she could happily wait a few years. But there was a compromise to be made, one that she was willing to make. She understood Paul's strong desire to enjoy his offspring's growing up while he was still young enough to appreciate it. But the appeasement, that was something else. It was a nice gesture, she knew. An adventurous, unusual holiday so different to their previous trips to Spain. One that she should be happy to experience. But all she felt was numb. Although, when she was honest with herself, she knew that she would probably, in the end, enjoy herself quite fully. She only wished that Paul would ease his over-excitement, his over-arrangement and concern.

'Penny for your thoughts,' Paul muttered softly, noticing her expression.

'Oh, it's nothing,' she replied, flashing a quick smile.

'You looked worried about something,' he persisted.

'I was just wondering about "Schweitzer" staying with Mrs Hogarth,' she said easily, consoling herself that it wasn't so much of a lie. She had, when leaving, concerned heself momentarily with that. 'You know, she has that part-time job and she's out a lot.'

'I know,' he agreed. 'But that cat's half-wild still, it could live through anything. Even if she doesn't feed it, it'll catch enough stuff in the garden, and if it's never let out . . . the last thing that Mrs Hogarth will remember is the hungry look in the cat's eye.'

'Don't joke about it, Paul,' she chided.

'I'm not, but if you have to worry about something, why can't it be a bit more meaningful – like our suitcases arriving in one piece or there not being a student riot when we arrive.'

'Student riot?' she questioned, raising an eyebrow.

'Yes, they had one a few months back. But tell me,' he concluded impatiently, 'why is it that women can't concern themselves with more important worries?'

'Oh, it's not just women.' Deborah rose up defensively. 'It's just that at times like this, people in general tend to worry about small things. I suppose it's because there's nothing really major to worry about. Surely there must be something back in England you're concerned about?'

'No,' he replied blankly.

'What about the business?'

'Heavens, no,' he said, this time more demonstratively. 'If I haven't taught Jack how to run the business in the last seven years, then I might as well throw in the towel completely. Believe me, that's the last thing on my mind.'

'You mean, there's absolutely nothing you're worried about, even in a small way?'

'No, how could there be?' he answered surprisedly.

'My God, Paul Ensor, I learn more about you each day,' Deborah sighed ironically, relaxing back in her seat, closing her eyes once again.

'Keeps it exciting,' he commented, almost triumphantly.

After a few minutes he leant over and kissed her on the bridge of the nose where a few freckles from childhood still lay. He was right, he knew. At a time like this there couldn't possibly be anything worth worrying about.

'Joseph, there have been some problems.'

'What kind of problems?'

Franz looked out of the open booth to a small group of people milling about aimlessly just inside the main hotel lobby.

'I can't explain now,' he said hesitantly. 'It's rather complicated.'

'Catch the next train,' the voice retorted sharply. 'It'll take you about twelve hours. I'll expect you late evening.'

Franz wanted to say something more, perhaps something that would sound quite ordinary to the passing ear, but would at least give some clue. He quickly decided against it. It could wait.

'Okay, I'll leave straight away,' he replied. 'Goodbye.'

He replaced the receiver and stood for a few minutes in thought. The lack of options rapidly became clear. He moved away from the booth.

Within an hour, he had booked out of the hotel, taken a taxi across mid-morning London and boarded the 10:45 a.m. train from Euston to Inverness. There remained only one thing on his mind. He became mildly aware that he hadn't concerned himself so deeply with any one particular incident since January 1965.

He remembered uncomfortably that the two incidents bore some similarity.

Gavin McNeil, Heathrow's Chief Security Officer, spent the first hour explaining the events of the day before to Steel – from Wilson's initial escape run to his final apprehension. He related Wilson's subsequent explanation, and its comparative plausibility; the fact that the wooden figure had disappeared and the possible effect of the 747's rotor blades and engine heat. McNeil's initial notification, followed by a check on a French import agency, had been almost a week ago now, and he had been left with direct lines of contact with the SIS at the time; this was his second meeting with Steel.

'The plane in question was heading for New York. When it landed we had the rotor blades checked, and some of them *were* damaged,' McNeil elaborated. 'Imagine the situation as it was presented to us at the time. As it was, if it wasn't for the Johannesburg seal we found in his pocket, we'd have had trouble even charging him with breach of Customs and Excise.'

It was hot. Gavin McNeil stood up and eased the tight collar beneath his starched blue uniform. He mentioned the police notification of Wilson's death as if it was the first hint of any strong suspicion.

'Is that what alerted you?' asked Steel.

'On its own, no.' McNeil sat down. He reached into a

side drawer and passed a bright blue thermos across the desk. 'The lads in the warehouse found it this morning – they think it was Wilson's.'

Steel looked at the flask blankly.

'If you'd like to look inside,' McNeil prompted.

Steel unscrewed the cap and peered into the neck. Its depth and darkness appeared profound, unusual. It was a large thermos, not quite the size of Rober Stockman's suggested shoe box, but certainly close enough to be a strong possibility.

'Of course,' McNeil said. 'Once this was found, it put everything in a completely different light.'

'If this *had* been used as a container for the diamonds, what would have been the chances of discovery by your security staff?'

McNeil paused. 'It's hard to say. Normally, they frisk each worker leaving; you know, some of these overall pockets can be quite deep. Apart from that, there's nothing really that can be done. As for the chaps that have a packed lunch, and there's a lot of them that do – they'd probably check a lunch box, or something of the kind, but a thermos . . . .' McNeil broke off, leaning across the desk towards Steel with an air of doubt. 'Well, it's not really the sort of place you'd suspect.'

Steel settled back into his seat. He recalled the photographs of Wilson's shattered body, and now McNeil's cold and factual explanation of events seemed out of place, almost sickening. In many ways he was the same as the Kentons and Mallinders of this world; more concerned with his *own* correct performance of duty, than its possible consequences. There were a number of things for which McNeil could be reprimanded, but now wasn't the time; there were other points of information he required – co-operation would be a vital key.

'Okay,' he exclaimed. 'We've established the flask as a likely container. But why take this wooden figure out at all. If the diamonds were already inside, why couldn't it have been picked up *after* clearing customs?'

'We have a question of weight here,' McNeil replied with noticeable enthusiasm. This was his subject. 'Customs inspections here at Heathrow follow a certain pattern of regularity. Now although this consignment was an unusual one, it was also, I'm told, of a regular kind. Customs officers, to a large extent, follow their observations. In essence they look for irregularities – broken seals, slightly open flaps, et cetera. One of the most important of those irregularities is weight. With regard to an unopened package, a weight difference might be noted to that of a previous consignment. As for a package that they decide to inspect fully, of course, that would spill the beans completely. The figures in this package, you see, were made from solid African teak. The specific weight of diamonds is almost twice as much. It would have been noticed straight away.' McNeil leaned across the desk. 'Of course, this also explains our Mr Wilson's anxiety to extract the diamonds before a possible customs inspection.'

'Were these other figures solid?'

'Yes.'

'Now, assuming that the diamonds had been emptied from the figure by Wilson, surely there would have been a weight difference the other way – a hollow figure amongst a collection of solid figures.'

McNeil nodded thoughtfully. It was a point that he had brought up himself with three customs officers.

'A large lead weight in the bottom or a series of smaller ones positioned to balance the weight distribution equally would have solved the problem.' He presented the explanation as it had been presented to him earlier.

'Well, we seem to have satisfied ourselves on Wilson's motives,' Steel commented. 'But what of your plane with the damaged rotor blades?'

'Could have been anything. A couple of birds on take-off or landing, a stone from the runway.'

Steel sat back. A straightforward, simple pattern of motives had been established. But that had never been the way with this case so far, he thought, resisting a number of obvious conclusions that came to mind. Already he was turning towards more intangible possibilities.

'Tell me more about this figure,' he asked of McNeil.

'It was part of a batch of thirty-six similar figures that arrived from Johannesburg early yesterday morning. We now have two consignments like this coming in regularly – from Johannesburg and Nairobi respectively. They're done on a "groupage" basis.' McNeil paused. 'That was, in fact, the main reason why your French import agency didn't find anything before – I'm afraid we didn't pick up on that until the other factors became apparent. . . .'

'Yes, go on,' Steel urged; already the loose ends were tying together.

'Well, that was it, really.' McNeil shrugged. 'It was an unusual bunch but that's about the strength of it.'

'What about size?'

'I'm only guessing here on the missing figure. You see, I only have the description on the import sheet to go by. But I would say it was probably a good eighteen inches long.'

'And width?'

'No more than four or five inches. Most of the figures were long and thin, except those on the lower layer.'

'You said "unusual",' Steel prompted.

McNeil relaxed back thoughtfully. 'Yes, very unusual lot. . . . Some had short bodies and long legs, others just the reverse. There were men holding spears, men with knives, women with elongated breasts – and some, quite honestly, were in configurations that would defy anyone's imagination. They were all "human-type" figures, but certain parts were distorted and disproportionate. It reminded me,' McNeil added, smiling faintly, 'Of those idolatrous figures you see on programmes about African witchcraft.'

Steel remembered Kenton's speculation regarding anthropological connections. At the time, he had considered it a case of spontaneous thought-association rather than a serious suggestion. He began to wonder now.

'Do you have some form of documentation detailing these figures?'

'There's a photostat of the import sheet,' McNeil replied, opening a drawer to his side. 'We used this to establish which figure was taken from the package.'

He passed a foolscap sheet across the desk-top. There was a series of numbers at the top, Steel noted, referring to the cargo flight, import batch and the custom's clearance at port of exit.

Steel could see the word already, halfway down the page, ringed in red ink; McNeil had identified it correctly. Tirelessly, he read down the page from the beginning, trying to form some type of symmetry, some other connection. Everything else had fallen into place so far. He skimmed through a chain of African words – *Ndengese*, *Bakuba*, *Balega*, *Tiv*, *Bamela* seemed more prominent because of the lengthy descriptions following them. *Basikasingo* was the sixteenth in the list.

Steel didn't feel any form of surprise anymore. It had been a thought during McNeil's earlier conversation and, on reflection, Steel considered he'd have probably been more surprised if the word had not been there. He looked back up the list, recalling the earlier tribal reference to *Balega* in Kenton's report. It was a strong possibility, Steel surmised – the figures named after their tribes of origin, or at least, some of them. He dwelt on that thought for a moment. The connection was most certainly there – Cleary's word, the reference to Heathrow Airport, the size of the figure, the necessity of planning Cleary's death. It would all serve to explain the theory. He looked up after a moment.

'Was there anything there to help you?' McNeil enquired.

Steel didn't reply. He stood up and strode towards the large map at the side of the room.

'So, somewhere between here and here,' he murmured questioningly, his back to McNeil.

'Yes,' confirmed McNeil, watching the diagonal path of Steel's hand. 'It's quite a mystery.'

Steel studied the conglomeration of main terminal buildings, scattered outer buildings, taxiways and runway. 'I'd like a photostat copy of this map and the import sheet, if I may?' he asked, over his shoulder. 'And also a look at the warehouse in question.'

Within the hour, Steel had completed his enquiries with the warehouse employees, customs inspectors and security guards involved the day before. Then he stood at the gate of the warehouse where Lawrence Wilson had started his escape bid and looked out across the wide proliferation of runways and taxiways towards Passenger Terminal 3, almost half a mile away.

At first, Deborah Ensor wasn't sure whether she'd heard someone shouting or not. Turning off the shower, she draped a towel around her and tucked part of it in between her breasts to hold it steady. The shout was more definite this time.

'Deborah!'

There was an urgency to the voice.

She came out of the bathroom and, with her hair still dripping wet, confronted Paul. His expression was surprised, contorted. He pointed towards her opened suitcase on the bed.

'That's not yours, is it?' he asked disbelievingly.

She stared at the case blankly. A tall, unusual, carved wooden figure lay there, she could now see.

'No!' she replied.

'I don't understand it,' Paul remarked confusedly. 'It wasn't there when we packed the cases.' And then he looked towards Deborah, a wry smile playing at the corners of his lips. 'This wasn't your idea of a joke, was it, Deborah?'

'No,' she pouted ruefully, adding, 'or yours?'

'Of course not.'

They stood there for a moment in silence.

'Could it have been one of our friends?' Paul quizzed hopefully. 'Sheila was around while we were packing.'

'No,' Deborah retorted. 'She never came into the bedroom. That's where all our stuff was. And anyway, what would be the point?'

'True,' Paul agreed.

They both stared at the figure as if sight alone would prompt an explanation of its appearance. Deborah was mildly disgusted by it. It seemed obscene, but in a demented, demonic fashion. There was a silence in the room. The windows were tightly shut and could not be opened, an assurance of effective air-conditioning at all times. Only faint, muted sounds filtered their way through from the busy Bangkok street, five floors down: high-pitched engine whirs, interspersed with equally high-pitched horns and klaxons that, at times, seemed to talk to each other. It was becoming aware of those sounds that made Deborah suddenly feel the silence.

'This is stupid,' she exclaimed, breaking it suddenly. 'There must be a simple explanation.'

'You first,' Paul invited.

'This is a joint effort. I'm not a detective.'

'Neither am I.'

Deborah held her hands up. 'Look, this is getting us nowhere. Now let's think, for God's sake. First of all, was there anytime that we were away from the cases?'

'No,' Paul replied blankly.

'You seem sure.'

'You're forgetting this was the case with the broken lock. The one that I had to keep my eye on all the time.' Paul smiled grimly with a mock salute. 'And I was a good Boy Scout, madam. The case never left my side.'

Paul leant forwards and picked up the figure. It was much heavier than he would have imagined such a figure to be. He placed it carefully on the dressing-table top at his side.

'So what do you think of our new ornament?'

'That's it,' Deborah exclaimed abstractedly, ignoring his remark. 'The open case. That's the reason for this.'

Paul was expressionless.

'It's obviously from someone else's luggage.'

'I don't see.'

'If you put yourself in the position of one of those handlers – among all the cases on the conveyor belt, either at Heathrow or this end, is a solitary wooden figure. No labels, no address, nothing. It can't go on the aircraft on its own, so he tried to match it up with a case. Ours is nearby, and it's also open.'

'Perhaps,' Paul conceded. 'But they could have also put out a tannoy call for a claimant.'

'I don't know. Once it goes to the handlers, would they be that bothered?'

Paul stared back at the figure. It was a weak assumption, he concluded after a moment, but it was as good an explanation as they were likely to come up with.

'Well, let's just say something happened at one of the airports,' he muttered. 'I'll notify our rep and he can check back with the airline. Let them sort it out between them.'

Deborah was smiling. 'You know what, Paul,' she said, tugging lightly at his shirt-sleeves, 'there's probably some poor sod at the other end of the globe wondering where his only souvenir from the deepest Amazon has disappeared to.'

'So how's the new Hercule Poirot feeling?' Paul joked, leaning over and kissing her gently.

'A bit wet from the shower,' she mumbled. She traced her hand delicately along Paul's shirt-sleeves and up his arm, finally resting her palm on a large patch of his bare chest. She popped open a few more buttons, stroking him in long, languorous motions.

'Are you trying to get me horny?' he protested weakly.

Deborah deftly opened his trousers and put her hand inside, cradling him from underneath.

'And what would make you think that?' she replied lewdly. She looked up at him soulfully, her eyes two deep pools.

'Damn you,' Paul resigned himself happily, clutching Deborah's damp hair, drawing her towards him. It became a long and sensuously wet kiss that left them both heady. Deborah felt him growing beneath her touch.

'Who's a naughty boy then?' she growled huskily.

'Bitch!' he taunted, smiling.

'Is that good, or isn't that good?'

'Oh, that's good,' he agreed.

142

'Well, stop complaining.'

He did stop. It was the way Deborah liked it at times, he knew: the dominant role. His pub friends had warned him that her behaviour was only one step away from total women's lib – a profession, burned bras and anti-men demonstrations. But he liked it. It was a change. 'We share everything else,' he would often answer them, 'why not the domination?'

He began to wonder at times himself. Deborah had left his underpants down around his ankles. She ran away from him playfully. He lunged after her impulsively, half-stumbling.

'You really are a bitch,' he exclaimed, more serious this time.

'But only for you, Paul,' she teased. She had moved around the opposite side of the bed from him.

He stepped out of his pants. 'You wait,' he threatened. Leaning towards her, he closed the suitcase on the bed and thrust it to the floor. 'Now I've got you,' he grinned.

In turn, when things became heated, he would often resume dominance. The sudden reversal, as always, excited them both. Deborah warmed to her role, becoming gradually passive. She moved away, feigning fear and surprise.

'Okay,' he said triumphantly. 'Now it's my turn.'

It was the game that was important, they had learnt, not the roles.

Deborah backed away. Paul gripped her hair, cradling her head in his hand, kissing her deeply. After a moment, she broke off, removing the towel and lying supine on the counterpane. She stretched out slowly and opened her slim legs in a posture of submissive relaxation.

They made love slowly.

The room was hot. Paul could feel Deborah's urgency, a subtle litheness shifting upwards to meet him, small droplets of sweat on her forehead, a thin film developing between their bodies, easing their motions. There was an impending feeling that he knew well; a sudden, sinking warmth, a shadowy mist over Deborah's eyes – her 'loving mist', as he

143

would often refer to it affectionately.

'Oh, God!' Deborah screamed. She brought her legs up from the surface of the bed and hooked them behind Paul's back. Her hands, which had clutched at the counterpane, she brought over, stroking at his shoulders, moving them in raking motions up and down the groove of his spine.

'Oh, fuck,' she hissed. 'Fuck me.' She closed her eyes. She wanted darkness, insular, comforting, a concentration of inner thoughts, not outer. At this moment of all moments. It was there now, she could tell.

But when she opened her eyes again, her head lolling mesmerized to one side, it wasn't Paul's face that she saw; it was another face, another expression – features demonic, eyes tightly closed, bulging, distorted; an obscene phallus, disproportionate, ever growing, becoming larger, more threatening.

Deborah screamed out in the final throes of her orgasm.

Half an hour later, while they were getting dressed, Deborah said simply, 'It startled me, that's all.'

Paul didn't say anything. There would be no point, he thought.

It was 3:26 p.m., Bangkok time. Paul knew, because he had already set their watches back five hours.

Jeffrey Steel loved London at night and always had done. He was above it all, looking down. It was particularly dark directly in front of him, among the rich expanse of Regent's Park; but on the outer edge of the darkness and in the distance, chains and columns of light twinkled magically.

Steel swirled the brandy in its balloon, savouring its aroma for a moment before tipping it back. He turned from the window, walking towards the centre of the large open-plan room, his bare feet padding softly on thick-pile carpet. He walked around for a moment, circling an expansive map, spread out on the floor with ash trays and book ends holding it down at each corner.

He reflected upon an earlier thought: Wilson had been dangerously near the Perimeter Road fence towards the end of the run. Why the sudden stop? Why not a frantic bid over it? And why, especially, the baggage-loading area?

Steel looked at the bottom corner of the map nearest him. There was a main terminal adjoining, he noticed, tracing a pattern from the straggled outer buildings to that much larger prominence. An extensive building, he remembered from his many visits there, invariably crowded with a vast and confusing conglomeration of people. An ideal place to get lost in. Again the question struck: why the baggage-loading area?

Steel sat down beside the map, tracing a path to the corner of the first, elongated extension. If Wilson was clear of all pursuers at that point, he reflected, he could have easily made it to either the Perimeter Road or main terminal building. There was a connecting door that opened from the warehouse side, and it would have been unusual for any of the baggage-workers to try to stop Wilson. Both options would have been clear. But would Wilson have been fully aware of that? came an afterthought. How well did he know that section of the airport? The perimeter fence, at least, would have been obvious. Steel studied the distance factor, referring briefly to the scale at the bottom. Sudden exhaustion, he asked himself, was that a possibility?

He took another swill of brandy. It was a full half-mile from the bonded warehouses to the main terminal, and yet the additional distance to the fence was less than a hundred yards. Steel sat back for a minute. He remembered the negro athletes at the Olympics just past, the sudden, finishing spurts on the marathon and thousand metres; that maniacal burst of energy when it all seemed finished; an indeterminable force from somewhere deep inside – the tape only needed to be just in sight, that was enough. And it wasn't just them, he thought, sitting straight again. It was anyone. If the objective was there, the adrenalin could be found.

No, it had to be something else.

Steel turned back to the window, gazing outwards. He remembered McNeil's final and careful reiteration of events.

If it had been accurate, Wilson would have had at least a full minute to himself inside the second warehouse. For a moment he considered the possibilities that such a time-gap would allow. His conclusion, though, was unsatisfactory. There was still the question of Wilson's death. If Wilson had used the baggage-loading area as a hiding place, the continuance of his life would have been a necessity, following the supposition that he would have been required to retrieve the figure. He dwelt for a moment on the question of other contacts. It was unlikely, he decided, recalling past affairs where outside contacts were, very often, considered an unavoidable risk and were subsequently dealt with abruptly and, as the Service so aptly put it – 'Invariably used only when the nature of a single disassociated action necessitates the use of such an operative.'

Political groups in particular, Steel remembered, were against outside connection of any form. An inside operative, too, was out of the question: the Service records of all the 'bonded employees' were both too long and too consistent, according to McNeil's files, for such 'political' or 'purpose' training to be induced effectively.

Steel slugged back the last of his brandy, placing the glass on the small table at his side. There had to be a connection, he cursed to himself, bringing to mind a picture of the baggage-loading area as it had appeared to him on McNeil's escorted tour earlier that afternoon. He recalled the ceiling-high locker-style shelving, main conveyor belt and wire-framed trolleys, tracing back still further through the description of Wilson's movements and the relative positions of baggage-workers at the time of his final apprehension. Steel clenched his fists at his side. He turned everything over in his mind once more, but again the answer was the same. There was a myriad of minor possibilities, many of them feasible but for one or more final but crushing factors.

Steel put it out of his mind, remembering that very often a solution to such problems appeared when not thought about – 'lateral concentration very often produces a spontaneous answer,' he recalled from the Service's resident psychologist – 'it is an extraordinary ability of the sub-conscious, not the conscious mind, to solve the intangible.'

Steel looked out across the London skyline: a faint pinky-red glow on the horizon appeared almost maroon in the thick band of concentrated light and fumes above the West End. A faint flashing light appeared to one side, advancing slowly aross the night sky. For a moment it seemed hypnotized by a set of similar flashing red beacons on top of the Post Office Tower, rising gradually above it before swinging away, south-east. Steel watched the flickering lights split apart and the aeroplane trail away over the more distant, duller promontories of the city. He started to turn away, but inexplicably he found something drawing him back; he watched in detached fascination the red-and-white flickers diminish until they had finally been absorbed into the glowing depths of the horizon.

Aircraft and baggage-loading areas, he remembered, had very direct connections.

Part Three

January, 1965

9

Joseph Matrai had led a tough life. 'The heroic exploits that helped his rise to power from a penniless refugee to his present-day position would amply fill the pages of any *Boy's Own Paper*, a close friend would remark, years later.

Matrai's arrival in South Africa came about in an unusual way. In September 1954, he was a young graduate with an agricultural degree from Budapest's Eotvos Lorand University. But the farmers of the time were much too basic and, in their own minds, practical. They had tilled the soil the same way for so many years, and their parents before them, and . . . what would a university boy know?

A combination of family pressures and a lack of options forced Matrai into the Hungarian army, and he had attained the rank of lieutenant when demonstrations against Matyas Rakosi's ruling Communist party showed strength. But in the following months, the all-too-close view of increasing bloodshed and atrocities turned Matrai's sympathies against the communists and in an ensuing 'rebel' incident, Matrai shot his army captain and fled overnight across the border at Bruck.

Matrai stayed in Vienna for a month, but his refugee journey led him eventually to England, where – due to his lack of command of the language – the only employment he could secure was in the Thurnscoe colliery near Doncaster. He was to stay in the same mine for almost two years. The work was dirty and rigorous, broadening his back and toning his muscles. At the end of a day he seemed as dusty, hard and black as the coal surrounding him. His outlook, too, became dark. He learnt to speak English quite well and yet he knew that if he was ever to make use of his agricultural degree, it would have to be on a farm of his own. Matrai saved, but the surplus of a miner's pay was insignificant and could never secure even the humblest small holding. He had already heard of a country where the mines were abundantly rich and full of opportunity and the farms were large, inexpensive and bountiful: South Africa. Men from his own mine had travelled there, writing back to friends in glowing terms, describing a world of raw and rapid fortune-finding.

Within another six months, adding to his previous savings, Matrai had enough money for the passage. He read as much as he could about the country from library books and then, in his best English, wrote off to the major gold and diamond mines. After six weeks he received an answer from the Dutoitspan diamond mine near Kimberley. He took the passage over within the month.

Matrai adapted well to the new atmosphere. He became fascinated by the produce he was mining, by the fact that such a small item could be worth so much. Diamonds held a magic for him. His interest spurred his ambition which, in turn, through the observation of others, aided his promotion. The first rung on that ladder was after fifteen months, as an underground team supervisor in charge of a working party of up to fifteen men, mostly drillers and pipeline 'feeders'. The second, Matrai waited another three and a half years for – as an underground works manager, co-ordinating the operations of over fifty men, both in the mine and at the early plant stages.

It was a welcome advancement, but then for some while Matrai had been observing that the men who bought and sold the diamonds could earn as much in a week as he could in a month. Already he felt he knew as much as them about the four 'C's – Carat weight, Cut, Colour and Clarity. He used a part of his extra pay to add to his already substantial savings and with the balance he bought small diamond packages. Trading outside of working hours, he made a small but regular profit. Over the following year, it built up steadily.

By the age of thirty-one, Joseph Matrai had attained his short-term ambitions. With his savings he secured a farm:

two hundred rurally rich, Orange Free State acres. He tended the farm as well as he could in his spare time. It became a dream that if he became a professional trader, his time would be his own; he would travel between Johannesburg and the mines of the Kimberley area. Matrai bought a small apartment close to Johannesburg's diamond trading centre, around De Villiers Street: a small, humble *pied à terre* with a sink and a kitchen table.

After eight months, Matrai considered his trading to have built up sufficiently for him to turn to it full-time. He left the mine at Dutoitspan, but over the next six months found that he spent more time at his apartment in Johannesburg than he had first intended. His farm became unkempt and finally he handed over responsibility to a neighbouring farmer for a share of the produce.

It was among the De Villiers Street traders that Matrai started to hear stories of abundant new finds on the southwest coastline. He considered this new information deeply, for at the time he felt he was faced with an ever-present and perhaps continuing problem: if he was ever to be able to trade in the style he wished, his business would require a large injection of capital. Many of the best packages available attracted top prices; already he had viewed the manner in which select groups controlled the market. A large prospecting find would solve such a problem, he decided.

Matrai sold his apartment in Johannesburg and travelled back to the Orange Free State, requesting his neighbouring farmer to tend his land for another year. He then sold his car, bought a Land-Rover, packed a rucksack, tent, tools, cooking equipment and essential supplies inside, and headed out across the five-hundred-mile stretch of 'Bushman Land' towards Port Nolloth.

Prospecting, as such, was strange to Matrai. He learnt a text-book approach, taking a few manuals with him that he felt would be as essential as his maps and compass. Mining underground had taught him what rough diamond rock, Kimberlite, and a rough diamond stone looked like, but coastal mining was another matter. Most of the diamonds to be found were in sand and alluvial beds close to the tidal margin.

He made camp south of Port Nolloth at the mouth of the Buffels River, just neighbouring the small mining settlement of Kleinzee. Many of the coastal mining rights to the north had been purchased and annexed-off long beforehand, but there were areas inland and further south yet to be exploited.

Matrai moved his camp southwards day by day, keeping about twelve miles inland, bordering the government concessions. Near Korignaas he met a group of three black African prospectors who described to him a district further inland, stating that they had already staked a claim there but would be willing to sell if he found the area worthwhile. Most finds, they added, would be close to the surface.

Matrai raked around in the hot sand for three days, but the only thing he uncovered which glittered to any extent in the sunlight was a scorpion; its bite was so venomous that even after biting out a chunk of his own hand and spitting it aside, he lapsed into a deep state of delirium that was to last almost eleven hours. He awoke in a strange camp to find a young blond-haired man in a safari suit leaning over him, smiling congenially.

'You stupid bastard. What were you doing out there?'

Matrai would always remember those first words with some amusement. As Matrai later discovered, the young man had a penchant for speaking flippantly, while concealing his deeper emotions. He introduced himself as Franz Zeifert.

Matrai responded to the stranger's cordiality, explaining in detail the offer of the three black African prospectors.

Zeifert smiled knowingly, commenting, 'It's an old trick. They were prospecting an unclaimed area when you first came across them and wanted you out of the way.'

Matrai swore vengeance on them. Zeifert was sympathetic, but reminded him of the main purpose in taking such risks.

'Don't let it upset you,' he added. 'That's what prospecting's all about.'

'You're right,' Matrai conceded.

Zeifert broke open a flask of rum and they sat there drinking, delving into each other's past and reminiscing. In many ways they had so much in common, Matrai thought.

'My father too,' Zeifert commiserated. 'He also left Europe because of his beliefs. He hated Hitler and everything the dirty Bosch stood for. I can remember to this day his warning – 'Franz, my son, it is the people who design a dictator after their own inborn hatreds, not the man himself.' He said that everything about Hitler was bad – too small, eyes too close together and that he only grew a moustache to hide a weak mouth.' They both laughed for a second. 'We left there in 1938. I was five years old. I had an uncle in Cape Town at the time, but now both my uncle and my father are dead. My mother died long ago in Germany while I was still a baby. I can never remember anything about her.'

'I'm sorry,' Matrai said. It was all he could think of.

Zeifert grinned ruefully, shrugging it off as if it was a casual experience. 'Look Joseph,' he continued thoughtfully, 'I've been told of a dredger operation just off the coast, south of Hondeklip Bay. It's past the government concessions and the rights are up for grabs. I was going to investigate alone, but an extra man is always welcome. If things look good we can work it together. I'd have to hire a bunch of Bantus anyway and it'll cut down on them too. I'll be dealing with a six-man, black African crew. What do you say?'

Joseph Matrai raised his glass.

'Prost,' he said simply.

He would remember that impromptu agreement for the rest of his life.

It was 3 January 1965.

The dredger was old and shrouded in a mist that, at points, seemed to merge into the water itself. There was something

155

ominous about it even at first sight. It was an oblong-decked, flat vessel floating about half a mile from the shoreline, with a pipeline fed down into the water and a convex metal plate welded to its barnacled hull. It moved slowly forward, a large pump sucking up a mixture of sand and rock disturbed from the shallow sea-bed, spewing the solids into a trough above deck and returning the water.

Of the crew, only four men were visible above deck, sorting out the solids in the trough; the other two stayed down below, tending the engine.

Matrai and Zeifert watched the operation for five hours. In that time they saw three good quality stones appear, each between two and three carats rough, and an assortment of smaller gems ranging from industrial up to just over one carat. It was an extraordinary find. They asked the Africans' price.

'Four hundred thousand rand,' the spokesman explained, using his calloused fingers for illustration. He eagerly showed them the registration for the boat and the concession papers for the area – a four-mile-long by one-mile-deep strip along the shoreline, with the mid-tide margin as its central marker. The price included the boat, the concession, the papers and the goodwill of the business, the spokesman elaborated, exploiting his gleeful salesman's talents.

Zeifert grinned to himself at the last expression. It was a long time since he'd heard the word 'goodwill' in the prospecting world. But it was all above board, he decided.

'Are you certain?' Matrai questioned, recalling his most recent experience.

'Joseph,' Zeifert asserted, 'this is the best find I've seen in all my five years of prospecting. We can't pass it up.'

If they were to work the claim an investor would be required, they decided in a short private conference. Zeifert had abundant prospecting experience, but it was Matrai who had contacts in South Africa's diamond centres. Their plans were set.

Matrai travelled back to Johannesburg, leaving Zeifert

in a makeshift camp between Hondeklip Bay and the dredger concession area. Ironically, although it was Johannesburg's De Villiers Street area where Matrai first made successful contact, it would be in Kimberley, he was informed, that such an investor could be found. He was given the address of an American there who had supported a number of claims similar to the one described.

Matrai travelled on to Kimberley overnight. The American was cordial but also precise and to the point. With shrewd reluctance he agreed to pass up some of his time to view the operation. He asked Matrai to leave directions to their camp and he would join them later.

It was almost another week before the American was to arrive and Matrai was surprised to see that he had traded his lightweight suit and cigar for a hunting jacket and a loaded gun. He was accompanied by three Bantus. Two of them, thin and clad only in loin cloths, were armed with machetes and carried a succession of supplies from his Land Rover. The third was much larger than the other two, wore a safari suit and carried only his weapons: a machete, a Luger automatic rifle and a chain of bullets strapped diagonally across his broad chest.

They looked an uncompromising bunch, Matrai thought at the time. Zeifert recognized such precautions well. The world of diamond-prospecting was cut-throat, he had learnt.

'A man well-prepared is nothing more than a man who values his life,' he explained to Matrai.

They all viewed the dredger operation as Matrai and Zeifert had done on that first day, almost three weeks beforehand. If anything, it was a more remarkable display than the first dredging run.

The American sat down with an air of congeniality with the crew's spokesman, talking of final terms, minor details. His terms with Matrai and Zeifert had already been established: a standard investor/prospector contract whereby they would put down ten per cent and he would furnish the balance. For that he would control fifty-one per cent of the operation and output. They would do the work. All finds

157

would have to be registered for that area, so that he would be able to keep track of their progress at all times.

They talked for some while and then the American offered the crew members some fine whisky which, he explained with a warming smile, 'I carry with me just for such occasions.' He sent one of his servants back to the Land Rover.

The crew accepted readily, not having tasted good quality liquor of any kind for some while. The spokesman was the last in rotation to be passed the bottle.

'You have two other men down in the engine room, I hear,' the American remarked casually but knowingly.

The spokesman showed surprise, a look that turned to horror as the first crew member to drink collapsed on to the deck, clutching at his stomach, a thick foam easing out from his mouth. He watched in a stupor his other two friends fall and then held out the whisky bottle at arm's length, staring fixedly at the label, oblivious to the rifle butt that came crashing into the back of his neck, felling him to the deck alongside his crew.

The large black Bantu, wielding the rifle as a club, went over to the engine-room door, burst it open, and went below. Seconds later sharp piercing screams rose upwards, followed by an uneasy quiet. The Bantu came to the base of the steep metal stairwell and called. The American waved his gun with mild impatience, directing Matrai and Zeifert to precede him. It was dark down below; the dampness and stench of diesel fumes hanging thickly in the air. But there was another stench, smothered but nauseating, warning them even before their adjustment to the dim light would allow them vision.

Matrai would try through the years to come, without ever quite succeeding, to blank out the memory: the two remaining black crew members, slashed savagely with machete strokes, eyes cod-like, staring fixedly into space, their blood mingling with the shallow pools of oily water that swilled between the rusted rivets bracing the engine-room floor. The Bantu wiped the blood from his machete with an oily rag, pointing at an area towards the dredger's bow. Set out almost display-like on top of a wooden trestle table was an assortment of rough diamonds. At the end of the table and resting on its edge was a plastic tube, trailing upwards and then through a hole in the dredger's hull. The Bantu flicked a switch to one side and another noise rose above the engine's persistent throbbing. With an air of dramatic illustration he picked up a handful of gems, placing them one by one into the neck of the tube, smiling faintly but meaningfully as they were sucked up inside, a succession of faint glitters disappearing with sickening ease. Within seconds his hand was empty.

'A very neat trick, gentlemen,' the American commented. 'You join it up to the pipeline outside and use the same gems each time the operation is viewed. Cuts right down on the initial outlay too. Very commendable.' He eyed them curiously, his gun pointed at them from waist level, adding in a change of tone, 'But I'm afraid I've seen this one before. Sorry to spoil your fun.'

Matrai was speechless. There were things that he wanted to say, but he felt numbed, as if any further surprise would have no effect on him. He wanted to explain, but the proper words wouldn't form in his mind and even simple phrases that were there seemed to catch in his throat.

It was Zeifert who finally interceded. Speaking softly but convincingly he explained how they too, like the American, had been fooled by the crew. That they had been told of the dredger by a black African prospector at a mining camp in Kleinzee and that there had been a witness to their conversation at the time. 'I would be pleased to give you this man's address,' Zeifert offered pleasantly.

The American looked unsure. Zeifert indicated the two bodies strewn on the dredger floor. 'I understand that now you have to ensure secrecy. My friend and I are seasoned prospectors. We are old friends to such discretion. If on the other hand you wish to kill us for our suspected involvement in this treachery, I only ask that you check our story first.'

The American looked back at them blankly for a moment. He remembered that if he killed them, there would be a connection through Matrai to him, from their common referral in Johannesburg's De Villiers Street area. At present, if secrecy was observed, there would be no possible connection between him and the dredger. He lowered his gun, holding up his hand.

'There's no need. I'll accept your story.' He ushered them above deck, asking them to leave quickly in a manner that suggested he still had some unfinished business on board. 'If I have reason to cross you on a prospecting claim again, I will have you killed on sight,' he warned in parting.

Later that evening Zeifert and Matrai sat in the glow of a camp fire in very much the same way that they had done on their first meeting.

'It seems we have something else to celebrate,' Matrai remarked jovially. 'This is the second time you've saved my life.'

Zeifert broke out the rum. 'It was you, Joseph, it was you,' he exclaimed, pouring two tumblers full. 'If it hadn't been for your mutual contact in Johannesburg, he'd have killed us both.'

'You think so?' Matrai questioned curiously.

'Men like that never take risks. They will always kill if it's safer, if it protects them. Believe me, I should know.'

'What about your witness in Kleinzee?'

'Non-existent.'

'And the man who told you about the claim?'

'I met him in the middle of the desert. He'd have made tracks long ago.'

Matrai made a swift evaluation. What Zeifert had said about his contact had been true, but then Zeifert had presented things in a way that had made it easier for the American to let them go and still save face. He reflected upon his own inability to speak at the time; drive and ambition got you nowhere if you couldn't cope with a crisis. Zeifert, he had seen, had intuitive and powerful persuasive skills and stayed calm under pressure. The very things

160

which he lacked.

'Franz,' Matrai said warmly, lifting his head up, 'I've been building up a small diamond trading business in Johannesburg. I work between there and Kimberley, getting rough stones from the camps, taking them to the market. I deal in some cut stones too, from the centres around De Villiers Street. My problem is that I can't be in Kimberley and Johannesburg at the same time. If I could, I would more than double my efficiency. I don't know how you feel about prospecting now, Franz, but if you would like to be that man in Kimberley – you'd be dealing with prospectors and rough diamonds, recently discovered; you'd be in your element. It would be a good arrangement.'

Zeifert looked deeply into Matrai's eyes.

'Hoch!' he spat gutturally, raising his glass; the first word of German to pass his lips since their first meeting.

When they shook hands, faces glowing in the flickering light amongst the vast openness of the coastal desert, their two figures appeared curiously isolated.

Although they could not foresee it at the time, it was a partnership that was to change the face of the diamond world. January 1965 was coming to an end.

It was 14 March 1969. In retrospect, there were two events that Matrai would consider had, above all else, changed his life dramatically: his marriage to Jennifer Colby and the death of her father, Patrick, only a year later.

At the time, the partnership with Zeifert was going well. Matrai had established in Johannesburg a trading agreement for small quantities of rough diamonds with dealers in London, Amsterdam and Antwerp. Their prospects were bright, but again an old problem had returned – to expand international trading, an extra injection of capital would be required.

Matrai had returned to the Orange Free State to sell his farm, and it was there that he met Jennifer Colby, a Scottish farmer's daughter visiting relatives in the province. Their common agricultural interests strengthened an instant physical bond. He was as attracted by her fair features and soft Scottish manners as she was by his dark rugged masculinity. As Matrai was to discover on a return visit to her Caithness home, in marrying Jennifer Colby he had become heir to one of the largest land fortunes in Scotland.

Patrick Colby had approved wholeheartedly of the marriage. Matrai appealed to him strongly as a man's man: intellect mellowed by physical presence, a broad back and ruddy complexion that reminded Colby so much of the gentlemen farmers he socialized with daily. A certain ruggedness that told of another, not so comfortable age. 'I admire a man with fire in his belly,' Patrick Colby would often proclaim to the assembled family, his back to the open fire, a tumblerful of Scotch in his hand.

When the news of Patrick Colby's death arrived – announced by no more than an awfully empty two-line telegram, Jennifer travelled back to Scotland to make the funeral arrangements; her only living relatives were an aunt and uncle with a small family in Aberdeen, and an uncle who had travelled south to London long ago, and was believed to have since become a professional tramp. The bulk of the estate, apart from small age-maturing financial trusts for nieces and nephews, had been left to her and Joseph.

It took another three months for Matrai to sell his interests in South Africa and take up the fireside position which had previously belonged to Patrick Colby. Zeifert purchased an apartment in Holborn close to London's Hatton Garden. They had kept their contacts in Johannesburg's De Villiers Street, acting as middlemen for rough diamonds from there and the now much more accessible European market-place.

Zeifert bought additional 'roughs' in London's diamond bourses and Matrai would make trips to Antwerp and Amsterdam if and when London prices forced them to. After eight months their trading appeared to have established a firm European base and Matrai converted a part of the sprawling Caithness mansion into offices.

In business terms, the money from Patrick Colby's estate

completely changed Matrai's and Zeifert's lives, enabling them to enact a long-awaited trading policy of Matrai's within the diamond industry.

It was something he had discovered in De Villiers Street: when gems of a specific weight, colour and clarity became scarce both their demand and the price that could be asked for them would rise dramatically. As more diamonds of that type became available, prices would level out again. 'We have enough money to control some of that flow ourselves,' Matrai explained to Zeifert.

Working as they had done before in diamond markets thoughout Europe and expanding their trading to markets in New York, Tel Aviv and Rio de Janiero, Matrai and Zeifert perfected a diamond 'transfer-hoarding' system. They would first select a specific category of gem, by size, colour and clarity; particularly of a kind which had already started to appear in short supply in any one diamond market. Then, purchasing all reasonably available stocks in that gem's category from both bourses and merchants in that same market and also resultant inflows from nearby markets, they would quickly create a heavy-demand/short-supply situation. Offload point was just before the peak – a quick, spreading sale touching each area of demand before news of such supplies spurred a return of price stabilization. Conversely, in markets where there was already a heavy demand in any one particular category, they would transfer gems from other areas, selling out in a similar manner. In closely connected markets, London, Amsterdam, Antwerp, and if the category of gem was not too large, they would buy up stocks in each area, creating a total demand and minimizing possible trading interaction.

In this way, Matrai and Zeifert grew from strength to strength. Within two years, in terms of total assets, they had more than trebled the initial capital from Patrick Colby's estate, but the money seemed unimportant to Matrai. On reading their trading balances, he would gloat over the conquests and then skim the figures as if they were purely a means to an end, his joy stemming from the power of control and manipulation, not its rewards. Inside, Matrai would always push away the recognition of that desire, striving on towards new ambitions, new conquests.

Matrai's strategy to expand trading still further was initiated by memories of his refugee days: the Jews fleeing from Hungary carrying quantities of gold and diamonds amongst their personal effects, refusing to hold any faith in paper money – they and their families in other Eastern European countries having seen its value eroded by breakneck inflation and currency devaluation. Matrai could see similar symptoms reappearing throughout the Western hemisphere, threatening especially those holding large sums of cash in banknote form.

Using banking centres of the free world, notably in tax-haven areas – the Channel Islands, the Bahamas, the Virgin Islands, Bermuda, the Cayman Islands and the New Hebrides – Matrai formed an international diamond investment exchange. The scheme attracted a chain of wealthy investors from all over the globe, driven either by the direct effects of devaluation and inflation or by the threat of it. In return for their often large payments, a pre-arranged quantity of certificated diamonds would be deposited in a duty-free vault of their choice. Identical certificates specifying carat size, cut, colour and clarity together with a laboratory authenticity stamp would be sent directly to them; an item very often held in a private safe as a form of 'title-deed' to their new-found property.

By a continuation of their rough-diamond trade direct to cutting-centre merchants and sales of cut-diamond investment packages, Matrai and Zeifert built up a trading empire. In March 1976, a private audit conducted in the Bahamas showed their independent diamond exhange to be amongst the world's foremost, though to a large extent the nature of their operations precluded both publicity and public awareness of that fact.

Joseph Matrai was not to become overly aware himself of the uniqueness of that position until later that year, in July 1976.

* * *

It was a hot day. But inside, in the cool, rosewood austerity of his mansion office, Joseph Matrai opened a black velvet bag and poured out a stream of diamonds, spreading them in a wide array on his desk-top until they appeared as they had done on that first day, back in July.

He remembered with mild irony his initial doubt. 'Franz, a bunch of crazy Africans say they have one of the finest collections of display gems ever assembled. They want me to buy them.' And then his cold, uncompromising calculations when their form of proof arrived – ten 'collection pieces', ranging between six and nine carats each.

'We would not have sent you such a valuable sample, if it was not a minor contribution compared with the total package,' the Africans were eager to add on further telephone contact. Their aims were made blatantly clear – a straightforward cash sale was desired for purchase of arms; transfer of money would be to a bank of their designation in Zürich, Switzerland. Above everything else, the transaction itself, their organization and the nature of their demands should be treated with the utmost discretion. 'Mr Matrai,' their final message concluded, 'we are conversant with your diamond trading operations and that such discretion has become your trademark. We look forward to receiving your offer.'

Matrai understood the implications of their last statement fully: through his diamond investment exchange he would be able to distribute large quantities of gems to bank vaults throughout the world on behalf of investors who would have no intention of declaring ownership for tax purposes. Within a year, the entire package could be disposed of without trace, including an allowance for safety by mixing in other lower-grade gems from European bourses to minimize the risk of package identity still further. It was a unique position, Matrai mused. Based on photographs, samples, carat weights and descriptions, Matrai had estimated the total package value to be in the region of sixty million pounds. He offered twenty million. It was a generous offer, he knew –

such a package would be almost impossible to offload through normal diamond channels, and fence prices usually ranged from twenty to twenty-five per cent. But then Joseph Matrai wanted to make sure. Suddenly it was important that only he could possibly be their owner. On reflection, he could quite easily see how the uniqueness of his position had led to the Africans contacting him and, to a large extent, that fact waived any initial suspicion he might have felt.

But then Joseph Matrai had other ideas outside his straightforward option of hiding the diamonds in investment packages: if such a quantity of diamonds could not be distributed easily, then, conversely, he had asked himself after the African's description of the total package, how had it been originally amassed? He drew on his diamond 'hoarding' experiences to work out an equation: how long would it take to collect such a package without attracting undue suspicion? Matrai filled up two foolscap sheets before arriving at an answer – six years, and even then, he considered, it was a conservative estimate: both the quality and quantity of diamonds described would preclude anything nearing regular availability in the market-place. And, he concluded, anyone who had built up such a collection in that manner would not consider selling out for a third of the market value. No, it had to be something else. The problem perplexed Joseph Matrai for days to come.

Ironically it was the involvement of Africans that turned Joseph Matrai's mind back to Johannesburg's De Villiers Street in the sixties and the 'shop-front' merchants speculating as to each separate diamond mine having its own form of distribution control.

'Don't be ridiculous,' Matrai would remonstrate at the time, 'it couldn't possibly be co-ordinated. The CSO's got everything under control, there would be no need.'

The merchants would be eager to point out that the CSO was purely an investors' work-horse and in having to publish annual accounts could not possibly offer total protection. 'If the figures aren't good, what then?'

Matrai had taken no notice at the time, but much later in

Europe he had heard the same speculation regarding separate South African control, this time in a more feasible form – a separate consortium to represent all the mining companies, at source.

When the Africans came back to Matrai, accepting his offer, he couldn't resist a final confirmation of his, by then, determined conviction as to the diamonds' origin. He sent a similar taped message to theirs, delivered by courier and to be collected at a London hotel reception desk. He stated, almost casually, that taking into account the difficulty he might experience in distributing such a package it would be necessary for him to know the nature of their origin. Not the *exact* source, but merely a general indication.

It was a reasonable request, Matrai considered; one that, perhaps, if not asked would have aroused some suspicion – rarely would diamond parcels of any size change hands without both parties being aware of total involvement.

Their tape returned almost a week later. Joseph Matrai played it over and over again, relishing it the first time and then trying to read further meaning behind the words. It was as he'd thought – although not specific on location, he concentrated on the vague reference – 'An organization designed to stabilize prices on behalf of various diamond mining concerns.' The tape ended, 'This organization relies heavily on discretion. Do not concern yourself, Mr Matrai, they will seek no form of publicity, either through the industry or other channels, to aid recovery of their diamonds.'

It was then that Matrai started calculating – the significance of such an organization and the part it might play in world diamond pricing. He would sit at his desk for hours, punching out a series of figures. The organization, as described by the Africans, he knew would be affiliated to the CSO in some way. He referred to files he kept on the CSO's sales, going back over the past five years. He worked out mining, market and public percentages of both rough- and cut-diamond pricing, filling a waste basket with trails of discarded adding-machine readouts, burning his desk lamp late into the night.

Zeifert remarked to him after one of those long nights, 'Joseph, is it really that important?'

Matrai turned to him, his eyes tired, weary and red, but with a burning compulsion and obsessiveness beneath their dull exteriors. 'Franz, this could be the most important thing that has ever happened to us. I can't let it go now.'

When Joseph Matrai had finally finished, he had lost eight pounds in weight, his back stooped slightly from constant leaning, his eyes ached and refused to focus on anything within two feet, but a single figure lay on a sheet of paper before him, underlined and circled in red ink: *£214 million*. It wasn't a firm conclusion in Matrai's mind; he knew that he might very well alter the figure at a later date. But as ten per cent of what he estimated the total immediate loss to the CSO must be, it somehow seemed right to him. It would make a good ransom, he decided.

When the Africans came through with final details – date of arrival, transfer point and monetary arrangements – Joseph Matrai's thoughts were moving on to other matters. A tape was to be sent to the CSO's London headquarters stating the ransom. It would threaten to offload the total package on to the market if it was not paid; an impending heavy market loss would be inevitable. Because of affiliated responsibility, either the CSO or the consortium they were shielding would pay the demand, he had calculated. It was important also that the Africans still held the belief that he would be distributing the gems through investment packages.

But again it wasn't only the ransom money that made Joseph Matrai's eyes gleam with intent. He had come close to recognizing the same inner instinct when involved in large diamond-'hoarding' operations. He could feel it now, almost as a burning at the back of his mind, a total, fearful preoccupation. 'No, it's *not* the power and control,' he would tell himself when it came too close. But in the end, Joseph Matrai felt it taking over, and he resigned himself, refusing to think about it. A decision had been made. 'Franz, you know how much this could mean to both of us,' he said simply, the day Zeifert had travelled to London to complete the negotiations.

But now everything had gone wrong. Zeifert had phoned just that morning, talking of 'complications'.

'My God!' he cursed to himself; had he learnt nothing from the two incidents in January 1965?

It was Jennifer's voice on the intercom, soft and un-assuming, 'Joseph, Franz is here.'

Matrai had come out from behind his desk by the time Zeifert had entered his office. They embraced in the old, formal European style towards the centre of the room. Matrai's rotund, stocky figure seemed to overshadow Zeifert. His was a much fuller presence than in their old prospecting days together – the result of countless, irre-sistible gourmet meals. Matrai's stomach thrust against his dark waistcoat, threatening to burst the buttons, and a trim black beard camouflaged the recesses of a double chin. Zeifert had retained his slimness, his age shown, if any-where, in distinctive greying sideburns and a succession of lines around his cold blue eyes, scored by months of squint-ing at the bright desert sun.

'Franz, what news?' Matrai enquired gravely, turning away.

Zeifert waited for Matrai to seat himself behind the large, leather inlaid desk and then settled into his own familiar armchair at its other end, nearest him.

'I don't know what to make of it,' he started. 'One day it was all set – the time, meeting place, everything – and then suddenly it was all off; or should I say 'postponed', as Magonde so politely put it. He said it was a minor problem and should only take a short while to sort out, but I tell you, Joseph, there was something wrong. He's usually so abrupt and formal, but this time he was polite, almost overpolite, and he was trying to make such a small issue out of the whole thing. Perhaps if he hadn't tried so hard I wouldn't have suspected, I don't know. On the other hand, I might be wrong completely. It was just one of those feelings I had.'

'And what now?'

'I have to phone him back in London. He wants to be assured that this will not in any way alter negotiations.'

Matrai raised an eyebrow.

'I said I couldn't talk for you,' Zeifert explained, in answer.

Matrai stood up and walked over to the large bay window to his side. 'I think you're right. I don't trust them either; as soon as I heard about problems, I knew. I'd been fighting the possibility out of my mind all the while, hoping that it wouldn't drag up all those old incidents, but somehow, things like that never really leave you.'

'I know,' Zeifert agreed with a reluctant grimace.

Matrai reflected for a moment upon Magonde. He had never seen the man, but from Zeifert's descriptions and the taped messages, Magonde already seemed different from other black Africans he had been involved with in the past; the polished English accent, cool temperament and soft, old-world manners all seemed to contribute towards that difference, he felt. Magonde remained an enigma. He turned from the window.

'We have a number of options, Franz; that is, if we are to assume there are more to these problems than Magonde would have us believe. The first is that someone within Magonde's own organization has played an unexpected trick on him. The second is a similar set of circumstances but with an outsider involved. It seems we can discard the possibility of this being a masquerade purely for our benefit. Usually things start going wrong when they've got the money, not before. And we are still, of course, holding samples worth over a hundred thousand pounds. Of the two, would you care to put your money on one?'

'An outsider,' Zeifert conjectured without hesitation. 'Political organizations of this type are usually too tight-knit.'

Matrai sat back down behind his desk. 'And then of course, we have the possibility that Magonde is actually telling the truth.'

'Yes,' Zeifert agreed, in a tone indicating the statement's total obviousness.

Matrai opened a broad cigar box to his right hand and slid its gaping mouth away from him, across the desk-top. Zeifert declined. Matrai picked out a fat havana, sucked its tapered stub and trimmed it with a set of clippers pouched just inside the lid.

'What do you think, Joseph?' Zeifert enquired.

Matrai lit the cigar. 'I think that, whatever the case, we can't afford to take any risks. You will travel back to London and phone Magonde, as arranged, but with one difference – you will give him the impression that you are phoning from here, or at least, not from London itself. There's one more Airbus flight from Edinburgh tonight. The number he gave you, do you have an address for it?'

'Yes, it's a hotel: the Chelsea.'

'That's Knightsbridge,' Matrai confirmed pensively.

'Yes, Sloane Street.'

'Is there anywhere within reasonable sight of its entrance, where you could make such a call?'

Zeifert envisioned the fashionable street for a moment; its furriers, hairdressers, clothes shops and jewellers. 'There's a pub just down the road, on the opposite side,' he recalled finally. 'The Gloucester Tavern. I could ask the landlord for the private line.'

'Did Magonde know of your movements while you were in London?'

'No, I kept away from my apartment as you'd instructed.'

'Good,' Matrai affirmed. 'It's an advantage to know Magonde's movements while he remains oblivious to ours. If you have to stay in London for any length of time, you will do the same.'

Zeifert nodded his understanding.

Matrai stood up and walked over to the side of the large room, where an Edwardian-style cabinet with bowed glass and delicate gold inlay stretched from the floor almost to the ceiling. Matrai produced a set of keys and opened the cabinet. Five rifles and three shotguns stood upright in line behind a bar and riveting chain. Zeifert recognized them and was well accustomed to several of them from sporadic hunting jaunts with Matrai. It was the lower showcase, though, into which Matrai reached. He took out a large handgun, re-locked the cabinet and turned back. He placed the gun centrally on the desk-top.

Reclining back into his seat, Matrai made no reference to the gun, looking above it in a direct line, ignoring its presence.

'When you've made the call, Franz,' he continued his previous line of thought, 'Magonde will make some type of move. It might not be straight away but then, on the other hand, I don't think he will want to waste too much time. You will follow him.'

'And what?' Zeifert asked, glancing at the gun.

Matrai ignored it still. 'Whoever has the diamonds or whatever has happened to them – either way, Magonde will be tracking them down in some fashion. You may be sure of that. He may have to leave the country – if so, keep me informed of his movements, but stay on his tail.'

'And what am I to do, if and when he has the diamonds again?'

Matrai leant forwards, exhaling a ponderous cloud of cigar smoke in his wake. 'I've been giving this a lot of thought, Franz. Even before your arrival, I asked myself what these 'problems' you described could have been. As you know, the Zürich bank-transfers were split into two equal parts – ten million to be paid on receipt of the diamonds, the remainder after my personal inspection, twenty-four hours later. It appears we may now have to change our plans, but the split transfer will come in useful, nonetheless. If Magonde ends up with the diamonds – we deal as planned. If it transpires that somebody else has the diamonds, we are free to deal with them on one transfer. The other may be held as a payment for the Africans; an insurance against reprisals, you might say. If the first party remark about the low payment, you may tell them what you have done. In a sense, it also ensures them against reprisals.

172

They would at the same time have a clear understanding that if they were to deal elsewhere, you would inform the Africans of their actions. You can play one against the other. This way we will be assured of receiving the package, whatever circumstances prevail.'

Zeifert both recognized and respected Matrai's talents as a negotiator, but it was the gun that preoccupied his thoughts most. 'And this?' he enquired, pointing to the desk-top.

'You will need it,' Matrai said simply. 'It could be dangerous.'

'Do you think that's wise, Joseph?' Zeifert remarked thoughtfully. 'Sometimes when you adopt another's tactics, you become no better than them. As the Africans seem dangerous to us now, we may at some time seem dangerous to them. At present they consider us no danger.'

'You're right, Franz, of course. But they will never know. It's purely for protection – just in case something goes wrong. Knowing you as I do, nothing will go wrong, and you will never need it.'

Zeifert picked up the gun, testing its weight tentatively. He hadn't been aware of his own nervousness previously, but now his palm sweated on the rough grip.

Joseph Matrai sat back, drawing deeper, more satisfyingly, on his thick cigar. There was nothing that he'd overlooked, he considered, panning back once again through the pattern of recent events. Everything had been covered. The diamonds would be his soon, he felt sure. He had remembered the lessons of January 1965 well.

10

Mark Collingson didn't like his job, but like so many clerks he was particularly good at looking efficient. He would never admit his dislike, even to close friends, electing by a form of vagueness not to talk about his work, and to people around the office he even managed to fake the desired amount of enthusiasm. But at three-thirty on a Friday afternoon, Mark Collingson's powers of forced enthusiasm were rapidly waning. Already he was thinking of which disco he would be 'shaking his ass' at later that evening, what type of girl he might be chatting up and what titles, duty descriptions and technical data he would recount for best effect when the conversation eventually came around to his line of work.

The day so far had provided a continuous line of routine papers across his small, but always neat grey desk-top, and at frequent intervals Collingson would gaze blankly towards a large window to one side, framing a bleak and monotonous panorama of the acres of flatness surrounding Heathrow Airport. When other workers looked his way, he was careful, though, to have a pen in his hand and look thoughtfully downwards. That was his position when the girl from the telex room approached for the third time that day. Collingson nodded imperceptibly without looking up.

When she had gone, he picked up the telex, studying the block of print at its centre –

KONI REP INFORMS – ENSORS – STAYING HOTEL NARAO – ITEM IN LUGGAGE – NOT THEIRS – CARVED WOODEN FIGURE – DESCRIPTION – 22″ TALL – TRIBAL-TYPE MAN – SUGGEST CHECK LOST-PROP LIST FOR DAY – FLT NO: BE 9461 – SCHEDULED 2:34 P.M. WED AUG 26TH – DELAYED – FINAL TAKEOFF 4:10 P.M. – REPORT BACK PLEASE – WILL REQUEST PROCEDURE IF POSITIVE.

Collingson referred to the top of the sheet: 2669 BA TH 2669 – BRITISH AIRWAYS BANGKOK 5 – 7TH FL – 95 RAJADAMN ARCADE.

He rose quickly, gripping the telex in a manner indicating its importance and headed towards the computer bank in the annexed office. He sat himself in front of one of eight visual display units.

'Have I got a line in on this one?' he asked an operator

seated at the furthest VDU.

'Yes.'

Collingson keyed into the computer, requesting a display of lost-property items for 26 August. There had been almost two hundred items lost on that particular day, the screen informed him after a few seconds; a complete listing would be displayed in five separate sections: PRESS PAI FOR EACH SECTION, it prompted him finally.

It was a normal day's lost property, Collingson reflected: cameras, jackets, umbrellas, hand-luggage, travel documents and assorted trivia. He scanned downwards methodically. The total irregularity of the request momentarily held Collingson's interest. It was the first un-routine thing to happen to him all day, but somehow he had a feeling that wooden figure wouldn't show on the screen. There had been eight requests earlier that day, most of them mundane, straightforward, but with little success in matching. What chance would a tribal figure in Bangkok have? he asked himself.

It showed up on the fourth display, but by then Collingson had adopted a more sober, more serious attitude to his work. Perhaps it wasn't such a bad day after all, he mused. He keyed in once more, requesting a print-out of that particular display.

Within seconds, the blue-lined paper tickered out from a unit at the room's end. Collingson took the telex, tore the print-out from its perforations and strode with renewed intent back towards his desk. He laid out both on its top, perfunctorily ringing the itemized wooden figure on the print-out in red ink. It was then that he noticed something alongside: a detail that he had overlooked on the VDU display. The coding signified a request from Security, not Lost Property. My, my, Collingson thought, the day really was turning out to be unusual. But there was nothing denoting urgency. He stared at the print-out and telex a moment longer and then pushed them aside. The excitement was over. The remaining part of the day would, no doubt, proceed as it had done before; it was time again,

Mark Collingson felt, for stoical and routine practicality. He would process the enquiry in the normal manner, along with the rest of his paperwork.

Franz Zeifert parked his car in Semley Place, just down from the thick, summery greenness of Ebury Square. From there he could just see the front entrance to the British Airways terminal in Buckingham Palace Road. The black Mercedes had edged slightly further along in the U-shaped approach road to the terminal but now had stopped completely. Once again, Zeifert picked up a set of binoculars from his passenger seat, adjusting them slightly from their last requirement, across a shorter distance in Knightsbridge. The lenses were scratched from the sands of the South-West African desert and the black metal was chipped and dented, but its moulded circles framed an accurate and close picture of the Mercedes' passenger: a dark countenance, serious, distinguished, tight-knit black curls greying heavily into sideburns. He followed the head until it had disappeared through the automatic doors to the terminal.

Time passed slowly. Zeifert scanned the shapes of three figures remaining inside the car; one of them was wearing a peaked cap, he noted. He put down the binoculars for a while, resting his eyes, taking in a more general view of the scene. There were momentary obstructions from passing vehicles and Zeifert watched carefully for any movement from the Mercedes or the terminal entrance doors.

It was almost fifteen minutes later when the figure re-emerged through the sliding glass entrance doors. Zeifert picked up the binoculars, fixing the man's head centrally in their view again, following it back resolutely to the car. The back door closed and the Mercedes swept away from the kerbside, heading east towards Victoria Station.

Zeifert relaxed for a moment. He waited until after the Mercedes had disappeared from view, placed his binoculars in the glove-compartment and then turned the ignition. Manoeuvring his car over to the far side of the road and along, he pulled into the terminal slip-road, stopping where, only a moment beforehand, the Mercedes had been parked.

The terminal was particularly quiet for a late Friday afternoon. Zeifert picked his way through a small group of people milling about by the entrance, quickly siting a backlit information sign above their heads. He approached the desk, smiling courteously.

'Excuse me, a friend of mine came in here a short while ago – a coloured gentleman, middle-aged, wearing a light brown suit. Could you tell me which counter he went to, please?'

The girl behind the counter smiled. 'Certainly, sir – British Airways desk, second from this end.' She pointed as if she were Columbus discovering the New World.

Zeifert followed her indication towards the end of the foyer. The girl behind the British Airways desk was a platinum blonde, hair ironed straight to her shoulders and then curled under just one inch. She seemed identical to so many he had seen before. Her smile was equally as uniform. 'Can I help you?'

Zeifert leaned forward on the desk, making his voice soft. 'I think you probably could. I do hope so, at least. It concerns a friend of mine, Dr Magonde. I dropped him off at the terminal here a short while ago. He had a hire-car arranged to the airport and I left straight away. Half way back to my office, I noticed that he'd left a part of his hand-luggage in my car. I understand he was at this desk just a moment ago, but now I've missed him?'

'Yes,' the girl nodded.

'This particular item of luggage could be very important. I would try and catch him at the airport, but I'm afraid I don't know which flight he'll be catching.'

The girl smiled again. 'No problem, sir.' The copy ticket stubs lay directly to her side. She had not processed them yet.

'Here it is.'

Zeifert took a pen and a scrap of paper from his inside pocket.

'Flight IA 238 scheduled for 16:45.'

Zeifert scribbled it down quickly. 'Where's that for, by the way?' he enquired as an afterthought, putting the pen away.

'Bahrain, Kuala Lumpur and Bangkok. Dr Magonde and his party are booked through to Bangkok.'

Zeifert tried not to let his surprise show.

'Thank you.'

He turned away. At the far end of the terminal, he could just see a vacant pay-phone. He picked up speed towards the booth, hoping that nobody else would take it first. It almost seemed unnecessary; already he knew what the answer would be. There would be a trip to make. And time was running short.

Jeffrey Steel was in the firing range when the message came through. He knew that it was important because Kenton had arrived to deliver it personally. He could see Kenton in the corner of his vision: a shiny dark suit, fingers in each ear and an expression that mirrored his disdain. The single sheet of paper appeared insignificant, clutched in one of his raised hands.

Steel fired off four more rounds, emptying the chamber, and yanked off his earmuffs before the echoing thunder and clatter of spent cartridges had completely died down in the coffin-shaped room.

'What is it?' he asked Kenton.

'Your alert at Heathrow. Something came through.' Curtly, he handed Steel the message.

Steel left Kenton standing, grabbing his jacket and making his way quickly from the basement room to an upstairs office phone. He glanced at the note on the way up. His first call was to Gavin McNeil.

'I'm glad you called,' was the first thing McNeil said. 'You obviously got my message.'

'Yes.'

'It was telexed through to one of our clerks dealing with lost property just this afternoon. I've got the full address of

178

the people concerned in front of me.'

'Go ahead.' Steel grabbed a pen and paper from the trough in front of him and wrote it down.

His second call was to the British Airways reservation desk, Heathrow Airport. 'The time of the next flight to Bangkok, please?'

'Boarding now, sir. Leaving at 16:45.'

Steel glared at his watch. 4:32 p.m. Damn!

'The next flight?'

'21:35 later this evening, sir.'

'Book me in please. Jeffrey Steel. . . .'

The girl took the details.

Steel turned over the sheet of paper before him and wrote down a series of names in block capitals – ENSORS – WILSON'S ORGANIZATION – VITCHIT CHARE-OMPOND. He spread the names out around the paper, wrote the word TIME at the bottom and left a blank space in the right-hand corner.

His last call was to Stannard.

'My alert at Heathrow came through eventually, but I've got a problem,' he explained. 'The figure's with a couple on holiday in Bangkok. Now it's very likely that Wilson's organization got this same information a couple of days ago, so we're left with a time-gap.'

Stannard mused for a second on the distance of Bangkok.

'I've just missed a flight out,' Steel continued, 'the next one's in five hours, and the flight itself takes thirteen hours – so that time-gap's widened. It'll be the best part of a day before I can get out there, but I can get a fast message through either by phone or by telegram. I've got two contacts in Bangkok, both from early DIS, four or five years back – a hotel manager and an officer with the Burmese military attaché.'

'How would they help?'

'Well, as for the hotel manager, I can trust him implicitly – the idea being that I ask the Ensors to go straight there and deposit the figure in his hotel safe. It would also, from the Ensors' point of view, still appear as a normal tourist procedure.'

'And your gentleman with the military attaché?'

' I don't think he can help – the red tape involved would be much too complex. But that's my *other* problem – we're left with a question of the Ensors' safety. We need a man out there, on the spot, fast. Who have we got?'

'The embassy staff, of course. But the nearest trained man is in Singapore.'

'What about the CIA?'

'One moment.' Stannard went away from the phone for almost three minutes. When he came back, he had a name.

'Okay,' Steel responded. 'I'll contact him straightaway and ask him to cover the Ensors as soon as possible.'

Steel wrote the name down in the blank space on the paper before him – GENE HASKELL.

Stannard indicated that clearance from Langley would be virtually automatic procedure, from what information was on file; also that he would pass on all the details to Jan Ostermeir – positive gem identification would be a vital factor. 'A representative of the CSO or the Consortium will contact you – with the time-factor involved, probably in Bangkok.'

Within an hour, Steel was able to contact the Ensors by phone and pass them the message; he made no reference to danger.

But Gene Haskell was not at his number so he sent a telegram instead.

And then Jeffrey Steel went back to the stark, fluorescently lit basement room and pumped a few more shells through the dark cardboard figure with a target at its gut.

Swaying palms and abundant tropical foliage on top of a sky-scraper might seem unusual in the centre of most cities, but Bangkok took it in its stride. 'Heaven on Earth' was certainly one phrase that had been used to describe the luxuriant surrounds of Bangkok's open-air, roof-top restaurant, the Chop-Chai steakhouse. The advertisement on the radio in the Ensors' hotel room had convinced Paul

Ensor that the Chop-Chai might be an ideal location for a first-night-out dinner surprise for Deborah. He looked from their small, thatched-roofed, table nook through a window moulded in dark, natural rock at their side.

'Have you ever see so many lights?' he commented abstractedly.

'No.'

'Just no, is that it?'

Deborah reached her hands across the table, gently placating him. 'No, really, it's beautiful, Paul. Thank you, love.'

Paul sensed a faint doubt still. 'Look, we've contacted the rep – he's contacted the airlines. For the moment there's nothing else we can do.'

'Yes, I suppose so.' Deborah had mentioned earlier that she just didn't like having the figure about, so it really wasn't worth repeating. And as Paul had said, women did tend to preoccupy themselves with unnecessary worries. She pushed the thoughts away.

They sat there in silence for a moment, an iridescent glow of a small candle between them, flickering in their eyes. A waiter in a bright flowery shirt approached with their drinks in two glass mugs engraved with bright, leering faces.

'How are the white shoes?' Deborah enquired thoughtfully, when he had gone.

Paul remembered with some awkwardness his two-hour shopping jaunt in Manchester's Piccadilly for 'tropically suitable' footwear.

'Humphrey Bogart wore a pair in Casablanca,' he defended in mock surprise. 'No, really, the wearing-in blister-stage seems to be just about over.'

Deborah started laughing. 'That chambermaid yesterday – her face when she looked at the bed. "Is it your honeymoon?" You know, I think it was less than an hour from arrival to sheet-tousling – we must have broken the record.'

'I hope we did.'

'Don't make me blush, vicar,' she admonished sarcastically.

'You know, this being our first evening out, we should have a toast.'

Deborah raised her glass.

'To sheet-tousling, morning, afternoon and night.' Paul said triumphantly.

The faces on the mugs reminded Deborah of something else, but again she pushed the thoughts away. There couldn't be a moment more magical, she consoled herself. Or more memorable.

'Paul, I love you,' she said softly.

And then she remembered with a discomfort that rose steadily and finally pervaded her whole being that just following the high points of her life there had often been a sudden and frightful downfall: her own brother's tragic death and the unnecessarily vicious divorce action from Paul's first wife.

In London it was 1:15 p.m. and more than four hours before Jeffrey Steel would contact them back at their hotel. At that time, it would be 1:56 a.m. in Bangkok, and perhaps if the combined factors of time and distance could have been remembered, Paul Ensor would have attached some urgency to the message. But any such urgency had been merely suggested, not mentioned directly, he reflected. And it was late.

What the hell, another six hours would surely do no harm, he decided finally, mumbling something about 'room service' to Deborah regarding the call. He would deliver the figure first thing in the morning.

Jeffrey Steel had thirty minutes to boarding call for Flight TG 911 to Bangkok. He had studied the report before leaving for the airport, but time had been limited, and now he sat in a quiet corner of the departure lobby, looking back through the paper, trying to absorb it more fully.

Gene Haskell's passport-sized photograph held his interest first of all. It was pasted insignificantly in the top corner of page three, but still managed somehow to command the page. Haskell's expression, as with most 'identikit' posing, was stern, but there was a warmth beneath his deep-set, dark eyes. His hair too was dark and cut short. Steel scanned downwards through the sections following: physical characteristics, qualifications, case experiences and commendations.

The following page outlined Haskell's current assignment: the location and infiltration of a Bangkok-based raw opium network. A Langley footnote indicated a degree of non-activity on the case in question; thus the availability for alternative assignments 'of a temporary nature'.

Steel turned the pages, extracting highlights from the remainder of the report: current diplomatic circumstances in Bangkok, contactable embassy officials, local legalities and an endless chain of minor 'do's' and 'dont's'. It was the more obscure, intangible qualities of the city that Steel was most concerned with. The type of nuances that couldn't possibly be defined, certainly not, at least, in typewritten official SIS reports. 'You can't get a "feeling" for a place from a report,' his in-field training commander had always said. 'You can only get that by going there yourself. Getting into the case. And those "feelings" will always be yours, different, in some way, to everyone else's. They will always be very *personal*.' Steel remembered that his own 'personal' feelings for Bangkok had, to a large extent, been moulded by a drunken American ex-GI and the manager of the hotel he was staying at, Vitchit Chareompond, on his first night in the city. The American referred to his country's recently past stake in neighbouring Vietnam. 'We fought the battle over there and lost, but I tell you, the main battle's going on right here. We've given these people such a taste for money, they ain't never going to want to be communist.'

And Steel had seen it later himself, in the streets. A country with one foot mired in a basic feudal existence and the other stretching relentlessly, almost hopelessly towards a dream of Western commercialism. Young, often beautiful girls drawn from outlying rural districts and suburban shanty towns towards the bright lights of the city, by money, and equally by necessity to provide for their more unfortunate, unattractive or aged relatives. With apparent fervour they would provide what the men from the West, the *farangs*, seemed so eager to part with money for. 'Yeah, it's a fuck for a buck city, didn't you know?' the American had elaborated, staggering out from his third club that night.

Chareompond offered a more benign view of the city. 'Call me Mr Tom,' he requested. He was used to that name from *farangs*, he explained, and showed Steel a business card with his own name and 'Mr Tom' alongside in brackets. 'In the tourist business it is not good that people are unable to pronounce your name.'

On that and one later visit to Bangkok, Steel had relied both heavily and persistently on 'Mr Tom' for information: insights into city life that very often only a true native could provide accurately. Despite the lapses in time and the distance between them, Steel had considered their friendship to have deepened, and even now after another two years, he knew that they would probably pick up as if it had been only yesterday that he'd left. He knew also that 'Mr Tom' would help the Ensors in any way he could – if he was not already too late.

A voice on the tannoy disturbed his thoughts; he looked up at the board. It was all right, still fifteen minutes or so. There was one other thing on his mind. He found the number at the back of his notebook and crossed quickly to a nearby phone booth.

'John Pender,' a voice responded abruptly, after a moment. Steel forced in a ten-pence piece.

'Mr Pender, my name's Jeffrey Steel. I'm sorry to contact you at home but I've been trying to get you at the Institute of Mankind for the last couple of days. They gave me your number.'

'Yes.'

Steel remembered that it was Stannard's secretary who had made initial enquiries. 'You were contacted earlier in the week by a Miss Harrigan requesting information on the Basikasingo tribe. I just wanted to clear up a couple of minor points on the same subject.'

'Yes, I remember. In what way can I help?'

'Well, we've ascertained that the word "Basikasingo" in fact refers to a carved wooden figure.'

'Yes.'

'Did you know that previously?'

'Of course,' Pender retorted. 'The Basikasingo tribe are noted for their wooden carvings. If I remember correctly, I mentioned all this to your Miss Harrigan.'

'Miss Harrigan didn't highlight that particular point, I'm afraid. She seemed to be more concerned with the tribe itself.' There was a short silence punctuated by the slow intakes of breath of a pipe-smoker.

'Well of course it's very difficult to generalize,' Pender commented finally. 'The name "Basikasingo" also refers to other objects associated with that particular tribe, as with other tribes – spears, shields and very often cooking utensils: bowls, jugs, et cetera. I suppose in many ways it's rather awkward to attach a singular significance to any item. Of course, primarily, Miss Harrigan is absolutely correct – the word "Basikasingo" does refer to the tribe itself.'

Steel had envisaged an outline figure from McNeil's import sheet, but the broad specification of 'Basikasingo' momentarily concerned him. 'How would I distinguish one of these figures? Is there a firm stereotype?'

'Yes, to a large extent they all look very similar. Basically, they're male idol forms in a praying posture – main body and arms extended, legs shortened and phallus exaggerated. Facial features are grossly enlarged, too. Commonly, they're known as "bearded figures" because of their finely notched jawlines, but then again that's more of an African art term.' Pender broke off for a second, pulling heavily on his pipe. 'I suppose the most immediate thing you'd notice is that they're extremely tall and thin. The original "Basikasingo" was about two-and-a-half feet tall, but only five inches across at its widest.'

'From a description we have, this particular figure is just over twenty inches tall,' Steel responded sharply.

'Ah, well, I can see what you have there, Mr Steel. To some extent, we seem to be at cross-purposes. You see, the "Basikasingo" I'm talking about is an original African tribal figure and the size that I mentioned would be applicable to any hopefully authentic "art" copies – for connoisseurs, if you see what I mean. Now, fortunately or unfortunately, depending on your viewpoint, African figures in the last few years have attracted a lot of attention in "fringe" art markets and even in slightly more exotic souvenir markets. Most of these are manufactured for export to tourist areas – souvenir, *objet d'art* shops; you know the type of thing. Your description would more likely fit one of these, Mr Steel. Generally they're made to fit easily on the normal mantelpiece.'

Steel recalled his earlier notes. 'Does the original "Basikasingo" have any deep African anthropological significance that you're aware of?'

'Not really. We're guessing, to a large extent, as to exact significance, but taken from tribal elders, the figures are purely ancestor memorials for chiefs or family heads.'

'And this souvenir market. How popular are they now?'

'Well, it all started around 1970-71, but now it's really on the climb. In the last couple of years the demand has tripled. And it's not just for "Basikasingos", it's for a variety of tribal carvings.'

Steel mused for a second. McNeil had, in fact, indicated that the Paris company was a bulk exporter; the Johannesburg manufacturer had been dealt with on a 'groupage basis', and had since disappeared without trace, although there were other similar South African companies dealt with on a regular basis. But the question of London as a delivery point came to mind.

'Mr Pender,' Steel said thoughtfully. 'At present, we are aware of manufacturers of these type of figures in both Johannesburg and Nairobi. But tell me, is there anywhere else that you know of where they're produced for export *en masse*?'

'A few of the West African states – Nigeria, Ghana,

186

Liberia, but it's a much smaller output. Obviously there's quite a number produced in Zaire, the tribe's homeland, but then again they're more authentic, for the connoisseurs.'

'And is London a popular import point?'

Pender murmured slightly, hesitating. 'Yes, to some extent. All the large European cities are big markets – Rome, Munich, Paris even more so, but for some reason most of them end up in Amsterdam. There seems to be a fantastic demand for them there.'

'This one's ended up in Bangkok,' Steel remarked as a form of casual reflection.

'How unusual,' Pender exclaimed.

The mid-evening bustle of the airport terminal momentarily distracted Steel.

'Yes,' he murmured. 'How unusual.'

Tonight was Peter Ngimo's second job. The first had been a small watch and jewellery store down on Joubert Street. Now he was on the opposite, northern side of the merchant's core of De Villiers Street, in a modest but highly productive wholesale goldsmith's on the ninth floor of one of the older-style office towers.

The corridor was dark and silent. The window he had just unlatched closed behind him, casting a faint incandescent glow from streetlamps far below. Ngimo glanced appreciatively at the flat roof two floors down and slipped deeper into the darkness and silence. He paused for a moment, adjusting his eyes to the gloom of the narrow corridor, gradually picking out its furthest extremity almost forty feet away. He started making his way along. The door he wanted was almost at the end: 'Hanbeck, Abrahams and Judd' was marked clearly on a small brass plate. But it was the small metal box by the door that claimed his attention.

Ngimo took a key from his side-pocket and turned it in the lock at the front of the box, quickly opening the facing metal flap. It was now a purposeful, measured procedure: the dialling in of the numbers and the pressing of the fingertips of his right hand against the opaque glass screen.

From the front, the door appeared the same as any other in the long corridor; the three thick steel bolts on its far side which Ngimo's action had slid back signalled its main difference. Ngimo deftly turned the handle and then closed the door quickly behind him.

He stayed there for a moment, allowing his breath to subside slightly, slowly taking in the overall dimensions of the room. The main object of his interest, the safe, was at the far side, highlighted beneath slats of faint light that came in from a venetian blind just behind. Ngimo moved quickly towards it, suddenly more aware of the age of the building as a floorboard creaked beneath his step. He examined the safe's front plate: Webb and Steadmann; the name meant nothing to him. the last job had been through an 'inside' connection, the combination supplied beforehand – but then again, as his friend in the mine had asserted, four sticks would handle the heaviest of safes. He took the dynamite from the inside folds of his windcheater, along with some thick brown tape.

The instructions were straightforward; Ngimo followed them to the letter: *Fix all the dynamite to the front of the safe, concentrated around the lock; make sure the sticks are equidistant; twist the fuses together – they should all come to the same length; find refuge behind a solid object to one side – not in front.*

Ngimo looked hastily around the room. There was a large filing cabinet backing against the same wall, but a good six yards away. Ngimo checked once again that everything was in place, lit the fuses, then secured himself quickly behind the metal cabinet, his back hard against the wall. He put a finger in each ear, and suddenly he felt curiously isolated from the nearby hissing sound – and what it signified. For some reason, at the last moment, he closed his eyes.

When the explosion came, it shattered the night-time stillness of the small business street. The total weight of the safe was forced suddenly back into the wall behind – the wall was solid, but parts of the floor and the window above were not, and these split apart at their weakest links. A section of the room containing Ngimo, the safe and the filing cabinet was spewed out almost as one, splitting slowly into a disarray of wood, plaster and glass as it tumbled the nine floors down.

Ngimo opened his eyes, aware only of a lazy, spinning panorama of the Johannesburg skyline and a sense of rushing air enveloping him with increasing fury. His ears were still ringing from the explosion as he hit the ground.

In many ways, Ngimo was lucky; a small collection of shrubs broke his fall – a broken leg and two sprained vertebrae were the only consequence. At the same time, one corner of the safe buried itself four inches deep in the concrete pavement a few feet away.

But it was the polythene glove on Ngimo's right hand that would, above all else, capture the interest of the South African Security Police. And Captain Calbeck.

11

The warm blue waters of the swimming pool provided Bradley Vansen with his early morning dip. It was a ritual that had taken place almost every day for the past four years and still preceded the eight hours of high-powered business that lay ahead of him. His black 'houseboy' hurried over as Vansen stepped out of the pool, wrapping a white terry-cloth robe around his shoulders, proffering a hand-towel draped across his forearm.

Swimming in Johannesburg was not unusual for the many 'garden district' pool owners, but in August, which represented the depth of a South African winter, Bradley Vansen was one of the few to keep up the pastime. His indoor pool was the one extension to the main house that, even in Johannesburg's opulent Houghton district, appeared slightly ostentatious. In summer, a succession of glass partitions flanking the side and roof would be slid back to let in the much warmer weather. A display of tropical plants bordering the glass frames thrived in the protected environment, a vivid, deeply rich contrast to the stark white wicker furniture of the poolside terraces.

Outside, a lush green lawn sloped gently down a quarter mile towards a neat row of jacaranda trees. Beyond them, in the distance, lay the centre of Johannesburg, faintly ringed by mist. As Vansen would often contemplate, looking out across the same view, it was his daily arena – where battles were fought and won. Never lost.

Walking from the pool, Vansen towelled vigorously, patting his stomach when he had finished: a playful self-indulgence, acknowledging a flat and firm stomach when so many men of his age had developed paunches. The only clue to his fifty-eight years was a slight thinning of hair on his crown which, if it worsened, Vansen had vowed to cure through hair transplants. Young socialite wives of fellow businessmen at upper-class Houghton dinner parties would guess his age at no more than forty-five, and it was obvious from his non-committal answers to such comments that he preferred to keep their thoughts that way.

But now Bradley Vansen lacked his normal, faintly arrogant composure. The telegram lay on the table at his side, where he had opened it. He glanced at it hesitantly. How he dealt with it, he knew, would seal his fate for many years to come. He was aware of little else at that moment. At first he had thought the events leading up to its arrival had been a form of indirect retribution for actions past.

If it had been the 'old days', Vansen reflected, he would have buried the problem as he had done in the past, along with the men that had stood in his way at the time. But now times were different. And, he remembered, there was just one thing that had never been completely buried. The past, he knew, would always live with him, at least for a fraction of every day. It had been that way for a long time, he remembered – ever since January 1965.

Bradley Vansen would always consider his first view of the Kimberley exchange as the turning point in his life. He was brought up as Brodloer, the only son of Erik and Helda Vanseumen, who had emigrated to America almost ten years before his birth and settled in New York's Bowery in a small, tumbledown tenement in Essex Street. Erik Vanseumen, by trade a respected diamond-cutter in Amsterdam, had re-established his business in a small shop on nearby 44th Avenue.

Erik's brother Tobias had settled in South Africa's Orange Free State over five years before, and a regular trade had already been arranged: Tobias would send on packages of rough diamonds that would ensure good commercial gems when finally cut and sold in the form of jewellery by Erik in New York.

Erik and Helda Vanseumen were to die within a few years of each other, and it was no surprise that Brodloer should then turn to Tobias. Erik had been aware of his own illness – a terminal stomach cancer – and in his fading years trained Brodloer in all aspects of the diamond trade, to ensure the continuing prosperity of the business after his death.

At the time, stories were already filtering back of mass Jewish persecution in Germany and Eastern Europe. Although Erik Vanseumen was Jewish, Brodloer had inherited the fair skin, light brown hair and green eyes of his mother. In a predominantly Jewish area, and particularly in a business that was almost exclusively Jewish – combined with his 'Aryan' appearance – Brodloer Vanseumen was not a good name to have. In January 1941, Brodloer changed his name by deed-poll to the more socially acceptable Bradley Vansen and his business improved almost overnight.

The Japanese attack on Pearl Harbour was to come less than a year later, and Vansen served his country well; he returned at the war's end with a Congressional Medal for his part in a daring raid on the Japanese installation at Guam. But the news of his mother's recent death decided his plans quickly. He sold the business for whatever property, goodwill and stock-value remained. Within weeks, his passage was booked.

Bradley Vansen was twenty-seven years old.

South Africa was a young, fearlessly striving nation at the time. 'A babe in a thorn bush,' Vansen's uncle commented over a bottle of local wine on their first night together. 'Its support is hard for the babe to bear, but each branch represents a different gold and diamond mine: the bush grows strong with the years and its thorns keep away the vultures.'

Vansen speculated on the farms and shipping he had heard so much of.

'They are merely hobbies, Brodloer. Believe me, the backbone of South Africa is built on mining.'

Tobias Vanseumen, in his thirty-six years in the Orange Free State, had moulded himself into its farming life in the tradition of the old Afrikaaners. But it was his localized knowledge of rough-diamond trading that Vansen wished to tap, a valuable insight into the Kimberley exchange and the fortune-hunter's world of diamond prospecting.

Bradley Vansen adapted well to the new life. He enjoyed the wide open countryside of the Orange Free State and its contrast to the concrete mass of New York that had surrounded him for so long. Within a year he was dealing on the Kimberley exchange while still, in his spare time, helping out on his uncle's farm, which had been the agreed form of repayment for his uncle's tuition.

His knowledge of the rough-diamond market increased, as did his fascination with prospecting as stories of new finds boasted their way through the exchange, becoming more glamorous and awe-inspiring from one person to the next. Some stories told of men finding a lifetime's fortune in a matter of hours and others of men finding their death in an equally surprising and speedy manner. It was always the success stories that attracted the starry-eyed prospector. Vansen was more realistic. He sensed the dangers as much as the rewards of prospecting, the often blind, wasteful folly of risking life and limb on the possibility of a fortune.

From tales he had heard and claims witnessed, one thing already appeared blatantly clear: when the prospector had finally reached his goal, he would invariably lack funds to mine his own claim to any great extent; he would be forced to accept financial aid, for which his new partner would often demand the controlling share.

Vansen's attention turned more and more towards claim financing, although for almost two years he was to sit on the sidelines, handling whatever small claims he was able to, and returning once again to prospecting during any heavy lulls. His golden opportunity was to come very much in the story-book manner of Erasmus Jacobs, discoverer of the 'Eureka' diamond: an old farming friend of Tobias Vanseumen had discovered a rough diamond stone while digging a fresh irrigation channel. The diamond was of poor quality, virtually 'industrial', but Vansen suspected that better quality stones lay in deeper veins. With the money he had brought from America, a financial and working partnership was agreed, although it was almost another six months before a more realistic value of the deeper veins was established and the rights finally offered to one of the large Kimberley mining corporations.

In August 1952 Vansen collected his share of the top bid at close to four hundred thousand rand, and his stake as a diamond claims financier was secured.

While claims were still being made in parts of the Orange Free State and Transvaal, more exciting and frequent discoveries were occurring on the south-west coastline and in the northern regions of Botswana. Vansen felt his diamond knowledge to be sufficient, but lacked geographical knowledge of these new prospecting areas and of the conditions prevailing there. Shortly, through the Kimberley exchange, he was told of an Xhosa tribesman named Mikeka Dinsengwayo, who had very little prospecting experience but had a strong diamond-mining background and had served as a hunter's guide on safaris throughout Southern Africa. On their first meeting, Vansen was impressed by Mikeka's strong command of the English language, his mental alertness and physical appearance. Although not very tall, Mikeka's frame was broad and square-set, his muscles bold as if bonded by strands of iron, traversed by darker, more prominent veins beneath his ebony skin. It was the powerhouse of strength that for eight years had drilled and shifted rock underground and had for five years saddled the burden of hunter's supplies across desert, jungle and swampland. Vansen had found his man.

It was agreed that with his tribal knowledge Mikeka would be left the responsibility of recruiting extra blacks, if and when they might be required. Mikeka always chose strong men who possessed good knowledge of the terrain and were equally at home with a rifle as with a knife or machete. Strength, reliability and arms power were the main criteria. 'We might be outnumbered,' Mikeka explained to Vansen, 'but if things turn nasty, with the right men, we can keep control.' Mikeka himself showed an almost unmatchable prowess with a wide range of firearms and the machete.

It was in this way that over the following years Vansen and Mikeka travelled extensively throughout South Africa, Botswana and South-West Africa, investing in a variety of claims from dry-desert discoveries to the harsh, tidal sea-bed explorations of the Skeleton Coast. Vansen's financial power and fame as a claims investor grew both in Kimberley and in Johannesburg.

Although most claims went without incident, in late October 1961, while investigating a surface claim worked by nine well-armed Afrikaaners, Vansen was reminded once again of Mikeka's initial warnings. On discovery of their fraud, the Afrikaaners reacted quickly and violently, the resultant exchange of rifle fire leaving Mikeka with a serious thigh wound and two of their Bantu helpers dead. Vansen was furious that his life should be so endangered. 'This must not happen again,' he admonished. 'We must prepare more or have extra arms and manpower.'

'That would be both more expensive and more difficult

to organize – but there is one thing,' Mikeka offered. He remembered that to the dusty-mouthed prospector, the long-forgotten taste of good quality liquor would most likely be welcomed above anything else. 'A mild poison tainting a specific bottle,' he suggested. 'While they are unconscious, we may investigate the claim fully and if it's fraudulent, leave quietly or kill them, whatever might be necessary. If not, a good offer when they come around will always compensate for a bit of drowsiness and discomfort.'

Vansen realized immediately the good sense of such a ploy. He used it often over the years, whenever there were grounds for suspicion. Through the often long and dangerous expeditions, their friendship grew and in true American style Vansen started referring to his companion and aide as 'Mik'. The nickname stuck and from then on the burly Xhosa was known by that name alone. Vansen also found himself relying more and more on Mikeka for diamond identification; a combination of a hunters' guide's sharp eyesight and a strong diamond-mining background warmed Mikeka to the task in a manner that even Vansen himself had lacked in his earlier years.

In July 1962 Bradley Vansen formed three mining companies through which he began to exploit the wealth of his sprawling claims empire in a more organized manner. He bid low for 'total rights', and where his offers were not accepted, he would starve future cash-flows, stemming full production and eventually forcing a sale. Partners who offered their shares to outside interest Vansen descended on swiftly, citing breach of contract for 'attempted re-sale without consent of holding party'. It marked the beginning of a process that even Vansen, at such an early stage, could not have foreseen.

The next two years Bradley Vansen would always remember as his most enjoyable and to a large extent most productive. His interests in South and South-West Africa and Botswana were virtually all now under his sole ownership. The stabilization of existing claims and their rapid progress became like a drug to him, driving him onwards, seeking other areas in which to invest in new claims. It was the remote tropical regions of Ghana, Sierra Leone and the small enclaves to the West African coast that were to capture Vansen's imagination, where stories of new discoveries were already rippling through the diamond world. The series of expeditions proved to be amongst Vansen's most successful. Shortly after his return and using his 'starvation' policy, he again made extensive bids for total control with great success, spinning the web ever tighter. By the end of the year, Vansen had solely-owned claims in almost every diamond mining district throughout Africa, and in terms of assets he was a millionaire several times over.

It was 7 January 1965. The day had started out quite normally, but then the call had come through later on. A distant, foreign-sounding voice, 'phoning from Johannesburg', detailing a dredger mining claim near Hondeklip Bay on the South-West African coast. Bradley Vansen would always remember it because, of the many claims he had been offered throughout his life, he was finally in a position to say 'No' and never have to invest in another claim again. And, on reflection, it was the total, wasteful folly of his actions that would haunt him through the years. However, at the time, the young Hungarian's voice intrigued him – what difference would one more claim make?

But already, the arrangements made, reaching for his safari hat by the office door, he began to doubt; a curious premonition halted him momentarily. Vansen shrugged it off – there were other things to be thought of.

Vansen would always remember the incident, looking back at it regretfully: Mikeka initially noticing something unusual, suggesting a full investigation and then the ensuing chaos, happening so quickly; the two Bantus slaughtered in the engine room, the final uncovering of their fraud. And, at first, he recalled, the young Hungarian had seemed so sincere to him. He had always prided himself upon his good judgement of character, and then suddenly he was deciding upon the Hungarian's and his partner's death, along with the black African crew.

From that day, he would remember in particular the young German's convincing explanation, swaying him, causing him to reconsider in what he would later think a rash manner, at a moment when he was numbed, faintly overwhelmed by the sudden development of events.

He knew that, at the time, if he had thought carefully, considering every possibility, he would never have let the Hungarian and German go with their lives. There was, he remembered, the question of a common contact in Johannesburg's De Villiers Street, but he had silenced referrals with heavy bribes before and, he had calculated, it would probably be a full week from their referral to his final inspection. If their bodies had been buried elsewhere, any possible connection would have been buried with them. Conversely, left alive, the young Hungarian and German were direct witnesses to the murder of the two Bantus. He began to think of little else, only moments after their departure, sitting on the shoreline gazing blankly out to sea in the direction of the dredger.

He could see Mikeka hauling the poisoned crew members from the dredger's deck, patiently drowning each of them and dragging their limp forms back aboard. The dredger gradually built up to its full speed amidst a tumultuous churning of grey froth, aiming towards a sharp rocky outcrop in the deep water; then the final, solitary figure diving overboard.

He sat there in silence for a few moments.

'It is all done.' Mikeka disturbed him, dripping wet from the ocean, but his breathing regular. 'It will look like nothing more than an accident.'

They watched, mesmerized, the dual, fiery-red explosions out to sea. The dredger pitched slowly on end and, when it had reached a forty-five degree angle, slid quickly downwards, foam rising seconds after as the only marker of its previous position.

'I have made a great mistake,' Vansen said calmly. He

explained his thoughts to Mikeka.

'There is nothing to worry about,' Mikeka said. 'They will most likely keep their word. In a way, they are as involved as us. Who is to say that *they* did not kill the crew. And we have more witnesses on our side,' he added, indicating their two Bantu helpers in the Land Rover.

Vansen considered mentioning his premonition, for really it was the combination of that and the following events that had given him second thoughts. But he stayed quiet, shrugging it off once more.

It was to return once again before the end of January 1965. 'What the hell, Mik,' Vansen remarked at the time. 'We have made our last claims-financing expedition. We must turn to other matters.'

And, for a while, the premonition disappeared from Bradley Vansen's life.

It was August 1969. Vansen had consolidated his interests still further, adding another four mining companies to control the interests of his more recent acquisitions in Ghana, Sierra Leone and the West African coast. In turn, his total seven companies had been brought under the newly formed corporate umbrella of Vansen Consolidated Mines, centring their registered offices, technical and clerical operations in Johannesburg's Jorissen Street. Within eight months shares were offered publicly on the Johannesburg stock exchange, but it was the surrounding furore and publicity that mainly concerned Vansen.

'Have you seen this, Mik?' he asked, throwing the *Johannesburg Star* across his desk-top.

Mikeka looked blankly at the paper.

'The photograph,' Vansen prompted.

Mikeka still didn't see the significance. 'It's a good photo, that's all. Don't you like the publicity?'

'No, it isn't that.' And then Vansen told Mikeka of his initial premonition and how he had pushed it away. 'It was an unusual feeling, all so real – that the young Hungarian and German prospectors would somehow be my downfall.

But there was always one thing that stopped it getting a total grip – and that was how? My premonition could never answer that for me. And then when I saw this, I knew.'

Mikeka shrugged. 'I don't see.'

'I'm now in the public eye,' Vansen elaborated. 'They may not have previously been aware of my position. And yet both of them witnessed directly two murders that we committed – can you think of a better situation for blackmail?'

'But they may not notice this,' Mikeka offered.

'If they are still in South Africa and in the diamond business, it will come to their notice sooner or later. You can be sure of that.'

The same premonition was to come again many times over the following months, with each new article in trade journals and business sections detailing Bradley Vansen's rise to power within the South African diamond industry. But as time passed and nothing occurred, he pushed it back again, allowing it to fade and turning to other matters.

By February 1971, it seemed totally unimportant to Bradley Vansen. Something else had come to the forefront, occupying him obsessively: the discovery of a rich new vein at one of his mines near Orapa in north-eastern Botswana. Employment of new plant and machinery at all of Vansen's commercially productive mines had helped shares rise dramatically on Johannesburg's stock exchange, but the new find boosted them to heights Vansen himself would never have previously believed possible. Within the year, VANSENCO was shown on the Johannesburg stock exchange as having crept into what was known locally as the 'big five' – the élite of mining conglomerates who controlled world diamond production. Shortly afterwards Vansen had elevated one of the two VANSENCO directors to Managing Director, relinquishing the position himself and retaining only the chairmanship. As such, he rapidly became more of a figurehead to Vansen Consolidated than a central entity around which everything revolved. 'I'm getting too old for all this high-powered commerce,' he commented self-effacingly to Mikeka. 'Let a younger man with a sharp mind take care of the things that require a younger man with a sharp mind. I want to put out a good image and I can't do that when I'm up to my ass in work.'

Supporting that image and his gradually developing semi-retirement, Vansen moved from Johannesburg's Hillbrow to its more select Houghton district, converting an early-thirties mansion house to suit his gargantuan, self-indulgent requirements.

Vansen's move towards lessening involvement with VANSENCO was highly significant, but in a way that he would not totally recognize until some months later – September 1972. He had been requested to attend a series of meetings discussing the continuing protection of world diamond pricing. At first, he considered the invitation to be nothing abnormal, having over the years attended similar Central Selling Organization-sponsored conferences. But then he recognized a significant difference: only the heads of major mining corporations and key members of the CSO were present, whereas normal conferences were more open affairs with representatives present from most sectors of the diamond world. In addition, the meeting dwelt on security and the political backgrounds of those present, with individual, private interviews interspersed throughout the total proceedings, which in all were to last five days.

Only Bradley Vansen, out of all the eleven men representing mining corporations, was to learn the exact nature of the meetings. For it was he, at their conclusion, that was to be selected President of the South African Diamond Consortium, following the recent and unexpected death of its President since its April 1965 inception, Dr Basil Heller.

Vansen, along with the other mining chiefs, knew of the Consortium as an organization designed to protect their interests with regard to controlling releases of any abundance of top-quality gems, as an extra, provisional safeguard. The people and procedures behind the Consortium remained anonymous, all representation to the mining corporations being made on their behalf by key members of the CSO. The appointment was strongly based on age and available time, which Vansen by his recent semi-retirement decision had unconsciously provided – the final, concluding factor to the adjudicating team of five CSO directors.

As with all other internal Consortium activities, the final deliberation was executed under a veil of secrecy. Following the meeting, formal letters were addressed to the other mining corporation chiefs thanking them for their attendance at what was described as a 'Special Security Conference', and trusting in their current and future discretion.

While aware of the uniqueness and stature of such a position, Vansen's enjoyment of his semi-retirement had initially made him hesitate. 'I have retained only the chairmanship of my corporation for a reason,' he had explained to the CSO adjudicating board. 'In fact, through the years, many of my affairs have been dealt with by my personal aide, Mikeka Dinsengwayo.'

The board accepted this singular statement. It was agreed that, with the provision of a security clearance, Dinsengwayo would share many of Vansen's Consortium duties, particularly in matters of gem identification. It was important to Vansen that he be able to personally verify incoming gem consignments, even though they had already been specified by the Consortium's laboratory staff and its expensive grading equipment. This safeguarded him totally against a possible internal fraud or discrepancy.

In many similar ways, Bradley Vansen carefully guarded himself against anything that might threaten his new-found stature. By January 1976, he was generally regarded by his peers to be among three of the most important men in the South African diamond industry.

On 19 June 1976, the pedestal was smashed from beneath Bradley Vansen's feet. But this time the premonition that had haunted him so many times through the years past was probably furthest from his mind.

It was 20 August 1976. Bradley Vansen stared at the telegram. At last there was some news.

The nightmare had started with the alarming, silent phone call. He had later established that the caller had been Dr Rosenkrands, the chief laboratory examiner. It was quickly followed by an alert from the South African Diamond Security Police: 'Our direct alarm with the vaults has been sounded,' they informed Vansen, sounding faintly surprised. The nightmare had continued with his investigation with Mikeka of the carnage strewn along the entrance corridors, and the occupants of the inner vault room, already unconscious, starved of oxygen.

'The men who did this were butchers,' Vansen swore to Mikeka. 'They will pay for this heavily.'

And then the long weeks of careful, painstaking strategy had started. Vansen was aware that the discovery of such a batch of diamonds and the possible subsequent uncovering of Consortium activities could topple the entire diamond market. The combined roles of Consortium President and South African diamond-industry leader gave Vansen more to lose than most. To him, such a consequence would represent a double loss – a personal failure and the collapse of a trade that had been his lifetime's devotion.

The way the robbery had been executed suggested to Vansen that there might well have been an inside leak of information. For that reason, he requested through CSO and South African Government channels that outside assistance be sought. Faces unknown to South African diamond security were required. Because of the enormity of both the financial and political implications, Vansen felt sure such a request would be granted. In addition, he asked that all communiqués regarding the diamonds be made directly to him, although at all times his name and involvement should be withheld. The planning of the diamonds' recovery was meticulous. Under Vansen's direction, key markets were kept under surveillance throughout the globe, and regular reports made to him through heavily guarded diplomatic channels. Vansen knew of only one name in his contact with such 'outside' channels: Colonel

Jan Ostermeir of BOSS.

The weeks following the robbery had been both quiet and frustrating, Vansen reflected: at their conclusion, there had been the recent death in Britain of the CIA agent, who had reportedly tracked down at least one tangible clue. The only clue so far. And now, Vansen concluded, only a week later, this!

Vansen lifted his arm. His 'houseboy' advanced swiftly, replenishing the glass of fresh orange juice on the white wicker table at his side. Vansen sipped from the glass abstractedly, reading the telegram for the third time that morning, trying to tease some extra meaning from its brief message –

LONDON * FRI 19TH AUG * 5:42 P.M.
IN PROCESS RECOVERING GOODS STOP CAN YOU ASSIST IN FINGERPRINTING STOP CONTACT JEFFREY STEEL HOTEL NARAO BANGKOK THAILAND STOP

JAN OSTERMEIR

'Fingerprinting,' Vansen recalled, even from as far back as his father's tuition, was a trade description of indisputable diamond identification. It worked on the same principle as fingerprints, from which it had derived its name, and was based strongly on the assumption that no two diamonds were exactly the same. A matching of enlarged transparencies of the recovered diamonds to those of the originals would ensure accurate identification by exact flaw positions in relation to the fifty-eight facets. There was only one man for that task, Vansen concluded, lifting his arm, beckoning once more.

'Send Mik in here.'

The original transparencies, Vansen recollected, had been taken from the vaults in the initial theft, but he had always been careful, in line with his 'internal fraud protection' policy, to keep a duplicate batch in his private safe for Mikeka to make 'spot verifications' if and when he felt it necessary. The two words IN PROCESS also concerned Vansen. It was obvious to him that a certain Jeffrey Steel would require aid in the diamonds' identification, and yet, from the tone of the telegram, such a recovery was not yet certain. No matter, Vansen mused, if there were complications, Mikeka's clandestine abilities would prove useful, a qualification further confirming Mikeka as the ideal emissary in Vansen's mind.

And in that final reflection Vansen took solace, blanking out those other thoughts, doing what he had done all too well through the years to combat his fears. But this time Vansen found it easier than ever before; the nature of retribution could not possibly be further from the current circumstances, he considered. It had always been a form of blackmail that this premonition had warned of in the past.

Mikeka Dinsengwayo approached deftly for his bulk, striding up the four marble steps from the Regency-style vestibule to the pool enclosure. His figure had a solid rotundity; his face was also rounded and full-blown, pushing out the normal lines that would show his age. The dark, closely matted curls of his hair had greyed extensively, contrasting deeply with his rich mahogany skin tone.

Vansen addressed him as he was only halfway across the expansive room.

'Mik, I want you to go to Bangkok.'

Part Four

Amwre Magonde

12

The streets of Bangkok were alive with the activities of morning trade that, like everything else, appeared to move just that bit faster than in any other city. Some of the merchants who had set up their food stalls offering various fruits, roasted meats and salt-fish at intervals along the Silom Road glanced up sporadically in mild surprise at the two figures striding purposefully along its tree-lined pavement.

The sight of two negroes in the centre of Bangkok was a rarity, but their remarkably disparate sizes and their obviously uncomfortable jackets in the ninety-degree heat made that rarity almost a phenomenon. Of the two, the smaller, slimmer one might have on his own passed by with little attention. His green two-piece suit was of a light-weight material, similiar to that worn by the businessmen of the Rajdamnoen district, who every morning could be seen scurrying to work with the impatience and excitability of soldier ants.

The larger negro was harder to ignore; his clothes were ill-fitting on his oversized frame, and perched on top of his head was a snakeskin-banded trilby hat, accentuating his already unusual height. The whites of his eyes appeared bloodshot, and his face was slightly scarred on each side, the flesh slightly puffed on the cheekbone, particularly on the widest part of the scars where the wounds had obviously stayed open for some while.

If the merchants of the Silom Road had troubled to look further into the stern, deadset expressions of the two men, they would have seen something else: an intense, deliberate purpose. A tell-tale bulge would have also served to explain why they wore jackets. But the merchants, as on every other morning, were too busy, talking fervently, arranging their bright produce on the angled stalls and looking upwards to the sky, trying to discern the first wispy trails of the next monsoon front. Earlier, along the Silom Road, a 'pineapple girl' had skinned and cubed a king pineapple with her curved knife, dropping the pieces into a polythene bag into which the large negro now reached, sucking greedily, his mouth and fingers coated with its sticky juices.

'Do you have to be such a pig, Karfi?' Bature asked.

The large negro stared back blankly. 'Sama shiru,' he muttered.

'Karfi', Bature knew, was all that had been understood by the giant. Before that, he had been known as Mahaukaci, 'the mad one', by the people of his village. It was a tale, he recalled, that Dr Magonde had recounted many times before, detailing his medical expedition to a small tribal village in his homeland to treat a reported malaria epidemic. 'The witchdoctor had tried to cure him,' Magonde would often reminisce, 'wailing fearfully in stark monotones of Hausa that he was a man possessed by the devil. But I knew that it was something else – even then I could see the symptoms of a minor brain tumour. It took almost a three-month course in acupuncture, but in the end it was worthwhile.'

And now Karfi could understand a number of words spoken in his native Hausa and enough simple hand movements to follow the directions that now caused him to be walking the streets of a city that was strange to him, his thoughts set on one purpose, one intent; Magonde was his master. 'I renamed him Karfi,' Magonde would conclude triumphantly. 'The Hausa word for strength, as that was the first thing to strike me about him – his strength.'

Bature's own new-found name had also been decided by Magonde. 'What sort of name is Nathan Tomlinson for a revolutionary? And it is too risky. The CIA may well have a file relating to your past activities. You will be named as are all Americans in my country.'

Bature remembered with affection the heady, idealistic days of the late sixties: Berkeley University's FSM and the Oakland chapter of the 'Black Panthers'. 'This young man has been given every opportunity,' he would recall the judge admonishing. 'He comes from a wealthy, respectable and deeply religious family. He has had the best in education this country has to offer – I fail to understand it.' Then, following his four-year imprisonment for armed assault, he had left for Ghana, where he first met Dr Amwre Magonde, already exiled from his own country. 'Eldridge Cleaver and Huey Newton are good tutors,' Magonde agreed, 'but with me you will learn the true spirit of Pan-Africanism.' There was also a brother, Bature knew, although they had never met; apparently, in the past, he had been equally as politically active in Magonde's home country.

Since then, Bature reflected, it had always been Magonde's wishes, Magonde's commands, driving ever onwards with maniacal intent for the 'cause' – a better life, a 'brotherhood', 'freedom' – his small army as mindless, willing partisans. There had been other projects, other objectives in the past, but none that Bature could remember seeming as vitally important to Magonde. 'We will not only have our long-awaited arms, but we will also sow the seeds of the destruction of Western capitalism.' He recalled Magonde's rousing speech during the tedious, camp-fire nights before the attack on the vault.

Magonde would never explain exactly how those seeds would be sown.

It was a question that perplexed Bature for a while, but his doubts were allayed by Magonde's final outlining of strategy, both in Amgawi and with the Sowetans.

And it was similar calm strategy, Bature reflected, that Magonde had employed when everything had gone wrong. '*This will be your own particular duty towards our overall plan. You alone are responsible.*'

Further along, Bature could now see the beginning of the Patpong Road.

'*It is important that neither I nor our car be seen in the vicinity of the hotel for any length of time. We will drop you off nearby and you will walk the remaining distance. We will arrive outside the hotel's back entrance at exactly ten fifteen.'*

Bature looked at his watch – 9:42 a.m. He turned into the beginning of the Patpong Road, Karfi close at his heels.

'The Patpong', as it was known by local Thais and lustful tourists was a collection of clubs, bars, restaurants and brothels crammed into a narrow street no more than a hundred yards long; at night it would be transformed into a confusing, massed conglomeration of bright lights, exotic smells and slitted, silken skirts: the ultimate sexual *potpourri*. But in the daytime it was quiet and almost deserted. At the end, across the much wider Suringwose Road, Bature could just see the ornate, expansive entrance of the Sheraton Hotel.

Bature smiled thinly. He was lucky to be allowed the execution of a duty alone, he considered, especially so soon after his last duty, the hiring of an independent assassin in Accra – Malusi Ugbaja.

It could be a long while, he reflected, before the total repercussions of that one incident subsided.

It was 9:28 a.m. Paul Ensor hailed a samlor heading along the Suringwose Road, and instructed the driver to take him to the Narao Hotel.

'Take care,' Deborah had smiled sweetly, giving him a light, parting kiss on the cheek. 'You take the key. I'm going to take a shower and then I'll probably do a bit of shopping. See you back here later.' She was happy that, at last, they were getting rid of the figure.

Paul did not mention the call of the previous evening, telling her instead that a message had been passed back to their hotel manager. 'I just have to deliver it to the Hotel Narao and then the whole business is finished. Someone will pick it up from there.'

The samlor putt-putted along the road, keeping close to the kerb; a rattling scooter frame supporting a small, cloth-canopied open two-seater carriage. Paul Ensor enjoyed samlors. 'They're too small', he had overheard other tourists comment. But to him they were ideal. Certainly, at least, for short-distance city travelling.

It took a full fifteen minutes to complete the one mile route between the two hotels.

Paul paid the driver and entered the bustling Narao lobby purposefully, approaching a red liveried clerk behind the reception desk.

'I'm looking for the manager – Mr Vitchit Chareompond.'

The clerk smiled. 'And who should I say is calling?'

'Paul Ensor.'

The clerk went away into the back office for a few minutes and returned accompanied by a slightly smaller man, dressed conservatively in a dark suit, white shirt and a soberly patterned college-style tie, the whole set off by a white carnation buttonhole. The smaller Thai advanced enthusiastically, proffering his right hand.

'Mr Ensor, I was expecting you.'

Ensor held up the wooden figure. 'I received a call asking me to deliver this to you.' He passed the figure across the reception desk.

'I'm sure Mr Steel will be most grateful to you,' Chareompond remarked with a disarmingly natural smile.

Ensor turned away slightly and then back again. 'What do you know of this?' he asked as an afterthought.

Chareompond looked blank.

'I mean there was such urgency attached to the message,' he added.

'I'm afraid I don't know. My message was very short and to the point. It told me only that you would deliver the figure here and that Mr Steel will come to collect it.'

'Mr Steel's coming here personally?' Ensor questioned curiously.

'Yes.'

'The thing that my wife and I have wondered about is how it got in our luggage in the first place,' Ensor commented laughingly. 'Maybe we'll get to find out yet.'

Chareompond nodded, smiling.

'What is Mr Steel, anyway?' Ensor added. 'An anthropologist?'

Chareompond shrugged it off. 'I'm afraid I don't know.'

Ensor looked disbelieving, but Chareompond smiled his smile again.

'If there's anything else I can help you with, Mr Ensor, please do not hesitate to contact me.'

'Yes, thank you,' Ensor answered vacantly, turning away.

He walked out of the Narao, hailing a samlor from the half-circle of its entrance drive.

There was something about Chareompond nagging at the back of Ensor's mind, although he was not to pinpoint it until the samlor had picked up speed back along the Silom Road. If Chareompond's part in all this was just that of a hotel manager, he thought, then why not his own hotel, the Sheraton? There was a question of both convenience and minimized risk. Conversely, if a position of trust was the answer, then why would Chareompond perform such a duty on behalf of someone he knew so vaguely as to be uncertain of his profession?

Although he could not completely dispel his doubts, he put it down finally to Chareompond's discretion. Spotting a small roadside bar from the open carriage, seemingly interesting enough to kill the time during Deborah's short shopping spree, he ordered the driver to stop. However, as he stepped through the bar's tasselled curtains, the same questions and doubts arose in his mind - people will have their secrets, he mused. But it was all over. And right now, he thought, that was all that really mattered.

It was time for a little celebration.

Bature spoke in the rounded, polished tones he remembered so well from Hillsborough. 'I'm looking for the Ensors.'

The Sheraton desk clerk responded alertly, flicking through the pages of a register to his side. 'Yes, sir, room five-seventeen.' The clerk turned momentarily, glancing towards a large display board to his side. 'But I'm afraid they're out right now, sir. Their key's on the board.'

Magonde was right, Bature reflected quickly. *The early morning excursions*. 'Thank you, I'll call later,' he said politely.

To one side he could see Karfi, as directed, making his way towards some seats on the far side of the lobby. Bature walked across, taking up a seat close by, but was careful not to show outward signs of recognition. A majestic fountain to his side sprayed water from dragons' mouths on to a large marble basin at its centre; the gentle, lapping sounds were soothing.

Bature sat there for a full four minutes, looking at his watch sporadically until the hands showed exactly 9:55; getting up, he walked directly past Karfi, mumbling without looking in his direction, 'Tafi sama yanzu.'

Karfi got up seconds later, moving away.

Bature walked on to the coffee shop in the far corner of the lobby, taking up a seat which offered him a partial view of the reception desk. He chose a moment when the desk clerk appeared to be preoccupied, then left the coffee shop and walked up the nearby stairs. As he'd directed, he found Karfi seated in the smaller first-floor vestibule only yards from the end of the sweeping spiral of steps. Bature ignored him, turning back towards the bank of lifts to one side, pressing the 'Up' indicator. He let a lift with an elderly couple inside pass. A moment later an empty lift arrived, Karfi joining him nonchalantly at the last moment. He pressed button five on the lighted panel.

Bature watched the indicator nervously. It would be best if nobody else entered the lift during the four-floor ascent. *It is important that you are not seen close to the room.* Magonde's directives were, as always, insistent.

On the fifth floor, a room-cleaner entered the lift. Bature quickly pressed seven, continuing on up and then taking the stairs back down the two floors. Karfi followed. At the end of the stairwell, to one side of the lifts, was a small vestibule. From the furthest of its four seats the main corridor extensions could be seen.

Bature glanced at the room indicator board, locating the direction he required. For ten yards past the vestibule the corridor was wide, then it narrowed abruptly. Both ends were lit by windows, but for a long extent it was dull, the overhead diffused lighting offering little relief. Bature could see that the rooms were grouped in sets of two in small recesses on each side of the corridor. 'Saura nan,' he remarked to Karfi, starting to make his way along. He left Karfi in the vestibule seat. Room 517 was almost two-thirds of the way down the forty-yard expanse. *Silence and caution will be imperative*, Bature recalled, increasing his stealth as he approached the door. He became aware only of the light scuffing sound of his own footsteps and distant, muted traffic noises becoming more distinct as he got closer to the window at the corridor's end.

Bature edged the last few feet, adjusting further to the silence, trying to hear beyond it any muffled but often instructive tell-tale sounds from the room's interior. *You must choose a moment when the room is unoccupied or alternatively dispose of any direct witnesses*. Bature leant closer to the door; the option, if at all, would have to be decided now.

After a moment he could just discern a sound, but it seemed to come from further away. He pulled back slightly, finally placing it next door or perhaps even two rooms away.

It was time to work quickly. He pulled a thick black wallet from his inside pocket, unzipping its centre and spreading out its four inside folds. A row of silvery-steel picks lay in three sections before him, an arrangement of tension wrenches in the fourth. He studied the lock on the door more carefully, and finally selected a raked pick and one of the longer tension tools. He inserted the tension tool into the lock, trying to get the right 'feel' through his fingertips.

The sound, when it came, seemed more profound than it

would have normally, crashing through the intense silence in which Bature had wrapped himself: Karfi's muffled cough and the simultaneous clicking of a door-latch at the far end of the corridor. But Bature had already sensed the start of some distant movement and settled into the recess by the door, glancing outwards momentarily, following the path of a middle-aged Japanese businessman out of his room, past Karfi in the central vestibule and finally to the lifts.

Bature waited a moment, then replaced the tension wrench in its previous position, working quickly and with impatience. He looked at his watch – 10:06. There was very little time left. He wiped a thin film of sweat from his forehead with his jacket cuff. He inserted the pick into the lock above the tension tool, working his way through the pins. He could feel the springs moving, the pins aligning, a gradual movement of the tension tool keeping each pin in line. His expression became forced, taut. For one pin to drop from place, he knew, would mean starting again; just the right amount of tension was required at all times to keep the springs from forcing the pins back from 'sheer' line. On the last two pins he felt a trembling through his arm threatening his steady hold; but he fought it off, staying it, gritting his teeth, a thicker, more profuse sweat returning to his face and neck. Through his shirt he could feel a clammy dampness building, aggravated even more by his constraining jacket in the close heat of the narrow corridor.

Then, seeming sudden and loud after the long silence, the lock finally freed, the latch clicking back. Bature's expression eased. He beckoned Karfi.

The giant approached remarkably silently for his bulk, drawing a Mauser 9mm from his shoulder holster, taking a silencer from his side-pocket and attaching it to the gun's end. Bature, although sure himself, did not mention that such an action would probably be unnecessary. Allow the animal his moment, he reflected, waiting for Karfi to come alongside him, an expression of pained, delirious expectation making his large face seem frighteningly childish.

When Bature finally swung the door open, Karfi was inside like a starved Doberman let loose from its leash. Bature followed calmly, closing the door behind him. He could see Karfi at the end of the entrance passage, looking into the room beyond.

'Babu ba jiki nan,' he commented.

Karfi relaxed.

But as soon as Bature had said the words, a faint sound became apparent to him from behind the closed door of the bathroom to his side. And suddenly, he wasn't so sure. He sidled closer to the door cautiously, drawing his own Mauser. Karfi had turned, noticing Bature's increased stealth and back-tracked along the hallway, coming to a stop just behind him. Bature held up one hand in a halting gesture.

After a moment the sound behind the door took form: the gentle, persistent lapping of running water. And Bature cursed to himself – the noise, muffled by two doors and a thick wall had made him site it initially as from another, adjacent room; a clumsy mistake that he knew he would now have to face the consequences of. He turned the bathroom door-handle slowly, careful not to make any sudden motions that might warn an occupant. The knob turned fully, Bature swung the door wide in one motion, his gun pointed directly into the open space.

What he saw inside surprised him: a steady dripping of water from a showerhead to its blue-tiled basin. Bature re-holstered his gun, crossed the few yards to the shower and turned the taps tightly shut.

They started searching the room.

Deborah Ensor browsed in a small group of open-fronted shops only fifty yards from the hotel. She had sauntered through the hotel's compact arcade shortly after her shower, but had quickly become more interested in the shops outside. She warmed immediately to the informal, almost ramshackle, attractions of the local stores, purchasing an unusual Thai-silk wrap-around dress at one of the first she came to. Aimlessly walking the remainder of the short street, she glanced abstractedly into the depth of each store, soaking in the general atmosphere. The narrowness of the street, the wide selection of goods, stacked on layer upon layer of shelving, and the bustle of people seemed to her both exciting and homely. This was *real* life, a sharp contrast to the plasticity of the hotel shops. But time was getting on, she thought, glancing briefly at her watch. She didn't want to keep Paul waiting too long after his return to the hotel. 'There's the Golden Buddha, the rose garden, the crocodile farm,' she recalled from Paul's endless sight-seeing itinerary, a gentle reminder not to take up the best part of the day with shopping. Deborah crossed the street, heading back the way she had come, but on the opposite side, walking brisker.

It took her only a few minutes to walk back to the hotel, clutching her purchase wrapped in bright mauve paper tightly under her arm. Looking up at the board behind the reception desk, she was faintly surprised that Paul hadn't returned yet.

'Five-seventeen, please.'

The desk clerk interrupted a ponderous entry on a form before him, turning back, unhooking the key from the board.

'Oh, Mrs Ensor, there was a man asking for you a short while ago,' he commented, passing the key across.

'Really?' was all Deborah could think of saying. She tried desperately to think who it could be.

'A coloured gentleman with an American accent,' the clerk added, noting her perplexity.

The only possible connection Deborah could immediately bring to mind was that of the wooden figure. Perhaps its claimant had been confused over hotels or had hoped to catch Paul before he left. 'Okay,' Deborah responded finally, 'thanks.'

'He did go into the coffee shop for a while,' the clerk added, pointing. 'You might like to try there.'

'He didn't leave his name?'

'No, but he did mention that he would call back later.'

'Thank you,' Deborah repeated, turning away. She walked across to the coffee shop, looking in for a second, but she quickly realized that without a name to hand it would be pointless unless the gentleman in question recognized her. Anyway, there were no negroes in sight. She turned to the lifts.

There was a small group of people on her floor waiting for a lift down, but as far as she was concerned they might not have been there; already her thoughts were turning to what jewellery and accessories she would wear with her new dress.

The hubbub by the lift faded into the distance and then suddenly disappeared with the sound of the next lift-bell. Only then did Deborah become aware of its previous presence, in the new silence as she turned her key and opened the door. She closed it quickly and walked into the main part of the room; it was empty. Deborah set about unwrapping her dress, laying open the delicate mauve folds of tissue paper.

The movement, when it came, was sudden, a large hand coming from behind, clamping hard across her mouth.

Then everything went dark.

In Johannesburg it was 1:40 p.m. and Jan Smuts Airport was crowded. Mikeka Dinsengwayo sat in the departure lounge, awaiting his final call, his main luggage already checked in. The flight was displayed on the board as RL 146 to Hong Kong. There would be a connecting flight to Bangkok within three hours, Dinsengwayo confirmed, consulting the tickets from his inside pocket.

He felt an unsettling but almost indefinable trepidation about this particular duty. There had been a thorough investigation three years before, he remembered, a total profile on each Consortium employee; surely that alone would have put the possibility of inside operatives out of the question – there had been no new recruitments since. But now, this was different. It was no longer a suspicion but a fact, irrevocable and potentially destructive.

And Mikeka Dinsengwayo also felt particularly unsettled about the fact that he had for years dismissed Vansen's 'premonitions', although it was also true that Vansen's fears had diminished slightly of late. Ironic, he thought. He could never tell Vansen that it was a combination of recent events and an ancient, inherent tribal instinct that had changed his thoughts. For Mikeka Dinsengwayo was also a proud man and would never admit that possibly, through almost twelve years, he had been wrong.

Paul Ensor sat slumped in a chair in Chareompond's small back office at the Narao, his eyes red-rimmed, his countenance tired and haggard. The doctor had prescribed tranquillizers, but Ensor could feel the glut of coffee he had drunk through the morning combating even their effect, jarring his nerves once again.

He found it difficult to comprehend what had happened; he found himself thinking of what he might be doing with Deborah now – sightseeing, swimming, love-making, lunch on a floating restaurant. All part of his intricate planning for the 'perfect' holiday. God, the whole thing couldn't possibly be more ironic. He had suggested calling the police, but his hotel manager, Cheddi Jhiang, had conferred with Chareompond, informing him that, 'It would be best if Mr Steel dealt with everything upon his arrival.' *What the hell did Jeffrey Steel know*? he cursed. And now he waited patiently through a succession of black coffees and tranquillizers for his arrival. 'My God, Jeffrey Steel, you've got a lot to answer for,' he hissed under his breath, his anger rising suddenly out of the pit of sorrow and bewilderment he felt deep down inside.

Outside were the sounds of a city on the move, with the build-up of lunch-time traffic; but inside, in solitude, Paul Ensor was to wait another six hours, the same anguished thoughts revolving slowly.

13

Captain Calbeck had been sitting in Jerome Ghelani's small office for almost an hour. At the back of the room and by the door stood two burly sergeants from the Port Elizabeth Police Department, looking on solemnly, sternly – as silent now as they had been since their arrival.

Through a small open window at one side, faint traffic noises rose up from Johannesburg's Jeppe Street, three floors below.

Calbeck was becoming impatient. He stood up and started pacing the room, tucking his short baton tightly under one arm. Ghelani was one of those 'coloureds' he disliked most of all; in general he considered all blacks to be below any 'coloured', but then there was a mistrust he attached to certain coloureds, dependent on their origin. In every respect, Calbeck had his own social strata. Ghelani was an East Indian with some Jewish blood, three generations back, from what they could find out by his registration papers. One of the worst types, Calbeck thought; invariably sharp and dishonest to the point of distraction.

It had taken Peter Ngimo three hours in detention to supply Ghelani's name; and Ngimo was surprised that the questions centred so much on his polythene glove, rather than on the robbery itself; as much as Ghelani was surprised that the police didn't seem in the least concerned with Ngimo, but more with a similar affair that had taken place almost two months earlier.

'I've told you already, I just don't have the names of the men concerned,' Ghelani protested.

Calbeck kept his back to Ghelani as he paced towards the side window. 'So let's re-cap – you left Datasec over six years ago and you took some of their design blueprints with you; but you say they didn't know that you also took copies of specific installation print patterns.'

'No,' Ghelani answered, studying Calbeck slowly through his horn-rimmed glasses, as if the thick lenses themselves would somehow shield his obvious contempt.

'And then you opened your own business.' Calbeck changed his tone. 'And you used some of the blueprints for your own designs . . . only *business* didn't go as well as you'd planned, and it was then that you decided to turn to other options. Is that about right?'

'Yes.'

'But then we come to the question of the Consortium print patterns, and this is where we hit a stumbling block – you claim you don't know their names.'

Ghelani adjusted his spectacles nervously, aware that Calbeck was suddenly staring at him intently. 'As I told you before, of course not – men in that type of business just don't give names.'

'I would have thought that a man in your line of business would ensure that he got to know a bit more about the people he's dealing with. Or am I wrong – is *trust* still alive?'

Ghelani didn't answer.

'Of course, when you think about it,' Calbeck continued fluently. 'Talking of options: those are now rather simple for you. No doubt if we have these two examples, there will be other similar cases to examine; in the meantime, you'll be held in custody. These things can be quite lengthy, you know – a year, two years even; and if the case is as serious as we think it might be, you'll be looking at another ten . . . minimum.' Calbeck paused significantly. 'On the other hand, if we have the co-operation we require, you'll only be charged with the Ngimo incident – we'll drop the rest out.'

'Is this some form of intimidation?' Ghelani inquired weakly.

Calbeck turned around sharply; there was a gleam in his eyes and a faint bead of sweat on his broad forehead.

'Lift him up,' he directed the two sergeants.

Ghelani was a light and frail man and the two sergeants lifted him from his chair with ease. Calbeck made his move swiftly, bringing the capped end of his baton hard into Ghelani's stomach.

'That's intimidation,' Calbeck emphasized. 'The other was a kind and generous offer which I am not often disposed to making. So shall we stop playing these games?'

Ghelani sank back into his chair, almost completely doubled with pain, his face pressed flat against the desk-top. 'Please,' he gasped. 'I told you, I don't know.'

Calbeck came in close, pulling Ghelani's head back by the hair, raising his baton once again. 'And *I told you* – that just isn't good enough.'

'For God's sake,' Ghelani screamed, holding one hand up feebly. 'Okay, okay . . . there is something.'

'What?' Calbeck demanded flatly.

'The box over by the corner, near the ceiling – there's another in the opposite corner.'

'Yes,' Calbeck urged.

Ghelani calmed himself. 'They're both activated by the door opening – that is, once I've switched them on. They take pictures, at three-second intervals, for fifteen seconds. Five pictures for each camera.' Ghelani seemed suddenly to be caught up with his own expertise. 'The angles ensure me of at least a few good pictures, so I pick the best and make up a file. . . . It's as simple as that.'

'A file?'

'Yes – most aren't their real names, or are just tribal names; so I take whatever information is given, and, together with the photograph, attach it to the specifications of the job in hand.' Ghelani faltered slightly, suddenly more aware of the implications of what he'd imparted. 'This *offer* that you mentioned earlier?'

Calbeck sat back, placing his baton and his cap firmly on the desk-top before him. 'Now why didn't you tell us all this to start with?' he smiled belligerently.

For the next hour, Calbeck questioned Ghelani on the two 'Consortium' files, relating the details to what little information Ghelani had already provided.

By late afternoon, Calbeck's report and the two files lay on Jan Ostermeir's desk: one was identified as a local rebel, resident in Soweto, but the other couldn't be matched against any police files; and, as Jan Ostermeir pointed out, if it wasn't a local 'boy', a name would be required before a positive trace could be hoped for through other agencies: SIS, CIA and SDECE.

Early the next morning, Calbeck deployed a group of men to Soweto.

When Jeffrey Steel left the air-conditioned VC-10 at Don Muang airport, he felt as if a steam towel had been thrown suddenly into his face. He had experienced similar temperatures during the recent heatwave in England, but nothing quite as humid and overpoweringly close. The flight had been long and tedious and Steel dealt with the rigours of customs and baggage collection impatiently. On the way from the terminal, some mild refreshment was afforded by a garland of fresh orchids draped over his taxi's rear-view mirror, the cool-air vents spraying the fragrance of moist blossoms throughout the car's interior.

The city looked much the same as Steel remembered it: muddy-brown shanty towns mixed with piecemeal industry and shops on the outskirts, giving way to more intense colours, sounds and smells, increasing in tempo as each traversing of a 'klong' bridge signalled the nearing of the city's heart.

'Tahn! You want Narao,' the taxi driver confirmed over his shoulder.

'Yes.'

After the forty-minute journey, Steel lacked sufficient energy to engage in the customary bartering that he knew from his past visits would normally accompany each purchase or service in Thailand. He settled his fare quickly as a porter emerged from the Narao's front entrance to assist with his luggage.

A small group of Thai men in bright, flowery shirts

clustered around the Narao's front doors, milling aimlessly, but turning their attention to Steel as he approached, each jostling for best position, invitations filling the air. 'Come to play-club, best fun you have in all city.'

'You want private showing? Lots of good films and girls at Larry's.'

One finally broke through to the front, taking the initiative by thrusting a business card into Steel's hand. 'My girls the best, you take my word. Will kiss you anywhere you want.'

'Steel smiled blankly at the group, still mildly numbed from his flight, pushing his way through. He could just see 'Mr Tom' above their heads, talking to one of his clerks behind the reception desk. He made his way across. Mr Tom noticed him halfway into the lobby, and came out from behind the desk with an enthusiastic greeting.

But there was also something suppressed, worried about Tom's expression; already Steel could sense that something was wrong.

For the first few minutes they reminisced, discussing highlights from their last meeting.

'Remember the last time you were here we had demonstrations against the UCTT?' Tom remarked.

'How could any weak-kneed visitor forget? The first thing my taxi driver took me to see was the bullet marks.'

Tom asked about the flight, the weather in England, Steel answering amicably but briefly. Almost as an afterthought, Tom instructed a porter to hold on to Steel's luggage until a room number had been decided; then he paused, his countenance darkening.

'I'm afraid we've got some problems, Jeff.'

'What type of problems?'

Tom turned away towards his back office. 'I think we can talk a lot better in there.'

The office was dimly lit and cool. Walking into it, Steel was aware of a man seated in its far corner who looked up briefly; he was middle-aged and smartly dressed but appeared tired and dejected. Steel guessed who he was before the introduction.

'Jeff, this is Mr Ensor.'

Steel walked towards him, offering his hand. 'I wondered if I'd actually get a chance to see you while in Bangkok. Pleased to meet you.' He noted that Ensor seemed reluctant to shake, forcing only a weak, ineffectual smile. Tom's mention of 'problems' suddenly seemed ominous.

For the moment he forced away the first obvious assumption to arise. He took up a seat across from Ensor, Tom placing himself behind his desk, opposite both of them. Tom sat back for a moment, surveying them.

'Jeff, this morning Mrs Ensor was kidnapped,' he started finally. 'Mr Ensor was delivering the figure to the hotel here, and meanwhile they took her from the Sheraton.'

Steel reflected quickly: he'd been wrong in his initial thought. 'You mean you still have the figure?'

'Yes.'

'That's all you're worried about, isn't it?' Ensor remarked bluntly. His voice was weak and quavering, but its tone cut through the silence harshly.

Steel sat up, staring across the room.

'You don't really give a damn about anything else, do you?' Ensor added.

Tom interrupted hastily. 'They left this.' He passed a buff envelope across the desk.

'They?' Steel quizzed, looking away from Ensor and taking the envelope.

'Two men, we think,' Tom elaborated. 'One came to the Sheraton reception desk about half an hour before the kidnapping, but the room-cleaner saw two men in the lift coming from the fifth floor just beforehand; both negroes – one was very large and the other's description fitted that of the first man given by the desk clerk.'

'Who collected all this information?'

'Cheddi Jhiang, the Sheraton manager; he's a good friend of mine – very co-operative. Just following the incident, Mr Ensor phoned me and I spoke to Cheddi and he assembled

225

all his staff for an interview. I went over to the Sheraton, had a look for myself, got as much information as I could and then brought Mr Ensor back here.'

'Were there any signs of violence?'

Tom shook his head slowly.

'No, not noticeably. If there was any, it must have been very little.'

Steel nodded impassively, opening the envelope in his hand.

'The note was delivered to the Sheraton by a young boy a couple of hours afterwards,' Tom said.

'How young?'

'Ten or eleven, a street-boy. He was barefoot, dressed raggedly. According to Cheddi, he rushed into the hotel, threw the note on the desk and then rushed straight out again. It was all very quick. I don't think the boy's important though, Jeff. They probably just paid him a few bahts for the errand.'

'Yes, I see.' Steel remembered well the multifarious talents of the barefoot brigade of children who daily tramped Bangkok's streets: mostly pedlars of one type or another or touts for brothels and seedy clubs. Many of them, he knew, would accept a simple task sweetened by money without question. The note itself provided little clue. It was plain, as was the envelope, a matching nondescript buff. Steel turned the paper and the envelope over, looking inside the flap for any identifying marks. There were none. He came back to the message written in heavy squared-off block capitals in black ink –

MR ENSOR. YOU WILL MAKE PREPARATIONS FOR THE RETURN OF OUR BASIKASINGO FIGURE IN EXCHANGE FOR YOUR WIFE. SHE WILL COME TO NO HARM IF YOU FOLLOW OUR INSTRUCTIONS EXACTLY. DO NOT NOTIFY THE POLICE. WE WILL CONTACT YOUR HOTEL AT EXACTLY 6 P.M.

It was a blunt message, cold in its brevity.

Steel raised his head. 'Why so much time?' he questioned

thoughtfully. 'Surely they'd want to get things over with as quick as possible.'

'I thought the same, Jeff,' Tom said. 'They may have assumed that Mr Ensor was out for the day and wanted to give him at least a bit of leeway after his return.'

Steel looked back at the note. A further clue lay in the word PREPARATIONS, he mused; whatever they thought Ensor might have done with the figure, they may have realized that recovery could take a little while.

'Were they seen leaving the hotel?' he asked Tom.

'Apparently not. But that's not as unlikely as it sounds. There's a back staircase leading down from the end of the corridor on the first floor to the end of the shopping arcade on the ground floor. There's another entrance right there. If they could have got down to the first floor without being seen, it would have been plain sailing from there.'

'Nobody?'

'Well, maybe a guest or two. But it's impossible to interview all of the guests.'

'How about when they took her from the room itself – perhaps somebody close was alerted.'

'Cheddi called on the nearby rooms – there were some people in a couple of doors away, but they saw nothing. They heard some faint thudding sounds, but nothing more. At the time, they thought nothing of it.'

Steel turned towards Paul Ensor, keeping his voice even. 'Mr Ensor, I want you to think very carefully. This is very important. Has an American at any time today called for you at your hotel or left a message there? A man named Gene Haskell.'

Ensor looked up dolefully. He had slumped back after his last outburst, watching the two men, amazed that they could talk so calmly about something that affected him so deeply. He had hardly heard the question, turning over in his mind time and time again Mr Tom's earlier reluctance to disclose Steel's profession. 'Who the hell are you, or rather what are you?' he asked. 'That's what I'd like to know for a start.'

'I'm just a civil servant,' Steel said flatly. 'Attached to British DIS – Defence Intelligence Staff.'

'Hoist up the flag,' Ensor scorned. 'Foreign Office, Diplomatic Corps and all that stuff – jolly good. Educated at Eton, were you?'

Steel looked back at Ensor calmly. 'The question, Mr Ensor.'

'What was it?'

'Gene Haskell, an American gentleman. Did he make a call at your hotel?'

Ensor looked vague. 'No.'

Steel turned back to Tom, his face stony, not reflecting his quick growing concern. 'There's something from my briefcase, I'll be needing, Tom.'

Tom flicked a switch on his desk intercom. '*Aw-fit nee*! Leong, is Mr Steel's luggage still in reception? I see. Okay, I'll come out,' and then to Steel and Ensor, 'I won't be a minute.'

The small office settled quickly into an uncomfortable silence. Ensor turned away, looking out of the window. Steel's thoughts turned back to the note; if the kidnappers had been able to plan their moves ahead, the note would surely have been left at the time of the kidnapping and if strategy was decided by an outside party, how could they be sure of Deborah Ensor's presence at that time? The questions turned over slowly in Steel's mind. He stood up, starting to pace restlessly away from his chair.

Collection of the figure had obviously been the main purpose, but at what point was kidnapping considered a good ploy?

'I'm sorry about all this, Mr Ensor,' he remarked finally, breaking his pace, suddenly conscious of the pervading silence. 'As you might have already guessed, your wife's kidnapping was more an unfortunate combination of circumstances than anything else – an accident.'

'Is that meant to console me?'

'No, just to make you aware of the circumstances.'

'I think I know already,' Ensor said testily. 'Let's not

play games. It's fairly obvious everything revolves around this figure of yours, but what I'd like to know is how the hell it got in our luggage in the first place!'

Steel related the pertinent events at Heathrow. '. . . It was purely an impulsive action by this particular baggage-worker – a mistake.'

Ensor lifted his eyes heavenwards. 'That's great.' And then looking back directly at Steel, 'And why is it so damn important?'

Steel let out his breath as if he was tired. 'Believe me, it's best that you don't know. You'll have to enter into negotiations with these people soon and in some way, perhaps unconsciously, you may make them aware that you have that knowledge. That would be fatal for all concerned.'

'It's *my* wife that's in danger and yet *you* know what's best for me,' Ensor said sarcastically.

Steel moved across the room, resting his back against Tom's desk, looking down at Ensor. 'There are a few things you should get clear,' he asserted. 'Now I'm sorry about your wife but what's done is done. At each stage. . . . If the baggage-worker hadn't put the figure in your luggage in the first place; if these people hadn't found out where you were; if the figure had been there for them; if your wife hadn't; if you hadn't been out of the hotel at the time, and finally,' Steel finished, pointing towards the telephone on Tom's desk, 'if the gentleman I'm going to call soon had done what he was supposed to do . . . *then* perhaps the situation might have been different. But now, I'm afraid, we're past that, we *have* to face things as they are. If you want your wife back safely, you'll have to rely totally upon me – follow my instructions to the letter. And if you're blaming the figure, go ahead, but right now that figure is the only thing keeping your wife alive, and it's also all we have to bargain with. . . .' Steel stopped himself suddenly; he had been aware of the conflict since his arrival, but now he was afraid he might have gone too far.

'I'm sorry,' Ensor offered after a moment. 'But the shock of it all – everything happening so quickly. It's all been so confusing.' His only totally coherent thought since the morning had been to blame Steel for all that had happened; perhaps because there had been no other tangible object at which to direct his frustrations, he now realized. He looked back down at the floor.

'I understand,' Steel said calmly, and studied Ensor a moment longer. He hoped now that he had assessed the situation correctly in the short time available. In a way he wanted to show Ensor the compassion he so obviously craved, but he thought that might demonstrate a weakening of resolve; Ensor would consider himself even more the injured party, and the strategy Steel had to formulate would then be that much harder to implement.

Tom had re-entered the office, standing silently for a moment by his desk and now interjecting, 'Jeff, I have your briefcase.'

'Thanks,' Steel responded, turning around. 'Can I use your phone?'

Tom nodded. Steel opened the latches of his briefcase, picking out a file and running his finger down a page towards its end. He lifted the telephone receiver and dialled out.

The ringing at the other end sounded distant and monotonous.

Steel let it ring, wondering more and more as it persisted where Gene Haskell could be; his telegram to Haskell, estimated from a quick mental juggling of time-zones, would have arrived first thing that morning in Bangkok. He left it a moment longer then replaced the receiver, remaining pensive.

Paul Ensor was on his feet for the first time. 'What are you going to do now?'

'I don't know,' Steel replied, 'I have to think.'

He looked at his watch – it was 4:22 p.m.

The rooms of the Dusit Thani Hotel were generally considered to be among the best in Bangkok. The drapes were French velvet, the heavy furniture for the most part the best quality teak, transported from the north and delicately

230

carved and inlaid with ivory in local factories. The light furniture, one chair, matching side-table and a foot-stool, was in rattan from Petchaburi.

Franz Zeifert sat on one of the intricately patterned peacock chairs and opened a well-worn but serviceable Italian leather briefcase. He lifted out two documents from the front pocket, examining them both carefully. Each one appeared more like a diploma than a bank form, gothic print, varying seals and stamps of authority lending a portentous air to their otherwise commonplace format. The figures on each sheet were printed clearly: 122,564,420 Swiss Francs, the Zürich exchange rate for £10 million as of 28 July 1976; only a few days after Magonde's final instructions, Zeifert recalled. The figures, however boldly displayed, Zeifert considered, seemed peculiarly blank, insignificant, unable to reflect the grandeur of the thick, steel-banded wads of banknotes stacked ceiling-high in the Zürich bank vaults. Two single documents with a typed line on each were the key to twenty million pounds.

Zeifert exclaimed softly. At the top of each page was a separate number, each one representing the opening of a new account. Towards the bottom was the signature of Joseph Matrai, countersigned by the bank manager directly beneath. Four further signature spaces were spread out alongside in two columns.

Franz Zeifert looked curiously at the space left for his own signature, wondering idly whom he might be signing in favour of on each document, if the occasion arose.

From Matrai's description of initial requirements and the bank manager's final directives, Zeifert was to countersign directly beneath the signature of the person in whose name the new account would be made. Once signed and countersigned the documents were as good as cash. It had been necessary for Matrai to transfer the respective monies to each numbered account before the documents could be raised. The new account-holder, after Zeifert's signature, would then travel to Switzerland, sign the document once more in the presence of the bank manager, who, if the signatures of the new account-holder matched, would conclude the proceedings by countersigning in the last space. Once completed, the new account-holder could make his first withdrawal. 'It will be quick, efficient and will give you on-the-spot powers of indisputable payment,' Zeifert recalled from Matrai's final assurances. 'It will suit our purposes ideally.'

Zeifert himself realized the tremendous strength behind his own signature. It would be his pen that could convert what would otherwise be worthless scraps of paper into millions of pounds. The sort of money that could buy dreams. He looked lovingly at the documents and, a smile playing across his lips, placed them carefully back in the briefcase. What a messenger-boy, he thought – a pen in one hand and a gun in the other.

He snapped the case shut.

The diamonds tumbled on to the counterpane like a free-flowing glacier. For a moment, Steel's eyes mirrored the gleam of the gems; he smiled, though not quite as widely as when he had discovered that the part of the figure to move, of all things, had been its extended, disproportionate phallus. The discovery was quickly followed by surprise that nothing immediately sprang open or could be detached. The remaining time had been absorbed in testing to see which part, if any, moved next.

The head seemed a more obvious choice than most. After seven, delicate, anti-clockwise turns, there had been the momentary feel of suction, as in a container released suddenly from a vacuum, although, as Steel had quickly discovered, it was in fact caused by a thick wad of rubberized cushioning on the underside of the head compacting the contents. Pressurized, the figure had appeared solid; a fact that had at first caused Steel some consternation, as he shook the figure for any apparent movement, thinking for one horrible moment that all his estimations and planning to date had been wrong.

But now there was no doubt any more. He whistled softly

at the sight and feel of the gems, the silence and solitude of the hotel room making them an awesome companion. Steel became faintly hypnotized by their aura, lifting handfuls of gems, allowing them to fall slowly through his fingers. The smaller stones, like beads, slipped through easily on to the mound leaving the larger ones, the size of bottle tops, in the palm of his hand. These he placed carefully one by one back into the neck of the wooden figure. Steel felt an obscure affinity with the diamonds that he hadn't felt before. They had always been distant, elusive, part of a chain of technical descriptions and trading reports he had absorbed in his first few days' briefing, and later through Rober Stockman's more erudite and intricate classifications. Now they were real, tangible.

It was the sight of the gems also that reminded Steel of current problems, although he had feared similar complications since the Heathrow incident, and in some respects, at least, had prepared himself. Now, he reflected, the return of the gems was necessary to ensure the safety of a British subject – the two objectives Stannard had stressed in his final briefing were perhaps now not both possible. 'Recovery of the diamonds is obviously your prime intent, but the Ensors' safety is also extremely important. It would be very awkward to explain their involvement in this if something should go wrong.'

Initially, in Steel's mind, it had been the fear that he would be too late; time was always against him. The figure would have been taken, the Ensors in some way harmed or perhaps dead. And then the chase would start again. Back to square one – combing the diamond markets. In many ways, what had happened was preferable to that, but the conflict of interests concerned him. The fact that some form of choice had to be made, instead of a straightforward *fait accompli*, was a tougher path, with no clear direction, he thought, balling his fist and staring vacantly at the gems as if for some form of inspiration.

Steel scanned frantically back through the options he had turned over in his mind time and time again. One thought stayed prominent – one that had been a constant consideration since the dilemma had presented itself, an immediately obvious way of achieving both objectives. But he had pushed it to the back of his mind as an option fraught with too many risks.

After a moment Steel refocused his attention on the gems, for he suddenly realized that it was really *them* that had stirred his subconscious. An isolated paragraph in one of the earlier technical reports had stated: 'With minimal magnification, in a poor light, it is impossible to discern a perfect or near-perfect diamond from a Yag (Yttriam, aluminium and garnate mix). It is the flaws and imperfections and the respective positions of these that are difficult to imitate.'

Steel picked up the phone.

Some brief re-routing from the Narao switchboard brought Tom to the other end. 'Yes, Jeff, how can I help you?'

'I wonder if you can, Tom – it's this exchange. If possible, that is, if everything can be swung our way, I'd like to be watching throughout. So, perhaps it could be arranged in some sort of crowd situation, where tourists don't appear too conspicuous?'

'Let me think for a while – I'll call you back. Anything else?'

'Yes – I'm looking for a couple of names.'

Paul Ensor sat in the small room allocated to him by Mr Tom at the Narao, turning events over and over in his mind; but his thoughts seemed numbed still. He remembered vaguely that the last thing said to him was that he would be called in his room and since then he had lost track of time, sitting alone, detached. But when the phone finally rang, breaking his reverie, he was not surprised to find Jeffrey Steel at the other end.

'Mr Ensor – everything's arranged for when the call comes through. If you'll go down to the reception desk at five-thirty, Tom and I will meet you there and we'll go on to the Sheraton; it only takes about ten minutes, so we'll have time to lay out some strategy beforehand. We'll also have the use of Mr Jhiang's office, so there'll be complete privacy.'

Ensor's thoughts were clearing slowly. 'Strategy?' he asked, conscious of the one word.

Steel related the essence of his conversation with Mr Tom, and Ensor could feel his initial doubts and concerns return. 'What makes you think I'll be able to do that?' he asked.

'It can be done – with planning,' Steel said simply.

'But my wife's safety – if we start fooling round with these people. . . .'

'Mr Ensor!' Steel cut in. 'This isn't a game of cricket where both sides play the rules fairly, and everyone comes away smiling. You have something *they* want just as badly as *you* want your wife's return. Otherwise they wouldn't have taken your wife in the first place. But it's once they have what they want that you both become in real danger, because then you're *both* dispensable. So you see, it's really a matter of bargaining – and strategy.' Steel paused heavily. 'You're a long way from Manchester and Old Trafford now – in every respect.'

'I know,' Ensor said; then it struck him. *How did Steel know*?

'It'll work out,' Steel assured him. 'You'll see.'

But placing back the receiver, Steel began to wonder himself about the meeting. He would need to watch Ensor through every step.

Gene Haskell stubbed out his third cigarette and walked away from his car, keeping alongside the large warehouse, close under its heavy shadow. At its end, a much wider expanse of the Chao Praya River and the small dock could be viewed. In the distance Haskell could just discern the sounds of the city at night. But ahead and to each side, along the lazy curves of the river, it was quiet and would have been peaceful, except that there was something about this particular quiet and what little activity there was that held a form of imperceptible energy. However, Haskell knew that he would not be able to relax there. Not tonight, of all nights, he mused. He lit another cigarette, the flickering light briefly illuminating a murky twenty-yard expanse of concrete leading to the water's edge. The same concrete extended for a few hundred yards on one side, and less than fifty yards on the other, some large warehouses bordering it at its start and gradually giving way to a mass of small tumbledown stores and sheds towards its end. There was only one crane on the dockside and the moorings were empty.

The *Branburi Rose*, Haskell reminded himself, drawing anxiously and long on his cigarette. Damn it! Where the hell were they?

There was a small barge he could see further up the river, but nothing near the size he'd visualized. And if the boat was expected, the loading truck would already have arrived, he speculated. *For them both to cancel? Impossible!*

Haskell stood there a few moments longer, becoming conscious of the smallest sounds; in the background, sporadic car horns and motor noises punctuated the blanket of silence and ahead a faint rippling was set up by the barge as it passed deeper into the channel. The river reflected a weak and hazy quarter moon close to the shore, fading out to sombre blackness towards its centre, and then again on the far shore a number of lights from small makeshift houseboats picked out the silhouettes of rows of coconut palms and thickly matted foliage. Further down the river on the same side as the docks, more houseboats clustered around floating wooden ramparts, and two fishing boats could just be made out, a quarter of a mile deeper into the channel at that point.

The silence was broken suddenly and harshly by the revving of a speeding car as it approached. Haskell turned, but the car flashed by on the neighbouring road, just behind the short entrance to the docks – a brief dazzling of headlamps, and then the noise, once again, fading into the distance. But it was enough. They had his car make, colour and number.

Haskell thought nothing of it, turning back to the river for another minute and then checking his watch. 'Another bum steer,' he cursed to himself, throwing the glowing stub of his cigarette to the ground in disgust. He watched the glowing ember die, and then walked back through the shadows to his car.

14

Cheddi Jhiang's office was mellow and sombre. There was a dark teak desk, cabinet and chairs, and matching panelling covering three walls; a Thai silk print in neutral tones of green, beige and brown covered the fourth.

The call was ten minutes late, abruptly breaking the uneasy silence. Ensor answered. Steel and Mr Tom were at his side.

'Mr Ensor, can you hear me?' The voice was deep and resonant.

'Yes.'

'We have your wife here. She is quite safe and well – but, as you know, you and I have some business to conclude.'

Again, 'Yes.'

'You have the figure with you.'

Paul Ensor faltered. It wasn't a question, but a statement – direct and purposeful, and asking only for confirmation. Nothing else. He felt his stomach churning, as it had done in the anxious moments preceding the call. 'No,' he answered finally.

There was a long, blank silence at the other end. Ensor looked hopefully towards Steel for one moment and then his concentration was wrenched back.

'Why not?'

'It's in a bank safe right now.'

There was another silence, longer, more penetrating than the first. Then finally, 'I find it interesting that you should place the figure in a safe place,' the voice remarked. 'Why have you done that, Mr Ensor?'

Ensor was regaining confidence. 'It looks valuable, that's all,' he said casually. *Keep it simple*, he recalled from Steel's final instructions. *For God's sake, keep it simple.*

'Yes, I see.' And then a deep intake of breath. 'Anyway, to the matter at hand. Do you have a pen?'

Ensor murmured a confirmation, reaching out for a notepad he could see at the end of Jhiang's desk.

'We will meet you in the small road approaching what is known locally as the Wat Traimit. You can give that name to your taxi driver. It's a small temple near the Bangkok railway station, famous for its Golden Buddha. In the daytime it's a tourist attraction but at night-time it's deserted – we shall not be disturbed. Nevertheless, it is a famous landmark and you should have no problem in finding it. We will be in a grey Toyota saloon car.'

Ensor was reading aloud parts of the address as if making notes, looking across the room for confirmation, and Steel was shaking his head, a deep frown apparent, his mouth forming a silent 'No'.

'What time can we set this for tonight, Mr Ensor?' the voice continued fluently. 'Taking into account that you have to retrieve the figure from where you have it deposited.'

Ensor denoted a hint of sarcasm, as if what he had said previously had been disbelieved or, at least, ignored. 'I'm afraid tonight won't be possible,' he said, fighting back the nerves once more.

'But my note, Mr Ensor – it was very clear.'

Ensor remembered Steel's instructions, picking phrases at random. 'Yes, I know, but I didn't see it until much later and by then the bank was already closed.'

'You expect me to believe this?'

There was a long pause. 'I'm sorry,' Ensor offered after a moment. 'There's nothing I can do.'

'So be it – the exchange will take place tomorrow. But

the Wat Traimit is not suitable then. One moment.' The voice faded into the background and Ensor could hear another voice, more distant and higher-pitched but still male, and then the first voice returned to the mouthpiece, repeating what had been said in the background. 'This other place is still near the railway station, but it is relatively quiet in the daytime. The intersection of the Song-Sward and the Sond-Yard Roads, by the river.'

Ensor was looking towards Steel again, relating part of the instructions aloud. 'I'm sorry, I couldn't meet you there,' he said, translating Steel's expression, suddenly surprised at himself and the ease with which the words came out. 'If it's that quiet . . . I would have to consider safety first – my wife's and my own.'

There was mild laughter at the other end; not humorous but cynical, mocking. 'I don't think you understand, Mr Ensor. Your wife's in danger – you do not have a choice.'

'I have a place in mind. . . .' Ensor submitted weakly.

'It still isn't clear, is it, Mr Ensor! First the bank and now this. . . .' The tone of the voice was rising, becoming measuredly vehement. 'It is almost impossible to deal with you. I have no compunction about your safety; and you should heed that as a warning. As we have already stated, we will kill your wife if our instructions are not obeyed to the letter.'

'But then your bargaining position would be lost – don't think I'm not aware of the immediate dangers, because I am.' Ensor didn't believe it, but suddenly he was repeating the words Steel had offered as a last resort. 'But in the end I have to consider our ultimate safety – otherwise everything else is futile.'

'Mr Ensor, you seem to have overlooked one factor – there are a number of stages before death; all of them fraught with much suffering.' There was a long pause and then the voice seemed suddenly calmer, but more purposeful. 'The introduction or, alternatively, avoidance of these stages is dependent on what is decided between the two of us now.'

Ensor didn't answer; the new threat threw him suddenly.

'We can delay that ultimate action at will,' the voice stated firmly, 'but you seem to have made your decision.'

'Please wait . . . listen.'

The voice continued immovable, decisive. 'When we call back, we will commence negotiating from a stronger position.'

'Please. . . .'

But it was lost in the dull monotone of the dialling signal.

Steel was shaking Ensor by the arm, as if to bring him back to reality. 'What is it?'

Ensor stood for a moment longer, the receiver held limply, mesmerized. 'They're going to harm Deborah in some way,' he said finally, his tone distant, almost disbelieving.

Although Ensor said no more, Steel could again sense that look of blame. 'Don't worry, they're bluffing,' he assured Ensor confidently. 'They've got too much at stake.' But suddenly, deep down, he really wasn't sure any more.

Amwre Magonde had found the small industrial unit ideal for his purpose; an abnormally high payment to a Bangkok property-dealer for one week's rental ensured 'no questions asked'. He sat in a chair by a small desk at the end of its single office after the call, signalling Bature towards the adjoining warehouse with a deft, purposeful motion of the leather-thonged stick gripped tight in his right hand. There were no words spoken between them.

This was one of many such setbacks, he reminded himself. There had been the recent events in London: the assassin who was never to complete his task, the inept cargo-worker; both because of Bature's judgement, he reflected – and now this! He turned the same thoughts over again, his face becoming taut, anguished. . . . And the danger of Leon's efforts being wasted!

Again the same thought struck, as it had done when their plans had to be so abruptly changed – that the fate of an ideology lay in a country far away, where all was strange to him. He had planned and fought too long for his 'brothers' to let things go now. Those of his own blood and those of the revolution, all joined by a common global bond of hope for people's power! The only true way. And the destruction of capitalism – the enemy of the *people*. There had been much blood, despair and frustration spilled on the road to freedom, he recalled; a journey fraught with corruption, treachery, and the disarming smiles of power and money-hungry capitalists – those who drained Africa's life-juices. The border fights, political insurgency and conflicts had all been successful in their own right, he remembered; but the fight against capitalism itself had always been a vain one until now. The fruition of years of intricate planning. No! he goaded himself, tensing his whole body, rising slowly from his chair; too much had gone before to stop now. He had vowed that it would be this way since the death of the first 'brother'. *A blood brother.*

And Amwre Magonde would never forget that time, for it was engraved boldly in Hausa, among the tribal faces of the Sarakunas on the ebony stick which he gripped so tightly in his hand – IN THE SPIRIT OF THE TRUE LOVE OF FREEDOM FOR THE PEOPLE OF AMGAWI – IN MEMORY – JOACHIM MAGONDE – JANUARY 1965.

Directly below was carved a single triangle.

Racialists, Bature recalled from sociology lectures at Berkeley, often remarked that all negroes looked alike, and that you could never tell when a negro was angry, that the colour of their skin hid the flushing that would show bright red on a white person. But you could, he knew. For he had seen the expression that Magonde now wore, as he swung wide the door to the small warehouse, so many times before.

The room was compact and oblong, a wide, garage-style door to one end and a jumbled mass of empty crates stacked against its walls. The light was starkly fluorescent, and in the centre a large fan fought vainly against the hot, oppressive air.

Deborah Ensor lay tied by her hands and feet, her mouth

241

taped, against a large crate in the corner of the room. Her eyes were tired and bloodshot, her hair dishevelled, a large mauve-and-blue bruise, mottled with broken skin and haemorrhaged blood on one cheek. Karfi was close at her side, Bature towards the centre of the room.

Magonde's look was direct, accusing. 'This is what you bring me in place of a fortune in diamonds. The man is hedging – as if he doesn't care for her welfare. He wants to delay everything till tomorrow.'

'That was all there was – what else could we do?' Bature protested.

Magonde looked away, back towards Deborah Ensor. 'Our bargaining position must be strengthened.' He turned to Karfi solemnly, eyes cast down. 'Dauka can wuka.'

Karfi reached on to the top crate in the corner, two above the one supporting Deborah Ensor's back, and took down a large curved knife with an inverted tip. It was a common Thai docker's knife; the curving blade was used for slicing through thick packaging and binding ropes and tapes, while the overhung tip made the ideal 'gaff hook'.

'Karye igayas!' Magonde directed.

Karfi brought the knife down, scything easily through the thick ropes binding Deborah Ensor's hands behind her back, and then again through the ropes at her feet.

'Kawo ta nan.'

Deborah Ensor felt her whole body lifted suddenly by Karfi, her feet taking the weight before her head had fully cleared. She moved her hands and feet to re-circulate the blood. Her main thought was – Doesn't care? hedging? *No!* that couldn't possibly be Paul. But her mind was jumbled, confused.

Karfi hustled Deborah into the adjoining office, Bature and Magonde following. Karfi gripped the back of her neck in one hand, ripping a wide band of brown tape from her mouth with the other; an ugly red rash of irritated skin appeared, and Deborah puckered her lips to allay the sudden raw tingling sensation.

Magonde turned to Bature, pointing to the phone on the

office desk. 'I wish to hear this conversation. Do whatever you have to do here.'

Bature nodded in understanding, studying the phone for one second and then he left the office, returning shortly with a small black leather bag. He had already ascertained that the earpiece covering could be detached and now unscrewed it hurriedly, attaching the two connections at its back to a five-foot length of wire which he produced from his bag and another, smaller earpiece similar to that used in a hearing-aid. He screwed the telephone earpiece covering back on, but not fully, allowing the wires to trail out of the side, stepping back with a faint smile of satisfaction. 'There you are – no problem.'

Magonde dialled out impatiently, staring hard at Deborah as if warning her of the task to come. It took only a moment to pass through the Sheraton switchboard and to hear Paul Ensor's voice at the other end. Magonde held out the receiver to Deborah Ensor, one hand blocking the mouth-piece. 'Your husband finds it necessary to cause certain complications. You will convince him, and us, of your worth. If that is not the case. . . .' Magonde's voice faded, an awkward silence implying intent. He picked up the small earpiece in his other hand.

Deborah gripped the receiver hesitantly. 'Hello Paul,' she said; what else was there to say?

'Thank God – I thought for a moment . . . No, it doesn't matter now. Are you all right?'

'I'm not really harmed, if that's what you mean.'

'Christ,' he hissed. 'I don't know. I don't know what to say any more. This whole thing is mad.'

'You thought that something *had* happened, didn't you, Paul?'

'Look, Deborah,' he started, and then he thought: it wasn't any use any more. Deborah's tone disturbed him, sounding so hopelessly lost, despairing, and he decided quickly – the pretence couldn't continue. He blurted out in one breath, 'I know what you're probably thinking, Deborah, and I wouldn't blame you, but you should know me better than that. . . . I was afraid that they might kill both of us once they have what they want, and that's why I tried to negotiate as best I could.' Paul paused, conscious of Steel at his side, but not caring. What the hell, he thought, these aren't my mental and verbal games; but he could sense that his own anxiety was causing his words to jumble. 'You see, I didn't trust him, that's why – but this all seems so ridiculously simple, telling you now. . . . It's that wooden figure from our luggage they want – you remember. I wish I could tell you more – explain; but it's all so vague and strange, and, anyway, I don't know any more than that, or why the hell this is all happening. It's a mess. All I know is that I want you back safely, Deborah. Believe me, I didn't know it would have that effect on him. . . .'

'Then why this delay? God, I'm so confused, Paul.'

'I can't get hold of the figure straight away – it's in a safe.' And then he realized: they were being played one against the other.

'But this man you delivered it to.'

'That was it,' he said convincingly. 'The man at the bank – I had to get his name from our hotel manager.'

Deborah paused suddenly; it was a lie, but more than that, it was an obvious lie, one that they were both openly aware of. And then she realized something else was involved – exactly what, she wasn't immediately sure. But she quickly sensed she must go along with it. 'Yes, I remember now,' she said, hoping to cover her tracks.

'It'll work out, Deborah, you'll see,' he said, breathing a silent sigh of relief.

But it was too late; Magonde had wrenched the receiver from Deborah Ensor's grip.

'On the face of it, it might seem unusual that you would go to such elaborate lengths, Mr Ensor, but at least things are now much clearer,' Magonde paused. 'Do you still feel the same way – that you cannot trust me?'

'I don't know.'

'It is important – you must be sure,' Magonde demanded.

There was a short but tense silence. Paul decided quickly to stay close to the truth – that the deep voice coming through the earpiece had the unusual power of discerning fact from prevarication. 'I'm afraid so,' he replied weakly. 'I still don't trust you.'

'You disappoint me, Mr Ensor,' Magonde reproached. 'I thought that by now I would have frightened all misgivings from your mind. Still, I appreciate your honesty. If you still feel this way, then no doubt you have a place in mind that will ease the burden of your mistrust.'

Another silence reflected Paul Ensor's surprise. 'Yes, but I don't understand,' he responded finally.

Magonde laughed mockingly. 'Mr Ensor, I am only interested in the return of my wooden figure. If your choice of meeting place will facilitate a smooth exchange without putting my own interests at risk, then so be it. I could alternatively force you into a meeting place of *my* choice, but then if you felt your own security was at risk, you might seek the assistance of the police – that would be unfortunate for all involved. I wish this transfer to be as straightforward as possible, with no outside involvement. It's quite plain. Do you have a place in mind or not?'

'But before. . . .'

'Before, Mr Ensor, your entire manner was heavy with deceit. I was unwilling to come to any arrangement with you under those circumstances. Shall we face the business at hand?'

'Yes,' Ensor agreed.

'Then where?'

Paul was momentarily non-plussed by the sudden reversal. 'The boxing stadium near the hotel,' he spat out finally. 'I thought it would be safer in a crowd.'

'What is it called?' Magonde asked.

'Lumpini. The Lumpini Boxing Stadium.'

'And how far is it from your hotel?'

'About half a mile,' Paul answered after a brief thought.

Magonde paused in a deep silence that passed no message, except of careful, deliberate planning. 'How many entrances has it?'

'I think two, but I'm not sure.'

'And what time does this stadium open?'

'Six o'clock. The first bout of the day.'

This time the silence was prolonged. Magonde mused: there was an advantage and yet a disadvantage – the space was confined, yet in a crowd Ensor's and perhaps any other suspect actions could be viewed easily prior to the exchange. The entrances could be sealed, but then so could any road, if that particular ploy was to be introduced; and even if Ensor did decide to contact the police, they would wish to avoid an armed conflict in such a crowded area at all costs. However, there was still a question of positioning. 'Tell me, Mr Ensor, what are the ticket arrangements there?' he enquired.

'At the gate, on entrance, I believe.'

Magonde cleared his throat as if still in thought, and then suddenly his tone seemed sharper, more purposeful. 'Listen carefully, Mr Ensor. This is how it will be. You will enter the stadium tomorrow night at precisely six o'clock, and you will take a ticket for yourself, and occupy a position with four vacant seats in one line, at the end of a row. You will take up the furthest seat in, leaving three empty towards the aisle, and you will make sure that nobody else occupies those seats. Is that clear so far?'

'Yes.'

'We will arrive and occupy those vacant seats sometime around six o'clock, but during that period you will be watched carefully. You will not know the exact time of our arrival, and one of my men will stay outside the arena throughout. I wish the exchange itself to be quick, so everything must be exact. As for identification, you will hold the figure in an obvious position – rest it on your lap perhaps. It is not necessary for you to know us, your wife will be present when the exchange is finally made.' Magonde paused for a moment, as if he might have neglected a detail, concluding 'Do we have a clear understanding?'

Ensor repeated the essence of the instructions.

'Are there any questions?'

'No.'

'Good, we are agreed – the Lumpini Stadium, six o'clock tomorrow night.' Magonde let out his breath. 'And as far as your safety in a crowd goes, Mr Ensor, I would not wish you to be under any misapprehension – if there are any complications, it will serve neither you nor your wife any purpose.'

The line went dead.

Paul remained silent, holding the receiver. Steel was at his side. 'You got it?'

'Yes,' Ensor replied, his tone dull, distant.

'Great!' Steel exclaimed, putting an arm around and jogging Ensor's shoulder. 'You've done your bit.'

It reminded Steel that his own arrangements were yet to be finalized: the gem transfer, monetary arrangements, a British Consulate diplomatic pouch, and still, he remembered, the daunting question of back-up; Gene Haskell was now more essential than ever.

Twenty minutes later, when they had gone back over the arrangements, Mr Tom took Steel to one side, out of the main office, commenting, 'I've found your gem merchant. It's all set for tomorrow – a man named Tanayo Pen.'

The Bangkok night was heavy, dark and damp, a threat of impending monsoon rain hanging like an ethereal cloak in the atmosphere. They were back at the Narao, and Steel dragged himself away from his fourteenth-floor window and the abstract fascination of the myriad of lights below, appearing distended and ghostly in the damp and misty air. He turned to the telephone on the bedside table and tried Gene Haskell's number. 'For the last time,' he swore to himself under his breath, dialling out the last few digits; but again there was no answer, and impatiently he put a call down to Chareompond's office.

'An interesting question, Tom – if you were tracking down a raw opium dealership in Bangkok, where would you start?'

Mr Tom mused for a second. 'The port authorities, dock police perhaps. . . .'

'How about taking it from the other side – the dealers themselves?'

'No question, Jeff – bars, clubs and brothels. Most of them are under the protection of organized crime. And it's no secret.'

'It's this American again,' Steel offered, as if sensing the inevitable question. 'I'm afraid it'll have to be tonight – there's no other time.'

'Have you thought of the American Embassy?' Tom enquired pensively.

'Yes – no good. He was 'out on a limb' on this one; they wouldn't have any record of his activities.'

'Okay, I can help out, Jeff. I know a good tout; his name's Samdech Suthayakha – everyone knows him just as 'Sam' or 'Sammy'. But I should also warn you, it's very dangerous. All these establishments are very close-knit – news travels fast.'

There was little other choice, Steel thought to himself; they made the arrangements.

It was 10:16 p.m.

Steel hauled his case on to the bed, flipping up its lid and picking out a medium-sized radio tucked in among the shirts and socks. He opened the back of the radio cautiously. A bank of small transistors and circuits confronted him; pressing three separate points, he removed the bakelite board supporting them. The underside of the transistor board, as with all other sides of the container, was lead-lined, impervious to standard airport X-ray. Steel lifted out a gun and two cartridge packs, all wrapped in polythene. The gun was a Browning 9mm, a personally chosen 'Renaissance' styling adding extra flair to the standard SIS and NATO sidearm.

He took a small rag from his case, and started cleaning the gun methodically, sliding its cylindrical magazine from the base of the handgrip and testing the trigger action by

248

sound as much as sight.

Leaving the gun in separate pieces on the counterpane, he rustled around at the bottom of his suitcase, finally lifting out a brown leather holster and two separate belts, which he interlaced together, standing up now, and strapping the two belts so that the holster hung to one side of his left armpit. He tightened one of the belts until it felt snug against his breast, and walked over to the wardrobe. The jacket he picked out was a pale fawn in lightweight material, but was heavier than you would expect such a jacket to be. 'Don't you think you're perhaps being overcautious,' Kenton had commented, on first noting the two flat knives on the requisition.

'It's purely for an edge – if required,' Steel had explained. The razor that had saved him with Ugbaja was still strong in his mind.

Steel moved back to the bed, opening one box of ammunition, filling the magazine of thirteen, and re-assembling the gun. The cartridges, thirty-six to each box, were KTW armour-piercing stock, supplied to the Service from a manufacturer in Ohio through a 'buffer' company in West Virginia and tested, according to Waldebridge from ballistics, 'to pass through a six millimetre sheet of compressed steel, fired from a distance of ten feet, penetrating an immediate alanine polyamide and wood pulp backing block to a distance of seventeen point three centimetres'.

Waldebridge remained an enigma within the Service; he had a comment on everything, whether within his department or not. 'I thought you'd be the first in with a request,' he had remarked to Steel, when the final tests were completed and requisitions 'rubber stamped' from upstairs. His cynicism appeared to indicate an inner doubt that a university graduate with a Defence Intelligence background, whether highest scoring of the trainees or not, could deal with the real thing. 'It's a bit different out there, you know – pumping your bullets through flesh and blood, rather than these paper targets.'

And Waldebridge had been right, Steel reflected, after

his first few assignments. But then at the vital moment, Jeffrey Steel's victims would magically transform from flesh and blood into paper and concentric rings of black ink; a crude but brief mental protection from the stench of burning cordite and the final inspection of human carnage. Flesh and blood once again. But then it wasn't important. And Jeffrey Steel never lived by regrets.

Early in the morning was Bangkok's most pleasant time, the sounds of birdsong the only break in the silence, the backstreets devoid of cars and people. Rain had been forecast for late that evening, but now a slight north-easterly breeze added an extra freshness to what was already the coolest time of the day. Harry Royston, as with many others in non-air-conditioned residences, slept with his windows open, a small top window at the front of the house and a larger side-window letting the slightly cooler air into his bedroom at the rear.

The house itself was small and typically Thai, half of it supported by concrete pillars to allow a carport for the small Datsun beneath. The other half was slightly larger, harbouring the front door and clearing the ground by just over two feet. In all, the house boasted two bedrooms, and the pocket-size surrounding garden plot allowed a small mango tree and an acacia hedgerow. The quiet suburban street supported another thirty-seven similarly designed houses spread almost evenly on opposite sides. For Harry Royston, the visiting American executive, it had proved the ideal habitat.

Regardless of the dawn chorus, Royston slept on in the back bedroom, oblivious also to the stream of light filtering through a twelve-inch gap in the curtains and picking out his shape on the bed. The curtains were of a thin material and more light seeped through to highlight the surrounding areas of the bedroom. It was of medium size, no more than fifteen feet square and the large double bed at its centre made it appear smaller than it actually was.

Harry Royston's body, long and heavy-framed, straggled

out diagonally across the bed, a single white sheet clinging to the thin film of sweat that he had found a constant companion since first arriving in Bangkok. One bodily function not yet acclimatized in his ten months' stay.

Royston's hair was black and lank, a disarrayed forelock hanging loosely over one eye. A faint smile lay frozen on his face – a dream perhaps of somebody sharing his bed. On the bedside table, as if to warn off any potential bed-sharers, was a picture of Royston's wife. A smaller picture beside framed two round-faced children, the girl a bit smaller than the boy, both inheriting their father's dark hair.

In the bedside-table drawer lay a gun, and in the dressing-table drawer an American passport: *Harry Royston – Occupation: Company executive.* The advent of the mass factory production of Thai shirts and their export to Europe and America made it not abnormal for a Bangkok manufacturer to employ an American with knowledge of his home clothing market. The oversized executive case in the corner crammed with off-cuts of Thai silks, cottons and polyesters in varying patterns supported that image. The cover was good.

Harry Royston slept through the intensifying light as the sun rose higher. He also slept through the slight clicking noise that was the only warning of the overweight Thai letting himself in through the front-room window. The Thai, his hair heavily greased back, grimaced as the latch forced itself the last inch. He pushed open the larger window below and crouched momentarily on the sill, his eyes almost closed in a tight squint, flashing at the empty room before him.

He let his heavy frame drop silently to the lounge floor. The window remained open behind him. Small, like most Thais, there was something muscular about his excess flesh that gave the little man a bull-like appearance. His yellow skin-pallor was faded and dull, his eyes jet-black, bottomless, glinting through tight-slit apertures. A single tattoo on the back of his right hand depicted a lion, one of its front paws raised from the ground and gripped like a fist around the handle of a large curved sword, the blade brandished above the lion's head in threatening gesture. The symbol of the fearless warrior.

He stalked silently across the lounge floor, handling his weight with surprising grace. He stood still by the door near the far end of the lounge and listened, his ear close to the door, then, opening it carefully, stepped into a small hallway section. To one side he could see the kitchen through a gap of light, and in the other direction the hallway leading back to the front door. Straight ahead, a small set of stairs led to the two bedrooms and the bathroom perched above the carport.

The Thai inched his way up the stairwell. As he approached the back bedroom door, he crouched down silently, cautiously, one hand stealing down and drawing a thick rod from his side-pocket, its length solid and of black polished ebony, save for two inches at the end which were capped in silver. He started unscrewing the silver cap, anti-clockwise. In close combat, the rod made a useful cosh, the silver end heavy and blunt, but it was the delicate workings inside the rod that he now sought.

He placed the silver cap back in his pocket. The exposed end showed a heavy lead ball almost half an inch in diameter and resting loosely but securely in a basin-shaped hollow. Attached to the other end of the lead ball was over ten yards of thin, sharp cheese-wire, most of it wrapped around a spindle at the centre of the rod itself and completely concealed. A sharp thrust of the rod would send the lead ball flying from its basin, exposing the length of wire from inside as it reeled smoothly from the rod's free-running spindle. From then on, the spindle operated on the inertia basis, a sharp pull locking it in place and securing the wire in position. The inertia rocker could be released by a small button on the side of the rod, which at the same time would bring a spring into operation, reeling the length of wire swiftly inwards until the lead ball rested once more in its small hollow basin. In the hands of an expert it was a deadly garotte, even at ten paces.

The Thai gradually rose from his crouched position, gently easing the bedroom door-handle with one hand as he slow-motioned upwards. There was no sound. He stood at his full height a few inches over five feet as the door swung open, revealing two-thirds of the bedroom. The large double bed at the centre was fully in view. A slight shadow hung over him as he stood in the doorway. In contrast, the middle section of Harry Royston's body lay highlighted below the white, clinging sheet by a beam of sunlight breaking through the gap in the curtains. The Thai's pupils glinted like balls of polished jet at the sight. Harry Royston lay in deep slumber.

The Thai stepped a pace inside the room and lifted the rod above his head. He pressed the button at the side to release the spring from its last action and flashed his forearm forward in one; the lead ball flew from its basin, the thin wire humming as it trailed swiftly through the air. Then with a flicking movement he brought the lead ball and the wire lashing down on to the sheets at Royston's side.

The whiplash noise brought the upper half of Royston's body sharply up from the bed, his deep brown eyes flickering, adjusting themselves to the light, then focusing.

The button pressed, the wire was swiftly looping back into the rod, the lead ball flying back to its cradle. But Harry Royston was quick. His large frame was already lunging sideways, his arm outstretched to the bedside drawer and his gun in an instinctive motion.

The Thai's forearm flicked, the lead ball hurtling once more across the room, steel wire whistling in pursuit, cutting harshly through the air.

The drawer was open, Royston's hand almost touching the gun.

Another flicking movement from the Thai, more delicate, more measured than the last.

Royston gripped the gun.

The lead ball wrapped around Royston's neck, once, twice, three times, rapidly drawing sharp steel wire behind it.

Royston's gun-grip weakened, fingers losing their hold on the smooth metal frame. The spindle locked, the wire humming like a guitar string with the tension. The Thai struggled with both hands, bringing the first beads of sweat to his forehead.

The power gone from Royston's hand, his gun clattered to the floor. His eyeballs bulged, as if in some final astonishment, his face already purplish-blue, but his body remaining upright. His hands flailed hopelessly at the wire around his neck and then started falling back to his sides in nervous, weakened contortions.

The sharp wire cut through the flesh of Royston's neck and into his jugular vein. His body shifted, turning slightly and then slumping forwards. The bed started shaking, his body dragging still further forwards as the wire sank deeper into his neck. His wife's picture fell off the bedside table, the glass front smashing on impact with the floor. The children's picture followed.

The Thai made a sharp, tugging motion, pulling the wire through the final obstruction of the cervical vertebrae, then pressed the rod's button, and the thin wire, glistening red in places, looped back on itself a few times and returned to its spindle. He stood inspecting the carnage from the doorway. Large red patches marred the crisp white linen and the decapitated body pumped out still more blood in a few final, involuntary motions.

Satisfied, the Thai turned from the bedroom into the adjoining bathroom. He poured hot water into the rod's end by lifting the lead ball and then, as if mixing a martini, cleaned the wire inside. He poured the discoloured water down the sink, screwed the silver cap back in place and then let himself out through the front door.

The stench of blood and body waste pervaded Harry Royston's bedroom. The birds outside with their uncanny sense of nearby death had stopped singing. The sun, not nearly so sensitive, continued rising.

Harry Royston's passport and clothing samples had proved worthless. The non-activity on the raw opium market had been the lull before the storm. His cover had been broken.

Gene Haskell was dead.

Two hours later the doorbell rang twice, and then thirty seconds later a small buff square of paper came through the letter-box and fluttered slowly to the wooden hallway floor.

It was a telegram.

Part Five

Lion's Quarry

15

The flashing neon sign spat its bright, gaudy double-nine into the night, its red reflection shimmering across the dark and hazy wetness of the road. The rain was heavy and the windscreen wipers whisked from side to side furiously, but still somewhat insufficiently, as 'Sammy' wheeled the car in alongside.

'They've got another place like this,' he remarked to Steel. 'The Triple Nine – just a bit larger. But I think we'll find the manager here.'

The building was white spar-dashed, with two Spanish-inspired towers at each end, and a tall coconut palm each side of the entrance.

It reminded Steel of an elaborate 'Alamo'; the fact that it was a brothel prompted some initial amusement.

Sammy was of average height for a Thai, but quite thin, his dark hair oiled and swept neatly to one side, his smile mischievous but endearing as he led the way briskly towards the entrance. 'Raining cat and dogs, eh?'

Steel followed, grinning ruefully. The Thais and their all-so-necessary displays of Westernization, he thought.

The main foyer of the brothel appeared to have retained its Spanish influence, Steel noted, but, to each side, elongated corridor extensions faded into 'barrack'-style architecture, the inspiration curtailing abruptly at the edge of the semi-circle of mosaic tiling they stood in the centre of. On the far wall was a reception desk, pretentiously ornate with Roman-style pillars.

The Thai behind the desk was old, his hair grey and thinning. He was dressed shabbily, apart from a dark jacket which seemed to be both an afterthought and an attempt at good appearance. He smiled sheepishly at them, the gaps in his teeth adding to his pathos. 'Dy pohm choo-ay koon,' he exclaimed.

Sammy approached him. 'Sa-waht dee krahp,' he nodded faintly, and asked about the manager.

To Steel, the conversation seemed much the same as in the earlier clubs they had visited; the discourse rapid and repetitive, going from one to the other, both men nodding and their tones changing quickly, the sounds guttural but dulled, as if they were, at times, having problems clearing their throats.

At one point Sammy paused, beckoning towards Steel, and Steel produced Haskell's photograph from his side pocket; but the desk man started shaking his head after a moment, and then the conversation continued for a while.

'What did he say?' Steel enquired in the first apparent lull.

'He says that he hasn't seen this man – and as for the manager, he's away for a few days, and anyway, when he is here, he doesn't see many of the guests. He says that *he* is the one,' Sammy emphasized, pointing to the desk man, 'who sees everyone and everything. He's here all the time.'

The desk man nodded as if he understood that the translation was accurate. They thanked him and made their way back out.

By the time they had manoeuvred out of the car park and down to the end of the wide, brightly lit avenue, the rain had eased off considerably. A few minutes later, passing an ornate green-and-gold temple that Sammy explained was the Wat Suthat, it stopped abruptly, and with as little warning as it had started. Just forty minutes of monsoon rain and everything was awash.

The perimeters of the temple were in white walling with red-roofed miniature monuments at intervals, and in front was an imposing tall redwood archway structure, the pavement bordering edged by a prominent white line. An ancient Eastern monument in a modern Western showcase, Steel thought. Somebody else's showcase. But now, at night and with the rain-water lapping in uneven pools against the white kerbstone, it had a drabness that contrasted with the regality of the photographs filling souvenir shop postcard racks.

'King Rama the First,' Sammy offered as if in answer to Steel's preoccupation. 'He started building it in the seventeen nineties. It wasn't finished for another forty years, and by then Rama the Third was king.'

'It's beautiful,' Steel replied, on an impulse. He cared, but not in the way he knew that Sammy expected; there were too many other things on his mind.

They sat in silence for a moment. The lights outside had become brighter and more frequent as they crept into the inner core of the city; the mass of small lanes and streets interlacing the wide avenues between Democracy Monument and Government House.

'They say that the archway on the Wat Suthat. . . ,' Sammy started, taking the conversation back to a thought he'd had as they had passed the temple. 'In olden times, in a ceremony performed for the kings, if you could swing on it and over the top, and snatch a purse full of gold in your teeth from its centre pole, you could keep the purse. Brave men would compete every year for it – can you imagine?'

'Yes, fascinating,' Steel agreed blankly, although he found it difficult to imagine – the archway was a good eighty to a hundred feet high. Combined with his earlier thoughts, he could see himself, as if in someone else's demented cartoon, swinging on the poles, trying to catch a purse of gold between his teeth. But he was never able to reach it.

As they turned, the streets were narrower and brightly lit; a jumbled mass of neon displaying both the Thai and English alphabets and, where words alone couldn't convey sufficient meaning, apt and often lurid shapes were formed by the dazzling signs and billboards, some clustering and overhanging others for best position.

'Where are we going?' Steel asked.

'A more respectable establishment,' Sammy replied. 'Not a brothel – a massage parlour. It's also supposed to be, for many reasons, as notorious as it is respectable.'

'Sounds interesting.'

'Even more interesting is that it's run by a woman.'

u 'And how notorious is she?'

'You'll soon find out,' Sammy grinned slyly. 'Her real name's a mystery – everybody just calls her Madame Chitra.'

Madame Chitra ran the Playboy Executive Massage Parlour with all the maternal attention and instinct of a mother hen. To the forty-two girls and three boys residing within the confines of her establishment, she was a mother, protector, provider, employer and confidante.

'All of them beautiful, sensuous and slim, and the oldest one is twenty-five,' Madame Chitra boasted.

'And the youngest?'

Madame Chitra declined to comment, turning away as if distracted. 'What do you think of my wares, as you say in your country, Mr Steel?' She changed the subject deftly, laughingly.

Steel studied the collection again: thirty-one girls and one boy, so well made-up and dressed as to initially go unnoticed by Steel, until pointed out by Sammy. 'The rest are on duty,' Madame Chitra explained.

The scene was like looking through the wrong side of a cinema screen towards a small audience, banked in five clearly visible rows of plush velvet seating. From their distracted gaze, Steel deduced that the glass was one-way, and the object of their attention, Madame Chitra clarified, was a television set. 'They like so much your Western films.'

The system of choice, the glass screen and the furnishings added a twentieth-century aura to what Steel felt was merely a variation on the Roman slave markets. On the 'slave' side of the screen the seating arrangement huddled its occupants closely together, whereas to those few making a choice, the seating was in expansive, open-plan lounge style, with the occasional potted palm, coffee-table and ash-tray. At the end of the sixty-foot oblong lounge was a wide, sweeping ruby-carpeted staircase with a gilded balustrade. 'That leads to the massage rooms,' Sammy informed him.

Madame Chitra was correct, Steel thought, looking back through the screen. Most of the girls, and even the one boy, the way he was presented, were extremely attractive.

In contrast, Madame Chitra herself was fat, heavy-faced, and seemed to be fighting off the ravages of late middle-age with gargantuan applications of make-up and accessories. An ornate wig was piled precariously on top of her head, and false eyelashes hung like dead spiders, almost completely concealing her slitted eyes. She wore, very wisely, a large flowing maternity-style gown in floral pattern. With each movement of her body, columns of jewellery jangled heavily.

'What do you think?' she prompted.

'Very nice,' Steel complimented.

At that point, Sammy interrupted, explaining to Madame Chitra that there was another small matter in which they thought she might be of assistance; he had already briefed Steel that the matter should be brought up as a sideline, if only as a matter of courtesy. Madame Chitra looked over curiously.

Steel took out Haskell's photograph. 'It's a friend of mine – he changed hotels and I've lost track of him. I thought that perhaps he may have called by and mentioned in passing to you, or one of your girls, where he might be staying.'

Madame Chitra took the photo, still with some mild apprehension.

'I know how popular your establishment is with visiting foreign businessmen,' Steel added.

This brought a smile to Madame Chitra's face, and she softened, studying the photo for the first time.

'I'm afraid I must get my glasses,' she said, and then looking up, smiling again. 'This is such a tiny photograph, Mr Steel.' She headed for a small room with a purple silk-cushioned door at the back of the lounge.

But Madame Chitra wore glasses only when inspecting the fine calligraphy of the parlour's ledger, and once inside the small office she held the photograph at her side, not troubling herself to look at it again, and bit hard on her knuckles, fighting to make a decision. She stayed by the door, her back to it for a moment, a pause that she felt appropriate.

She came out of the office beaming apologetically. 'I'm afraid not, Mr Steel. A good-looking man though – Madame Chitra would not easily forget a face so handsome.' She handed the photo back, mentioning as if as an afterthought, 'Although on the other hand, so often I am busy in my office and the girls take care of customers. Perhaps it would be as well to talk to some of them too – combine business with pleasure, as you say.'

Steel looked back towards the glass screen.

'Sunnee speaks the best English and Nittaya the best French; she's from Cambodia. If I'm not here, one of them is always taking care of things.' Madame Chitra pointed out their positions.

Both of the girls, Steel noted, had long, straight, dark hair; one just below shoulder-length, the other almost to her waist. All of the display-room occupants wore white shorts and matching bolero tops, their midriffs and legs bare.

'Why don't you take them both?' Madame Chitra egged him on.

At first, Steel hesitated – then he remembered Sammy's advice that their enquiry should appear as a sideline to what Madame Chitra would consider the main purpose of their visit; once resigned to it, he found himself faintly intrigued by the proposition.

'One of my girls will fulfil your needs in a way you will have never before experienced – but two, aah!' she exclaimed, lifting her eyes heavenwards, softening her voice. 'You look a strong enough man to take it,' she added, in obvious appeal to Steel's pride.

Without waiting for an answer, she made the arrangements.

Steel vaguely sensed from Sammy's bemused expression, although he could not immediately fathom why, that Madame Chitra's enthusiasm was perhaps more marked than normal.

She introduced Steel to the two girls and excused herself abruptly. 'I have some business to attend to.'

Madame Chitra was pleased with herself. She had told the truth, not trusting herself to lie at such a juncture. But then, she knew that Steel could have no idea of what she really meant by 'business'. The *Bpratahn* himself would have been proud of such an action. In the meantime, she would gain a bit more information from Sammy.

She walked back into the office, to a velvet-panelled wooden desk at its centre, picked up the phone and dialled a number implanted indelibly on her memory. She had known that number for many years now, she mused, but had so rarely used it. For she knew, as did so many others in Bangkok who would remain faceless to her, that it was a number that could never be written down.

The room was sixteen feet long but no more than ten feet wide with a large oval bath at one end bordered by a strip of patterned tiling. The thick pile carpet which extended for the remainder of its length was a lush expanse of snowy whiteness broken only by the rich green of two Palmetto palms in wicker tubs, one in each corner. The massage table was also covered in white, a stark linen that would have seemed clinical but for the surrounding decor. The bath was running, its steam filtering up through more palm and green foliage grouped in a large well behind; and on each side small grilles offered delicate piped music.

Steel watched the two girls. The longer-haired girl turned the bath's gilded taps, while the other selected one by one a variety of bottles from the back shelf, tipping no more than a few drops of each into the now foaming water, a touch of amber being the final addition. Both girls were bent away from him, the slimness of their limbs accentuated by their tight-fitting white shorts.

The longer-haired girl beckoned him over finally. 'It is ready now.'

Steel had traded in his clothes for a white terry-cloth robe, careful to extract his gun and the photo from his jacket; he slipped the gun into the robe's front pocket, placing the photo on the tiling shelf at the back of the massage table. He left the robe to one side, padded naked the few feet towards the bath. 'Tell me,' he asked, 'which one of you is Sunnee and which is Nittaya? You look so much alike.'

The long-haired one giggled like a schoolgirl. 'My name Sunnee, and that Nittaya,' she exclaimed, pointing.

'What's so funny?'

'Nothing,' Sunnee said, hanging her head coyly, adding flatly, 'If you please to get in bath.'

Steel submerged himself in the steaming water and Sunnee took a large round sponge from the side, Nittaya following her example. They spread a thick foam of lather across his chest in easy strokes.

Sunnee lifted her head, still smiling mischievously. 'Funny you should ask name,' she said. 'Englishmen call all the time for Sunnee but always ask for 'Parrot'. Only ten girls in the parlour speak English, and all the Englishmen who call say me and one other girl speak it the best, but me even a bit better than her. Madame Chitra say I talk too much. She the one who give me nickname 'Parrot'. What do you say – you think I talk too much?' She looked concerned.

'No,' Steel replied. He turned to Nittaya.

'She talks French, but only a few words in English,' Sunnee offered. 'All she knows is "Hello, you want good time?" I tell her – that no get you very far in Bangkok, only in trouble. Since then she not say anything in English, just keep her mouth shut all the time.' Sunnee laughed slightly, and then added musingly, 'Best thing anyway. One day I teach her English damn good.'

They continued lathering with the sponges, now in long circular motions.

'Stand up, please,' Sunnee gestured after a moment, lifting her sponge. They had finished Steel's arms, chest and back, and now lathered his legs, Nittaya breaking off first, putting down her sponge and drying her hands. Sunnee continued, holding Steel's manhood gently from beneath and lathering with a particular care and attention that she had paid to no other part, her almond eyes glinting up at him teasingly, mocking. 'Now you clean – all over!'

They dried him with large, fluffy white towels and laid him supine on the massage table, covering him with a small hand-towel.

The towels were folded in a neat pile by the bath and then they commenced undressing. The bolero tops they wore had lacing at the front, and Sunnee pulled at the taut string between her breasts, sliding the scant material off her bamboo-brown shoulders. Swiftly she stepped out of her shorts. Her breasts were full and round on a slim torso, her skin-colour from head to toe the same bamboo-brown, except a lighter shade in those areas always guarded from the sun. The heaviest part of her breasts, surrounding the nipple, appeared the lightest of all, and her long dark hair hung straight and blue-black in the stark light, at times overlapping the coarser darkness of her small pubic triangle. Nittaya was also naked now, her breasts smaller but proud, accentuating the slim boyishness of her hips. Her skin was darker, and her hair had the same straight blue-blackness.

'You're both very beautiful,' Steel said. 'How old are you?'

'You're very flattering, Mr Steel,' Sunnee rebuked, hanging her head. 'But still is not enough for woman to admit last and most important secret.' She giggled out loud again, and it was obvious to Steel that she was practised; as natural in her joyful flippancy naked as she was with her clothes on. He guessed their ages at not more than nineteen, Nittaya perhaps a bit younger.

The two girls took small ivory slides from the back shelf of the bath, twirling their hair on top and fastening it in a bun. They stepped into the bath and took the same sponges, lathering each other with the thick suds, smiling as if in some silent enjoyment between only the two of them.

Steel asked, as though in passing, if all the girls were so slim, and very quickly the conversation led to comparisons – Steel deciding spontaneously on a note of melodrama. 'You see, where I come from we have this particular disease you don't have here. It enlarges the bottom and hips to gross proportions,' he emphasized, holding his hands out wide at his sides. 'But they haven't found a name for it yet, and it affects mainly the women of our country. Now if they can find out how Eastern women stay so slim. . . .'

'Oh, Mr Steel, you make fun of Sunnee!'

'Would I do such a thing?' he demanded defensively, looking towards Nittaya. She just smiled back blankly at him.

'Anyway,' Sunnee retorted, as if faintly upset, 'what you say not true. Many of your Western women very nice, very slim. I go to cinema and see with my own eyes – Brigitte Bardot, Ursula Andress, Jane Fonda . . . Ali McGraw,' she added as an afterthought. 'I saw her in a film with Steef McQueen.'

'Steve McQueen,' he corrected.

'Yes, Steef McQueen.' She stepped out of the bath, Nittaya following, and they started drying. 'No!' she concluded finally, as if convincing only herself. 'What you say not right.'

They dried each other swiftly and moved towards Steel on the massage table, their small rounded faces deadset, as though the previous conversation had been forgotten and only duty remained. They spoke a few words in Thai to each other and then Nittaya took a tall wooden container of sandalwood-essence powder from the back shelf, passing it across, and Sunnee spread the powder liberally on Steel's body, rubbing it deep into his skin. Then followed an oil, purple in colour, from a long cylindrical bottle with a bulb at its base. Its scent was jasmine with an underlying redolence of varying flowers and herbs, too fused to be identified individually.

'I had an old boyfriend once,' Sunnee reminisced, her head tilted, eyes dreamy, her hands moving as if detached, deep into Steel's shoulderblades. 'He had muscles like this – but larger, and his skin was dark, like mine, but more brown. His muscles weren't as hard as yours, though,' she added hastily, shaking her head, suddenly attentive, worried that she may have offended Steel's pride. An unforgivable act in Thailand, from a woman to a man, though quite acceptable in reverse. 'He used to come here all the time,' she said, returning to her dreaminess. 'He asked for me every day, except one Friday and a Tuesday, for two months. I remember, because I wrote the days down in my diary. . . . Always asked for Sunnee. And we would see each other even out of the parlour and I would put off my regulars for him. Madame Chitra was very annoyed, I remember well. He came from near your country, Mr Steel. I know, because he mentioned going to, how you say . . . Liwerpool. He talked of football all the time, although I never understand . . . all these men running about, kicking ball – hah!' She looked back at Steel, raising one eyebrow in salutation of the memory. 'He was Greek – a sailor.'

'All Greeks are sailors,' Steel commented dryly.

'Oh, Mr Steel,' Sunnee retorted, waving her finger in warning. 'You make fun of me again. . . . Anyway he wasn't a sailor when I knew him, he owned a garage. It was just that he was a sailor for so many years that he looked at himself as still a sailor.'

Steel mumbled, 'I see,' resting back, surrendering himself to the mobile precision of their small hands, the tension easing from the bunched muscles at the back of his neck. Sunnee transferred her attention to the fingers of one hand, cracking each knuckle in a straight pull, and then those too seemed to relax. Nittaya took his other hand and they started working their way upwards on his arms, kneading deep into his flesh, their hands gripped into loose fists, knuckles rounded, probing.

After a moment, Sunnee requested him to turn over, and Nittaya climbed up on to the massage table, tentatively positioning herself, then stepping on to his back. She concentrated around his spine, spreading her toes outwards from that point, rolling her feet back and forth, following a forty-five degree angle in specific areas that she would stop at from time to time. It seemed, by the flow and rapidity of her movements, that at no time did the full weight of her body come to bear. And then after a moment, as the delicate motions increased, he could sense, as though a warm veil had been drawn over his outer skin and was sinking gradually deeper, a more mellow, more total relaxation enveloping him, and he thought, lying here with these girls, all so natural, so uninhibited, all problems seemed distant, unimportant; and yet in another way it was an unsettling contrast to what he feared was impending. Again Haskell! He glanced towards the back shelf, indicating the photograph.

'A friend of mine, I lost track of him,' he said casually, answering Sunnee's expected curiosity.

She had noticed the photo previously, but leant over as if she had not. 'He looks familiar,' she commented, studying the photo a bit longer; and then, as a hasty afterthought, 'Have you asked Madame Chitra?'

'Yes, but she told me that you might know better.' Steel smiled faintly. 'After all, you'd probably get to see much more of him.'

Sunnee frowned, veiling it quickly. 'Madame Chitra have a very good memory. If she say she not remember him, then you can be sure he no be here.' She lifted her head, a clear indication that the conversation was finished, continuing her massage, deeper, more forcefully.

'That's okay,' Steel acknowledged calmly, and he wondered what Sunnee was thinking behind the steadfast yet placid softness of her rounded features. First of all Madame Chitra's open offer, he thought, and now this plain contradiction.

'What's Madame Chitra like?' he asked after a moment, careful to make it no more than a passing comment.

'She's very good – some places very bad to work for, you

know. We get all the food and clothing we want and one night off a week. And our rooms are good here too, but then this is my first 'house'. Nittaya worked for another 'house' before though, and that man very bad. He beat her all the time.'

Sunnee broke off and spoke a few words to Nittaya. Nittaya made a few more probing motions with her feet between Steel's shoulder-blades and then jumped down.

'I'll show you what that man did to her,' Sunnee continued enthusiastically.

She reached out and parted Nittaya's long black hair and there, just below her right breast, was a scar, Steel could see now, although he hadn't noticed it before; it ran diagonally, almost four inches long.

'He did this with a kitchen knife,' Sunnee spat.

By sight Steel judged it to have healed a good few years before, but it had an open, delicately pink quality, as if it had not been stitched at the time. Steel reached out and touched the scar, although it looked so delicate. In a way he was afraid he might hurt her, but when he did touch her skin, she just smiled, and he felt a special affinity with Nittaya he hadn't felt before. 'This is bad,' he said, stroking the scar tenderly.

'It's all right now,' Sunnee said. 'It's almost four years ago this happened now – very dangerous. He keep all the girls in all the time, so she not allowed to go to hospital. Only bandage allowed and she almost die. I told her to leave that 'house' even before this happen. He was a bad, bad man.' She spluttered the words out as if the memory of the man alone had soiled her mouth.

'I'm sorry,' Steel said, looking gently towards Nittaya.

Sunnee had noticed Steel's injuries before – the strapping on his shoulder and the scar on the back of his left calf – but only now did she pass any comment. 'You seem to have had some problem too, Mr Steel.'

'It's nothing,' Steel commented lightly.

'Anyway, not problem time,' Sunnee forced a smile, as if in understanding. 'You must relax, enjoy.'

Sunnee reached for a bottle behind him and tipped it up, pouring a generous quantity of its contents into her palm. It was oil, warm and sweet-smelling and she carefully reached down, saying softly. 'I give you rub now – you relax.' And it was only then that Steel noticed how small her hands were, fluttering attentively like two love birds at the sensitive skin of his groin, while a warmth spread through him like an insistent ache from deep within.

'Ooh, Mr Steel,' she exclaimed reprovingly after a while, and she lifted herself up on to the massage table and spread her slim legs wide apart either side of him, lowering herself gently. She guided him with her hand, gasping slightly at the initial shock and then sliding confidently until her pubic bone rammed hard against him.

She closed her eyes, silent now in concentration, and she started writhing slowly back and forth, her mouth parted slightly as if in some distant ecstacy, her long hair moving slowly back and forth, flowing, caressing, small beads of sweat breaking out on her forehead and just above her top lip. She leant forwards, fitting the length of her body to his, and her hair hung like a blanket around them, dark and total, as if insulating them from the world outside. She kissed him deeply, probing and sensuously damp, her tongue writhing inside, and he could taste the saltiness of her mouth and sense the warmth and passion building deep within her loins.

'Oh, so good, *Keu soo-ay!*' she muttered dreamily; and then suddenly, as if possessed, she started bucking violently, her eyes closing gently, low groans emanating from her slightly parted lips as she leant backwards, stretching out like a cat.

At that moment, Nittaya caressed the muscles at Steel's shoulders, leaning over and kissing him lightly on the forehead, and he felt momentarily distracted, although in another way her slight touch relaxed him totally, his own pleasure rising without warning, exploding outwards from somewhere towards the centre of his spine and dissipating in mellow warmth.

272

And in that storm he was only faintly aware of Sunnee's own orgasm, her weight collapsed hard on his chest, her breath in low, repeated gasps, warm and moist against his cheek.

They talked for a while – restful, polite conversation with no aim. 'You as good as Greek boyfriend,' Sunnee complimented him. They rested a while longer and then she goaded him to make love to Nittaya while she watched. And then again to her. Always impatiently attentive.

Pleasurable oblivion.

Oblivious also to the small, fish-eye lens watching them impassively from the far corner of the room.

Madame Chitra accepted the small man through the side-door of her office curtly. 'Dtawn rakp,' she muttered, a forced smile defying her unease. In her heels, she stood slightly taller than him, but still he entered with an air of superiority. She knew him from many past visits as 'Kalchorn'.

He was middle-aged, dressed casually, his dark hair swept back and greying faintly at the sides, some faint freckles mottled brown on the shiny yellow of his forehead.

'Sa-waht dee krahp,' he bowed, in greeting. 'I came as soon as I could.'

'I would not have called you earlier than your normal time like this, unless it was absolutely necessary.'

'Of course,' he said, making it obvious by an impassive smile that this was purely a masquerade; he would not easily understand unless he thought that his duties had been requested with good cause.

Madame Chitra walked ahead of him, towards the far side of the room, her flowery ankle-length gown flapping around her. She turned to face a set of three display screens positioned neatly on a bench, side by side.

'He is on the second screen, the man that I spoke of,' she indicated. The first showed a generous but hazy portion of the main lounge and the third was switched off.

The small man moved closer to the second screen. 'And

he is an Englishman, this one?' he confirmed thoughtfully.

'Yes.'

He stood immobile for a moment, eyes flickering, attentive. 'It is good that you called us.' He glanced again at the screen, ignoring the lurid movements of the three figures, concentrating on the face of the Englishman: light-brown hair, tall, stocky, he noted. Larger and better-built than average, even for a *farang*, he thought. He had become accustomed to their unusual size from the influx of Americans through the years past, and although he had at first been awed by this, he had later found it to be an advantage, making them clumsy, awkward. Feeble opponents. He looked on with obvious contempt. 'How did he find his way here?' he enquired.

'Through a local tout recommended by the manager at the Narao, Vitchit Chareompond.'

'So, so. It is becoming clearer,' Kalchorn nodded, contemplating.

'It seems that he is an old friend of this manager,' Madame Chitra explained further.

'No more than that? There is no other connection, eh?'

'No, no. I am quite sure.'

Kalchorn stood for another moment in the same position, studying, impassive, and Madame Chitra turned away. 'He will be in there for at least another twenty minutes, you can be sure of that,' she said. 'However, we shall know when he's done. A small buzzer will sound by the screen when the door to that particular massage room is opened.'

Kalchorn bowed slightly at such ingenuity. 'Yes, good.' And he followed Madame Chitra towards her desk. 'It is perhaps an appropriate time to deal with our usual business,' he suggested. 'We are only a few days away at this point. . . . That is, if you have the figures ready.'

'I was to propose the very same myself. I am always at least a full week in advance,' she beamed courteously, 'so there is no problem.'

Kalchorn smiled. 'That is admirable,' he said, although he had expected no less.

Madame Chitra perched a pair of rounded, wire-framed spectacles on the end of her nose which appeared somehow out of place among her lustre and bright colours. She drew a wad of notes from a desk-drawer: one-hundred, five-hundred and one-thousand baht notes, bundled tight and two inches thick with a neat row of calligraphic-style figures on a white slip of paper which, folded over and slipped under the elastic band, fastened it all together.

She studied the figures on the top slip and passed the wad across the desk-top.

The small man accepted these curtly. 'Ka na bata.' He started counting the money, at intervals comparing his arithmetic to the calligraphy.

There were three other wads, and these he inspected with similar deliberation. 'My compliments, you have had a good month,' he said finally, lifting his attention. 'Our *Bpratahn* would have been displeased if it had *not* been a good month.'

Kalchorn bundled the four wads into his pocket, and they sat facing each other, talking very little. This suited Kalchorn, for he was not one for polite conversation and the silence allowed him to think clearly; there was much to be considered – the *farang* Englishman foremost of all.

When the buzzer finally sounded, almost ten minutes later, it came almost as a tiresome interruption to his thoughts; Kalchorn went back to the screen and watched the Englishman, now dressed, leave the massage room. He stood there for a moment staring impassively, until the door on the small room had been closed.

'Kawp jy,' he said. 'We are concluded. Good.'

'My bpen nahn,' Madame Chitra reciprocated. She opened the side-door and let the small man back out into the misty darkness, into a small, shadowed alleyway which finally led to Ratchdamnoen Avenue. And she bit back the fear and revulsion she felt deep down inside for him.

16

They sat next to each other in the front of the car and didn't talk until they were out of the maze of small streets, and when they did, it was Sammy who asked, as if in passing, what Steel thought of his massage. 'It is an experience, no? Especially with two girls.'

Steel recounted the events briefly, gazing distractedly at the passing streets, at vendors with open-fronted, board-frame shops, a stark fluorescence illuminating a miscellany of goods, too crammed to be picked out individually.

Then Sammy talked of his own experiences in the parlour, although these he seemed to be tiring of, mentioning them as if there was nothing else to talk about, filling the lull. 'She's meant to be one of the best there, but I go so often nowadays that she becomes almost like the wife I never had, so in the end, I tire of her.' He glanced out the window and turned a corner. 'Maybe I'll take my money somewhere else in future. Accept something inferior . . . but then at least a bit of variety.'

The lights at each side passed as brightly coloured blurs, reflected in sheets of water on the road and pavement. After a short while, they turned into a wider, more elaborate avenue with teak-wood and glass fronts displaying jewellery, furniture and Thai silks; a sign flashed Club Daisaku – with a Thai equivalent alongside – above a dress shop.

At the end was a large square opening out in front of them as they merged with the traffic to one side of the roundabout at its centre; a vista of billboards around its perimeter advertised various films, mostly American made with Thai sub-titles. All were large, gaudy artist's impressions depicting the anguished melodrama of love, blood and lust that supposedly could be viewed inside the expansive cinema halls.

The traffic was heavy. Samlors putt-putted in among the cars and buses. Bicycles, some supporting small trailers full of wares, hugged the kerb.

The car following them had gone unnoticed and was now even more insignificant in the heavy flow; twin beams among a proliferation, always at least a hundred yards behind and keeping mostly to the inside lane. Kalchorn, as ever, patient and attentive.

They turned into a wide avenue leading off the square, then made another turn.

A sudden contrast: market stalls grouped close, canvas tops and sides, open at the front, and bare electric light bulbs dangling; an array of clothes, jewellery, foods and general provisions. Colours, contrasts, movement and noise overlaid the otherwise drab ramshackleness of the narrow street with excitement.

At intervals, canals could be seen running beneath small, often ornate bridges, faint lights reflecting on water showing the humble dwellings of those who made their homes bordering the 'klongs'. Small-framed and constructed from old wooden boarding, palm fronds and corrugated iron, the shanty houses boasted little more than the running water washing their doorsteps. Some of them were open and movement could occasionally be picked out inside – people washing and cooking, bare flames from small paraffin-burners; but still there was a quiet solitude in comparison with the bustle of the streets close by. 'Add a splash of rainbow colours to an old silent movie, give the people big smiles and slit eyes, adorn with exotic art forms and that's Bangkok for you,' Steel recalled Cullen at the British Embassy saying.

It had been one of Cullen's more colourful statements, Steel had later discovered, but it had been accurate. He could sense it now, as much as ever. The danger and excitement of Bangkok was there, as always, open and exuberant in its soiled innocence.

They drove for another twenty minutes and then the

roads became rougher, narrower and devoid of street-lamps. The only lights were from small, outlying industrial units and the occasional passing car.

'Where now?' Steel asked, breaking the silence, and suddenly more aware of their surroundings.

'A closed establishment,' Sammy said. 'The places we've been so far are open and operate inside of the law but pay protection to a local "bandit" for a favour past – a loan perhaps, or a bribe paid to a law officer for a minor infringement.'

'A "bandit"?' Steel retorted, picking out that one un-likely phrase.

'Yes – in a way, it's just like olden times, but now they no longer roam the countryside, but have set areas of the city allocated, and sometimes control small armies of men. Like your American "bosses" and "godfathers".' Steel sat silent and Sammy glanced over at him momentarily. 'But the place we're going to now is different. It's fully protected and operates mostly outside of the law, so payments are made for that purpose.'

'Does that explain its remoteness?'

Sammy glanced in the mirror and turned into another road. 'Ah, yes – that is very important,' he exclaimed. 'These men are honourable and, if humoured, reasonable, but even though they are paying and could "call the tune", so to speak, they would not wish to be clumsy or obvious and so these establishments are well hidden. To do other-wise would be flaunting a vice and indiscreet and everyone would lose face. It would be like puting a false idol inside the Wat Phra Keo, and then paying the Buddhist monks to ignore it. But then, of course, these "closed establish-ments" require much heavier protection too.'

Steel nodded his understanding.

They turned again, and the road was narrower and for the most part straight, closely bordered on each side by sugar-cane. Kalchorn followed a good half-mile behind and far from sight. It would not be necessary to tail so closely, he had calculated – there was only one main road now, which they were on, and very few turn-offs, and it was pitch black. If they were to take one of the smaller roads he would be able to see the glow of their headlamps above the sugar-cane.

They turned once again, after a mile or so, and continued for almost another three miles, the road narrower still; and then the last turn, but this time only for a few hundred yards, for it was little more than a track, blocked-off at the end, the sugar-cane higher still and so closely encroaching on the road that there would hardly be room for another car passing.

A large gate confronted them, twenty feet wide and half as tall, consisting of a series of thick bamboo poles roped tight in a vertical line. The fence on either side was similarly constructed and carved into spikes at the ends. The darkness outside was a thick blanket, the trilling of crickets almost deafening.

Sammy pushed on his horn – one long blast and two short ones, several seconds after the first – and then he flashed his lights once.

A small hatch opened up in the gate, four feet from the ground: a set of eyes, beady and inquisitive in the stark beam, appeared, and then disappeared with equal rapidity.

Seconds after, the gate started to open, heavy and slow and swinging in a wide arc on two old bicycle tyres, one either side.

The two men pulling were large and stocky, printed cotton shirts hanging loose over cream trousers, and both barefoot. They looked on as Steel and Sammy passed with no sign of welcome or otherwise, and closed the gate swiftly behind them.

They were in the centre of a large courtyard, and the bamboo fence, they could see now, went all of the way around; a hundred-yard-square area of neatly penned, hard-packed brown earth.

They got out of the car.

'The fence is to keep people out.' Sammy gestured in an off-hand manner behind him. 'The guards at the gate too, that's their job and they stay in that position all the time and never move, whatever happens. Even if the sky falls in,' he dramatized, holding his hands up high.

Steel glanced back at them.

'There'll be another one inside,' Sammy added. 'Maybe two.' And they walked on ahead.

There were four buildings: three were small, single-storey cabins twenty feet square and made of slatted green board on which the paint was flaking. The main building was of the same boarding, oblong, and two storeys high, one window visible downstairs, but heavily shaded, and several upstairs, mostly curtained with varying colours and prints, tattered and soiled. Above the door was a small sign board, etched in gaudy red lettering – 'MAA-OH HAWNG', and underneath (CAT CLUB).

They headed towards the sign and walked inside.

It was an oblong room. The stage was to their side as they entered, and the music deafening. It was hot, the same clammy atmosphere as outside but smoke-filled and dense, a dark mauve haze prevailing. They moved towards a table and the full extent of the stage appeared, garishly bright among a series of purple spotlights, the remainder of the room a pitch-blackness in contrast; a small bar in the far corner was the only other thing clearly visible, backlit in red and circled by fairy lights. There was a perfume in the air too, they could now sense, adding to the mugginess; thickly veiled and yet both erotic and nauseating in the heaviness of its scent.

On the stage an attractive Thai girl danced in an incessant, thrusting rhythm to a disco beat, her skin a faint golden brown, glistening with sweat from head to toe but more noticeably on her forehead and flat, undulating belly. She wore only a tasselled bikini bottom — the silver sequins reflecting the purple spotlights – and high platform shoes with criss-cross rope straps rising to her calves. Her breasts were rounded and firm, and moved only slightly in spite of her motions; her hair too remained oddly unruffled, dark and cut short in page-boy style.

A waitress came out of the darkness behind them. 'Can I get you a drink?' she enquired with a faint American accent. She had noticed both Sammy and the *farang*, but the club was predominantly tourist, and as always in such a situation, the language was English.

Sammy asked for a Coke; he had learnt the limitations of Oriental livers on drinking sessions past. Steel asked for a scotch and ice. 'A double.'

'Scotch on the rocks,' Sammy translated, and when she had walked away, added, 'That's the problem here. A lot of people speak English but there's far too many American-isms – all GI and cinema language.' Then after a second, he added, 'What about the photo?'

Steel glanced around at the bar. 'When she comes back.'

'You'll have to be careful, Jeff,' Sammy said, leaning over. 'It's a bit different in a protected club like this. Okay if Haskell was just passing through like anybody else, they might give you a time, or more hopefully the contact who brought him here, a taxi-driver, or a street tout like myself who would know of this place. Perhaps you might then be able to track him down from their information. . . . But if they were suspicious of him in any way. . . ?'

It was a possibility, Steel mused; Haskell was 'out on a limb', and so direct contact with any official American representatives would have been vetoed, although by the same token, he reminded himself, in such a situation, Haskell would probably have exercised extra caution, and if a cover break had been suspected, contact would have been made with an area 'operative' and finally re-routed to Langley. 'It's okay, I'd have known before now.'

'Just a precaution,' Sammy held one hand up. He knew very little of Steel's work, and didn't wish to be involved any deeper.

They were distracted by a building furore in the audience.

The girl on stage had hooked her fingers into her bikini bottom and it was now pulled down to her knees. She lifted out her ankle-strapped calves with as much grace as such an action would allow, and kicked it aside; dark pubic hair stood in a large, proud triangle between glistening tan thighs.

Groans of approval rose from the back of the room. An American voice shouted an obscenity, suggesting what he would most like to do at that moment.

'She's from the north,' Sammy said to nobody in particular. 'Chaing Mai.' He studied her a moment longer and then, as if in answer to a silent question, 'You can always tell from their skin colour, it's a good bit lighter – you can see it on her bikini marks.'

Steel muttered an inaudible agreement, his main attention on a door to one side of the stage. 'How many times have you been here before, Sammy?'

'Thirty or forty, maybe more.'

'And do you know what's upstairs?'

'It's nothing special,' Sammy shrugged. 'Just a collection of rooms, about a dozen or so. The girls you see on stage and some in the audience too – you take your pick and that's where you go with them. They're all identical layouts – one bed, wardrobe, chair, sink and a bidet. Purpose-built, you might say.'

Their eyes had adjusted to the light and more of the room was discernible now: another two rows of small tables were behind them, some larger tables in alcoves to one side and rows of seating in theatre formation stretching back into the darkness. The back of the room could be made out only at one point – the bar in the far corner. The rest of the far side of the room, from one end of the bar to the entrance, was in pitch darkness, except for an ultra-violet bulb above a cigarette machine.

The waitress returned with their drinks, taking them from a round tray held *camarero*-style and setting them down on small mats. 'One Coke, and a scotch on the rocks.' Steel paid.

'Kawp jy,' Sammy nodded amiably, gesturing across the table with a thoughtful air. 'I wondered if you could help my friend with just one thing before you go.'

Steel left a generous tip and laid the photo face up on the side-table, making reference to a 'tall, heavy-set American'. 'He may have been in recently and if you know who recommended him here, I'd appreciate it.'

'We get many Americans in here,' she said quickly, and then picked up the photo and turned it towards the light from the stage.

'It's the last few weeks I'm most interested in,' Steel prompted.

'No, no, I don't think so,' she said finally. 'One man a bit close, just a week ago, but not the same. No! Sorry.'

Kalchorn entered while they were talking. It would not have mattered if they had been watching, for he was only momentarily visible in a slat of light, his dress dark and ordinary, and he made his way swiftly to the bar at the back of the room. He looked towards the stage first of all, then scanned the haze from that point to where a waitress was standing just past the centre of the room, turning towards a table at her side. Although Kalchorn could not clearly discern the man she was speaking to, he had, nevertheless, an interesting profile, he thought – the same brown hair as the man on the video screen. No, perhaps a bit darker, or was it the same? Could it be him? He looked around at the other faces visible, mostly heads turned away. There were many *farangs*, but his attention was back quickly on the same man. He could now see the waitress walking away, coming towards him, but he kept his gaze on that one point. The hair? The profile? 'Pra yeh-soo!' he muttered to himself. It was too dark, too hazy to tell, and he cursed the atmosphere – the smoke, the heat of the room, the clamouring crowd, the noise, the whore on the stage! 'Rohk Nawgny!' he exclaimed quietly but disgustedly, leaning over towards the barman. 'Is it always like this?'

The barman held his hands up to heaven.

'Some nights we are very busy, full to the rafters and others we are almost empty. And these Americans,' he sighed, waving a small tea-towel, 'They are the worst of all – so noisy.'

Then Kalchorn leant closer to the barman, and with the same impassive smile, introduced himself – a small sign made with the crossing of his hands; and the barman paled visibly. 'I'm sorry, I had no idea,' he offered hastily. 'It is usually Cheang who calls on us.'

'That is of no matter now,' Kalchorn said. And then he asked about the *farang* Englishman, drawing as accurate a verbal picture as he was able to. 'It is of the most vital importance to our *Bpratahn*.'

The barman remained vague, lifting his hands towards heaven once again. 'Chahn see-uh jy.'

They talked lightly for a moment, and then the waitress was at their side and Kalchorn turned his conversation towards her, talking longer this time, and using his hands for illustration.

The waitress's answer too, when he had finished, was expansive and graphic, punctuated by frequent nods and delicate pointing with her free hand. 'Soo-hakk!' she finished excitedly. 'I thought it was unusual – so many questions.'

And for the first time, Kalchorn's expression eased. They talked a moment longer and then the clamour of the audience built to a crescendo.

Another girl had walked on to the stage, joining the first girl, but to the small man it was unimportant, for he had already stepped behind a small black curtain, nodding knowingly to the large club bouncer positioned stolidly at its side and disappearing among the darker shadows at the back of the room.

The second girl was already completely naked, her breasts full and jostling, her entire body liberally oiled and shining beneath the spotlights. She was barefoot but still stood slightly taller than the first girl. Her hair was long, straight and dark, hanging a full six inches beyond her shoulders and held back off her forehead by a brightly coloured Red Indian-style headband. In one hand she carried a small stool, which she positioned behind the first girl; and in the other a red box, eight inches square, which she placed to one side.

The first girl leant back almost into a crab position, resting her back against the stool, and spreading her legs, her platform heels braced firm and flat on the floor. She traced her hands smoothly along the expanse of her flat belly until they lay at the apex of her open legs and then carefully slid two fingers into her open vagina, easing herself gradually into the motion until her bare knuckles pressed hard against her clitoris. She moved the fingers slowly, searchingly, her eyes almost completely closed and just visible above her breasts, slightly flattened by her reclining posture. She writhed in the same position for almost a full minute.

Appreciation grew louder from the audience; there were low growling noises and clapping from the back of the room.

She removed her fingers and lifted them in slow motion to her face, licking them cautiously at first, and then sucking them deeply, her eyes now completely closed in abandon.

The atmosphere was hot and oppressive. Steel took the first slug of his drink, feeling it cut through the sudden apparent dryness in his throat, exploding in warmth towards the pit of his stomach.

The girl with the headband came in closer, swinging a long tan leg from the floor, straddling the first girl's face, leaning forwards and resting her weight on the spread-eagled knees beneath. Her long black hair hung down in a curtain between the first girl's legs, shielding the rapid movements of her tongue. They stayed in the same position for some while, the second girl parting her long dark hair at intervals, lifting her face towards the audience with an embracing, salacious smile. She started sliding her body slowly back and forth on the girl beneath, slithering easily, fluidly, the oil easing the movement between their bare flesh; at the lowest point, her head almost touched the ground, her thighs sliding across smooth shoulders and resting on the breasts for a moment, wiggling slightly to effect a massaging rhythm.

It was a close, unsufferable, building heat. No air-conditioning! Only two fans twirled pathetically towards the centre of the room, Steel noted, easing the bands of sweat breaking out across his back. Somebody lit a cigar at his side. Or was it a Gauloise? The first stream of smoke came across, acrid and pungent in the already stale, muggy, perfumed air.

The two girls reversed positions, the first girl on top; then she swung around, pivoting easily on her abdomen, her legs opened wide and bent at the knee, mirroring the girl beneath.

The waitress was back at their side. 'So sorry.' She forced a smile. 'The man you were asking of earlier?'

'Yes,' Steel nodded pointedly.

'Our barman suggests you talk to Datuk, the other waitress. You see, I am not here for two nights a week, and if he was to have called one of these nights. . . .' She trailed off slightly, indicating the door to one side of the stage. 'You'll find her upstairs, room five. You can go through there if you like.'

'Thank you,' Steel responded politely. 'I'll ask her.'

'My bpen ry.' The waitress nodded courteously to both of them, and then turned and walked away. Her instructions had been short and uncomplicated, and she felt pleased with herself, although, at the same time, mildly apprehensive; the Englishman had a certain air, she mused, one which she had observed in many Japanese men and was widely revered among them, but in very few *farangs*: a detached but pleasant scepticism, the ability to give one impression while feeling something else. And it was that, she concluded, which unsettled her most. Was it too late to tell the small man? Yes. And foolish, she chided herself. Such things could not be explained.

'If she's off duty,' Steel asked of Sammy when the waitress had gone, 'what is she doing still here?'

'It is quite normal,' Sammy shrugged. 'Most of the girls "live in".'

Steel glanced back towards the stage for a moment.

'Okay, I'll go up,' he muttered, still looking away from Sammy. He took another slug of his drink. 'You stay here.'

It was only a few yards to the small door, but the lights close to the stage were dazzling and the music deafening. He made his way through quickly, closing it behind him, and it was dark once again.

He stood there for a moment and light became apparent above him and to one side. The stairway was rough and wooden, doubling back on itself from a small vestibule. The boards creaked as he made his way up and the sounds from the club were muted below, a dull, persistent, throbbing beat. At the top, the same boarding extended along a narrow corridor, starkly lit, scrubbed and spartan. A thin red strip of carpet dulled the creaking of the boards as he strode along, and from the rooms each side there were other sounds now, those of pleasure: squeals, giggles and gentle murmuring.

Steel counted the numbers down from seventeen, which was closest to him; five was towards the far end. There was another stairwell at that end, he could see now, and he judged that he had all but walked the length of the club below. The music seemed even more distant, although the throbbing was still there, monotonous, all-pervading. He stopped in front of the faded wood-stained door of room five and listened; there was no sound apparent from inside and he let out his breath gently, rapping hard on the wood.

There was a muffled exclamation from inside, and then more clearly, 'Kow mah!'

Steel turned the handle and stepped inside. A Chinese bell above his head tinkled faintly with the movement, a circle of brass among six hollow chiming tubes. Only half of the room was lit, by a shaded lamp by the bed on the far wall; the opening door let another gradually widening beam of light in from the hallway.

A Thai girl lay naked on the bed, her legs wide and drawn up high, her fingers playing like a team of worms between her open thighs. Steel was momentarily transfixed.

There was another movement; the Chinese bell jangled again.

A faint warning, but enough. Steel sensed a flicker of white in the corner of his vision and he was already leaning forwards, away from it.

The blow caught him high across his back, numbing nerves and muscles and forcing the air from his body, its solid impact throwing him forwards.

Another flicker of white. Steel ducked down this time and to one side, and it passed somewhere above his head in a rush of air.

He straightened and backed up. It was clearer now, movement taking form – a man, a small dark silhouette in the light from the door, a slim white object almost as tall as his body gripped tight in both hands.

Steel reached for his gun. Everything was happening quickly, and speed would be vital, he sensed vaguely. But the silhouette reminded him of the dummy figures in the firing range and it was too close, too easy; then his gun was out, and pointing.

It flashed white in an arc this time, coming in from the side, surprisingly fast, and Steel felt the shock and crashing pain before he had fully registered the movement, his arm jolted sharply to one side. In an action already started but now involuntary, his gun fired, slipping from his grip, skittering across the floor; a flash of blue trailed out in the darkness, an explosion of plaster coming from the far wall.

The girl on the bed screamed. She was frightened now and was up quickly, turning a switch at her side, clutching a part of the sheet to cover her nakedness.

A light came on above them, bright, stark.

It was a baseball bat, Steel could see clearly now, clutched loosely at one side, and the man was Thai, dressed plainly, drably, his face contorted, grimacing in the downward beam of light, the sweat thick on his forehead.

The small man edged in closer and swung the bat viciously, but the movements were easier to anticipate now, and Steel dodged and side-stepped, the tip of the bat just brushing one thigh. And then it came back quickly, on reflex; a wide, sweeping semi-circle, high and threatening. Steel ducked down sharply and the solid wood crashed into a dressing table at his side, clearing an array of perfume bottles and jars from its top and shattering a large ornate mirror in a deluge of noise.

As the last few shards of glass tumbled to the floor they stood there motionless for a moment, now calm, both scrutinizing, measuring, assessing. It would be essential to get in close, Steel realized, for the widest point of the bat's arc was its most lethal; yet it was that same arc that could also prevent such a movement.

The bat came across high again, and the small man had edged in; there was no backing up, so Steel crouched down, lunging forwards swiftly, instinctively. He felt the bat graze his back and shoulders, but his full weight had crashed into the small man's chest, his head butting low, and at that moment, that was all that was important. He rammed hard against the far wall and he felt the small body go limp against him for a moment; then the man's muscles were tensing again, arms raising.

Steel gripped them up high before they could come down, and he struggled for a while, trying to wrench the bat from the small man's grip. Their hands were slippery with sweat, sliding and gripping, muscles strained, aching; but he finally got one free, and then it was the right arm, he could see, swinging the bat out and towards him again.

He grabbed it in mid-swing, swivelling his body, forcing his back against the small man and gripping his right arm. Almost in the same motion, he brought his knee up, breaking the straightened arm across it, snapping the cartilage and forcing the ball socket out from its elbow-joint.

The small man screamed shrilly, a glut of haemorrhaged blood from a severed tendon quickly appearing dark purple beneath his skin, the baseball bat clattering to the floor. He clamped his left arm hard around Steel's neck, drawing upwards, ever tighter.

It was a frantic, desperate action, Steel sensed, but already he could feel its effect, the air coming short, a constriction in his throat, the small man applying surprising pressure for his size. He tried to turn, but the movement brought more pressure, a flow of blood rising sharply to his head.

Flailing his arms out frantically, Steel could only just reach inside his own jacket, perhaps the only movement allowed to him now, and he did it quickly, ripping at the lining. Then the flat knife was firmly in his grip. He twisted his lower body sideways and lunged upwards in one, and he felt the blade tearing flesh and then something solid, the tip breaking off on a lower rib. He cursed to himself. But then the grip weakened, and immediately breathing was easier; he broke free, swinging around again.

The small Thai staggered, the broken knife falling to the floor, a gout of red on his white shirt. His eyes were blood-shot, and he lunged forwards drunkenly, movements sluggish, stunted. Everything seemed suspended, slowed. Steel picked up the baseball bat casually, swinging wide.

Kalchorn kept coming.

The bat stuck him squarely in the centre of his chest, the full force exaggerated by his own momentum, throwing him back over four yards. He lay on his back by the door-way, turning over gradually, trying to fight back on to his feet, but his body, now shattered, defeated, collapsed back in weak, sporadic contortions.

Steel walked over and nudged the prone figure with his foot. 'Who sent you?' he spat.

A weak grunt rose up. 'Dy Lohng tahng.'

It meant nothing to Steel. 'Who?' he fired again.

The small man looked away. Still nothing.

Steel gripped him by the shirt-collar in one hand and trouser-belt in the other and hauled him to the edge of the stairwell, hanging him over its edge threateningly. 'For the last time – who, you bastard?'

Again, silence.

The small man weighed no more than a hundred and forty pounds and Steel swung him easily back and then let go. The body appeared rubbery in mid-air, flailing spasmodically; there was a short gargling scream, and then the head connected with the far wall. Steel heard the small man's neck snap like a piece of dry wood, the whole body careening back on itself until the legs stuck out awkwardly into the air at crooked, opposed angles.

Steel looked on for a second. There was no movement, and he turned back into the room. The girl had backed into the far corner, the sheet wound totally around her and clutched tight at the neck, her eyes wide and blank.

'You tell me!' he demanded. 'Who sent him? Who do you both work for – your boss? "Tochuan"!' he added, now exasperated.

'My poot,' she muttered pathetically, pointing to her tongue. 'No ahng-grit!'

Steel stared at her hard, disgustedly for a moment, and then turned his back on her. She was not important in this, he decided quickly, and he started looking for his gun, back-tracking his movements, finally discovering it by the far side of the bed where it had fallen. He opened the chamber and checked the firing pin for damage before re-holstering it.

The girl mumbled some Thai under her breath, but Steel ignored it and was on his way out of the room. He almost missed the object at first because it appeared so insignificant, lying on the floor close to the door. As he got closer he could see that it was a thick wad of money tied with an elastic band, a thin strip of paper attached to its topside.

He picked it up and studied it for a second, and he remembered seeing similar calligraphic print in Hong Kong, although for the moment that was all he thought. Extracting the paper and tucking it inside his side-pocket, he threw the bundle to the girl in the corner. *Buy some clothes and get him a decent funeral* was on his lips, but suddenly he didn't feel like talking any more, the aftermath of shock and jaded nerves catching up with him, taking their toll. Anyway, she didn't speak English, he reminded himself. He turned silently, trying to ease an insistent ache from his injured shoulder-blade as he strode back along the narrow corridor.

The brightness gradually diminished at the end of the passage as he went back down the stairwell, the music growing louder, ever-persistent, throbbing; he could feel it in his head this time, but still muffled, veiled.

The full atmosphere of the club hit him again as he opened the door: the noise, smell, the thickness of the air, the gaudy lighting, as if his short absence and the chain of events had allowed him to forget it all. But he could see Sammy clearly, and he made his way back towards the table.

Something flashed by at his side, although at first he didn't see it, finally picking it out as it fell among some second-row tables: a white ping-pong ball.

There was a sudden, climactic uproar from the audience.

Steel looked around to the stage, and it gradually took shape amongst the haze: the girl with the Red Indian head-band lay recumbent, her back against the small stool, her legs wide and facing the audience. The first girl was at her side, taking another ping-pong ball from its small red box and placing it in her own mouth. She lolled her tongue sensuously and languidly around the white sphere, extracting if after a second, glistening and damp, and placing it in the recumbent girl's open vagina. The vulval lips resisted slightly at first, but with a delicate probe from a single azure-tipped finger, the ball lay full inside.

There was a contraction of stomach muscles, a slight shuddering from her widely spaced thighs, and then the ping-pong ball flew out into the room, clearing the third row of tables this time.

More loud cheering, some wild cat-calls from the back of the room.

Steel turned back to the table, slugging back the last of his drink, nodding to Sammy. 'Let's go.' The words were silent among the noise, but the indication was clear.

Outside, the air was fresh, the clouds clearing away quickly with a slight breeze, a part of a quarter moon and some stars just visible.

292

'Nice show, eh, Jeff?' Sammy remarked as they headed back across the dried earth courtyard.

Steel just smiled blandly. 'Yes, Sammy, nice show.'

They got into the car.

Some faint noises filtered through into the concrete shell. A few trucks or buses somewhere in the distance. Deborah Ensor strained her ears – it was impossible to tell their direction, and she settled back again. There were some other sounds there but they were faint, indiscernible. The murmurs of the night. She relaxed once more, trying to urge on much-needed sleep. It didn't come. For almost an hour she lay trying to sleep, seeking the oblivion that would take her into tomorrow and Paul; away from the horrors of the day passed and once more into the comfort of his arms. Then it would all be forgotten, she thought. Something to tell their children about. An incident too horrible to dwell on at the time but a fantastic adventure in retrospect. Yes, that would be it, she told herself in the semi-light. Something for them to laugh about at a later date. A family heirloom that would be handed down as Paul's father's stories of the war had been – perhaps even more interesting because of its difference. Almost everybody had war experiences, but how many people had been kidnapped in Bangkok? Yes, she told herself, a unique story. Something they would remember forever. She could almost imagine small faces glowing in the light of a log-fire, eyes twinkling with excitement, small mouths open in awe. Yes, that would be the way, she concluded, and then she looked at the slouched figure in the chair at the side of the room.

Bature lay half-seated, half-asleep, his legs at angles, his gun hanging loosely from his right hand. She stared at his figure, silhouetted from the light coming through the partially open door of the connecting office. The only visible light. She knew what she would have liked to shout at that moment if the tape was removed from her mouth, but then in another way she found something pathetic about him. Earlier that night, she had watched with interest his childlike eagerness as he'd dismantled an automatic rifle, sliding each piece out methodically, cleaning it, greasing it, and reassembling the parts again. And then, in contrast, his taunting when he pointed it towards her as if testing the sights and easing the trigger with a final dull click. Smiling cruelly, sardonically – appearing almost as pathetic as he had done when the man she referred to as 'the cultured one' had been shouting at him. He looked even more pathetic now, half-asleep, she thought. Of the three, she feared him least of all and 'the cultured one' the most – a reflection on his earlier, demented preoccupation: 'Hedging! As if he doesn't care'. And she had thought, no, not my Paul. He loves me. And then the sudden change. Placating, full of reason. A complete reversal. A psychopath with an education. She feared him more than ever now. There was a fear she felt for the 'large one' too but it was a physical fear more than one of the mind: a bear with no brain. Only at the command of the others did she consider him a danger.

That morning, she had felt her whole being violated by his initial physical attack, but later her thoughts of him had mellowed as she'd observed the interplay of the three. And now, in an obscure way, he was the only one she felt any compassion for. A lost figure, she thought – misguided and unable to master his own fate. The other two *were* able, and for that alone she felt sorry, although she weakly admitted to herself it was for that reason she felt an unusual tie with him. For at that moment, she realized, she was not able to control *her* own fate: a fact that frightened her now, a sense of the day's events building up from within, her dreams dwindling and fading. She recalled some of the words of one of her favourite songs, 'Go placidly amidst the noise and haste', and she told herself again, come tomorrow and everything will be okay. Wait till tomorrow and you'll be all right. But then it was too much. The exhaustion, nerves, emotions, and the thought of a love and warmth she did not have at that moment overwhelmed her. It came forward in a tidal wave. She felt herself choking with the gag as her cries were blocked and seemed to be forced back down into her throat. Only the tears came freely. She felt her cheeks moistening, her whole body shaking uncontrollably, now completely racked by sobbing.

Bature sat up in his chair and flickered his eyes, alarmed by the sound. He could not clearly make out her figure in the light. 'You all right?' he enquired in a matter-of-fact tone.

Deborah controlled her sobbing and nodded her head slowly, and Bature, vaguely seeing the movement, relaxed back in his chair once again.

Deborah came back to her dream of how it would all be over the next day and how one day they would tell their children the story. A dream of being in Paul's arms the next night. A dream of sleeping in a clean bed with fresh linen. A dream of breathing fresh air again. A dream of not being frightened any more. After tonight, Deborah thought. Just tonight, and then my dreams will be there.

But nights can be long and, without sleep, reality has a habit of returning.

It was almost 3 a.m. when they arrived in front of Gene Haskell's house, the rattling of their car engine breaking the quiet suburban solitude.

Steel had related the incident at the Cat Club to Sammy on the way, showing him the small slip with calligraphic print; neither the bouncer at the back of the club room or the two gate men had been alerted, so they were not disturbed in leaving.

'The slips are a "take" record from a club,' Sammy remarked. 'It's likely there were problems with Haskell,' he concluded, weighing all the information.

'I know,' Steel said blankly, staring up at the house. 'We'll soon find out.' He got out of the car, leaning back to the open window. 'You stay here and keep a look-out, eh, Sammy.'

Sammy nodded, staring ahead.

There were no streetlamps, and with light apparent from

only a couple of houses on the small estate, the street was peaceful and dark.

Steel rang the doorbell four times at one-minute intervals, and then on the last ring allowed a full three minutes before moving back from the door to look at the house for signs of life from any of the windows. It was a window at the front of the house that caught Steel's attention. He moved closer towards it; a small hatch window was open at the top, and a larger window beneath had the latch off, swinging freely, not secured by the arm at its base.

Steel opened the larger window and clambered upwards, letting himself easily into the house. He drew his gun out and waited a moment for his eyes to become accustomed to the semi-darkness, then moved out across the length of the room. Steel searched the house stealthily. The bedroom at the rear of the house was the third on his check-list after the lounge and kitchen. The door was slightly ajar, but it was a curious, pungent smell that hit Steel first. He pushed the door wide open. A faint light picked out something on the bed and Steel strained his eyes. It looked like a body but there were other things on the bed, something rounded. Not the head – it was too far from the body. A football? No. Perhaps a knee at an impossible angle? Perhaps the whole thing wasn't a body but a trick of light played by a jumbled array of sheets and pillows. But the dark patches. What were they?

Steel turned on the light at his side.

He turned it off just as quickly and, reeling towards the adjacent bathroom, was violently sick. He staggered along the small hallway, out of the front door and away from the house, his stomach still churning. Once in the car he made an abstract waving motion for Sammy to drive them back. He said only one word on their return to the hotel.

'Animals!'

He bade Sammy a solemn 'goodnight and thank-you', and made his way back to his room. In his private bathroom, preparing for bed, he was violently sick once more and then later between the crisp single sheets he muttered the same word.

'Animals!'

Then he tried to wrench away the images of carnage implanted so vividly in his mind. Mercifully, within an hour, sleep laid a darkened blanket over his clear thoughts, but at some time later a nightmare formed, a mixture of strong realistic images and impossible horrors. It was sometimes difficult to discern which was more frightening, which the real image. Then it became real. It was happening. *Or was it?* A head on its own, slowly turning and then suddenly it was on a spit and roasting and a man was at the side and smiling. Then his head too was decapitated. It was on the spit. Then came familiar heads. Decapitated, horrific, bloody. Sunnee, Nittaya, Sammy, myself? Myself! Me! *No! No!*

'No!'

The safety-valve snapped, the subconscious unable to accept its own images, a blanket of sleep rudely lifted. Steel heard the last reverberations of his own scream, sitting up straight in bed, his body soaked in sweat, his nerves strained and jaded.

He got up, walked to the bathroom and for the third time that night was violently sick.

17

Dust rose in turbid clouds from the Soweto street. Captain Calbeck sat in the front of the Land Rover, his two burly sergeants in the back, rifles held upright, at the ready, and a Warrant Officer behind the wheel. To each side, houses were grouped tight, mostly single-storey, constructed of cheap boarding and stucco, and fenced-off by chicken-wire.

The sun was still quite low. A few hundred yards behind, a helicopter whirred a dizzy path, climbing slowly over a small ridge, the sound of its engine and giros now more prominent. Calbeck checked the mirror; the dust behind gave the helicopter an almost ghostly appearance as it crossed the sun's path, winging still higher.

Calbeck reached for his radio-microphone. 'Hold back a bit, Kenny,' he snapped. 'We still want to surprise the buggers, you know.'

Both the pilot and his passenger, an SASP sniper, wore earphones. 'Okay, will do,' the pilot responded.

The helicopter had a more total view of Soweto: the streets were mainly in grid formation, the large proportion no more than dust tracks; those few that didn't conform to the pattern were the 'shanty' developments, houses constructed from urban waste – corrugated iron, old boarding and straw, some with straw roofs built in tribal Bantu style, with mud and clay. At intervals, burnt-out buildings – mostly schools and business premises – lay as a testament to the recent troubles.

'Hang back even further and swing round to the south-west,' Calbeck came over on the radio-phone again.

'Got yer.'

They could see the path of Calbeck's Land Rover clearly, now turning into a new road, still a dust path.

'It's about eight houses up on the left,' Calbeck added. 'The roof is a sort of dull green slate.'

'There's a few like that, Captain,' the pilot responded.

'Okay – the windows are painted a mustardy-orange colour; the front door too. I don't know about the back.'

'Yeah, we've got it,' the pilot said after a moment.

The Land Rover stopped almost thirty yards short of the house, and the helicopter started circling around to the back, still a good way behind. The two sergeants got out of the Land Rover and started edging their way further up the road, crouching low.

'They might try and spring out of the back, so make sure you're covering,' Calbeck said into the radio-phone, and then to the driver, 'Let's go.' They got out and followed behind the two sergeants, drawing their revolvers cautiously as they got closer to the house.

One of the sergeants ran ahead and kicked the door open. The other was right behind; they positioned themselves quickly either side of the door, assessing the situation in that same split-second: three black men sat at a table before them, their eyes wide with surprise; another was awaking slowly from a set of bunk beds to one side, and in the adjoining kitchen a woman was cooking.

The furthest black turned and reached for a rifle in the corner but was felled by a salvo of fire as he made his first move; the other two, virtually in the same motion, sprang from the table – one towards the back door, the other towards the same rifle.

The first sergeant had committed himself to the man heading for the back door and momentarily blocked his partner's line of fire, then suddenly realized that the black sprawling in the corner had almost reached the rifle. He side-stepped smartly, swinging his rifle butt into the back of the man's head. At the same instant, the woman from the kitchen came out screaming, wielding a short, glistening object high in one hand.

The second sergeant turned and fired twice into her chest, and she sprawled back against the stove behind, upsetting a pan of boiling water.

Up above, the sniper in the helicopter spotted the lone figure sprinting from the back door almost immediately, and quickly beaded a line. Only one shot was required; it was clean, through the skull.

When Captain Calbeck entered the house, it was all over. He looked first towards the black sitting on the bunk beds to one side, but now backed up hard against the wall behind, his hands up high, the first sergeant guarding him staunchly.

Calbeck walked towards the black in the corner; one hand still gripped the rifle and the indent on the back of his skull could be made out quite clearly.

'You're a bit heavy with your rifle butt, Sergeant,' Calbeck commented casually, and he turned the figure over; the eyes were showing only the whites and had a slightly pink tone. 'I was hoping for more than one alive, but if that's what we're left with, so be it.'

Calbeck walked slowly towards the kitchen. 'Why did you kill the woman?' he asked.

'I thought she had a knife,' replied the sergeant.

Calbeck looked thoughtfully at the spatula still gripped in the woman's hand. 'Don't worry, when the report's made up, it *will* be a knife.' And then he turned with an air of finality towards the black on the bunk beds. 'Okay, let's get this cunt downtown – let's see what he knows.'

Less than an hour later, the man in custody had been identified from SASP files as one Bokwe Tshuma, and Colonel Ostermeir summoned Calbeck into his office immediately prior to the interrogation, commenting, 'There's some sort of meeting taking place in Bangkok at six p.m. – they're five hours ahead, so right now it's almost three p.m., their time. Anything you can find out beforehand will be crucial.'

Calbeck went to work; it was a sound-proof room, two storeys below the main floor of the compound.

'Gus' Cullen faced the tall window, glancing out, his hands clasped loosely behind his back. The day was bright and traffic was already heavy in both direction of the Ploenchit Road directly in front of the embassy.

'The sheer arrogance of some of these local bandits is incredible. And you know – we can't do a bloody thing with them. Even the police can't handle it, so the best thing is to keep completely out of it.' Cullen turned back to his desk. 'Bloody cheek!'

'I know,' Steel said, although he found it hard to understand the strength of Cullen's feelings on the issue.

Cullen had commenced the proceedings by passing Steel a 'sealed' report, 'received just this morning from London', which Steel had decided – as a matter of caution and protocol – to study when he had a moment alone. Then Steel had broadly outlined the Ensor situation, mentioning the attack in the Cat Club, but neglecting all information regarding Haskell. Cullen's classification, he remembered, was only R-11, and as such he couldn't 'by the book' be passed such information without an official CIA go-ahead. An early call to a South-East Asian liaison operative in Singapore had sufficed; the details would be relayed from there to all key agency sources in Langley and London. Stannard would know later that day. 'Sometime around eleven a.m. in London,' the operative had informed him; from there it would be relayed once again to Ostermeir in Johannesburg. Steel had considered asking the operative for assistance, but it would have been pointless, he quickly calculated – the exchange was at 6 p.m. that evening, less than eight hours' time, and the shortest flight time from London was thirteen hours. Singapore had already, earlier, confirmed their inability to spare an operative. And so now Steel dealt with things as best he could, mentally panning forward through the various stages of development as he envisaged them.

'I'll need a diplomatic pouch,' he remarked, pulling out some earlier notes. 'That's first and foremost.'

'When by?'

'Sometime this evening. Certainly before nine, at least. I'll also need some back-up in the arena and the same man, if possible, can escort the Ensors to the airport, although he certainly shouldn't be seen leaving the arena with them – we can meet up back at their hotel or mine.'

'You know we don't have any "trained" men,' Cullen said.

'That's all right, I just want him armed with a camera – and he should be unobtrusive. That's about it.'

'What time's this meeting again?'

'Six p.m.'

'That's a bit short notice,' Cullen mused slowly. 'And what time's their flight?'

'There's a British Airways at seven-twenty, but it's full up, so I'm waiting for a cancellation. If not, it'll be the same as mine, nine-forty: that's the next one out. But if it has to be the later flight I'd appreciate you keeping them here as late as possible before check-in.'

'Will they be in great danger, do you think?' Cullen raised an eyebrow, folding his hands on the desk-top.

'They *could* be,' Steel amended. 'I don't want to take any risks, that's all.'

'I don't think there should be any problems with that,' Cullen nodded approvingly. 'Always here to do our best for you chaps, you know. Now just a minute, let me make a note. . . .' Cullen rustled among some papers in a side-drawer. 'Shame about your experience with the local bandits though,' he remarked, still with his head down; although in fact, it wasn't Steel's personal attack that he was particularly concerned with, but more the threat of its implications to himself, and his own way of life: the tea parties on the lawn at four, the game of bowls every Thursday, the various functions with visiting diplomats. It seemed ironic. He was respected among the highest-ranking of both law and government officials, and all those worthy of entry in Thailand's *Who's Who*, and yet a local bandit, he knew, could take his life with as much thought as breaking wind. The audacity of it! 'I'm sorry,' he exclaimed, looking back at Steel, placing a note-pad on his desk-top. 'Now where were we? Oh yes – the diplomatic pouch.' He scribbled something down on the pad. . . . 'And a back-up man with a camera, the Lumpini stadium, six p.m. this evening,' he muttered aloud, as he wrote. 'Any further information I should have?'

'Yes – there'll be a payment for the British couple, a standard official Secrets Act compensation. It'll be made from London, but they'll discuss the details with you. Just so you know what sort of ground you're on, I'm recommending twenty thousand.'

'Isn't that rather excessive?'

'There are some unusual circumstances. Anyway, that's the picture for you. Oh, there is just one other thing,' Steel added, as if as an afterthought. 'I'm going to need an immediate transfer of funds.'

'How much?'

'Nine hundred and twenty thousand bahts,' Steel read from his notes. It was the figure provided for him earlier that morning by Pen, the gem merchant.

Cullen did some quick calculations. 'My God,' he uttered. He lifted his eyebrows. 'That's over twenty-five thousand pounds. What's it for, anyway?'

'The same as the diplomatic pouch,' Steel smiled thinly. The words were empty, but the implication was clear: it was above Cullen's classification, and unlike Mr Tom who was involved peripherally, it was unnecessary to provide such information in order to expedite matters. 'If you like, I'll fill out a section eight transfer form while I'm here,' Steel said. 'You can enter the amount, and if you let me have one of your "house" seals, I'll send it through straight away. I'd imagine it would be balanced through the Foreign Office in a matter of weeks.'

Cullen mumbled an agreement, rustled quickly in another drawer, and pulled out a buff form. 'Unusual weather we're having, eh?' he commented, as he filled in the boxes. 'Bloody rain last night, sunny this morning, rain forecast again for tonight. Doesn't make any sense.'

'Yes,' Steel agreed sympathetically.

'Still, I suppose we're still at the end of the monsoon season. So – can't complain, eh?' Cullen swivelled the form around and Steel filled in the last details, signing at the bottom and folding the paper over. Cullen passed him an envelope and an embassy seal. 'It's the closeness that I hate so much,' Cullen mused aloud. 'It gets so bloody sticky when it's damp like this.'

'Yes,' Steel nodded sympathetically, sealing the envelope flap and slipping it in his inside pocket.

Cullen disliked approving monetary transactions for purposes of which he was ignorant through high classifications, but he had no choice, and so he tried not to give too much away by the manner in which he viewed Steel's movements. 'So, old chap – all you'll be needing is a cheque from us, and that concludes everything, eh?'

Steel just smiled lightly, but Cullen didn't expect an answer, and patted his brow with a handkerchief from his top pocket, opening a locked drawer this time. The cheque-book folder was a rich red leather with a large gold *ER* crest set at its centre. Cullen scribbled inside it furiously and then took a rubber stamp from the side, endorsing the cheque with an elaborate motion. 'Money's not the same nowadays,' he remarked, tearing the cheque out and passing it across the desk-top. 'The values have all gone crazy.'

Steel studied the figures: twenty-five thousand, six hundred and forty-four pounds.

'It can be cashed immediately,' Cullen prompted. 'The Hong Kong and Shanghai Bank on Suapa Road. The exchange rate for today will give you nine hundred and twenty thousand bahts, as you requested.'

They concluded their business, Cullen asking about affairs back home, and Steel answering shortly but politely, omitting the details, at all times aware of Cullen's security classification. They shook hands and turned towards the door at the back of the room. Cullen's expression changed slightly.

'Oh, there is just one more thing. Now normally I wouldn't worry one of you chaps with something like this, but you know, sometimes you never can be too careful.' Cullen kept in close to Steel as they walked towards the large double doors, as if in some special confidence. 'It's this little fracas you've had with this local bandit,' he said, his eyebrows crowding over slightly. 'I might be wrong, because they are, by nature, very unpredictable. But unfortunately, very often they will seek revenge in the most voracious manner. Almost maniacal! I've seen it happen many a time before. Now here comes the only dividing line I know of: if it was just a normal soldier, a *tahahn* as they're known, you're all right. On the other hand, if it happened to be one of their generals, a *ny-pohn*, that, under their law, constitutes a direct insult to the *Bpratahn* and there could be reprisals.' Cullen opened the doors. 'As I say, I might be wrong, but it's just a thought.'

Steel thanked him again.

Outside it was hot and Steel hailed a taxi to take him through the busy two miles to the bank. Seated in the back, his thoughts dwelled, almost monotonously, on the same issue. The diamonds and the exchange were still a problem, and had been since his arrival, but now it was something else, looming ever larger. Images of Haskell were still strong.

The interior of the bank was cool and austere, a combination of polished rosewood, marble floors and ultra-efficient air-conditioning. Steel remained oddly detached while the clerk busied himself with the paperwork, his thoughts returning once again to something Mr Tom had said earlier that morning: 'Haskell was probably killed for something he knew, and your attack was for fear of you gaining that same knowledge. The fact that you have killed one of their men will not matter. As long as there are no further enquiries on your part into their operations, there will be no repercussions. I am quite sure of that.' And now Cullen's contradiction! He would be seeing Tom again for the meeting with Tanayo Pen, he reflected, and perhaps then more light could be cast on the issue. Although if it transpired that Cullen was right, Steel concluded, there would certainly be an extra element to consider: the involvement of another party in such a precarious set of circumstances and planning, at this stage, he knew, could be disastrous. For all concerned.

The bank clerk passed across four steel-banded wads and some loose notes, and Steel tucked them in his side-pockets, thanking him. Then he pushed back those thoughts which now he feared the most and walked back out into the heat, bustle and noise of the street outside.

The twin islands of Hong Kong and Lantau cast heavy shadows from their peaks into the harbour. At points, because of the mass of jagged inlets it was almost impossible to discern the islands from the mainland, until the plane circled lower for its approach. Victoria harbour gradually appeared, the clustered skyscrapers of Kowloon and Hong Kong Island closely bordering each side, although those on the Hong Kong side were so closely grouped that it seemed the hills behind had thrust upwards sliding them down into whatever space remained on the shoreline. Dusk was approaching, a faint red glow hanging low over the hills of Lantau, a few lights in small blocks dotted among the tall buildings below.

Mikeka Dinsengwayo turned away from the small window, watching with interest an air hostess attend to an elderly gentleman three rows ahead. He wasn't particularly concerned with what ailed the passenger, but the air hostess's bent posture had a distracting quality. He found that most of the other men in sight, the majority elderly, respectable, white South Africans, were enjoying the same distraction. Some looked away as he caught the direction of their gaze and the baffled fury which strongly indicated the rarity of blacks in the first-class compartment. The fact that so many white passengers were clustered behind in the second-class compartment of the 747 made his presence even more unacceptable. The large number of orientals in the second-class compartment was accepted because of the plane's destination, the blacks because apartheid was impracticable to apply to international airlines.

The air hostess straightened up, smiled through the neat frame of her blonde hair and walked back through the connecting curtains behind him into the second-class compartment.

Mikeka took a calculator out from his top pocket, one that he frequently used for additions of carat weights among diamond packages, and commenced a calculation: he took the time of his flight out from Hong Kong, its scheduled duration, and subtracted the time difference. He looked at the result.

An exacting man, a habit that increased with age, he switched off the calculator and placed it back in his top pocket, glancing out again at the slowly advancing panorama of the harbour below; lights and buildings taking form now, a myriad of small boats between concrete clusters, framed by rich green hills. He was thoughtful at that moment. It would be dark by the time he arrived in Bangkok. Not by much, but dark all the same.

Tanayo Pen appeared a typical Thai, except that he boasted a small pencil-line moustache, which was untypical, and his skin colour was light. His ancestry was, in fact, Chinese from both parents, although he would never readily admit it. The Chinese already owned a good proportion of the business in Bangkok and were, in some quarters, resented for it.

Mr Tom had introduced Steel formally, and they sat opposite Pen, the faint mechanical sounds of the gem factory straining through a thin partition behind them.

Pen turned apologetically towards Tom before excluding him from the conversation. 'Mr Chareompond explained the position to me quite carefully yesterday. I hope that I have been able to prepare everything satisfactorily for you.' Pen turned his palms towards them. 'Now – have you brought the container with you?'

Steel reached into a holdall at his side. 'I have it here. It's a piece of African art,' he added, as if that one detail would compensate for the total irregularity of the request. The figure was empty and light, the head already detached. Tom had earlier informed him of Pen's stipulation and together they had emptied the figure's contents into a large draw-string bag, which they had then deposited in the Narao's safe.

'Soon we shall see, then,' Pen remarked invitingly. His English was good.

Steel placed the two pieces of the figure on the desk-top, the head lolling clumsily for a second.

'Very unusual,' Pen commented. 'I hope you didn't mind bringing this, Mr Steel, but as I said to Mr Chareompond, the size and weight are very important.'

'Yes, he told me,' Steel said, looking over at Tom.

Pen folded his hands and leant forward. 'You see, the problem with fake gems is that they are normally heavier than real diamonds. As you are probably aware, Mr Steel, diamonds are measured in carats, which refers to their weight.'

'Yes, I know.'

'Well,' Pen continued fluently, 'When you request so many carats in diamonds, the fake gems of the corresponding weight are smaller. This means that if you took the carat weight of the diamonds taken out of that container, you would be short when trying to fill it with substitutes. This is why I thought it best that I asked for the container itself.' Pen turned momentarily towards Tom. 'As I indicated earlier, the 'diagems' that you mentioned to me initially would take too long to manufacture and we don't keep a large selection of these. But what I have done is to provide as many of these as possible, and the balance is made up with parcels of what are known as 'zircons'.'

Steel studied the tray crammed with small envelopes that Pen indicated. This was something he knew nothing of. He looked up at Pen curiously. 'What's the difference?'

Pen waved his hand indifferently. 'Very little, Mr Steel. To the naked eye, certainly no difference at all. You did say that the diamonds you wish to duplicate were largely flawless, didn't you?'

Steel glanced at Tom. He had mentioned that fact purely to indicate the relative ease of matching 'collection pieces'. For a moment, he wondered just how far Tom had taken the gem-dealer into his confidence. He turned back to Pen. 'Most of them, yes.'

'Then there should be no problems. There are some 'diagems' made up for the larger pieces that you mentioned, but the majority are 'zircons'. What sort of examination will they be subject to?'

Steel looked vague. 'I'm not really sure. Whatever it is will be fairly quick. Perhaps a short surveillance with an eye-glass.'

'No laboratory examination?'

'No.'

Pen relaxed thoughtfully into his large leather swivel chair. 'Then you should be quite safe,' he said abruptly. 'A lot of people think that because diamonds are the world's hardest substance, you can test them by hitting them with a hammer or mallet. Of course, this isn't true. They're hard for cutting, but they're also brittle and would smash to pieces. The 'diagems' are a mixture of yttrium, aluminium and garnet – the 'zircons' a hard paste. Both will stand up equally well under the hammer, and in addition, the 'diagems' have reasonable cutting qualities. What I will do is to place all of the 'diagems' towards the top of the container, since these will fare better under all forms of testing.'

'What about somebody who knows diamonds?' Steel asked guardedly.

'Under the lens, they wouldn't know the difference. The light reflection qualities of the 'zircons' are slightly poorer, but you need a particularly good light and magnification to judge this. The 'diagems' reflect excellently. The only thing that could be looked for are flaws, and since I understand there are few of these in the originals, I don't see any problems.' Pen seemed smugly confident; then suddenly his look changed to faint apprehension. 'There's only one acid test to watch out for, Mr Steel, and that involves oil or grease.'

'How does it work?' Steel leant forwards.

Pen used his hands for illustration. 'A diamond placed into a small amount of oil on a flat surface will stick like a ball-bearing to a magnet. Even if you turn it upside down, defying gravity, it will still adhere. 'Diagems' and 'zircons' will not. It's the only thing to watch out for, but it's a very clumsy test. Most will just settle for an eyeglass.'

'Anything else?' Steel asked tentatively.

'Only with the 'zircons'. If they are submerged in water, they'll become cloudy after a while.' Pen waved his arm in a dismissive motion. 'This takes quite a while and shouldn't affect you. The main thing is the oil.'

Steel nodded his head understandingly. There was no other choice. An oil test would have to remain an acceptable risk. He passed the figure across the desk-top. 'Okay. Let's see how we get on.'

Pen gripped the main body of the figure and glanced into its open neck. The aperture was narrow and there was not enough light let in to judge the internal dimensions to any extent.

'Very unusual,' Pen muttered again, this time with a questioning tone. He placed the base of the figure flat on the desk top and took a small brown envelope from the front of the tray to his side. He trickled a collection of small stones into the open neck of the figure. They tinkled hollowly on their descent. With a deliberate measuring action, Pen left a few gems in the bottom of the envelope and placed it back in position. In this fashion he worked his way through the tray, the diamonds becoming progressively larger as he went. Halfway through, Pen started to take the largest gems in separate polythene envelopes from the back of the tray. These he dropped carefully into the neck one by one, tipping the figure slightly to ease their fall; then he continued working backwards on to the brown envelopes, until he had reached an envelope with its corner turned down. He tipped in the remaining gems in the bottom of each brown envelope, and then started on some green envelopes nearest him. The sound of gems trickling into the figure was now quite dull and muffled. Pen tipped the figure slightly and looked once more into the neck.

'Just as I thought!' he exclaimed smugly, acknowledging Tom once more. 'I have put in approximately the carat weight mentioned by Mr Chareompond to me yesterday, and I am still a good way short of the top.'

'I see,' Tom affirmed, sitting up.

Pen tilted the figure away from him. Steel half-raised himself from his chair, caught a glimpse of glistening whiteness a few inches down from the figure's aperture and nodded his agreement. Pen shook the figure slightly to effect a loose arrangement and then continued working through the last of the green envelopes, emptying the few remaining gems in each. His movements became increasingly measured and his attention alternated between the loose head, the envelopes and the level of gems in the figure's neck. Almost at the end of the box he stopped suddenly, as if instinctively, his hand raised above it. He looked towards the figure's loose head.

'How does this fit on?' he ventured.

'Anti-clockwise turns,' Steel illustrated with his left hand. 'The cushioning presses hard against the diamonds. It's a very tight fit: there should be no movement apparent from inside if it's on properly.'

Pen acknowledged this with a thin smile as he commenced the first few screw turns. It was too tight. Removing the head and tilting the figure, he trickled a few gems out of the neck and then repeated the process. On the third attempt Pen appeared to have found the ideal quantity balance. He replaced the head and then tested its tightness, more as a show of accomplishment than of assurance.

'There you are, Mr Steel, all packaged and ready.' Pen passed the figure across the desk. Much heavier, it made a dull but ominously deep sound, its base resting solidly on the wooden surface.

Steel picked it up, tentatively testing its weight. 'Is there much difference in the weight?'

'There is a bit, of course, but it shouldn't be noticed. It depends. Is the person you're dealing with used to handling this figure and testing its weight?'

'Hard to say,' Steel said thoughtfully. 'If so, they won't have been able to sample its weight recently.'

'Is it possible that it could be weighed accurately – a merchant's scale, for instance?'

'No, it's unlikely.'

Pen considered briefly. 'If you wish for a tip, Mr Steel, there is quite a lot of wood in this figure and it is possible for some ingrained dampness to explain away a small weight difference.'

'Yes, thank you,' Steel acknowledged, although he

quickly realized that a weight test would be impracticable to apply within the arena. 'So,' he recapped, 'an oil test and the weight difference are the main things to watch out for. Nothing else?'

'No.'

Steel turned back to his holdall and confirmed the monetary arrangements. 'Nine hundred and twenty thousand bahts was, I believe, the agreed price.'

Pen nodded agreement, and Steel piled the banded wads on to the desk-top: each of the four was two hundred thousand bahts in thousand-baht notes; the loose notes Steel spread out on one side.

Pen looked at the money blankly.

'If you'd like to check it,' Steel invited; he had not done so himself, merely taking out all the money passed him at the bank earlier.

'There is no need, Mr Steel. I have dealt with many English businessmen in the past, and I have found them all honest. An Englishman's word is his bond, as they say.' Steel grimaced.

It took only a moment more to finish their business, Steel placing the figure back inside the holdall and re-zipping it, and Pen folding the money, almost carelessly, into a side-drawer.

They shook hands heartily over the desk-top, courteous 'Thank you's' coinciding, and then Pen came around, ushering them out of the office with the same broad smile and a few muttered pleasantries, Pen finally turning to Tom. 'Dee ngahn. And thank you, Mr Chareompond, for introducing me to this worthy customer.' It was the custom in Thailand to acknowledge a good business referral.

'Pohm kwahm yin dee.' Tom nodded faintly, and they turned from the small office along a narrow corridor which cut alongside the busiest section of the factory and then out into the relative quiet of a car park.

'How much did you tell him?' Steel enquired, once they were clear of the main building.

'It was difficult, Jeff. He wouldn't do the deal without

312

some information, it was too irregular and much too short notice, he said at first. And then with each piece of information I gave him, he wanted a little more.'

'He doesn't know why or where?'

'No,' Tom confirmed, shaking his head resolutely, looking back down at the ground. 'It was just that he said fake gems, under certain circumstances, would be no good as substitutes.'

Steel accepted what Tom had said without question, but he dwelled a moment longer on Pen's over-enthused courtesy, unusual curiosity and, in particular – though this was more instinct than observation – a certain detached coldness beneath his smile, empty, calculating.

It had been hot when they entered Pen's factory, but now, just passing midday, it was stifling, almost unbearable, and Tom turned on the air-conditioner as soon as they were back inside the car. 'It'll probably rain again tonight,' Tom commented sourly. 'I can feel it in the air.'

Minutes later, as Tom drove them back through the straggling industrial estates towards the city, Tanayo Pen had fallen to the back of Steel's mind; there were other things to consider and time was running short. The figure would require re-depositing, and the embassy bank, as an immediate thought, seemed as good a choice as any. And, Steel contemplated, it would be necessary to arrange another meeting with Paul Ensor. But this time, away from either of the two hotels.

Franz Zeifert loosened his tie a bit more at the neck. He was used to wearing a tie constantly due to hectic rosters of business engagements, but more recently in England's unusual heat-wave, and certainly now in the stifling midday heat of Bangkok's city centre, he much preferred an open neck.

It was the open neck he'd opted for, following Magonde from the airport, a short taxi journey to a nearby car-hire firm, then trailing the grey Toyota saloon towards the city centre. There were still the four men, Zeifert had noted: the blond chauffeur, Magonde, and the two negroes in the back.

When the car had finally stopped, it was suddenly, halfway along the Silom Road. The two negroes stepped out quickly. Zeifert decided to stay with the car itself, ordering his taxi on again. 'Kow bpen ngoh!' his taxi-driver had commented. 'They are crazy – going in circles all time. You wish me still to follow?'

'Yes.'

A similar pattern continued for almost an hour, and then the grey Toyota turned into the Suringwose Road, and sharply into a side-street. It had been a rapid action and Zeifert's taxi was a good distance away; he thought he saw the two blacks bundling into the back again, carrying a large object in white, although he could not be completely certain. Only when his taxi moved closer, could he pick out their outlines in the car. The Toyota stopped again in the Siphya Road and a young street-boy was summoned to the window. He stood there for a moment and then was passed something quickly. The car pulled out again from the kerb. The next stopping point was, to Zeifert's puzzlement, a real-estate office. After another twenty-minute wait, he trailed the grey Toyota slightly away from the city centre, towards the river.

It was a small warehouse this time, fading yellow cement and tumbledown, and Zeifert had seen the object clearer – large, elongated and wrapped tight in a white sheet as the four men disappeared quickly through a side-door.

He had stayed in the same position, watching, waiting, for over an hour. It had appeared that nothing was happening immediately, and so it seemed an opportune time to check in at a hotel, hire a car, wash and freshen up.

Zeifert had checked back in two hours and stayed again for another hour, but there was no movement. And then again in the evening, but with the same result. The purpose of the warehouse began to preoccupy his thoughts: was it a delivery point? Transit point? Or perhaps the goods were already there and awaiting shipment out? And then what was the large white object? It was then that he remembered the real-estate office; perhaps there would be some answers there. He would check first thing in the morning.

A tie had seemed appropriate for such an enquiry. Within an hour of the opening of business that day, he had his information. The locals were so easy to bribe, Zeifert mused. The real-estate agent had refused to give any information until the appearance of a five-hundred-baht note had softened his attitude. 'The rental is for one full week, payment in advance, and an extra premium not to make out the usual registration.'

And so now Franz Zeifert was back in front of the small warehouse, suddenly aware of the constraint of the tie at his neck, and the building heat outside. Nothing had changed: the grey Toyota was still in the same position, the shutters drawn in a small side-window, the front corrugated gate firmly closed and bolted. *When the hell are you going to make your move, Amwre Magonde?* he cursed to himself. He glared once more, disapprovingly, at the small warehouse and settled further back in his seat, preparing himself for a much longer vigil.

To Madame Chitra, the man appeared similar to the last, except that he was slightly taller and his hair was heavily greased and thick black, without any grey. Their dress was identical, she noted. Black trousers, white shirt and canvas shoes; the dress of the common labourer. 'Dtawn rahp!' she acknowledged, nodding slightly. 'I was sorry to hear of your colleague. It came as quite a shock.'

The small man accepted her greeting in silence with a reciprocal bow. She did not know his name and he did not offer any.

'I have the film in question,' she offered hastily, breaking the tension. 'It is, as I mentioned earlier to you on the phone, a part of the film shown to Kalchorn.' She paused suddenly; she was momentarily unsure that it was the same man. 'So sorry! If it was you that I spoke to, that is.'

The small man remained silent.

Madame Chitra led him to the side of the room. 'It is of

extremely short duration,' she remarked uneasily, oddly unnerved by his silence. Her hands trembled slightly as she operated the video tape. It was a short run that she had put through the machine in case Kalchorn had failed to arrive in sufficient time. 'I hope you find it of some use,' she offered, summoning bravado. 'The *farang* Englishman, you will notice, can be viewed quite clearly.'

She ran the tape through and the small man watched intently. It flickered to an end after only thirty seconds, but he remained immobile.

'I can run it through again if you wish,' Madame Chitra commented obligingly.

The small man held up one hand. '*Kawp-jy*. That will not be necessary.'

'You will be looking for the *farang* Englishman no doubt?' she enquired. She had been relieved at the break in his silence and felt now able to be more open, although as he turned towards her, eyes glaring, she suddenly realized the directness and clumsiness of her question regarding a business which rightly should have been none of her concern. 'The only reason I ask this,' she added hastily, 'is that I have information that would lead you to him quite easily. He was introduced to the parlour through a tout recommended by a local hotel manager – Mr Chareompond, at the Narao.'

The small man remained stony-faced, nodding slightly. 'Such information will be of no concern to me or my *Bpratahn*. Kalchorn was merely a *tahahn*. As far as your interests in this are concerned, Kalchorn will be replaced and the collections will proceed as before. There will be no alteration in schedule. *Sa waht dee krahp*.'

'*Chann kow-jy*.' She bowed deeper this time, although she thought to herself – what gave this man the right to remain so arrogant, so aloof? Dressed like a peasant or a common labourer, and yet he spurns my most pleasurable assistance. *Huh!* 'Kawp koon,' she nodded again, smiling.

There was only one thing which appeared slightly out of the ordinary about the small man, she noted, insignificant

316

and yet striking, setting him aside from others of that dress: the back of his hand as it gripped the door handle showed the blue tattoo of a lion. One of its paws raised and clutching the handle of a large, curving sword.

The symbol of the fearless warrior.

18

The only light was directly above him, bright and stark and suspended by a single cord. For a moment it had swung lazily back and forth, the tin shade caught on one edge by the sudden upward motion of Calbeck's baton, but now it was still, casting its ghostly rays over his half-naked body.

Bokwe Tshuma sat in a solid wooden chair at the room's centre, strapped tight with leather thongs on his arms, legs and waist; the chair, in turn, was bolted with iron rivets to a rough flagstone floor. A thin cord trailed from the far wall, splitting into two at the base of the chair, each end capped in a shiny metal disc, one fastened to Tshuma's left arm by sticking plaster, the other hanging loosely at one side.

Calbeck's two sergeants had ripped the shirt brusquely from Tshuma's back, and now the light glistened on the thick sweat gathering on parts of his ebony skin. The two sergeants stood at the back of the room, looking on blankly as Calbeck continued, although now both the questions and Tshuma's responses were becoming repetitive, predictable.

A pair of thick rubber gloves on Calbeck's hands looked awkward but still somehow ominous as he twirled his baton slowly back and forth. He had already attached the electrode to Tshuma's arms, and then higher up, to his stomach and chest, but with no result.

'*Bature, Bature,* is that the only name you can give me?' Calbeck mocked. 'You must think me an idiot. A tribal name among thousands. . . . And am I also asked to believe that a trained, close-ranked rebel force accepted such a name without question.'

Tshuma stared back blankly; in the space of a few minutes he had seen three of his closest friends and his wife die, and suddenly everything seemed unimportant.

Calbeck pulled his head back sharply by the hair. 'I mean he could so easily have been an SASP or BOSS infiltrator. What's wrong – don't you trouble yourselves with such formalities any more?'

Tshuma fixed him with the same stare and then smiled thinly. Calbeck brought his baton down hard and sharp on Tshuma's left shoulder.

'Inja!' Tshuma hissed, the same smile still fixed perversely.

For a moment Calbeck stood there immobile, his face bloated and ruddy, and then the full extent of the outrage began to tell. *Inja*, he recalled, was the Xhosa word for dog, but had a much more serious connotation than in English or Afrikaans. Calbeck began to tremble, but was speechless, momentarily overcome by exasperation. As the feeling of rage totally overwhelmed him, he struck out again with his baton, first to Tshuma's stomach and then to his mouth, splitting his top lip wide and snapping two teeth clean at the gums.

Tshuma spat out some of the blood and Calbeck came in closer, leering down at him. 'You can still talk, you Kaffir bastard, so let's be having it now.'

Tshuma smiled again, only now his teeth were coated thickly with his own blood, and he spat out some more of it into Calbeck's face.

Calbeck gripped Tshuma's hair again, then reached for the electrode with his other hand. 'Okay, cunt, now you've done it. What's his full name. . . . Now or not at all! It's your last chance! So let's have it.'

Tshuma stared back blankly and Calbeck reached one finger down and pulled up Tshuma's left eyelid; his eyeball appeared suddenly ragged and distended in its socket.

'Who?' Calbeck snapped bluntly.

Calbeck brought the electrode over slowly, purposefully, giving Tshuma a final chance to respond. But Tshuma remained oddly impassive. Calbeck trailed the wire the last few inches in a measured action, finally touching it against Tshuma's eyeball.

The scream that rose from Tshuma was instant and heart-rending. Calbeck could feel the tremendous jolt, even though he was protected from the shock itself by his thick rubber gloves. At first, Tshuma's eyeball pulsed high into its socket, then settled back slowly, the cornea almost totally bloodshot, a few involuntary impulses still moving it slightly, as if it was detached.

For the first time Tshuma appeared defeated and Calbeck quickly seized hold of the opportunity, repeating the shock treatment to Tshuma's stomach and neck. At one point, Tshuma's bravado returned, the same blank, indifferent belligerence he had confronted Calbeck with initially; but then slowly he found himself clinging to a form of vague, somewhat bewildered hope, and whatever life remained within his broken body. As one of Calbeck's sergeants stood above him, ready to throw a full bucket of water, his resolve was abandoned completely.

'Tomlinson,' he muttered.

Calbeck leant closer and tilted his ear in a deliberate motion.

'Nathan Tomlinson,' Tshuma mumbled weakly, his accent so pronounced that the 'th' sounded almost like a 'd'.

Calbeck got Tshuma to repeat it once more and then asked how such information could be verified; it was as Calbeck had thought: infiltration from 'outside' *had* been a main criterion. Calbeck concluded the interrogation with a few minor points that he considered relevant and then ordered that Tshuma be held in one of the cells on the same floor. Without delay, he reported to Jan Ostermeir. It was 2:10 p.m.

London was one hour behind Johannesburg, and by mid-afternoon, through the wire service, the information lay on Commander Stannard's desk. From there it was relayed to the CIA in Langley, who were able to cross-reference the details with a key-note from an FBI file. The FBI, in turn, passed the now slightly expanded dossier on to their COUNTELPRO division.

The roar of the motor was muffled in the murky waters, two parallel lines of white foam showing the boat's path. 'Why this place of all places?' Ensor enquired.

Steel gazed distractedly towards the far river bank, picking out groups of wooden shacks and small groups of children, naked and swimming in the shallows. Kneeling at the waterside were the woman of the Klong villages, backs bent and shoulders hunched in the midst of the weekly wash. 'It's reasonably isolated,' Steel commented, looking back at Ensor. 'It was important to keep away from the two hotels.'

Ensor glanced towards the people in front of them on the boat. He and Steel were towards the back, another four behind them and a Thai crouched low in the stern, operating the outboard motor.

'Just tourists,' Steel remarked, picking up on the intimation. 'It's also quite natural for you to be here and strike up a conversation with the tourist seated next to you. This is quite a popular spot among the excursion touts.'

Ensor's expression lifted. He seemed suddenly to understand.

After a moment Steel started to explain the purpose of the meeting and Ensor sat back and listened carefully. Most of it was a straightforward procedure: a bank receipt for claiming the figure and a diagram showing respective positionings inside the arena, two rather insignificant slips of paper that Steel would pass across before they left the boat. As a final point, Steel brought up the question of their having to leave Bangkok as soon as possible afterwards, and it was then that he could sense Ensor's resentment.

'It's an unavoidable consequence.' Steel pressed his point home. 'I'm afraid we have to face things the way they are.'

'And which way is that?'

'Please, Mr Ensor, I don't want to cover the same ground time and time again. This is in your own interest.'

Ensor was faintly bewildered. 'You must have known about this earlier, so why this sudden information?'

'There are certain risks,' Steel retorted sharply.

'Risks, risks!' Ensor mocked. 'More like bloody risks to your precious wooden figure. That's all you care about, you bastard!'

Steel bit back his anger. 'You'll be well compensated,' he appeased, outwardly calm, moderating his tone.

'What's that supposed to mean?'

Steel outlined the terms of the compensation he had discussed with Cullen earlier. 'My recommendation is going through now.'

'Oh, I see – *your* recommendation. And what exactly does that represent to me? And *Deborah*?'

A slight wash from a distant merchant's boat rocked them slightly. Steel looked up, studying Ensor coldly, calmly. It was the same problem as before, he reflected. Quelled in that one moment of conflict, but always returning. He was aware of the hard image he had presented to Ensor, but then he had made that decision from the outset; if necessary, he was prepared for Ensor to dislike him, if it meant that implementing his plans would be easier. If he took a weaker stance now, it could lead to disaster for *both* of them.

'It's quite straightforward – just a matter of some paperwork,' he said, with an air of detachment. 'After the exchange, you'll instruct a taxi back to your hotel and an official from the British embassy will meet up with you. From there, you'll go to the embassy itself, where the time of your flight out will be confirmed.'

'You don't know for certain yet, then?'

'No.'

Ensor looked over curiously. 'This payment. If I was to accept it and go along with everything, when would I receive it?'

'A few months at the most. Of course there are certain conditions. . . .'

'Of course,' Ensor mimicked, a faint belligerence returning.

Steel pressed on, explaining the finer points of the compensation. 'Cullen will start processing everything for you at the embassy, or it can be done in London. Your choice.'

This time Ensor, too, stared abstractedly towards the far river bank. The realization of the payment, its implications and the nuance of danger were all there for him. He laughed inwardly. It was ridiculous, insane, but suddenly and inextricably he found himself scheming. He asked some more questions about the terms of such an arrangement, and with each of Steel's answers, began to question that same unsavoury choice. 'There are other things to consider,' he said. 'Certain principles, for instance.'

'Oh yes?'

Ensor looked lost for a moment. 'It just seems so trite thinking of money at a time like this.'

'I can understand that,' Steel agreed, and he looked more directly at Ensor. 'But then what else can we do?'

'And what if I didn't want to play along?'

'Where would *not* playing along get you?'

Ensor looked blankly downwards. 'I don't know, it's just that. . . .'

'Why don't we stop playing games, Mr Ensor. It's been the same since our first meeting – back and forth – a game of bloody tennis. We're really on the same side, only you haven't come to realize it yet.' He glanced thoughtfully at Ensor's white shoes. 'We both know what you'll do. . . .' There were some sounds to one side and he turned back towards the water, his voice trailing off.

Ensor winced. He hadn't realized that his eagerness regarding the money had shown through. He knew that in that one moment, he had wanted the money; and now Steel knew it and so nothing more needed to be said. He thought again of Deborah, of her lost voice on the phone the night before, and everything else seemed suddenly unimportant.

322

He looked over at Steel hesitantly. 'My wife, will she be safe?'

Steel sensed Ensor's concern, almost desperation. 'They won't harm her before the exchange, you can rest assured.' He paused. 'But *that* is where the planning comes in.'

Ensor contemplated Steel a moment longer. 'Okay,' he said in a low, defeated voice. 'Is there anything else I need to know?'

For the first time, Steel sensed that an understanding had been reached between them; Ensor's anger and indignation had finally wound itself down.

Steel turned his attention to the river bank on the other side of the boat. They were within a hundred yards of the floating market. It showed at a tangent to the main course of the river in a small offshoot canal, rows of wooden shacks clustered on each side in terraces and supported by wooden stilts, allowing a clearance of a full six feet between floorboards and water. The narrow channel between the two terraces was crammed with a flotilla of small boats, each narrow and long with mostly one occupant seated at the rear, the remainder of the boat crammed with a wide selection of vegetables and fruit-produce ranging from beanshoots and watermelons to peppers and plantains. Colours were reflected hazily from the little water space allowed between the jostling wooden frames.

'Fascinating, isn't it?' Steel remarked. 'A whole life on the water.'

Ensor, joining him momentarily in appreciation of the scene, weakly grimaced his accord; but Steel turned away equally as abruptly, his thoughts clearing. 'There's a couple of things to watch out for,' he said pensively. 'The first thing is not to hang around with the figure for too long once you've picked it up. The main part of the bank closes at three-thirty, but the safe deposits stay open until late tonight.' Steel looked quickly at his watch, a precise gesture. 'It's almost two-thirty now, so you've a few hours to spare. Leave it up until the last minute to pick up the figure and then take a taxi. Don't stop on the way; and

323

don't hang around outside the arena, get straight inside.'

Ensor nodded his understanding calmly; it was quite straightforward. The boat had cut down to a low chugging reverberation, spluttering white foam behind them as they coasted towards a narrow wooden landing platform.

'Tom's busy packing your luggage with some assistance from Cheddi Jhiang,' Steel continued, measuring his words carefully. 'So you'll stop off only long enough to load your luggage and meet up with this chap from the embassy, and the same taxi will take you straight on. Cullen will meet you, confirm your flight out, and go through any final details.'

'What if something goes wrong?'

'It won't,' Steel asserted. 'Everything's been carefully worked out, and I'll be watching you all the way.'

Ensor studied Steel curiously; his confidence was evident, but Paul wasn't sure about his sincerity. After a moment, he grinned a reluctant acceptance, 'Okay.'

Steel visibly relaxed. 'I'll wish you good luck now. Don't look around for me inside the arena, I'll be there all the time. Just act as naturally as you can.'

The boat nestled in towards the landing platform and a Thai boatman gripped the bow, winding a rope around a starboard pole quickly. The Thai at the stern flung another rope ashore, which was quickly picked up by the same boatman and fastened to a large pole on the landing deck. People started moving off towards the front.

Steel took two slips of paper deftly from his shirt-pocket and passed them to Ensor. The movement was natural – that of men transferring business cards or telephone numbers. 'That's the bank receipt and the diagram I mentioned. Keep them safe.'

Ensor tucked the papers into his trouser-pocket and stood up. Steel was just behind him as they walked up on to the wooden dock.

They followed the trail of tourists up the steps to the wooden walkway bordering the terraced shacks high above the water. The shacks on closer inspection proved to be

324

shops, providing all types of amenities from tinned goods to a haircut. At intervals, steps led down from the walkway to the water.

Steel looked at Ensor. The moment's silence and the short walk had allowed him time to reflect that everything had been covered. 'That's it. There's nothing else for you to know. Again, good luck.' Steel smiled warmly, almost ruefully, turning after a short pause and heading further along the narrow boardwalk.

Ensor rested on the wooden beam bordering the walkway and looked down into the murky green waters. He'd sensed the sincerity in Steel's parting words, but there was something else, something that he couldn't immediately put his finger on.

A Thai boatwoman floated her colourful wares into his vision and fired a bright, toothy smile at him from beneath the rim of her wide hat. Ensor smiled in return, his thoughts fading momentarily; but then in a more obscure way, they were renewed and invigorated by the passing cordiality, an indirect, unconscious reminder of Steel's sincerity. He bunched his fist on the wooden railing ahead and tried to wrench the ever-spiralling contemplation away. But however hard he tried, staring blankly into the water below, the same thoughts returned. That he and Deborah were a small part in something much larger, more complicated than anyone would admit.

Pawns in a game of chess.

Part Six

Mongkai

19

Chalerm Mongkai was king of Bangkok, though not in terms of royalty or political standing. Neither kings nor politicians could aspire to his level of absolute power. His money ensured the service of the police, his powers of corruption the loyalty of politicians and fear the homage of the common people. 'Modern day royalty with bright regalia and ceremony remain as figureheads – the true rulers came in less obvious forms.' 'Ny pohns', seeking favour, would compliment him in his eclipsing years. Mongkai would accept graciously, for to be considered royalty in Thailand was indeed an honour, although at no time did he truly, inwardly, consider himself below such a station.

His palace was in gleaming white stone, tinted glass at intervals spread along the balconies and displaying various split levels. His carriages, sprawled in a wide trailing array from the front forecourt, served as excellent advertisements for Rolls Royce, Mercedes, Cadillac and Ferrari. The driveway was in red ochre, a colour copied from the Mall approaching Buckingham Palace; a souvenir of one of Mongkai's tourist visits to London.

His servants, mostly young, alert and armed men, guarded the electronic gates at the end of the long expanse of manicured lawn and were dotted around the palm-fringed boundaries of the estate. More personal bodyguards and employees occupied strategic areas of the house itself. His 'messengers' would return at set intervals and attend court, their humility befitting their duties. Those of the lower order, the *tahahns*, would bow deeply, showing appreciation for Mongkai's age and apparent wisdom. Although smiling, their eyes would often betray mild fear;

but above all, such meetings were pervaded with an air of the respect that can only be demanded from the servile by an indisputable master. These messengers would be allowed duties as guards for drugs shipments alongside the normal 'Lahus' and as touts or bouncers for establishments owned and protected by Mongkai: bars, restaurants, gambling dens, brothels and massage parlours. When required, they would execute Mongkai's dictates of murder and extortion in the humbler districts of the city.

To those of the higher echelon, the 'Ny pohns', little was denied. At the least they were trusted with monetary transactions for drugs shipments and monetary collections from protected establishments. At the extreme, their tasks included the corruption and assassination of politicians and police chiefs.

Mongkai's dictate on such matters followed the pattern of a systematic examination of man's basic principles. He often preached that those who were incorruptible were rarely invulnerable. Those who possessed both qualities invariably had friends who didn't. Betrayal was common. Those who built their reputations as monuments to honesty and unswervable decency found themselves alone; a character assassination destroyed not only the monument but also the foundations of the principles themselves. The people following learnt their lessons from those before them: that corruption, and not honesty, was the way. It was a consolation to those of lesser morals that they were not alone and a lesson to those of higher morals that they too would soon fall.

Mongkai's rule of law was obeyed to the letter. The elite of his force spread like tentacles throughout his kingdom, offering his subjects comfort, protection and an infinite largesse from a leader often described but never seen.

Captivity, ruin and death were equally available. This elite was small, a ruthless force of five men. Mongkai would hold council with them in a businesslike manner. Gestures of respect were amicable rather than servile: a rare appreciation granted Mongkai by men whose respect for life itself had long since diminished.

Even among a force of men trained to the peak of their profession, there is always one who stands out from the others - for his ruthlessness, his individualism, his appearance, or sometimes an invisible, intangible quality, an air of danger. Sometimes the qualities that make him different cannot be categorized. Everybody recognizes the difference and cannot explain it, but at the same time would never question what their animal instincts tell them.

Surak was such a man. More ruthless, more cold-blooded and more individual than the other four, he was most definitely apart from them. Mongkai recognized him as such, but would disguise his strong favour for Surak for fear of creating a power struggle among the members of the higher echelon. Similarly, Mongkai would never visibly show his respect for Surak nor admit, even to himself, that such a feeling was tinged with fear.

In return, Surak's allegiance to Mongkai was undying, as it had been from that first day with the mixing of their bloods above crossed swords, sticks of incense burning at their side, his service bonded by the words of his vow, as with those through the centuries before him. For Chalerm Mongkai was his master and confessor - his *Bpratahn*.

In retrospect, Surak Kalhya would remember above everything else the events that led up to his first meeting with Mongkai. At seventeen, Surak was working in the docks of the Chao Prya River, having left school almost three years previously. He was lithe and fleet of foot, and had been taking Aikido lessons for the past year from a local master, Subha Chaleo. Surak's appreciation of physical and mental skills in perfect and harmonious balance increased through time.

He very soon became a favourite of Chaleo's, claiming a special attention and training from the master given to no other. Surak paid for such indulgence with total dedication. Over a nine-year period, Surak had attained Chaleo's previous rank, that of seventh Dan, Chaleo himself progressing, by then, to eighth. 'It is as far as I am likely to go,' Chaleo would remark self-effacingly. 'But you, Surak, you are still very young. If you willed it, anything could be possible. Perhaps even attainment of tenth Dan - that of Grand Master.'

The words haunted Surak through the months to come. A divine ambition of which he had never before dreamt. A simple dock-worker – *Grand Master!* Oh, how his friends at the dock would talk, and all those around him. Their gestures of respect, so much more satisfying. Yes, that would be the way.

His outward calm hiding a deep, almost maniacal intent, Surak drove ever onwards. He increased his training under Chaleo, at the same time seeking specialist advice from a Japanese ninth Dan master, Mohanara Kaihito, who would visit Chaleo's school seasonally. At the end of that year, Surak had achieved eighth Dan, and his dream was becoming ever closer.

It was at this time that Surak's family life began to change, although at first he was not to recognize the significance. Surak had always held a deep respect for his parents. The small bar/restaurant they had owned since his early teens had been humble, but always profitable. Surak, in order to continue his Aikido lessons had stayed with them, paying them sufficient for his keep, and the arrangement had always been a harmonious one. Now times were suddenly different; a new road had taken the trade away from their district and Surak was faced with a pleading father. 'If it is our karma, what else can we do? You are the only one who could help. Perhaps times will get better.'

It was as if there was a new man before him. Surak hated to look at his father in that way, but he finally relented, passing as much as he could spare from his dock-worker's pay without affecting his Aikido lessons. Very soon the business absorbed that money also, and within months the only emotion Surak could find for his parents was pity – and strong resentment towards them for the position forced upon all of them. The poverty of Bangkok that he had seen and pitied since birth was now in his own home. A hatred grew within him, a sense of rebellion, as if he was taking the problems of all the poor upon his shoulders. He had always deemed the poor as ignorant, deserving their position through their weakness, their lack of will-power, lack of enterprise and their humble acceptance of their position. Surak knew that none of these were part of his character and yet he, of all people, was plagued with poverty. And for that he felt deeply aggrieved. By the end of that year the business required further support, and with his finances sapped Surak found he could no longer continue his Aikido lessons. His dream was dead.

The following months were particularly agonizing for Surak. He began to resent his parents for the poverty that affected all of them. Each day he viewed new aspects of his parents' character, traits that he had loathed over many years. His father, previously strong and wise in decisions and character, appeared frightened and frail, but at the same time accepting a powerlessness to change things. His mother, who had shared in his strength, now shared in his frailty and fear. At night through the walls of his room, he would hear the sounds of their crying. He would hear their weak pleas to Buddha to help their tragic plight. The sounds distressed Surak. That his parents, now so weak, left their fate in the lap of the gods was an admission of absolute defeat; one thing that Surak, an Aikido warrior of the eighth Dan, could never accept. Surak tried to fight the emotion, but inextricably, day by day, he grew to hate his parents. Over the months it enveloped whatever pity remained within his heart for them. As a family, they were broken.

Begrudging the money with which he supported the family business, Surak began to question its use. His father's answers were invariably vague, as if his own confusion had blanked those parts of his memory. 'It would be very hard to explain, my son. Only your mother and I fully understand the books.' Surak began to question both their integrity and their sanity. The gap widened.

It had been almost a year since their business downfall

when Surak, returning from the dockside, found his mother crying. His father lay bruised and bloodied at her feet, a deep gash running from his cheek to his chin. He too appeared to be whimpering. When Surak demanded what had happened, his father's answers were vague, saying that he had fallen and that Surak should not concern himself with such things.

Surak disbelieved his father, as he had done increasingly over the past months, but now his suspicion reached a peak. He asked what they had left of the money he had given them the day before, and again his father was vague, adding that everything was being taken care of. Surak looked first in the till on the bar counter. It was empty. Again he asked what had happened to the money. 'Tee ny?'

The old man stared blankly and then started evading once more. When he spoke, his voice trembled; never before had he seen his son so enraged.

Surak stated that if there was any money, he should see it; but the old man was stubborn. With a few lightning paces, Surak crossed the room and yanked a set of keys from his father's pocket. The old man struggled, but Surak slapped him hard across the face, sending him sprawling back on the floor. His father's eyes held a curious look. It was the first time that his son had struck him, and yet in his eyes was not contempt or hatred. It was forgiveness – for what his son would soon discover with the keys he now held, for the past year of poverty, for all the things a father would like to explain to his only son, but somehow realizes that it is far too late for explanations. That what was, is no longer.

Surak sensed the look's meaning. In that moment he felt remorse. For his father's expression told him what he would find in the small safe beneath the work counter. In a low voice Surak asked where the money had gone. He did not need to press, because he sensed there would be no more lies, that the unity his father and he had lost over the past year had momentarily returned. Now at last the truth came

334

out: how for the past years two men had come regularly to their small establishment and collected protection money; that even with the downfall of the business, the collections had continued, despite protest. As the business sank further, the amounts became harder to pay. His father finished, stating that he was afraid to say anything, although he knew that he should have. Again his eyes begged forgiveness. 'Chahn see-uh jy. What else was there for me to do?'

Surak asked why, and his father began to explain, in lucid detail, the sprawling empire of Bangkok's main 'Gawng john' under the command of Chalerm Mongkai. When he asked where Mongkai lived, his father shook his head. Surak accepted this. It was unlikely that his father would know of such a man's whereabouts. He decided quickly that there was only one way to locate Mongkai.

Surak asked his father when he next expected the two collectors. Then he began to plan.

Surak's hatred for his parents' weakness now turned to the men who had shown them in such a light. And towards Chalerm Mongkai. For he knew that without them, his parents might still appear strong in his eyes. His childhood memories and happiness might have remained intact and the business as it had been before. Surak decided that he would ensure the future safety of his parents' business, but that what had been taken from him personally could not be replaced, it could only be avenged. The two collectors would tell him of Mongkai's whereabouts. That he would make sure of.

He would free his parents from their burden and make his own way in life, perhaps never to see them again. As a true Aikido warrior he would fight for what he believed in and would dissociate himself from lesser mortals. Only fighting men and men of conviction would have his friendship and companionship! But first he would deal with the two collectors and Mongkai.

Over the next week, Surak's planning was faultless. The positioning in the shop of the two collectors, his father and

335

himself, he worked out carefully. He would be hidden, but it was vital that his father remained on the far side of the two collectors, not for one moment coming between them and his own concealed position. There would be one further element to Surak's plan – one which would give him the advantage of but one second and yet the difference between life and death, if the collectors were professional men. That they were, Surak had no doubt.

For the two collectors, the visit to the small bar in Bangkok's Thonburi district appeared the same as any other had been in the past years. True, the bar front had become more dilapidated over the past year or so, and the small owner ever more fearful of their demands. But he was still paying and that was all that mattered.

That the owner appeared more nervous than usual did not perturb them. That his wife, always behind the bar, was not visible, did not alert them to what was about to happen. Only a slight shuffling noise served as any form of warning, but then that was too late to be of any use. Simultaneously, a succession of firecrackers exploded on the far side of the room in the opposite direction to the shuffling noise.

Both men turned abruptly towards the sound. The first caught the full impact of Surak's wooden staff across his temple, and was knocked unconscious. The second started to take a gun out from his jacket, half-turning as the other end of Surak's staff whiplashed down on his forearm, sending his gun spinning across the wooden floor. The third blow caught him squarely in the chest, knocking him to the floor and taking his breath away. Surak asked him where he might find Mongkai.

The collector was reluctant to pass any information, and Surak brought his staff down swiftly, without warning, smashing one of his kneecaps. 'Ny pra jow chew!' the collector spat.

It was systematic now to Surak, the breaking of each limb. He was oblivious to the steadily rising screams and had crushed the joints in each leg and arm and cracked two ribs with the bulbous end of his staff before an address was muttered between clenched teeth.

Surak took careful note. He paced the room, picked up the collector's fallen gun and fired twice.

The collector shrieked feebly as the first bullet entered his stomach, the second his heart. Surak walked towards the first collector, still unconscious, and from a distance of three feet was slightly more accurate: both shells struck the heart. Everything was set now; Surak felt only a cold determination.

Surak dragged the two bodies into the kitchen at the far end of the main restaurant area. Taking the sharpest meat hatchet from a long line of hooks above the work counters, he hacked their heads free from their bodies. He placed the two severed heads inside an empty rice sack. The two headless bodies were placed in separate sacks, which were then filled with a collection of rubble and bricks from local waste ground and tied securely at the neck with thick rope. The sacks, in turn, were tied with the same rope to each end of his long staff.

Surak carried the staff like a yoke, trudging the three miles from his home in Thonburi to the southern reaches of the Chao Prya River, a section noted for its depth and size. He found a secluded spot behind a pandanus and bamboo forest area bordering the Charoen Krung Road, throwing the sacks as far from the steep bank he stood on as possible. He returned quickly to the restaurant, picked up the third rice sack and then headed towards northern Bangkok and the domain of Chalerm Mongkai.

The last sack Surak slung over one shoulder, his staff carried freely in his other hand. If there was to be any chance against Mongkai, Surak realized that his staff must remain unencumbered. There would be no surprises against Mongkai and so Surak resigned himself to relying upon his wits, taking things as they came.

It took nearly three hours from his arrival for Surak to finally see Mongkai. The guards had asked what was inside the sack and Surak had told them repeatedly that it was something for Mongkai's eyes only. That if he couldn't see

Mongkai he would go away, but that no one else would he allow to view the contents of the sack. '*Gep bpy!* Such an action would betray my purpose in seeing your master.' He bowed graciously.

The guards were wary of the lone stranger, but after several consultations by telephone between the large front gate and the house itself, it was Mongkai's curiosity that was eventually Surak's passport to enter the bandit's domain.

By the time Surak sat opposite Mongkai in his 'throne room', all thoughts of murderous revenge had gone. Apart from the fact that a bank of eight armed men stood at the back of the room and two either side of the bandit's high-backed chair, Mongkai possessed an appearance, warmth and charm that Surak found disarming.

Mongkai asked how he might help his new visitor – he could clearly see there was something amiss and hoped that he was not the source of such displeasure. 'If so, I would be pleased if you would inform me – speak clear and loud now, my friend.'

There was an openness to the introduction that made Surak think anew – he did not forget the purpose of his visit but, clutching tight the neck of the rice sack, he began to explain the events of the past years. How his parents had run their small business in the Thonburi district successfully, providing him with a comfortable and happy upbringing. How when the new highway had been built, business shifted away from them. Surak described the poverty, sadness and deceit of the past year. He talked soulfully of his previous respect for his parents and how it had diminished, only to be replaced by bitterness and hatred. 'They claim it is their karma. But a fate as such is so unfulfilling after so many happy years, *ney?*'

Mongkai listened with patience and indulgence, his balding, grey-haired head nodding imperceptibly, his expression mirroring the weight of Surak's words. The descriptions of poverty and the growing gap between father and son was a familiar story. Mongkai himself had experienced a similar upbringing.

Surak finished by describing his final disgust and annoyance at discovering about the regular 'collections'. He did not mention the murder of the two collectors but with a simple, distracted movement he drew the thick rope from the rice sack, rolling the two severed heads to the floor. A few of the guards at the back of the room shifted uneasily, already reaching for their guns, but awaiting a signal from Mongkai. It did not come.

Mongkai stood up. The sight of the two heads did not shock him. Instead, his face flushed with anger and a chain of vehement words spilled forth that surprised all present in the room, although none more so than Surak.

Mongkai addressed the guards at the back of the room, stating that the sight of the two heads should be a lesson to them. That he only claimed protection money from successful businesses, and that any collector who disobeyed his order could expect a similar fate. 'Prajow! I have said it often enough – those who are less fortunate should be allowed some leeway.' He pointed to the two heads. 'If the rules of these two dogs were observed, my empire would surely crumble.' Mongkai sat down resolutely, his flush subsiding gradually. It was a constant problem to him: collectors were offered a small percentage of their take, and such a situation was often an incentive to foolish oversight.

Then Mongkai waved his hand towards Surak, adding how such a young man had risked his life in order to follow his principles. 'This should also serve as a worthy lesson to you all.'

Mongkai leant forward and studied Surak directly, warmly. 'If I had known of this, I would have had these two dogs put to death personally.' Mongkai sighed deeply, and then his expression changed quickly. He chastised Surak for not allowing *him* their executions, and Surak paled, chilling slightly in that single moment; for already he could sense Mongkai's awesome power and unpredictability. 'As the *Bpratahn* it is my duty and mine alone to mete out punishment to my *tahahns*.'

There was a moment suspended between them, and the

room was quiet, unsettled; Surak tensed, his hand gripped tight on his staff, but Mongkai's expression warmed again. He spoke lower and softer than before. '*Peu-un*. Since I owe you a great debt for the past year of suffering, I will overlook this undermining of my authority. I hope you will do me the honour of the acceptance of this favour.'

Surak looked up solemnly. 'Dtohk lohng,' he nodded finally.

Mongkai stared directly into Surak's eyes and after a moment he sensed an understanding had been reached between them. The wild look that had been apparent when Surak had first entered the room was now dissipated, giving way to a solemn serenity. To Mongkai, Surak possessed the qualities of independence and bravery only his best men could boast. Conversely, to Surak, Mongkai was already replacing all the qualities he had found lacking in his father over the past year. Qualities of strength, forcefulness and leadership mellowed by a warmth, sincerity and honesty that already, in their short encounter, Surak had found apparent. Only in the highest ranking of the old Aikido masters had he observed the same. Irresistibly, Surak found himself respecting the man he had come to kill.

Sensing no further danger, Mongkai ushered all but one guard from the room. He asked that a servant bring them *cha* and some hot food for his guest. 'Tahn-tee!'

In the hours that followed, they talked of many things: Surak's background, family, Aikido accomplishments, and future hopes and aspirations; but the events just past were foremost throughout. Mongkai explained that it was not his code of practice to demand money from failing businesses. That if he did, the businesses themselves would cease to exist, and then where would he be? 'Such a ploy serves no purpose, *ney*?' He promised that Surak's parents would never again be troubled, and that some money would be paid back to them in compensation for their unnecessary hardship.

Mongkai stroked his chin thoughtfully, carefully considering his final question. He started it cautiously, stating that while his own rule of law remained within the boundaries of fairness, it was increasingly difficult to find honest collectors. That with the loss of two men, replacements would have to be found, but those of principle and honesty would be preferred. He asked if Surak might consider himself as such a man. 'It would be yet another way of repaying this heavy debt of hardship I carry for you and your family. For I alone, as the *Bpratahn*, in the end, must hold myself responsible.' Mongkai sensed faint indecision, and he added quickly. 'If not for those reasons, then purely for those of professionalism – rarely are we honoured with one so highly trained in the 'arts' among our ranks.'

The fact that Surak had cut his family ties weighed heavily in his decision. Already Mongkai had become a temporary replacement for what he had wished his father to be and, to some extent, a model of all those he had ever respected. Surak asked a few questions regarding the conditions of such a task.

The offer was generous. Gratefully, Surak accepted, 'Kawp koon.'

Mongkai appeared equally pleased with the impromptu agreement. 'You are welcomed - *gahp kwahm sook*.'

And later that evening, in the traditional manner, the final vows were sealed and Surak Kalhya sworn in as a *tahahn*.

Over the years, Surak's respect for Mongkai increased. He found a firm yet fair quality in Mongkai that led him not to question the duties he was set. To kill for a cause was not wrong. *The cause of the Bpratahn could never be wrong!* Such an act could only be deemed as an affirmation of all that was previously right through the eyes of one's master and, more importantly, a show of undying allegiance. The vows of *Sawahn laa lohk* were firmly made.

For Chalerm Mongkai was king.

In Surak, Mongkai discovered a brave and fearless servant with all the qualities of the finest warrior. Within three years, Surak had fought his way from the lower ranks to become part of Mongkai's elite force - the *ny pohns*. His service was bonded by a second vow, an allegiance to Mongkai ingrained as deeply on his soul as that of the blue lion on the back of his right hand.

The symbol of the fearless warrior.

It was almost seven years from the day of Surak's first vows that Mongkai's drugs empire was threatened with collapse. A CIA agent had gained vital information regarding raw opium shipments from the north: a potentially disastrous threat that could not be overlooked. A prime action had been set.

For Mongkai, the day held a special significance. His personal servant had informed him that Surak had arrived and was requesting council at the earliest possible convenience. Mongkai was aware of two issues requiring discussion. One involved the recent death of a regular collection's *tahahn*. The other, foremost in Mongkai's mind, concerned the CIA agent. He would hasten a meeting as soon as his servant had cleared the array of silverware from his dining table.

The sun was breaking through a tall window, at the side of the room, highlighting the majesty of a group of palms set in a bamboo trellis alcove. A white macaw uttered a stark cry from behind, subsiding quickly. Mongkai settled himself into the quiet of the large room, trying to open his mind to the forthcoming meeting.

When the servant returned, he informed Mongkai that another man awaited a private meeting. Mongkai sent a message that the other would have to wait. The servant left the room with a sharp bow, but within minutes had returned. 'Peu uh see-uh jy.' This time he explained that the new visitor was insistent, claiming that it was a matter of the utmost importance and that time was most valuable. 'I have passed him your message, *Bpratahn,* but he wishes an immediate audience.'

Mongkai was reluctant. The name of the new visitor was one which displeased him, that of a man who had a small yet unrepaid loan; a gem-dealer, who, as yet, had returned nothing but promises. Finally, through curiosity alone, Mongkai nodded solemnly to the servant standing just inside the doorway.

He would see Tanayo Pen.

The sun had turned fully on the tall window and Tanayo Pen sat in its extended light, Mongkai remaining in faint shadow towards the room's end.

'If the amount had been any larger, I would have had you killed. You are aware of that, I hope?' Mongkai said casually, one eyebrow raised as he finished. A test for physical reaction at least.

Pen shuffled uncomfortably in his seat. It had taken him a full five minutes to settle in the soft-padded low chair whilst Mongkai's servant cleared away the silver dinner-plates. The grandeur of the room and the size of Mongkai's chair did not help to ease Pen's disposition. Now, once again, he felt ill-at-ease. 'I know,' he muttered, 'I only wish that things could have been better. I would have repaid you twofold by now.'

Mongkai waved his arm in a discarding motion. '*Bproht!* That is of no matter now. State your business quickly, I have some other matters to attend to.'

'It's regarding the loan,' Pen interjected.

Mongkai leant forward and lifted his hand in warning. 'You have a habit of making futile promises. Don't test my patience any further.'

Pen shuffled again in his seat. The right words were beginning to form in his mind. 'I cannot pay you directly,' he said, 'but I have some information. If I am right, this information could be worth many times the value of my loan.'

'I'm not in the mood for conundrums,' warned Mongkai. 'What is the nature of this information?'

'It involves diamonds,' Pen offered, trying to spark some interest.

'How much?'

'It's difficult to say.'

'*Pra-jow cheu!* Try anyway,' Mongkai said, becoming impatient again.

Pen paused for a second. 'With respect, *Bpratahn,* there are many variables, but I would believe it to be somewhere between three thousand and four thousand million bahts, if what I am thinking is correct.' Pen had been calculating the figures in his mind since Steel's first contact, but he hoped the pause would demonstrate careful thought.

At first, there was no reaction. Mongkai stared blankly ahead. He had heard Pen without any trouble. When his thoughts cleared, they told him that Pen was lying, and then he realized perhaps that was what had triggered his initial instinct to question what he was sure he had heard correctly. He decided to tackle it another way. 'How do you arrive at such high figures?'

Pen leant forward with new intent. 'It was a gradual deduction – *Ny nee tahng.* . . .' He sensed that he now had Mongkai's interest. There was a lot of doubt still apparent, but there was now, Pen felt, at least sufficient interest for him to elaborate his story and assumptions. After the first few opening sentences, Mongkai sat back and listened carefully, his head, at times, nodding with a casual, reluctant acknowledgement. Pen explained in detail the initial contact by an old friend of his, now a hotel manager, on behalf of a visiting English businessman and how he had at first shied away from the order without some further information. '*Doy pra-jow!* Such an unusual request, *ney?*'

Pen paused again, looking up. Mongkai nodded imperceptibly, making a small signal with one hand, his attention now complete. Pen continued with increasing relish. He explained how there was an urgency to the Englishman's request, but also an insistence on the quality of the fake gems which needed to pass as real diamonds.

Mongkai leant forward again. 'Correct me if I'm wrong, but are you saying that the *farang* Englishman intends to dupe another party? Surely this is far too large an amount for such a plan?'

'I agree, *Bpratahn,*' Pen responded courteously.

'Far too elaborate a scheme to be conceivable, *ney?*'

Pen held his hands up. For the first time since his arrival, he felt masterly. He was in control. This was his subject. 'You are perfectly right, of course. A monetary payment is a possibility, but not very likely.' He shifted slightly forward with obvious enthusiasm. 'This type of transaction is much too large. Even a person trading diamonds worth only twenty thousand bahts would have a thorough examination first. Most of the fakes I provided this Englishman were 'zircons'; just a mixture of pastes. They wouldn't stand up to much examination. There are 'yags' which stand up to testing very well, but I could only offer a few of these towards the total package - that was all I could prepare in the time.'

Mongkai was deeply interested, but his past experience of Pen still laid some doubt in his mind. 'Then what makes you think that there is any money involved?'

'I don't,' Pen said, sitting back for a second. He sensed the obvious next question forming in Mongkai's mind. He quickly decided that Mongkai's presence was too great and patience too short to actually allow time for it to be asked. 'I believe diamonds are involved,' he continued. 'The real diamonds to match the fakes I have prepared. As I say, perhaps as much as four thousand million bahts' worth. I am almost sure that is the case. You see, there was this figure,' he blurted out as an afterthought, trying desperately to support his case before Mongkai's interest, once again, subsided.

'Yes,' Mongkai encouraged him. 'What of this figure?'

Pen quickly took control of his rational thoughts. 'The Englishman insisted that I put the fake gems inside a tall wooden figure. It had to be filled exactly to the top, with no apparent movement.'

'This is an unusual request again, *ney?*'

'Yes – and the *farang* Englishman was most exact in this requirement.'

The macaw cried out again from the side of the room, and Pen turned abruptly towards the sound, fixing on the bird's position momentarily. Mongkai's gaze had remained constant. 'I still do not see the relevance of this figure,' he said impatiently.

Pen wiped his brow. This was the cue he had been waiting for, but for some reason he still felt inordinately nervous. Nevertheless, the *coup de grâce* of his meeting with Mongkai was within his grasp. '*Kaw toht* – I believe this figure must for some reason be associated with the real diamonds,' he answered, gathering his composure. 'This would explain why the fake gems would be subject to only a short examination. It would also explain why this Englishman insisted on it being used as a container. The people he's dealing with must fully expect the figure to contain real diamonds. Perhaps the last time they saw this figure it contained real diamonds or alternatively they may have been informed by someone they trust implicitly of its contents.'

'*Dahng nahn!* And where does that lead us?' Mongkai enquired, holding up the palms of his hands in offering.

'There are a number of options,' Pen replied. 'First, that the people he's dealing with are acting on behalf of somebody else. . . . That seems quite likely, as I would imagine they do not have a great knowledge of diamonds. The other party involved may already have the real diamonds and is allowing the Englishman and his clients to go through these motions purely to put everyone off the scent of the real diamonds' whereabouts. Secondly, the Englishman may be acting in his own interests or may have been hired by this third party for exactly the same reasons, but in reverse.' Pen halted momentarily, waiting for the expression on Mongkai's face to indicate that the last piece of information had been absorbed.

Mongkai had never liked Pen. The granting of his loan had been purely a business matter that Mongkai later wished had been based more upon his evaluation of Pen's personal character. Whatever his past thoughts, he couldn't help now admiring Pen's partly intuitive, partly logical deductions. Mongkai nodded his continuing tolerance. 'Dtaw bpy!'

At the small signal, Pen resumed fluently. 'Finally, and this really goes back to your original thought of monetary involvement, although as I mentioned earlier, it is not quite as strong a possibility. . . . If the people involved have recently examined the figure containing real diamonds, they may be preparing a payment based purely on that evaluation. They may not consider a second thorough inspection, not suspecting that the diamonds in the short space since their last viewing could have possibly been switched. This is the only way there could conceivably be any money involved.'

Mongkai remained thoughtful.

He had resisted asking for a repetition of the amount involved earlier. Now he considered that the time passed could allow for a possible lapse in memory. '*Bawk pohm!* How much did you say these diamonds would be worth?'

'Between three thousand and four thousand million bahts,' Pen repeated, with more composure and authority than he had at first.

Mongkai sat back in his chair, then, leaning slightly forwards again, he picked up a gold letter-opener lying at his right hand and started a series of short tapping motions on the desk-top, a distraction which Pen found unsettling in the short silence following. It was a common ploy: Mongkai would always delay in decisions of such vital importance, whether he felt sure of his answer or not, in the belief that an impromptu silence at such a crucial moment might bring to light the visible awkwardness or insincerity of a dishonest visitor. If nothing else, he considered it would at least serve to quell some of Pen's more distasteful and obvious over-eagerness in his presence. He remained in doubt. '*La dee-oh nee.* How would I discover the existence of these diamonds or whatever money there might be?'

'Whatever this Englishman proposes to do will be done quickly. I am quite sure of it – his request was so urgent, you see.'

'Yes, yes,' Mongkai waved impatiently. 'Go on.'

Pen lowered his head slightly. 'I would like to humbly

suggest. . . . If the Englishman was to be followed for a short while, I am quite sure something would transpire.'

'Something to the effect of which you have already mentioned?'

'*Wahng*. Yes.' Pen fumbled in his side-pocket for a hand-kerchief, mopping his brow quickly.

'How am I to locate this Englishman?' Mongkai enquired impatiently.

Pen exhaled audibly. He was now sure of Mongkai's interest, but the fact that his questions were posed as if part of some tiresome ritual perpetuated his ill-ease. 'I am quite sure that he is staying at the hotel of the man who first made the contact,' he stated finally.

'*My dee*. And you believe he will shortly be making some form of exchange with the fake gems you have sold him,' confirmed Mongkai.

'Yes.'

Mongkai twirled the gold letter-opener between his fingers thoughtfully. He was still as surprised at the size of the transaction as he had been at its first mention. There was one difference – he now chose to believe Pen. He had dealt with transactions of that size before, but never in hard or negotiable cash terms. It was the kind of sum that his raw opium, once cut, refined and processed in Turkish and French laboratories, would fetch on the Western European and North American heroin markets. Of late some had been processed locally and shipped direct to Australia and the Western Seaboard ports of North America. Mongkai's was only the first payment. Out of those gargantuan sums came pay-offs for customs officers, ship crews, laboratory workers, port authorities, and then finally the local mobsters and dealers who completed the distribution networks. Mongkai realized that this one could be all his. No distribution bribes! No pay-offs! He eyed Pen cautiously. '*Bawk pohm*. Is there any other information I should have?'

'No, that is all I can tell you.' Pen mopped his brow again. It had taken him over an hour to calculate his figures and formulate the varying options that the unusual visit of the *farang* Englishman could possibly open up. A long, laborious thought-process. And harder still to explain to the *Bpratahn,* he reflected.

Mongkai continued his contemplation of Pen. His acceptance of Pen's story had been as much because of its total absurdity as anything else; if Pen had intended deceit a more credible story, at least, would have been concocted. Still, he felt it necessary to deliver an appropriate warning.

'For the moment, Mr Pen, I choose to believe your story. However, if I later discover any discrepancy in what you have told me . . . that would be unfortunate.' Mongkai said no more. It was unnecessary, he had discovered through the years, for a man in his position to deliver direct or clumsy threats. The intimation was clear. 'I hope we have an understanding.'

Pen's expression glazed over faintly with the sudden hollow realization of the worth of his involvement. 'Pohm kow-jy.'

Mongkai relished the effect briefly, then changed his tone. 'On the other hand, if what you are telling me is correct, your debt to me will be wiped out, and you will be handsomely rewarded. By comparison, Mr Pen, you should be quite a wealthy man. I hope that pleases you.'

'Kawp koon.' Pen's faint smile quickly demonstrated that it did. They settled the final arrangements.

When Tanayo Pen had gone, Mongkai sat back majestically, laying down the gold letter-opener at his side. There was but one further consideration. Thankfully, he mused, it was a short, uncomplicated one. For an assignment of such magnitude there was one obvious choice, he concluded; a percentage of the total bounty would ensure him of a particularly zealous pursuit. Since time was of the essence, it would also be a matter of convenience; an introduction to Pen could be made following the normal day's counselling. If all proved fruitless, he considered finally, the bounty on Pen would serve as an ample reward. *It was ideal!*

Mongkai grimaced faintly at the prospects, ringing a small gold bell to one side.

A servant appeared promptly inside the doorway. 'Tee kawng koon baw-ri-gahn.'

Mongkai instructed him with a wave of one hand. '*Dee-oh nee!* Send in Surak.'

20

Folsom Prison is one of California's toughest maximum security prisons. In the early seventies it had been the home of Charles Manson but, more significantly for Maximilian Boyce, in the previous decade it had housed Malcolm X and Eldridge Cleaver, and both, through that period and since, had been recognized as an underground rallying-point for hard-bitten black Muslim militants.

Boyce had been in the thick of it in the sixties: J.Edgar Hoover had proclaimed that the Black Panther Party was *the* greatest threat to the country's internal security. The aim had then been to initiate disunity among black militant groups and prevent a coalition of any kind; to this end, an FBI division, COUNTELPRO, was greatly extended, employing mainly negroes from both the FBI and state police ranks who had some familiarity with black militancy. Boyce had been one of the early recruits, and had seen the inside of Folsom Prison quite frequently during that period and since; now, as he passed once more among its rambling steel confines – the weightlifting 'den', the hard-sand quad, the men with their marbles – nothing seemed to have changed that much. Deeper inside, the atmosphere became more oppressive with a sense of caged humanity, either defeated or defiant, and the all-pervading and closely mingled smells of sweat, urine, clean laundry and disinfectant.

The man he had come to see, Larry Gaines, was ensconced in 4-A, the highest security section. At the height of the Black Panthers' activities, Gaines had been a strong-arm man in their Oakland chapter, but it was a short, chaotic bout of 'scoping pigs' just after the assassination of Malcolm X that had earned him his sentence. Boyce was familiar with the case, but had still re-read the file diligently beforehand, in particular, the details of Gaines' past relationship with Nathan Tomlinson, of the same chapter. It was more recent contact with Tomlinson that Boyce was most interested in, and for almost the first half-hour with Gaines his questioning was centred around that point. At first, Gaines was mildly cordial, but noncommittal; and then suddenly he changed.

'You sold us out, man – why should I help you?' Gaines glared disapprovingly towards the heavy steel door to one side. They were alone in a large cell, and at intervals a guard on the other side would peer through a small glass square.

'You've got nothing to lose, probably more to gain,' Boyce stated simply; the extent of COUNTELPRO'S role in splitting negro Muslim factions had become the object of such wild conjecture that Boyce considered both explanation or denial pointless.

'Yeah,' Gaines drawled slowly. 'An' that brings up another interesting point. I'm doin' life three times, so yours ain't worth shit. You know, one o' them pigs, I broke his neck. . . .' Gaines rose in one measured, purposeful motion and moved in closer. 'I could fix you right here and now'.

'You wouldn't have time, "brother".' Boyce edged a derogatory tone into his voice. Gaines didn't see the movement, but he heard the faint flick and then the cool press of the knife-tip under his ribs. 'I'd stick you like a pig, and when they hauled your dead ass out of here, it'd carry the State department stamp of approval.'

Gaines stared Boyce out a second longer and then turned away; there were moments of defiance still, but the last seven years had dulled that final edge. 'Okay, lay it out straight.'

Boyce put the knife away and rested his back against a table. 'At present you're facing another eight to twelve. I can guarantee you out in three to five.'

'Looks like you put quite a value on this information.'

'I don't set the values – you know that.'

Gaines looked up dolefully. 'What about protection?'

'This particular freedom fight's a long way away – in a few years it'll all be history.'

'In here, man, in here,' Gaines emphasized. 'Every heavy West Coast Muslim dude worth a shit's in this joint.'

Boyce considered the question a moment longer. 'We can keep you in 4-A a while longer, but I just don't think this one will come back down the grapevine.'

Gaines remained mildly doubtful. 'As I said, it's a few years since I heard from the dude.'

'That's all right - whatever you've got.'

Gaines asked a few more questions regarding the 'guarantee', and then looked up again after a moment. 'Okay, what do you want to know?'

'First of all, weapons. You used to be the strong-arm man, so what did Tomlinson get into once you were in the can?'

'Automatics mainly. . . . Oh sure, there were a few handguns from time to time – .38s, .45s, a magnum or two, but M l6s and Armalites were the main things.'

For a moment, Boyce angled his questioning around the extent of Tomlinson's expertise with automatics, then came back to Gaines' earlier mention of 'contact'. 'This last letter a few years back – what did it say?'

'Nothin' much,' Gaines mumbled, and Boyce knew immediately that he'd have to work for the information. He went further back, enquiring about earlier letters, and slowly a pattern emerged: one of the first containing fresh information from Ghana, another from Amgawi, Mozambique, South Africa, then Ghana again. . . Ghana and Amgawi seemed the most common denominators; but it was the main character of the letters that Boyce was most concerned with, and as yet only a slim profile was evident.

'This Magonde – tell me more,' Boyce prompted.

Gaines stopped suddenly and looked down at the stone floor. When he looked up again, his eyes seemed faintly glazed. 'I tell you, man, that Magonde sounds like Samuel, Moses and Elijah all rolled into one.'

'And what exactly do you think he's going to lead you away from?' Boyce mocked faintly. '. . . Or is it to – I can never remember.'

Gaines glared back. 'In your own cute way, you wanta know what's going down. . . . Well, I'll tell you, an' I'm going to use Tomlinson's own words, so I can be sure you don't get it wrong. Now let me see. . . . "A huge blow to white capitalism – the same capitalism that has enslaved the negro the past hundred years." . . . Yeah, that was it.' Gaines was on his feet again, and Boyce was aware that his own mocking tone was being imitated. 'The only trouble is "brother", that's all I know – I don't know the "whys" or the "wherefores", they only fed me the rabble-rousin' stuff. . . . Fo' instance, Tomlinson reckons that all o' that "blood of the white man" stuff is now no more than chicken shit. That we only dealt with things on the "physical level" because that was the role the white man expected us to take, an' that's what we related to easiest. But now it's time for somethin' else. Financial! Political! Hit whitey where it hurts the most.'

'Looks like your little foray a few years back's been wasted, brother.'

'Yeah, an' you've just bought yourself a pig in a poke, Uncle Tom.'

'Why's that?' Boyce demanded flatly.

'Because it's already been done, man – cut an' dried months back. They're just going through the motions now. . . .'

The sun was lower in the sky, but the clammy heat persisted.

The rush-hour traffic outside was heavier now; monotonous motor churnings and sporadic horns and klaxons filtering up through the fourteenth-floor window, the small room now a familiar companion.

Jeffrey Steel put down the internal telephone after speculating with Mr Tom on the likely time of the couple's return to the hotel. 'The Ensors' luggage is packed and ready,' Tom had confirmed.

Cullen had phoned earlier to say that a man called Rawsthorne would be present with a camera, and Steel had quickly run through respective positionings. Shortly afterwards he had had his first real opportunity to study the file that Cullen had passed over that morning, and now he looked at it again, picking out relevant details: a rebel group traced through an electronics engineer, four killed in a dawn raid on Soweto, and a photograph. . . . The photograph was from above, Steel noted, from a high, sharp angle, and even though both men were facing the camera, the angle gave their features the appearance of being slightly flattened, shallow. 'One man was identified as a local rebel, the other as yet "unidentified" – a "trace" will be initiated through all agencies, although until a name can be attached, positive ID is unlikely. *You will be kept informed through regular channels etcetera, etcetera.* . . .' With the time-gaps involved, there wouldn't be anything else through till the next morning, Steel considered, glancing briefly at his watch.

What else was there now? he asked himself. Cullen? The diplomatic pouch? Flight arrangements? Gem exchange? Ensor's final briefing? He scanned the mental check-list once again. No, that was it. Whatever else there might be was either superfluous or impossible to arrange, Steel mused. No point in reproaching yourself from here on in.

However, there was one thing remaining, he reminded himself. Small yet vital: at least twenty per cent of the arena would comprise *farangs*, Tom had estimated. But those that there were, he knew, would be scrutinized as well as the circumstances might allow. Appearance as a normal tourist would be essential.

With that thought in mind, Steel made his final preparations. He hung his jacket in the wardrobe close by, unfastening the leather straps of his shoulder holster and picking out a sports shirt: royal blue, short-sleeved. The fresh shirt felt good against his skin, cool, refreshing. He turned his attention back to his gun; a shoulder holster was impracticable, clumsy, and most certainly too evident to a watchful eye.

Steel walked over to his suitcase by the far wall, rummaging quickly inside. The soft leather bag was towards the bottom. It was small and oblong, a camera and accessories crammed awkwardly inside. He emptied them out on to the bed and placed his gun in their place. It fitted snugly from end to end, and he filled the loose side-spaces with a dozen or so spare cartridges.

There was nothing else to be done, he concluded, re-zipping the bag. Very soon it would all be over. Soon he would know *who* and perhaps even *why*.

But first the Ensors.

It was 5:42 p.m.

The inside of the car was like an inferno. At first it had been only mildly hot, but that was over two hours ago. For the second time that day, Pen wished he had never got himself involved. Already the affair was becoming too tiresome, too tedious to be worthwhile, he felt.

The small man in the driver's seat beside him stared fixedly out of the side-window. It was a familiar position to Pen, one which the small man had upheld stolidly since their arrival, not breaking off even for the few words of conversation that had passed between them in that time; a forced, unnatural silence. He had felt unusually uncomfortable with the small man initially, but now things had escalated. It was now something akin to nervous exhaustion. Pen sweated profusely. Reaching into his trouser pocket and producing his already dampened handkerchief, he mopped his brow once again; anything to break the tension.

Pen followed the line of Surak's vision across the broad Silom Road, past intermittent flashes of slow-moving traffic towards the expansive entrance of the Hotel Narao. Another group of tourists emerged: bright shirts, sun hats, eager gossip, a few parting gestures as they entered separate taxis, but nothing interesting. Pen looked away.

He had already provided Surak with a description: large,

355

light brown hair, casual but smart dress, athletic-looking. Surak had alerted him a few times since, but it had been nothing; someone only remotely similar to the image he had, by now, imprinted indelibly on his mind. Now he was lacking patience and energy. Perhaps he was wrong. What if it was another hotel? What if the transaction had already been completed? He remembered again the urgency of the Englishman's demand, mopping his brow automatically now, easing himself further into his seat. The covering was a Japanese vinyl which in the bright sunlight had baked almost red-hot and was only slightly cooled by the covering of Pen's trousers. Now, two hours later, combined with Pen's body heat it had succeeded in bringing his arse to the boil, his capillaries pumping a steam of sweat, soaking his underpants and trousers in a frantic cooling operation. A small rivulet had also developed on the ridge of his spine, running downwards to form a lake of perspiration at its base. Pen shifted his position slightly in a vain but nevertheless comforting attempt at relief. '*Mahn bpen nahn*. It should not be much longer now.' He looked over at the small man hopefully.

'Hy rao kwahm wahng,' a non-committal grunt came in reply.

'Yes.'

'*My chah*. We shall see.'

Pen looked out the window again. There had been the normal coach, taxi and assorted car arrivals, but nothing to block their view of the main doors for any significant periods of time. The third coach since their arrival moved into position, its rear section obscuring the hotel's central swing doors; but they could still catch the outlines of heads through its rear windows. Time passed slowly.

It was almost ten minutes later, and the coach was still there, when a profile appeared momentarily and then dis-appeared again among the people milling around on the pavement outside the hotel. There was something familiar about it. The head appeared again, but it wasn't until it turned towards him that he was totally sure; 'Nahn bpen kow!' he blurted out. 'The man in the royal blue shirt.'

Surak squinted at Pen momentarily and then stared in the direction Pen was indicating. 'Pohm hen!'

Pen was pointing unnecessarily; Surak had already fixed on the movements of the *farang* as he emerged into full vision from behind the coach. He noted that his movements were lithe and fluid, certainly athletic, and that the man was indeed large; not abnormally, but over six feet, he judged. Surak scanned the figure more attentively for any possible places.in which a gun or concealed weapon could be positioned. He registered slim-fitting slacks and a short-sleeved shirt, but no outwardly obvious irregularities. Then he noticed a small black leather bag in the *farang*'s left hand. It was a possibility. He would keep it in mind.

Surak was especially looking for any telltale signs that might set this man apart from others he had dealt with in the past: a subtle movement, sometimes only a certain expression, a nuance of confidence, or even arrogance; and after a moment he would have been satisfied that this wasn't his man, but there was something about the profile, and he drew his attention closer, although it wasn't until the head turned, studying traffic streaming from behind along the Silom Road, that he was completely sure: it was the *farang* Englishman on Madame Chitra's video-tape.

It would be well to be cautious!

Steel walked the length of the Silom Road and then into the wider Rama IV, his thoughts revolving slowly, peripherally, oblivious to the small blue Datsun that turned after a moment and followed a short distance behind.

Only a few yards into the Rama IV, Steel could clearly make out the Lumpini Stadium on the far side: there was a small park bordering it, trails of people at the ticket counters, and a profusion of taxis and samlors. A group of traders had set up a line of stalls in front, but in a couple of hours the traffic and the crowds would dissipate, and some of the traders would move their stalls further along the Rama IV.

21

A high-pitched and rapid drum-beat echoed around the large arena. The accompanying tones rising from two flutes should have mellowed the incessant drumming, but they too were high-pitched and constantly wavering. The mood was set for a nest of cobras to rise obediently from a line of wicker baskets.

Both music and attention were directed to a roped and canvassed platform, twenty-four feet square and raised four feet from the ground in the exact centre of the auditorium: a stage on to which two young Thai men would soon walk, a sacred cord holding a small buddha or herb tied around each one's head: the symbolic protection of the gods. They would diligently pray to the spirits, lest they should die or be seriously injured during combat, and then the cord would be removed.

Beneath the gaudy lustre of their shorts, a hard sea-shell protected the groin. Their hands gloved and their feet bound with nothing more than cloth tape, they would soon perform a ritual that regularly drew thronging crowds to the Lumpini Stadium.

Today's contest was an important one, a crowd puller; groups of Thais, mostly men, rapidly and excitedly filled the seats and terraces. There was also a number of obvious tourists. To them, far in mind and spirit from the Queensberry Rules, the prospect of two men engaged in uncontrolled combat held a form of morbid fascination.

Steel watched the arena start to fill. There had been only a few people present when he first arrived, now it was over half-full. He could see a man he thought was Rawsthorne moving towards the back, but it could just have been another tourist with a camera; it didn't matter anyway, inconspicuousness had been the main criterion. *But where was Ensor?* There were four entrances to the arena following the natural enclaves formed between each terrace and seating areas. The bulk of people streamed in from two entrances to one side and Steel turned his attention almost exclusively to those.

The Thais entered quickly and anxiously, taking little time or trouble in selecting their positions. The air was filled with the ever-increasing echoes of their excited and animated conversation. In contrast, the tourists entered slowly, almost totally preoccupied with the selection of a good seat.

The minutes passed slowly and the arena was filling rapidly, noisily.

A white-shirted referee climbed up into the ring, commanding its centre, tentatively testing his microphone as a roar rose up from all sides.

Two young Thai boxers emerged from tunnels in the terraces at each end, holding their arms up spasmodically to receive the rising appreciation of the audience. They knelt ceremoniously at each side of the ring, the 'seconds' removing their rich silk robes; then inside the ring, another, shorter bout of prayer was performed.

The referee started the announcements. '*Sah-waht dee!* Welcome, ladies an' genelmen. In the red corner we have Dan Sai Tiger . . . furious master of foot an' han' combat who seek to bash opponen's head until it no think on canvas. And in the blue corner we have Chareon Cobra . . . the deadliest strike this side of Ayutthaya. . . .'

Steel could see Ensor entering on the far side of the arena, a full head and shoulders above three jostling Thais directly in front of him. For a second he looked lost, then turning towards the raised walkway to one side, he made his way swiftly between the musicians' pit and the far bank of terraces. He moved up from that point, as instructed, choosing a seat four in from the end of a row, leaving three empty towards the aisle.

The music around the arena had slowed to a repetitive, incessant drum-beat. The two boxers moved around the ring as if in some purposeful, mesmeric dance, interspersed with sudden, sharp flurries of movement.

Paul Ensor sat stern and upright, staring towards the stage, his eyes glazed and distant, seemingly oblivious to the building furore around him. He held the Basikasingo figure like a stunted flagpole, its base resting loosely on one knee.

The bell rang, and then again, but Ensor remained unmoved. It rang twice more, but it wasn't until the Tiger sent a gout of blood spilling from his opponent's mouth with a jaw-line kick, that Paul Ensor finally registered some movement in front of his vision.

'Yaek,' the referee screamed, moving one arm between them. He directed the Cobra to spit into a bucket produced by his second at the side of the ring, then inspected his mouth perfunctorily. 'Dtaw by!' He ordered the fight to continue.

The boxers came back together in a tangled clash of limbs.

Steel looked beyond them towards Ensor's seat. There was some movement: two Thai men, one of them pointing with his programme.

The boxers obscured his vision.

Steel altered the angle by leaning to one side to determine exactly what was happening. It was harder than he had previously envisaged – Paul Ensor's seat was a good hundred feet away and shielded by sporadic motions of hands and feet; his vision at times was totally obscured, although he could now see the two men walking off.

It was another movement though, occurring in that same instant, that drew his attention – a man entering the arena to his far right and staying at the end of the long aisle. At first Steel wasn't sure of his identity – the man was most certainly negro *and* painfully thin, but somehow his features appeared more prominent and angular than in the photograph. For most of the time, the man watched the boxing, although at intervals his head would turn, taking in the full span of the audience – an action that dispelled whatever doubts remained; for a brief second his profile almost totally matched that of the photograph's sharp angle.

The man moved a few paces further into the aisle. He stood still for a moment, and then again his head turned. He stayed in the same position for another few minutes, at intervals repeating his observations; then turned quickly and strode purposefully back through the passage behind.

Steel had considered it a possible reconnaissance, but as time passed with no further movement, a suspicion began that something had gone wrong – that some small irregularity had warned the man that everything was not quite as it should have been. The suspicion grew stronger as the boxing continued. *Damn it!* Time passed slowly, agonizingly; the ringing of bells; the shouting of the referee; low grunts as sweated limbs received sickening blows. *When would they finally arrive?*

The first bout had finished and the second was already in progress.

Shit! Steel looked at his watch – 6:45 p.m.

The second bout developed into a slow, tedious slugging match, and Steel sat through it paying little attention. The boxers were clinging almost constantly, and an uneasy clatter of conversation grew around the arena. Then suddenly, surprising all present, the 'blue corner' floored his opponent with a clumsy, flailing punch that appeared more walked into than intentional.

'Neung, Sawng . . . Sahm,' the referee counted dramatically, the final 'Sip!' emphasized with outstretched arms. 'Poo cha na!' he shouted, walking over and hoisting the smiling, bloodied boxer's hands up high.

The faster drum-beat and chanting flutes rose gradually with the applause.

The boxers left the ring, and in the following lull, the referee once again took the microphone. 'An' now ladies an' genelmen. The highligh' of the evenin' . . . a masterful we'erweight contest. . . .'

There was another movement at the periphery of Steel's vision, vague as the referee started his announcements, but now clearer. Two negro men: one of medium build, middle-aged, distinguished, the other abnormally large, a fawn-coloured trilby hat particularly distinctive. And a girl, pretty in an innocent way, Steel noted – dark hair hanging lank and tired to match her worn, harrowed expression, a large, dark bruise on one cheek. It was almost certainly them. The girl reminded him somehow of Christine – something in her walk, her manner. . . .

The two boxers emerged boldly from their respective tunnels, a climactic roar building suddenly around the arena.

The two negroes were moving along the aisle and up, and Steel's thoughts turned again to the slim negro from the photograph. Reconnaissance? An outside watch now perhaps? Yes, that would be it! 'One man will stay outside the arena throughout', he recalled from what Ensor had related of the previous day's telephone conversation.

All three had their backs to him moving up the aisle, then they turned again, taking their seats; he could now see the large negro loosely gripping Deborah Ensor's wrist. But there was something about the first negro, the distinguished one, and he focused his attention back on the finely-chiselled ebony features, the distinctive greying sideburns, the taut, refined expression.

The profile before had been a fleeting one and had told him nothing, but now the face was turned towards him, and although it took him almost a full minute the recall was finally there: an article in the *Daily Telegraph* that Kenton had brought him in hospital, detailing a build-up of rebel forces in the African state of Amgawi, and an earlier related photographic profile and article in *TIME* magazine. The first article was over a year before the rebel uprising, he reflected, reporting the exile, for undisclosed political reasons, of the country's most eminent physician – Dr Amwre Magonde.

An insignificant footnote, by comparison, had been regarding the surprising growth of Amgawi's newest industry: *diamond mining and exploration.*

Slowly, Steel mused, a picture was beginning to form.

The roar around the arena gradually subsided. The fight was in progress.

'I see you have the figure,' Magonde said.

Paul Ensor looked at him. 'Yes.' A flat indignant tone.

'I hope you have come alone.'

'Yes, of course.'

'I hope so,' Magonde warned, 'because if not, I would not like. . . .'

Ensor cut in sharply. 'Let's get on with it, shall we? I have a holiday to continue and I'm quite sure you have better things to do.'

Magonde eyed him cautiously, making it obvious that he suddenly saw this new stranger in a different and unexpected light.

Ensor stared back coldly. The hurt and hatred had made him feel more confident. *It made the lying easier too!* 'I wouldn't risk anything by doing that,' he added calmly, shifting his gaze momentarily to Deborah. 'There's too much at stake. I just want to get things settled and then get out of here.'

Magonde nodded solemnly. He appeared to accept the logic behind such an emotion. 'That is all I want too,' he agreed.

Ensor eased off. He felt nothing but hatred for Magonde but sensed that a temporary understanding, at least, had been reached. Something that, for all concerned, would ease the moments to follow. Especially Deborah, he reminded himself, biting on his lip. She had been through enough. He had tried to smile when she had first come into sight, walking up the rough aisle steps behind the two negroes; but it hadn't come out right, and she looked so empty, so withdrawn, he thought. *Oh God!*

He passed the Basikasingo figure to Magonde without

speaking, now suddenly subdued, empty of emotion. Even if there were words on his mind at that moment, he knew he would be incapable of speaking them. His mouth felt dry, his senses distant, numb. The weight was gone from his hand. Magonde took the figure from his grasp, but it all seemed abstract. As if he was an onlooker to this scene and not playing a part in it at all.

'It's quite a work of art, don't you think?' Magonde remarked, his eyes gleaming with expectation.

Ensor nodded blankly, 'Yes.' He had always hated the figure, but then the lying *was* becoming easier. *No, more than that. It was becoming a habit!* He remembered thinking of the figure as particularly ugly, demonic. Perhaps it was an inborn reluctance to disagree with somebody so obviously enrapt, he thought. When Deborah was passionate about something he would so often agree, never even thinking of what his own opinion might be.

He watched Magonde grip the phallus of the Basikasingo figure, turning it carefully. Magonde's expression was ebullient, almost theatrical.

It was ridiculous! Ensor mused. Only yesterday everything had been perfect – beautiful: sights, sounds, feelings. And now it all seemed so strange; how quickly such magic could be shattered! Whatever happened now, Bangkok would always seem different to him. He would still love the city, but it would be a cautious love, as if one previously believed faithful virgin was found to be a whore.

He looked blankly towards Magonde, and yet he still felt more an observer of all this than a participant. *It was unreal*, he thought. *Everything*: the leer on Magonde's face, Deborah bruised and dishevelled, the giant constraining her, the boxing – a shouting, screaming crowd . . . building, becoming louder, deafening, crashing through his mind in one final, awakening climax. He would open his eyes, and the stewardess would be leaning over him, saying in a soft voice that they would soon be landing in Bangkok. *Oh God! But it was real! It was happening!*

Magonde was more serious now, turning the head of the

figure, the sweat thick on his brow. The giant was looking on expectantly and sweating too, and Ensor could smell the damp fear rise from his own body.

'You are surprised?' Magonde tested, tipping a few gems from the open neck.

'Yes,' he answered impulsively, as numbed now as he had been at the first movements of the phallus and head; he had already accepted that the figure would be of great value, and so now his surprise was muted. 'I hope you have what you want now,' he remarked dully.

'Yes, I hope so too,' Magonde retorted. 'Diamonds fascinate you, do they, Mr Ensor?'

'No, not particularly.'

'I am disappointed,' Magonde admonished him with mock gravity. 'Usually diamonds attract people's eyes as does no other natural substance – a hypnotic magnetism, you might say.'

'I'm not troubled,' Ensor said shortly, looking away and down, sounding uninterested, although there was another feeling, arising quickly, a sweeping, sudden realization – if anything were to happen, it would be now. A decision of life or death in a moment. No. It couldn't be that easy. There would be more to it than that. . . . 'Why should I be?' he offered quickly, fighting back a sudden dryness in his throat. 'I just want my wife back safely, that's all. Nothing more, nothing less.'

'I can see that,' Magonde said flatly, but his expression bore some doubt.

Ensor stared ahead. On the stage the referee had broken the two boxers apart. One seemed noticeably larger than the other and had a small cut above his eye. When they came back together, the smaller boxer in red shorts was obviously faster, letting loose a rain of vicious punches.

Through the gap that had formed momentarily, Steel caught a fleeting glimpse of Magonde's last expression. Now he remained unsure. He could see that Ensor had paid no attention.

The boxers parted.

Ensor was still staring straight ahead, Steel noted quickly. *God!* I hope he's not staring at me, he cursed impulsively.

A heavy torso shifted, blocking his vision. There was a head movement and then a knee and then just as quickly it moved away.

He could see again. Ensor was still in the same position, gazing directly ahead, but his eyes were glazed, distant. Magonde was looking down and reaching one hand inside his jacket.

There was a flash of blue shorts and then a broad back moved around. A set of bull-like shoulder-blades worked like pistons for a second and then the body was staggering, falling , but still at the same angle.

Damn! Steel cursed. This was no time for speculation. He drew one hand down to his leather bag, unzipping it cautiously, guarding the motion with his other arm.

The view was there again. Magonde had a small black object in his hand, raising it in a measured action to one eye.

The blue-shorted boxer was still staggering. His aggressor bore down on him mercilessly.

Steel gripped the butt of his gun and turned the silver barrel, still in its leather pouch, until it pointed directly at Magonde who sat with his head slightly bowed. He held his other hand close to the small black object. Ensor was still looking blankly ahead.

The boxers came together. The large one clung on to his opponent, trying desperately to smother the flow of punches. Above one eye, blood trickled copiously and the other was almost blinded by a bruise the size of an ice-cream scoop.

'Yaek,' the referee screamed. 'My jahp!'

And there was Magonde. He was examining, turning something small between his fingers. Then another object, and yet another. His expression was taut, an intense mask of concentration.

Towards the back of the arena, unseen to all of them, Rawsthorne moved in closer with a zoom lens, cranking hard on the motor drive, the repetitive clicking lost among the building furore.

The boxer in blue shorts was clinging again. He sucked in his breath to tense himself, but let it out in low, defeated groans as the blows transferred to his stomach. The referee moved between them.

Steel stared intently. The view was clearer now than it had ever been. The large negro would be an easy target. The seat directly in front of him was empty and most of his torso was exposed to view. In that instant, Steel remembered the blood-splattered Park Lane bathroom, and felt a flow of adrenalin. His palm moistened on the pearl grip. Magonde would be more difficult. His body was slightly stooped and a small head bobbed excitedly in front of him. Then the view was gone.

The boxers were tangled. A fast, stinging exchange of punches and high kicks. The shorter one stepped back deftly, his opponent staggering, his knees weak, jelly-like. Excitement and tension rose rapidly around the arena; an animated, high-pitched turmoil.

Magonde had finished examining the diamonds. He was screwing the head back on to the figure, his face dead-pan, expressionless. Steel was looking for just a small hint – a small gesture or facial movement. *That would be enough!* But there was nothing.

The blue-shorted boxer came in close, clinging on desperately. He looked finished. His gloves were locked behind his opponent's neck and his weight seemed to be supported by them. The blows came to his stomach again. And then he took a deep breath, as if a new surge of adrenalin had taken over, its flow coursing suddenly. Bracing his whole body taut, he brought one knee up sharply into his assailant's face.

Magonde stood up. So did the large negro.

The knee smashed against the red-shorted boxer's nose, the bone cracking loudly and a torrent of blood splashing on to his chest as he straightened up.

The crowd rose in a bursting crescendo.

Magonde and Karfi walked out of the aisle.

It was all over.

*　　　*　　　*

The small man had sat inconspicuously among the many Thais in the large arena, hardly aware of the boxing. Stolid and hawkish at the centre of the far end terraces, his eyes mostly in a tight squint, he stayed, ever watchful, thoughtful, maintaining an unencumbered view of the *farang* Englishman a full fifty feet away. He could easily pick out the royal blue shirt among the crowds, as he had done upon first entering the arena.

Early on, a tourist with a large 'Buddha' had raised a question in his mind, but was discarded quickly. It was a slim, warrior-type figure he had reminded himself. Tribal, demonic!

It wasn't until the approach of the boxing's climax that he had fully appreciated the relevance of Pen's brief description. Two negro men rose from a position he had, by then, fixed in his field of view, following the direction of the Englishman's obvious absorption; one negro was clutching a tall wooden figure and the other, to his mind, was obviously a bodyguard. *Yai dtoh!* Even by negro *farang* standards, a veritable giant, he thought, scanning the two men more closely.

It was in that same instant that Surak had noticed another movement, at first apparently irrelevant – on the same side as the Englishman but several rows behind, a man in a grey suit rising suddenly and walking out of his aisle; a tall *farang*, well-dressed, Surak had noted, with blond hair with grey streaks swept back over his ear.

It was the way in which the man had stood up only moments after the two negroes, his vision following them in an unbroken line, that had increased Surak's curiosity. Something else was rapidly becoming obvious. There was more involved than he had first estimated.

Unbeknown to him, the man in the grey suit shared that growing, uneasy resolve.

Clouds were dark against the sky, heavy, threatening silhouettes in the fading light. The lights were on outside the arena and in the street now, and bare bulbs illuminated the closely grouped merchant stalls.

Paul and Deborah moved briskly away from the entrance among a throng of Thais, hailing a taxi from a rank just inside the slipway.

They didn't talk to each other until they were in the back of the taxi and moving away; and then Paul was holding Deborah's hand, gently touching her cheek and the bruise above, heavy and blue on her cheekbone. 'My God, what have they done to you. . . ?'

'It wasn't so much that,' she muttered, clasping his hand tighter, fighting back the aftermath of nerves. And memories. The night before. The final moments.

'It looks so painful,' he continued, sounding curiously detached. 'Does it hurt still?'

Deborah didn't answer, and he looked deeper into her face, at the lines and dark circles around her eyes that he hadn't seen before, her lips drawn tight. 'You're still beautiful though,' he offered, forcing a smile, lightly touching her other cheek.

But then he quickly sensed that the smile was misplaced, ineffectual, and Deborah was looking away, her eyes moistening faintly, her lips trembling. 'Oh, Paul,' she quavered, 'there were some times. . . .' She came closer into his arms, wanting to say more, but unable to.

'It's okay,' he soothed. 'It's all over now.' Then suddenly speechless himself, he looked away, the streetlamps outside passing slowly as they moved with the heavy traffic-flow away from the arena.

'*Koon dtawng gahn* . . . Sheraton?' the taxi-driver swung around on them.

'Yes, Sheraton, *Sheraton!*' Paul prompted impatiently.

The silence was uncomfortable for a moment, and Paul held Deborah tighter than before, her body still quaking gently beside him.

'I don't understand it all,' he spluttered, annoyed at the silence, and at his own inability to find appropriate words.

And then he stopped himself quickly, realizing the total futility of such annoyance, now vague, senseless. *As with everything else.* Only two days before, he thought. The restaurant. Sightseeing. *Plans!* And now there seemed a gap between them, as if that had all been in some past lifetime, and that what had transpired since was irreversible because neither of them could come to understand its full meaning. 'I hope . . .' he started, his voice trailing off. 'No, it doesn't matter – it's just good to have you here and hold you again like this.' And he clutched Deborah reassuringly, as if that physical closeness would compensate.

Deborah wiped her cheeks gently with the back of one hand. 'You were going to say something else?' she ventured, controlling her breath, looking up at Paul more directly.

'Just that I hope we can forget it all quickly.' He returned Deborah's gaze, clasping her hand again. 'But then that's rather obvious anyway, and doesn't really help at all. If anything, it just reminds us . . . and so I didn't mention it.'

'I'm sorry,' she offered.

'That's all right – it's been difficult for both of us.'

'Yes, I know, but I just wasn't thinking,' she reproached herself, now conscious of the previous edge in her voice, fighting, once again, for composure. 'I shouldn't talk – I'm not fit. . . .'

'No, don't say that. It's good to get it out.'

'Said the actress to the bishop,' she said weakly, and it was the first time Paul had seen her smile; he was amazed at how such a small phrase could change everything, melting so much of the tension between them.

Deborah turned blankly towards the side-window, her smile subsiding quickly. 'Do you think it will be easy to forget?' she asked, her voice as lost as her gaze.

'Forget's the wrong word.'

'I mean for both of us,' she added, almost ignoring Paul's comment.

He looked out of the same window. 'We'll always remember – I don't think we can kid ourselves otherwise. But we can at least hope for it to slip into the background.

Different things will happen. Home, friends, other holidays . . . a family. It just won't seem important anymore.'

'I hope so,' she said, but the words meant nothing to her, the tone of Paul's voice being the only comfort.

Paul bit on his lip. He had wanted to mention their having to leave Bangkok on first entering the taxi, but then suddenly it had seemed too soon, and now the time was as right as it could ever be. 'If we're to stand a chance of putting this all behind us, we certainly won't do it while we're still in Bangkok,' he said.

'I know,' Deborah agreed blankly.

And Paul knew immediately that she hadn't fully understood. He turned to her again, clasping back her hand. 'I'm sorry to spring it on you like this, I'd have liked more time. But believe me, it's for the best – we have to leave Bangkok immediately.'

'Have to?' Deborah stared back incredulously.

'Yes.' Paul looked straight ahead now, a traffic-jam at the neck of the Dejo Road stopping the taxi from turning. 'My reaction was the same as yours initially, but then I thought about it for a while, and then I realized – after this we couldn't possibly get any enjoyment out of the holiday . . . Bangkok, the whole damn thing! It just wouldn't be the same anymore.'

Deborah thought about things for a moment, looking down at the floor. 'When did you know this?'

'Earlier today.'

She reflected quickly upon his reference to 'my reaction'. 'This obviously wasn't your idea, Paul, so. . . .'

'The man's name is Jeffrey Steel,' he interjected, exhaling audibly, not wanting her to continue. 'He's attached to the British government in some way – defence or something.'

Deborah stopped herself suddenly. Paul was right, she had been thrown initially, but purely by the suddenness of the information. 'And I suppose this Jeffrey Steel decided all this?' she asked.

'Yes – he made the arrangements for the exchange and our flight out.' Paul glanced up hesitantly, pointing a thumb towards the rear window. 'He was watching the whole thing inside the arena, and he's probably following us right now. We'll meet up with him back at our hotel.'

Deborah shook her head from side to side in disbelief. 'For God's sake, Paul, what's happening?'

I don't know.'

'But you must know something. From this Jeffrey Steel, if nobody else – surely he knows what's going on.'

'He does, Deborah, but he just won't talk about it. Please, I really don't know.' Paul looked down, and he could see that he had been gripping Deborah's hand tight in exasperation, releasing it gently now, and thinking how his reaction had been the same. In fact, he had expected no less from Deborah – perhaps would have even been disappointed at any emotional subterfuge. And now he was defending those very same stipulations which earlier had so incensed him.

Funny how quickly we justify what has to be, he mused. 'I'm sorry, it's just that I've been trying to find out exactly the same things myself, and it's a blank wall every time,' he said, looking up hopefully again.

Deborah turned away, and then so did he, adding as if by-the-way, 'You saw the diamonds inside the arena?'

'Yes,' she nodded faintly.

'Well, at least that explains that part,' he said. He became aware of a heavy silence settling between them, growing stronger with the passing minutes – that same gap. Deborah unresponsive, distant! And he knew immediately that he wouldn't be able to mention the compensation – there would be far too many possible misinterpretations. If Cullen mentioned it, he would feign outrage at the arrangement, quelling or at least redirecting Deborah's anger.

'Which one of them gave you the bruise?' He changed the subject deftly, touching Deborah's chin lightly, turning her back to face him.

'The large one,' she muttered, clearing her throat quickly.

'Was he the worst of the two?'

'There were four of them, including the chauffeur.'

He stared blankly ahead. He had never really speculated about details like that, he realized.

'The oldest one with greying hair was the worst,' she answered finally. 'His control over the others was awesome. You never knew where you stood with him.' She turned away quickly, not able to look at Paul directly, the memory too painful. *The telephone call! The long night following!* She put one hand over her eyes, cradling her forehead, a slight trembling back in her lips as she gazed distractedly at the passing shops of the Suringwose Road.

'I know, I hated that bastard too,' he commiserated, still staring straight ahead. 'He was so damn smug. On the phone, in the arena. So bloody supercilious! I'd like to have taken that precious wooden figure of his and rammed it right up his arse!'

Paul sat back deeper in his seat, letting out his breath, suddenly aware of the melodrama of his outburst, and its faint comedy. But something else too – Deborah's movement beside him; a gentle rocking, her face turned away, one hand shielding a part of it; but he could just see a trickle of moisture below the edge of her palm in the half-light – part of a beam from a passing streetlamp. He looked straight ahead again, not knowing what to say anymore. A faint rumble somewhere in the distance sounded above the traffic.

The first drops of rain hit the windscreen as oversized globules, spreading dramatically, spaced at two-second intervals; and then after a moment there was a torrent.

Paul had just sighted the Sheraton a quarter of a mile further along the road, but now it was lost in the thick mist of the downpour. 'See what you've done now?' he commented lightly. 'You started crying, and the whole world's decided to join in.'

And he saw her smile again, although he knew deep down that for a while the smiles would be infrequent, and that same gap would remain; at least until they could both come to terms with exactly what had been lost between them.

Paul glanced back to where he had previously picked out the hotel's entrance; the taxi's headlamps were now on, their glare lost in a blanket of water as the taxi edged further along the rain-swept road.

Racha Jawatsuri had operated the same stall on the Rama IV for almost twenty-five years, and had lost all his teeth after ten – a sad legacy from his constant chewing on the salt-fish that he would string in a line above the copper oil basin set at the stall's centre. However, as so many passers-by would quickly discover, this affliction had never troubled him, as he'd become accustomed to selling his wares with meaningless grunts, cries and elaborate arm movements.

In the daytime, he would set up his stall at the entrance to Lumpini Park, catching the tourist trade from the gardens, but in the evening would move further along to the slipway of the boxing stadium. He would keep close to the ticket counters and the main entrance, encroaching slightly on the thoroughfare itself so that his was one of the first stalls people would come to on exiting, and also the most convenient for the long queues that would often form on entrance.

Tonight, as with other 'crown contest' nights, trade had been brisk at the entrance, and now Jawatsuri prepared for the crowds coming out, glancing hesitantly up at the night sky and pulling his canopy further over so that it covered both his fish display and the oil basin. A constant gas flame underneath the copper basin cast some light so Jawatsuri, unlike so many other traders, did not require an electric bulb to light his wares.

The crowds milling out of the arena grew rapidly, a heavy clamour increasing with their excited conversation; taxis and samlors jostled for position in the few ranks directly outside, moving hurriedly away with curt directions, leaving behind them a fight for the vacant space: horns blaring and peeping, accompanied by emphatic words and gestures.

Karfi came out of the arena, a full head and shoulders above the bulk of the jostling crowd; trailing slightly behind

Magonde, but his attention was drawn towards Jawatsuri's small fish stall, fascinated at the sight, sound and smell of the delicate frying.

'Yai dtoh farang,' Jawatsuri mumbled in a private joke to himself at the sight of Karfi, covering his toothless grin with one hand. 'Gleu-uh-bplah!' he exclaimed, pointing to the line of fish. 'Nahk dee! Nahk dee!'

Karfi grunted back, rustling in his pocket and then holding out a few coins in the palm of his large hand.

Jawatsuri picked at the coins like a small child. 'Hah. . . . Bpaat. . . .' Then he held a few up triumphantly. 'Gow baht! Nahk dee!'

Karfi nodded solemnly.

Jawatsuri took one of the white fish from the line, feeding it through a small mangle at the end of the stall. It came out almost three times larger and paper thin, and he salted it on both sides, throwing it into the bowl of oil. It bubbled up quickly and was fried a rich golden brown in seconds, appearing more like an oversized potato crisp than a piece of fish. Jawatsuri wrapped it in a slip of white grease-proof paper, passing it across with gleeful expectancy. 'Nahk dee! Koon chawp.'

The flow out of the arena was thicker now, and Magonde had paid little attention to Karfi's movement, turning towards their car at the far side of the slip road, then quickly asking Bature, 'You noticed nothing unusual out here?'

'No.'

'That is good,' Magonde said, and looked briefly in both directions, sighing audibly. 'It is all over now, my friend. . . .' He broke off, passing the Basikasingo figure through the open window. 'There is but one step to make. From there our fight will no doubt be a more noble one – I hope you will join me in it.'

Magonde held his right hand through the window, and Bature clasped it firmly. 'You can be sure of it,' he nodded emphatically. 'As far as we might have to go.'

Magonde smiled, then turned back towards the stadium.

'Where's Karfi?'

Bature had sighted Karfi a moment before and could still make out his prominent figure at the other end of the slip road, despite the traffic and mass of people. 'Over there,' he pointed, picking out the second stall in the long line from the entrance.

Magonde could just discern the flicker of the gas flame through gaps in the crowd, and Karfi above it, dwarfing the small stall and its proprietor, his features gleaming and ghostly in the reflected light. He walked across, pushing through the bustle, addressing Karfi from a few yards behind. 'Mu dole tafi yanzi.'

'Na'am ba fahimta.' Karfi swung around, nodding eagerly, some small crumbs from a second fish at the corner of his mouth.

Then suddenly Magonde held one hand up, staring at Karfi's side. 'Jira akwai daya abu!'

'Fa nan?'

But Magonde didn't answer, intent on the copper bowl brimful with oil, another sliver of fish bubbling furiously inside.

'Gleu-uh-bplah!' Jawatsuri shouted. 'Nahk dee! Nahk dee!'

Magonde moved closer to the stall, his eyes steadfast on the same position, and he bit hard on his lip. *Sama jini!* His hands gripped tight at his sides in anguish, the image now much clearer in his mind: giant drums and belts coated in thick oil spinning slowly, and gravel, dust and glitter spilling freely down on to them, but only the glitter remaining as they came back around again. And he cursed again, *Sama jini!*

It had been in the new diamond sorting plant in Amgawi's Nuaga district. The guided tour was a well-planned public relations exercise by the mining corporations, he recalled. So beneficial! So cordial!

A test by sight and a cutting instrument had seemed appropriate and sufficient, but now a portion of the tour-director's speech began to haunt him: 'Not only is oil the most efficient means of diamond separation, but under laboratory conditions, it is also an ideal "acid" test – so many diamond substitutes nowadays reach almost optimum standards of hardness and brilliance.' There would have been time: almost forty-eight hours, he confirmed, glancing at his watch and panning back through events. *It was a possibility.* But then again for substitutes of such quality? *Surely not!* Magonde edged closer to the stall. 'I would like the use of some of your oil.'

'Ah-ry? Chahm my kow-jy,' Jawatsuri retorted.

Magonde eyed the small stall-holder curiously. 'Your oil!' he emphasized impatiently, clutching a plastic container at one side of the counter.

Jawatsuri took hold of its base defensively, waving his other arm away from him. 'Mahn kawng pohm. Bpy!'

Magonde's rage was rising rapidly, uncontrollably. He delved into his wallet, drawing out the first note to come to hand: a fifty-baht. 'There you are, you fool. In the name of Allah. *Sama Jini!* Your oil! Your oil!' He gesticulated furiously back towards the container.

Jawatsuri took the crisp note and held his hands out helplessly at each side. 'Chahn see-uh jy. My lahm bahk,' he uttered, nodding faintly; a clear indication that for fifty bahts, the black *farang* could do whatever he wished.

Magonde took a gold pen from his inside pocket, studying its base to judge its suitability in both circumference and flatness. 'Mun gani,' he mumbled to Karfi.

Turning his attention back to the plastic oil flask, he unscrewed its cap, dipping the pen inside. He took it out with a globule of oil glistening on its end, fishing in his side pocket for a few gems he had placed there from his inspection. The second largest proved the most ideal choice: just over one carat, he judged, not too large in circumference and yet heavy enough to create possible separation.

The bustle of people and traffic was still heavy in front of the stadium, but Magonde remained oddly detached, delicately setting the gem at the centre of the oil gobule. It remained suspended for a second, then separated with a

377

slight glistening trail and fell back into the palm of his hand.

Magonde's expression became taut, anguished. 'Sama jin kai!' he spat, glaring indignantly towards Karfi. He waited a moment, regaining his briefly lost composure, and placed the same gem purposefully back into the globule. But with the same result. And then he tried another smaller – then one larger.

'Sama jin kai!' he cursed again, as the last gem fell into his palm.

'Ah-ry bpen mahn?' Jawatsuri quizzed perplexedly. 'Ah-ry peet?'

'It is all right,' Magonde nodded, barely containing his anger. 'Thank you, thank you.' He turned resolutely, pushing his way back through the crowd, directing Karfi with a small arm movement. 'Mu dole tafi.'

It was almost forty yards across the front forecourt of the stadium, but Bature could sense the impending air of disaster as they approached. Magonde's countenance was dull, grim. Bature stepped out of the car, confronting them worriedly. 'What is it?'

'We have been duped,' Magonde said simply.

Bature's expression held disbelief. 'But that's not possible, you. . . .'

'It is not a matter for discussion,' Magonde cut in sharply. 'What's done is done, and time is short.'

'What can we do?'

'We must prepare.' Magonde glared back contemptuously, then paused. 'As it was to have been with our first alternative plan.'

Magonde turned away. 'It is a foul night for such business,' he commented as an afterthought, glancing towards the sky and inhaling the heavy dampness of the night air.

They got back into the car and Bature reached for the Armalite automatic rifle resting on the back seat, which he had so meticulously stripped, cleaned and greased the night before. He slammed home the base-feeding magazine, released the safety catch, and pushed two rather insignificant wads of cotton wool deep into each eardrum. 'Okay, let's do it,' he mumbled, and he stared stony-faced out of the side-window, across the Rama IV towards the palatial façade of the Dusit Thani Hotel on the far side.

Magonde directed the chauffeur.

Thirty yards away, through the thickest part of the exiting crowd, Rawsthorne had watched patiently throughout, and now he attempted furiously to hail a taxi.

As Magonde's car turned out the stadium sliproad, it had started to rain.

22

Flocks of sparrows were perched between the telegraph poles, on a line of wire trailing into the distance along the Suringwose Road. At intervals, they would quiver their feathers slightly in the heavy rain, shaking off the excess moisture, their heavy chirruping audible even above the deluge.

It was an unusual sight, and Steel watched them a moment longer before turning back to the passenger window.

'As I said, you did well,' he acknowledged, and he looked past Paul Ensor, smiling faintly at Deborah on the far side of the car, shadowed in the poor light. 'I know how much of an ordeal this must have been for you, Mrs Ensor,' he added, his expression becoming grave.

'And if this is any form of consolation – I'm truly sorry.'

'Thank you.' Deborah smiled awkwardly, turning quickly away. This all seemed so strange, she thought. So vague. Unreal. And she wanted to say something more, without knowing immediately what.

'It's okay,' Paul commented, as if consoling both of them, but he clutched Deborah's hand tighter than before.

Steel straightened up. 'Rawsthorne should be with us soon,' he said thoughtfully. And then he repeated the essence of his previous instructions, concluding. 'Cullen will be expecting you.'

Steel went back towards the main entrance and arranged for the valets to put in the last of the Ensors' luggage. The taxi was at the end of the covered turn-in, the only available space at the time, and there were small bustlings around from other departures and arrivals.

At first, the movement was vague: a distant figure among the mist, moving close fast – large, striding out boldly across the wide road, between the traffic flow; and then, suddenly, awesomely aparent.

Steel stood mesmerized, his camera bag held loose at one side. . . .

The large negro from the arena! Discovery? Time! *How?* And then automatically reaching and opening, still with the questions unanswered, the pearl grip firm in his hand. No reasoning. No time. Now! *Now!*

The sudden burst came close to his side – deafening, drowning all his senses, throwing him off balance as he eased the trigger; and for a moment he was unsure whether he'd actually fired or not, aware only of shattering glass and singing metal all round him.

It was a split-second view as he threw himself down to the concrete – the large negro, gun in hand, opening the Ensors' taxi door, stepping in. . . .

And then the arc of hammering gunfire was coming closer, swinging across, more glass exploding behind him, screams now intermingling. The bedlam rose to a crescendo, the flocks of sparrows fleeing the telegraph wires, a tumultuous fluttering filling the air above.

The arc swung across viciously, and people were running, scattering before its indiscriminate destructiveness: one of the porters, struck in the hip, fell agonizingly to the ground, a copious red blotch spreading quickly on his crisp green uniform.

Steel lay flat, his cheek pressed hard against the cool concrete, and he could just make out the bursts of red across the far side of the road. There was a split-second pause, and then the arc came quickly back, lower this time, raising cement-dust before him, and he could taste it in his mouth as it subsided: a white, dry dust, filling the air. People huddled close to the walls and floors of the lobby as if clinging to slippery rock.

The Ensors' taxi was moving away, he could see now, turning out and back along the Suringwose Road. There was a further short burst from a car on the far side, a final dying red flare; and then it too moved out quickly, trailing closely behind the taxi.

Through the wide span of the lobby and the entrance slipway, the hubbub had died down, people getting slowly to their feet, nursing injuries. Steel glanced back briefly, then ran out towards the road.

The rain hit him in a heavy torrent, taking his breath away, soaking him quickly, but he remained oblivious. He could just discern the back of the second car, the Toyota, towards the end of the Suringwose Road among a hazy proliferation of tail-lights.

The Suringwose Road was a one-way street, and Steel swung around, quickly panning the traffic streaming from behind.

He could just make out a taxi for hire in the far lane, a few hundred yards away. It was a pale grey, only its small green light gleaming through the dizzy flow. He stepped out into a more prominent position, flagging it down fervently.

The taxi cut sharply across the three lanes of traffic, horns blaring and lights flashing from behind as it pulled into the kerb.

'Bpy ny?' the driver shouted through a quickly opened window, leaning over.

Steel jumped in the back. 'There,' he gesticulated frantically. 'That car! The Rama IV! Quick – follow!' He stunted his English, aware of the driver's possible lack of vocabulary.

The taxi pulled out again, cutting sharply back, a different set of horns blaring from behind this time. '*Tahn.* You 'merican?' the driver enquired.

'No, English,' Steel said blankly, distracted by the coming

traffic-lights, changing now to orange. 'Go through! Go through! he shouted. 'Turn right – right!'

The Toyota was gone from sight for a moment as they turned, and Steel picked it up again as it pulled out from in front of a large truck in the distance. The Ensors' taxi was still directly in front, but they were both further away than before. 'Please, a bit faster – faster!' he urged impatiently.

They picked up speed slowly, swinging out to the far lane. 'Frien's of yours?' The driver swivelled half towards him.

'Not exactly.' And Steel laughed inwardly at the irony for a second – *master of the understatement!* Suddenly he was more aware of the gun gripped tight in his hand. It was shielded below the back of the front seat, he judged, although he was certain now that he had hailed the cab with it; the driver seemed not to have noticed.

'*My dee!* Bad weather,' the driver cursed, switching the wipers up another notch. Traffic was heavy, the inside lane almost jammed solid, but the outside mostly free, a mass of lights glimmering distortedly as they sped past.

A motorbike to their side pulled out suddenly and they swerved a fraction, sliding faintly with the motion. 'Ngoh kohn!'

There was a faint light flickering ahead but it was partially obscured, and then the traffic moved again and Steel was sure. 'Turn left – left!' he directed.

They were passing Lumpini Park again and a small tail-back had eased slightly ahead, so that they were only a couple of hundred yards behind as they turned into the Witayu Road.

The traffic was lighter there, although there was some caught behind a car turning left, and they switched quickly inside and then out, the tail sliding again, but righting and straightening up as they accelerated. The road was virtually clear ahead now, only three cars between them and the Toyota, spaced at wide intervals, and the driver pushed his foot hard on the floor. They built up speed slowly, Steel sinking deeper into his seat as the needle flickered hesitantly upwards. '*Doo!* I catch 'em soon now,' the driver commented enthusiastically. 'You see.'

The Toyota was looming up fast as they weaved through the sparse traffic, the back fish-tailing on the slippery road, the driver's loose sandal flapping between the accelerator and the brake pedal. '*My-cha!* Soon now,' he emphasized, half turning around.

Already Steel could make out shapes inside the car. 'Not too close,' he warned, leaning slightly forwards.

'*Dtaa*. You no wan' me to catch?' the driver quizzed surprisedly.

'No, *follow*,' Steel said emphatically, trying to differentiate. 'Follow!'

The driver looked puzzled still. 'I don' understan'. *Bah farang!*'

'Please – keep back!'

They eased off slightly. But too late.

A head turned in the back seat and for a second Steel was sure there was a glimmer of recognition, although it turned back quickly, resolutely, facing the road ahead again.

'Further back! further!' Steel stressed, and he used one hand for illustration.

They slowed, although the distance still seemed the same between them. It was sudden – expected and yet unexpected – the long barrel creeping almost insignificantly out of the side-window.

'Get back – for God's sake . . . brake!' Steel spat, now flushed with exasperation.

It meant nothing to the Thai. '*Bah farang!*' They fell back a bit more, but still dangerously close.

The head was fully out, turning, sighting. . . .

'Quick. . . .' Steel hunched tight behind the front seat.

'Yah hoo-ung. . . .'

The explosions seemed to come from all around them, the front windscreen shattering in a swirling shower of glass, then the far side-windows. A chain of bullets thudded into metal lower down, and the whole car appeared to shake with a high-pitched whistling and rending.

'Pra-jow!' the driver screamed pathetically, and then the whirlwind deluge rose upwards again, consuming him totally. There was a weak gargling as bullets ripped through the flesh of his neck and face, the back of his skull splitting outwards in a gout of blood and fluid.

The heavy hail spewed relentlessly through, taking out the back window on exiting, only the glass flanking Steel's side remaining intact.

At first, the lurching was lazy, slow; then sickeningly violent as the driver slumped away from the wheel, the rain lashing heavily in through the burst windows.

The avalanche of gunfire stopped suddenly, although Steel was momentarily unsure, his ears still singing; and then with everything suddenly much clearer, he straightened and dived forward in an instinctive motion over the front seat, trying to grip the wheel as it spiralled further away, the sudden motion throwing the driver's inert body almost flat.

They were diagonal to the oncoming traffic, he could see now, swinging ever deeper into the flow. . . . He had one hand on the wheel, struggling to turn it back, and a blur of red appeared suddenly to one side, a quick blaze of lights, and then he felt the glancing blow as the car swerved around his far side, buffeting his tail, straightening him slightly, and then he was skidding. . . .

A large bus approached, throwing up a heavy spray of muddy water from all around, announcing itself with an array of lamps and spotlights around a gleaming radiator grill, blinding, dazzling.

Steel grappled and struggled with the dead weight, pushing it further away, sitting straight now – *God in hell!* – forcing his own foot in place. . . . But the taxi was in fourth, chugging, surging forward slowly, almost stalling . . . .

There was a sudden blast of air horns, overwhelming light and sound. The bus swerved slightly, passing – a dull, ponderous form to one side, rending and tearing metal from somewhere behind, swinging the back of the taxi away. The bus continued in a straight line, as if undeterred by the impact, braking and stopping a bit further on.

Steel controlled the swaying taxi, easier now because of its sluggishness; he could see the driver getting out of the bus, but *no time now!*

He was conscious of the gun still gripped tight in one hand, and he laid it to one side, pushing the tangled body of the driver further away, fishing for the gearstick, clutching down, slamming it into second and accelerating away. . . .

The taxi picked up slowly, and Steel scanned the road ahead. It was difficult. Rain lashed hard against his face, through the broken windscreen, stinging, numbing, running down in torrents. *Jesus!* The darkness of the road, lights, colours and shapes all merged together: a murky, distorted kaleidoscope. Against his back and on the vinyl seat, he could feel the driver's blood, warm, sticky, pungent. Suddenly the rain was a welcome refreshment, washing, cleansing, the carnage swilling to the floor in small pools.

The touch of metal came suddenly, distractingly to one hand, the windscreen wipers swinging like two spastic arms betwen the dashboard and steering wheel, and he fumbled around, switching them off impatiently.

There was a familiarity about a set of tail-lights in the distance, towards the end of the road, and Steel slammed the car into third, accelerating fast then swinging again into the outside lane, changing quickly to fourth. . . .

At first, it was a small flickering, becoming gradually clearer as he closed the gap, an indication for a left turn, but still he wasn't sure if it was the Toyota. *Fucking weather!* he cursed, wiping the moisture from his face, deciding to make the turn anyway. Steel reached the intersection a few seconds behind the Toyota, turning quickly into a gap in the traffic, and he could see the lights again on the inside lane, the gap a bit closer between them, but the shape and colour still vague. Damn! The streetlamps were orange, casting incandescent, stark beams of light at regular intervals, and after the fifth he had gained considerably, the next one highlighting the shape and colour of the car ahead more clearly. . . . *Grey. Squared-off back. The outline of heads inside.* And then he was sure.

He could see the Ensors' taxi now, fifty yards or so ahead of the Toyota with another car in between. There were some traffic-lights looming ahead, and he put his foot down more, passing through on green, then easing off again, staying his distance.

Steel stayed in the inside lane and let the gap grow between them; a quick visual assessment at a good five hundred yards, and he was about to pull out again when the Ensors' taxi, and then the Toyota, pulled sharply into the inside lane. They were lost from view for a moment – five cars wide-spaced in a line directly between them – but became visible again as they turned off just past a railway crossing in the distance.

Steel accelerated towards the turning, slowing slightly for the cars in front, but picking up quickly afterwards, sighting the back of the Toyota again, concerned not to lose it in a sudden double turn. He eased off immediately, slipping back as far as he could without losing the identity of the tail-lights through the blurring rain.

The road was narrower than the last, the streetlights less frequent, and for the first time Steel was conscious of the unevenness of his own front beam; one of the headlamps was obviously out. *Damn!* he cursed. It wasn't so much the lack of visibility that troubled him – it was *such an obvious marker!* He tapped the brakes impatiently, pulling back still further to compensate.

Under the next streetlamp he could see a head turned around fully, although he wasn't sure how long it had been that way. It disappeared again in the next segment of darkness and by the time the car passed under the next light it was facing the front again.

Steel let out his breath – the darkness hit again. For a moment he felt sure he had been recognized, but as the minutes passed with no further movement, he remained in doubt.

The passing lights formed a vague, mesmerizing pattern, and for the first time Steel thought deeply about the situation in total, as if he was suddenly outside, looking in. It had been less than a week since the Cleary incident, and yet here he was racing madly through the streets of Bangkok, the passing lights and streets, as they picked up pace, seeming to represent the events in between: Wilson, the Ensors, Haskell, Sammy, Mr Tom, Pen . . . but in a vague, senseless way; lights, colours and movement all merging slowly together.

At one point he was sure he saw the barrel of the automatic extending, but just as quickly it was retracted, whether because he was too distant and couldn't be sighted easily or because of something else, he could not be sure.

They were coming into some busier streets and Steel took stock: it was probably the Phra Mane area, he judged from the surrounding landmarks. And then suddenly the pace picked up again – a quick turn through two side-streets – and Steel could see the danger area as soon as they emerged: a large roundabout looming quickly ahead, the traffic thick on each side.

The policeman at its centre was on a small rostrum, his back towards them as they entered; a starched khaki uniform, immaculate white gloves beckoning the oncoming traffic.

He turned stiffly and furiously as they trespassed on his guarded domain, one hand held high in flamboyant illustration, an accompanying shrill scream, 'Yoot!' and then again after a short, disbelieving pause, re-emphasizing with his hand as they swept across the intersection. . . . 'Yoot!'

The oncoming traffic was braking and swerving as he reached for the white holster at his hip – a gleaming pistol hoisted, fired blankly into the air. . . . But they were already swinging off sharply, the shot sounding behind them. There was another shot, more distant, insignificant.

The street was wide, but the traffic was moving slowly, choked, the start of a bottle neck ahead . . . and they turned sharply again. . . .

It was a market street this time, a yellow dragon symbol on a red billboard hanging proud above a shop at its entrance

– lights and colours blinding, dazzling; stalls crammed haphazardly on each side; people crowding, talking, selling – little space in between . . . sweeping quickly past now . . . stark bulbs flashing intermittently. . . .

A trader stepped out in the distance ahead, pushing a wooden barrow, and Steel saw the Ensors' taxi connect at one corner, throwing the man to one side and splitting the barrow, an array of wooden planks and vegetables filling the air, some of it cascading on to the Toyota behind.

Steel was closer now, measuring the distance prudently, but the movement was quick, the dark barrel extended, turning, sighting . . . and then the sudden spurt of red.

There was a singing and whining from the bonnet, a solid thudding from the front, low and tearing, the radiator spraying a sudden jet of steam into the air.

Steel turned sharply – a samlor loomed up suddenly on one side, connecting somewhere towards the back – and then they were racing off again.

It came only a few yards after the turn, and Steel saw it too late – a small klong-style bridge, bright trelliswork in red and green each side, an insignificant three-foot hump. The car hit solidly, still moving with the turn, and the driver's bloodied corpse lurched suddenly back against one arm, sticky and foul. Steel pushed it away frantically, turning hard at the wheel . . . now straightening, accelerating. . . .

The street was dark – small, industrial, run-down; and then another quick right turn. . . . Up ahead, a light flashed between the Toyota and the Ensors' taxi; once, twice . . . and then a final double flash after a few seconds. Steel concentrated fiercely, watching again for the tell-tale flickering between the two cars; but there was nothing more.

They had driven over a mile along the same road and the signs of industry were now almost non-existent; small warehouse units to one side with broad flats of waste ground interweaving. On the other side, the waste ground was continuous, a slight bush growth apparent, becoming thicker in the distance, faint sparse lights between the trees picking out a small klong village.

The two cars ahead slowed; then, without warning, the Ensors' taxi made a left turn; the Toyota continued on straight ahead.

It was a curious action, and for a moment Steel asked himself, *why?* But there was also a *decision* to be taken.

He turned off, swinging fast around, trailing the Ensors' taxi deeper into the narrow road.

The distance had increased slightly between them now, the darkness more intense. Steel pressed on a bit harder, fighting to pick up the dim form again through the haze of driving rain.

But when a shape did finally become apparent to him, a distant and ghostly glimmer in his lop-sided beam, it was the taxi turning broadside, braking, reversing slightly, and then finally stopping.

There was a warehouse wall on one side, a steep canal bank on the other; not enough room either side. Again, *why?* . . .

Steel's reaction was impulsive, but prompted by a faint flickering of lights from behind – an ominous reflection in the small frame of the rear-view mirror, at first distant, but then turning fully . . . *the Toyota again!* Twin beams straightening, advancing slowly, dazzling . . . all-encompassing. . . .

Suddenly everything was much clearer.

The klong was dark and wide at the bottom of the deep bank, sparse clusters of trees bordering it at intervals. On the other side, the warehouse wall stretched a full hundred feet, a small gap apparent just beyond the Ensors' taxi.

Steel had already passed a similar gap at its beginning, coasting gradually forwards, measuring his options. The lights behind advanced purposefully, the surrounding shadows becoming gradually more prominent.

It was too late now to head for the warehouse gap, Steel realized and the blank wall itself presented nothing more than a ricochet trap. . . . *No*. It had to be the klong.

The banks would be fairly steep, he judged, picking out the faint reflections of light on the water down below – the

389

car broadside, blocking, shielding – if necessary, an escape down the bank, through the trees; the heavy darkness would make a good cover. Steel swung the car sharply over towards the klong's banks, coming as close as possible to the edge; then turned around, keeping the far side flanking the road, almost directly parallel to the klong itself.

The deafening explosions came before he had stopped fully, and he lay prone, clutching his gun from the seat, swinging the side-door open quickly and rolling through the gap. . . . The ground below was muddy and warm with the rain, the nearside tyres pulled a good two yards off the asphalt of the road. Steel hunched close to the side of the car, his cheek pressed hard against the cool metal, feeling his breath pumping frantically, then gradually subsiding, easing. . . .

Another chain of fire came rapidly after the first, only a split second gap in between, and there were sporadic single shots from behind the Ensors' taxi now. Steel gritted his teeth against the hammering of metal on the far side, a few of the shells spreading out in a fan, spewing up mud along the rim of the klong's bank.

The lights of the Toyota beamed across for a moment, then turned away, the sleek expanse of its side now facing him. It was a curious precaution, Steel thought – his having a gun could only be pure supposition on their part. But then he could see that it was the gunman's side window, the logistics of such positioning now obvious.

Shells buffeted through the burst windows just above him, then, swinging gradually across, glanced off the bonnet and tore through the trees behind . . . coming back slowly, methodically, lower this time, kicking up asphalt underneath the car – ricochets burying themselves deep into the chassis.

The explosions stopped suddenly, a last vestige echoing off the blank wall of the warehouse across the far side. Everything settled for a moment, the still sounds of the night returning – crickets and geckoes along the banks of the klong; a faint, lost voice trailing across the water from the village in the distance.

Their three cars had formed a neat triangle. Steel assessed the situation in the lull. Fifty yards past the Ensors' taxi, picked out by the beam of the Toyota, the road changed into a dirt track, the rain frothing it up to a thick mire. In the other direction, the main road was over half a mile away and only pin-pointed by the beams of passing cars, Steel noted, as he followed the path of another; the third so far that he had been aware of.

Another short burst came without warning and Steel fired off a token shot immediately afterwards, raising his head a fraction, watching a splay of metal appear near the front of the Toyota and then ducking down quickly again.

A clicking sound came from the far side – car-doors closing again, metal on metal – and then a faint shuffling. It stopped abruptly . . . no movement, no sound, nothing – the surrounding darkness becoming an awesome companion, as if enveloping all present. A blank silence.

The rich voice broke through it harshly.

'Please . . . this will serve none of us any purpose.' There was a short pause; a stark emphasis as the overtones died among their own echoes. 'You hold the key to something I desire strongly,' the voice continued, slightly louder now, as if addressing a wider audience. 'You have crossed me once. Now I have restored the *status quo* and the same choice is offered you. Except, of course, that this time *your* life, too, is part of the bargain.' Magonde's voice rose, addressing the Ensors as well as Steel. 'It may be that only one of you has what I want; the others are worthless to me. It is not necessary for you *all* to be subject to retribution for the sake of *one*.' There was a laugh. 'Of course, you are hopelessly outnumbered, and your fire-power is far inferior – there is no possibility of your escaping – or rescuing your friends.'

It was the voice of the well-versed military strategist, Steel reflected – *psyching the enemy!* He didn't answer.

Across the street, huddled against the gunfire and rain on the far side of the second taxi, Paul Ensor also listened attentively, for already he considered that Magonde was endorsing a view he had expressed to Deborah during the chase.

'What did I tell you,' he remarked quietly, looking away as Karfi swung round on them, his dark countenance gleaming and ominous. They had already ascertained that the giant negro spoke no English. Sporadic questions and commands while in the taxi, yes. But no fluency and certainly no coherence.

'What I am proposing is some form of co-operation,' the rich voice boomed.

Again there was no answer, the silence returning – thick, enveloping.

'We're worthless in all this,' Paul whispered vehemently as Karfi turned away, attentive again to the sounds and activity of the street. 'This Jeffrey Steel has what they want, and when that's passed on – if what he's taken so much time to make clear to me is correct – we'll be killed!'

Deborah shook her head dreamily, hiding again in her tears. 'I don't know, I don't know,' she said, now totally confused.

Karfi started to swing around again, but a voice from the far side distracted him.

'What do you have in mind?'

'We have discovered your fraud.' A bland statement. 'Obviously you have the real diamonds?'

'Yes!' There was no point denying it now, Steel realized – he would be disbelieved.

'I find your involvement in this quite intriguing,' Magonde remarked.

'It's not important.'

'Was it Vansen . . . perhaps the CSO itself?'

A blank silence.

'Yes, yes . . .' Magonde surmised of his own comments. 'That would be it . . . but as you say, it's not important.' He paused. 'There is only one course of action that I could possibly offer. The Ensors will remain hostage until the return of the real diamonds.'

'No, no – I couldn't agree to that. They're not a party to this in any way.'

'What would you suggest?'

'Myself as hostage – a transfer in a mutually agreeable location – as before.'

The cynical laugh returned. 'Your worth in such a transfer is questionable. At least I know that the Ensors can be used quite effectively in a bargaining situation. And as for the strength and reliability of such an agreement – I do believe, if I'm not mistaken, that has been tested quite admirably in the exchange just passed.' The laugh became almost mocking, ridiculing. 'It seems that you still do not fully understand the position. Perhaps a further demonstration would be in order. . . .'

There was a few seconds' silence, and then the hammering gunfire rang out again.

Steel braced himself tighter against the side of the car, trying to shut himself off from the sound and the cataclysm of destruction all around – the smell of cordite strong in the air as it subsided, repetitive echoes dying, silence returning gradually. . . .

'That is purely a reminder,' Magonde said forcefully. 'This is not a bargaining table – if necessary, I can gain what I wish by force. I am merely providing those present with the opportunity of settling this in a more amicable manner. The final terms will be mine.'

Steel remained prone. There was something nagging at the back of his mind concerning the articles on Magonde; a reflection on his main studies as a doctor and a key note from an SIS file on the activities of the ex-Ghanaian president, Dr Kwame Nkrumah, relating to the same: Christ College, Oxford – yes! That explained the accent, but there were other details; a daunting significance, vague! And slipping further away now. . . . *Damn!* 'Okay, you've made your point,' he answered finally. 'What. . . .'

'Gut ah-ry keun?' The Ensors' taxi-driver cut in suddenly at the sound of renewed discourse. 'Nee bpen bah. . . .' His voice stopped abruptly as the base of Karfi's Mauser butt crashed heavily into the back of his neck.

Paul Ensor watched the driver slump clumsily to the ground, a copious red trickle appearing below his hairline. 'Jesus. . . .' he muttered under his breath, clutching Deborah tight in one arm, comforting, consoling her. 'The bastard's mad!' And he met Karfi's furious gaze for a second, the conversation across the road resuming as the movement faded, distracting them back.

'I have stated my terms quite clearly,' Magonde re-iterated.

And Paul Ensor knew immediately, as he had done during Magonde's opening gambit, that the negotiations would amount to nothing – everything was falling apart; at best, they would be hostage again. *At the worst?* . . . 'Deborah, we've got to do something,' he spluttered frantically, suddenly surprised at the ease of the words.

Deborah looked up dolefully, her hair lank with the rain. 'What can we do?'

The tone revealed an innocent hopelessness, but in another way it created a new determination in Paul. Now, stroking her cheek softly, he was more aware of the frailty that had always been a part of her femininity, now more open, vulnerable. She had been through enough, he thought. . . . 'I don't know,' he said, considering her question for the first time. 'But something . . . just something.' And he turned away, controlling his emotions, not wanting them to show. *We can't both appear weak; not at this moment of all moments!*

The conversation across the street continued, although to Paul it formed only a dull background. . . .

He was aware of Steel remarking, 'There doesn't seem to be much room for negotiation,' at the end of a long and furious exchange; an anxious reminder that things were going the same way. . . .

The gap between the warehouses wasn't far behind, he noted, swinging around quickly. If only he could distract the large negro for a moment, they could make it . . . *Distract!* *But how?*

394

The gun was the main thing! he reminded himself – if only he could dislodge it from the negro's grip for a second. He studied Karfi's oversized hand, the giant frame crouched, taut and expectant. In the normal course of events, it would be impossible, he surmised, but then at some time the magazine would require re-loading, and at that moment his grip would be lighter, more lax – and then and *only* then would there be a chance. He started taking stock of shots fired.

On the far side the minutes passed slowly for Steel. Further conversation with Magonde seemed almost wasteful, futile; yet whatever other options remained appeared equally hopeless. He braced himself hard as the sporadic fire resumed, interspersed with some single shots from behind the Ensors' taxi. At one point he raised himself up, firing back a token shot, but after that he sat back, conscious of needing to reserve as much of his fire as possible. For a while he seemed to lose track of time and a sense of tangible purpose, and so when the movement came, it took a moment for everything to become totally clear; a faint scuffling from behind the Ensors' taxi, the shadow of an arm, some other vague movements, and then the skittering of a gun on the wet tarmac. It was directly underneath the car, Steel could judge, the only object to show clearly, glinting faintly among the surrounding darkness and shadows. And then he could see Deborah Ensor moving away on the far side, towards a gap between the warehouses behind.

Karfi was down on his belly quickly, scrambling – his trilby falling forgotten to one side. He got a few fingers curled around a part of the gun, hauling it back sharply.

Bature heard the movement late, swinging an arc of hammering fire gradually around. . . . But as he raised his arm above the bonnet, Steel had already sensed the action, firing off two shots in quick succession, pinning him back down again.

The air was thick with rain and mist and Paul Ensor found it difficult to breathe, his clothes wet and clinging, his legs moving slowly, stunted with the saturated weight, but gaining on Deborah now as she headed towards the gap. . . .

Karfi slammed the half-full magazine into the gun as it was. There were cartridges there, he knew – he had already started re-loading when Ensor had knocked it from his grip – but how many? It didn't matter, the spring would align them to the chamber.

The gap was looming up fast, fifteen yards, ten . . . and Paul could see clearly into it now, the shapes and shadows gradually taking form from out of the depth of its darkness. . . . And he knew that soon . . . soon!

At first, the single explosion seemed insignificant among the furore, somehow lost, dissociated; and then there was a second, and he saw Deborah stumbling slightly and still it had no meaning, coming up alongside, clutching her weight as she staggered, feeling her grow limp in his arms.

'God, no,' he breathed.

Deborah looked up faintly, pathetically – wanting to say something, but the wave of confusion continued as it had done so strongly, so relentlessly in the long hours past, robbing her of words.

There was a weak gargling deep in her throat, a small trickle of red appearing suddenly at the corner of her mouth.

'Please . . . Deborah,' Paul whispered; then louder, his voice echoing in the narrow street, shaking her limp form desperately. 'Please! . . .'

As if defying him, her body slid down. He was unable to grip on the damp slickness of her clothing, her blood flowing in ever-darkening pools with the torrential rain. Even the warmth slipping away, he thought – and now he wanted it to stay a moment longer. . . .

To Steel the whole thing appeared like some ghostly scenario being played in slow motion through the damp and misty darkness. Deborah's body was now almost lying flat at Paul Ensor's feet. But he still stood there, and Steel could clearly see that Karfi was about to fire yet again.

'Go!' Steel shouted, lifting himself up slightly. 'For God's sake, get away!' And then the automatic fire returned quickly, pinning him back down again.

For a moment Paul Ensor remained frozen, as if in stunned acceptance of what was impending. But then the silence was broken abruptly by a dull click from Karfi's gun; then another. And he was already turning, striding out once again, the dark gap between the two warehouses becoming ever closer.

Steel saw each of the movements, but they were still vague: Paul Ensor merging quickly with the depth of the shadows on the far side, and Karfi re-loading hastily from his side pocket and taking pursuit, disappearing through the same gap and only seconds behind.

After a moment there were two single shots, echoing blankly from the heart of the warehouse complex.

In the moments following, Steel tried to reconcile Ensor's actions in his own mind: perhaps he had pushed him too hard prior to the exchange, presented him with a set of ever diminishing options, of which this was one? But then again, he thought, that had been as much a reaction to Ensor's increasing belligerence as anything else. Under the circumstances, Paul Ensor had earned a right to it, but it was unproductive, so awkward to deal with, and in the end he had countered with coldness and efficiency – the safest possible ploy. Or so he had thought. And now Deborah, and perhaps Paul Ensor as well, were dead. *Was that the price*?

At times he could see the two sides of his own character so clearly – and it was almost the very same two identities that he considered separated his work from his home life: coldness, efficiency and infallibility representing his work; warmth, understanding and fallibility the moments away, or at least those parts that he could fully separate from his work. But at other times the characters merged, becoming indiscernible from each other, and it was then that the conflict would begin! It was important, Steel had learnt, to keep the two apart: how could any semblance of normality co-exist with this madness? He looked out again towards Deborah Ensor's body across the far side of the road.

Behind Magonde's car it had been quiet for a while, bar the low murmur of conversation; but then the hammering gunfire resumed quite suddenly. Steel tried to get a glimpse of Deborah Ensor: her body was straggled at an awkward angle, and it was difficult to distinguish it from the surrounding shadows. At one point he felt sure he saw it move, but as he strained his eyes closer through the rain and mist, there was nothing more. And then he quickly realized that the reflected glow of Magonde's headlamps on the far warehouse wall tended to distort shapes, seeming almost, at times, to animate them.

Steel leant back again. He was unsure of exactly how long the burst of automatic fire had lasted, but now he became aware of a certain irregularity, growing stronger as the pounding of bullets continued – *the intonation!* Previously they had sprayed up and down the length of the car, some passing over the top and to the sides, the tones fluctuating with the varying thicknesses and angles, but now? There was a certain consistency, Steel mused; a pinpoint emerging as he listened harder. . . . They were concentrated towards the back. . . . *Why?*

It was an old car – the metal couldn't easily be penetrated by a single shot. . . . But a succession in one position?

The full realization swept suddenly forward like a wave. . . . *Jesus! the tank!*

Steel leapt forwards in one frantic motion and single shots started to kick up the mud around his feet, the edge of the ridge now only a few feet away.

The explosion came as he was at the apex of the muddy bank, tumultuous clouds of red flames billowing upwards and to each side. A wall of heat thrust suddenly outwards, and Steel could feel it against his back, searing, scorching, an accompanying rush of air throwing him still further forwards. And then there was darkness again, the muddy bank of the klong wet and cool, accentuating the contrast, quickly quelling the pain as he slipped deeper below the rim, grappling and sliding among the sparse brush. . . .

The gunfire stopped abruptly.

Further below, the darkness was deeper, more ominous, Steel could now see. Taller trees and thick foliage bordered the klong; the garish red flames were a stark background, lighting up a wide expanse of the rim, but only a few yards down into the bank itself.

Seconds later the vividness of the flames had died a fraction, thick clouds of black smoke now trailing upwards, and the heavy roar had diminished. Rapid, urgent footsteps were just audible from beyond.

There was a faint shuffling as they came to rest. 'This is a wasteful exercise – totally unnecessary,' a voice remarked into the darkness.

Magonde's voice again! Steel cursed, glancing back fleetingly. Two figures stood on the rim, the flaring backlight turning them into ghostly, ominous silhouettes.

'You cannot escape,' the voice added. 'Please . . . we are both intelligent men.'

Steel scrambled a bit deeper down the bank, stopping for a moment behind a small bamboo thicket, catching his breath, a near silence slowly enveloping him, the calls of crickets and geckoes much weaker in the aftermath of the explosion and only a faint crackle now sounding from the plume of flames on the ridge. All reasoning had gone, Steel thought; discussion would have no purpose.

'Cigaba wuta!'

The harsh command held as little meaning to Steel as the faint click following, but the hail of bullets ripping through the foliage above was vicious, all-encompassing – a tearing, cataclysmic trail sweeping across, fast, irrepressible. The smaller limbs of bamboo and eucalyptus snapped like so many matchsticks, the staccato flares lighting up the front line of brush.

Steel leapt desperately forwards, but the mud was thick, clinging in heavy lumps to his clothes, holding him back, the denser brush almost impenetrable. A steep shelf loomed suddenly out of the darkness, and he tried to grip on to the surrounding shrubs, but too late – the thin branches snapped easily as he slipped suddenly sideways, floundering, stumbling, a sheer black sheet before his eyes.

And then he was in the water, its depths quickly enveloping him . . . and he could taste it in his mouth – salty, putrid; inhaled in that one burst of surprise, a nauseating slime slid deep into his throat, the pit of his stomach retching involuntarily. And then he was fighting back, emerging slowly, spitting out the sour bile, the air a sudden relief.

The chain of bullets came back lower, picking up mud at the edge of the klong and Steel thrust frantically forwards, the water high on his legs as he straightened.

Across the far side of the klong, he could just make out some small canoes, partly shielded by the shadows of some surrounding wooden ramparts. They were about eighty yards or so away, Steel judged, and he started making his way across, keeping low in the water, the automatic fire sinking further behind him, most of it concentrated near the edge of the bank.

For a moment the gunfire stopped, and just over halfway into the channel Steel submerged, swimming the rest of the distance underwater, sensing his way purely by instinct, the thick algae and mud being almost totally opaque. He knew that they had lost him among the deeper shadows at that point, and when he came up again, he was partly concealed by one of the smaller ramparts.

Steel let his breath ease back slowly, but kept a watchful eye on the two figures on the rim as he started working his way between the boats, finally selecting one by a criterion of both easy access and the power of its motor. He untied its rope and edged it out slowly, swimming alongside in the water on its far side. He planned to push it as far out as possible before climbing in and starting the motor, both of which would quickly pinpoint his position.

A silence settled slowly as he eased his way still further out: the gentle lapping of the water, the sounds of crickets and geckoes along the canal bank now seemed much more pronounced.

There was an ominous click and a quick latching-back, and Steel knew even before the first renewed burst of gunfire that they had picked him out. He swung up into the boat and started the engine on the second pull of its ignition cord, and was just starting to edge away as the splatter of white foam chased it in an arc, becoming lost among the boat's own trail of propeller churnings.

Steel kept low as he glanced back. Still a few bullets chased his path, but he could quickly see that the two figures had given up the ghost, running back towards their car. At first he had a good lead, but it seemed only moments later that the car was almost alongside, powering its way along the dust road bordering the klong. He could see its lights flickering intermittently through the sparse trees and another vicious chain of fire began splattering the water up to each side and behind.

For a while he managed to avoid the hail of bullets, but then he could see that the arc had moved directly ahead of him, swinging ever closer.

At the last moment he tried to turn away, but the bullets ripped right through the centre of the boat, and then there was a sudden explosion of red, a red that turned gradually to black, merging with the darkness of the water below; and a warmth started rising slowly through his body. It felt somehow comforting, soothing, like the soft, heavy blankets he remembered from his childhood. And when it reached his eyes, he found he could no longer see.

Part Seven

The Triangle

23

Mikeka Dinsengwayo was tired and jaded. The last leg of the flight from Hong Kong had been particularly turbulent, the rain heavy on landing, though easing slightly as he'd made his way by taxi from Don Muang to the Narao.

Initially, he had thought the desk clerk's attitude unusual when he had asked about Jeffrey Steel. The clerk had studied his business card without troubling to look in the register; then had disappeared twice with mild perplexity, finally saying 'the manager, Mr Chareompond will assist you, sir.'

And now Dinsengwayo sat in the comparative peace of Chareompond's office, the deep chair offering welcome relaxation.

Chareompond studied the business card with a similar air of perplexity. He wished to establish Dinsengwayo's status first. 'You are a consultant of this . . . Central Selling Organization?' he enquired, looking up briefly.

'Yes.' Dinsengwayo responded non-committally, outwardly conscious of the information on the card, identifying him as an accredited representative of the CSO with the addresses of the London and Johannesburg offices printed at each side, like supportive pillars for his name just above.

'And you say that Jeffrey Steel contacted you for some form of verification?'

'Not exactly – instructions were received from London by my employer in Johannesburg,' Dinsengwayo amended courteously. 'No doubt Mr Steel made some previous contact with London.'

'And it concerns diamonds?' asked Chareompond, studying the business card curiously once again.

405

Dinsengwayo leant forward, appearing suddenly uneasy. Already he had provided more information than he considered expedient – most certainly in regard to what had initially appeared a simple exercise; and in particular to a hotel manager who, as yet, had not stated his interest in such affairs. 'Tell me, Mr Chareompond – why do you ask this? Such a procedure is most irregular for a normal visitor, like myself, enquiring about one of your guests – is it not?'

Chareompond laid down Dinsengwayo's business card resolutely, folding his hands above it on the desk-top. 'Forgive me, Mr Dinsengwayo,' he said, exhaling as though in mild relief. 'I think I should start by saying that Jeffrey Steel is a good friend of mine, but I am not in any way involved in his business affairs. . . . I have some knowledge of them, yes,' he admitted, opening his hands outward a fraction. 'But that is all I could possibly lay claim to.'

It was Dinsengwayo now who appeared perplexed. 'I was informed that Mr Steel was staying at your hotel. . . . Is that not the case?'

'Yes, yes, Mr Steel is staying here,' Chareompond agreed. 'But I'm afraid that's not the problem at hand at the moment.' The call from Jhiang had come through less than half an hour earlier and he had not, as yet, even fully assimilated the information – let alone considered any deeper implications. 'I should correct that information slightly, Mr Dinsengwayo, by adding that Mr Steel is registered here, but that unfortunately his current whereabouts are something of a mystery.'

Dinsengwayo's frown deepened.

'Is there an explanation for this . . . disappearance?'

'From what I know of Mr Steel's activities over the past few days, there are a number of options.' Chareompond avoided the intensity of Dinsengwayo's gaze, standing up and walking casually towards the far window. A set of wide lace curtains were drawn across and sporadic car lights filtered distortedly through. Chareompond kept his back to Dinsengwayo, raising his voice slightly to compensate.

'However, from the call I recently received there appears to be one particularly strong possibility. . . .' Chareompond related the events passed him by Jhiang – the return of the Ensors' taxi from the stadium, and the horrendous 'shoot-out' at the Sheraton's front entrance. . . . 'Following which both the Ensors and Mr Steel drove away and have not returned since.'

Chareompond turned back towards Dinsengwayo. Drawing his breath, he continued, explaining the Ensors' significance, the original kidnapping and final exchange. 'I must apologize again, Mr Dinsengwayo – and please, this is no reflection on your race or colour – but from the very first descriptions provided by the Sheraton desk clerks, the Ensors' abductors were described as negroes, and one of them quite large, I believe. I hope that you might now understand my initial hesitation regarding your enquiry. I'm sorry if I offended you in any manner.'

'No, no – I understand,' Dinsengwayo offered, although his frown had remained constant throughout. It tallied with Vansen's initial surmise and a later interim report from the security networks, he reflected: 'Black Africans – probably communist-backed', although the latter was still a matter of supposition.

'Obviously you have no names?'

'No.'

'Or perhaps a car-licence number?'

'No, I'm afraid not,' Chareompond sighed, resuming his seat. 'Apparently, it was all much too fast and very dark at the time. Unfortunately, apart from the descriptions I've given you, there isn't really any information.'

Dinsengwayo reflected quickly on Chareompond's reference to the 'exchange'. 'As you said before, Mr Chareompond, to your knowledge Mr Steel substituted fake gems and the exchange was made with these. And as for the real diamonds – do you know of their present whereabouts?'

'I can only repeat that I am not deeply involved in Mr Steel's business affairs,' Chareompond hedged cautiously. He now trusted Dinsengwayo, but there had been no mention of such matters by Steel, and so any initiative on his part would be far too presumptuous, especially concerning an affair of such magnitude. 'However, I do understand that Mr Steel has them deposited safely somewhere. I'm afraid it seems we can only wait for his return to gain such information,' Chareompond concluded, smiling politely. 'I wish I could be of more asistance. However, the police should still be at the Sheraton. You may be able to pick up some information there that would give you a small clue.'

'Thank you,' Dinsengwayo said, trying at the same time to picture what information there could be. *What if Jeffrey Steel didn't reappear?* He pushed the thought away. 'If you know this. . . . is it Mr Chung? I'd be pleased if you would inform him that I *will* be calling.'

'Mr Jhiang,' Chareompond corrected amiably. 'I'd be happy to.'

Dinsengwayo recapped on some of the events Chareompond had detailed in their short conversation, concluding: '. . . And I would be obliged if you could notify me the moment Mr Steel returns, or if there is any other information.' He quickly realized the obviousness of the request, and broke off lamely . . . . 'I understand you have a room available for me here.'

'Yes, of course,' Chareompond answered to both questions. He hailed a valet through the intercom.

It was a comfortable room on the third floor and Dinsengwayo showered and changed his clothes. He considered putting a call through to Johannesburg, but decided finally to wait. Within forty minutes, he had completed and made his way by taxi the half-mile to the Sheraton.

Chareompond was right, he concluded, after some brief opening enquiries – there were some useful clues: according to eye-witnesses there had been three men in the car on the far side of the road, and one large negro who had made his way across to the Ensors' taxi during the affray. 'Four bystanders were injured by gunfire, one seriously, and another seven suffered superficial wounds from flying glass,' Lieutenant Dwaonong of the Bangkok Central Police

Department added, after some initial hedging. When Dinsengwayo had presented his card, mentioned Chareompond, and referred to 'international investigations', Dwaonong relaxed.

However, it was the mass of spent cartridges littering the hotel's front entrance and slip-road, that Dinsengwayo found most intriguing: 5.56mm – *identical to those found in the corridors of the Consortium vault.*

'You may take one if you wish,' Lieutenant Dwaonong offered. 'We have more than enough for our own analyses.'

Dinsengwayo accepted, and took a few more minutes to study the devastation before returning once again to the Narao. On the way, he examined the small cartridge more closely. Almost in the same fashion as in 'fingerprinting', he remembered, the faint grooves in the sides of the metal could be matched against those found in the vault.

With the same thought in mind, he put through the call he had previously contemplated on his arrival. This time, though, he had some tangible information.

But there was no answer.

It was 4:20 p.m. in Johannesburg, he calculated, quickly running through the time-differences – Vansen would probably be playing the last few holes at Kyalami golf-course. . . . Damn! he cursed, slamming the phone back down. He knew it would be vital to contact Vansen as soon as possible. Each hour would go against them now.

At first the darkness was total: black, opaque. Then the colours started drawing away from it, radiating outwards in blurred segments – mauve and then red, a subtle haziness in rainbow hues in the foreground, masking, distorting, the colours fading gradually in towards the base; and then suddenly, from behind, a stronger light – blinding, dazzling, coming forwards now, ever faster . . . breaking through the haze, obliterating all else – pure and bright white in one solid, enveloping blanket, separating slowly into three strips as it descended . . . shapes gradually taking form, the edges becoming sharp, harsh.

The lights were coming from above, Steel became aware, as the wave of consciousness swept further through: three fluorescent strip-lights on a grey cement ceiling.

Sounds came slightly afterwards, a faint shuffling from one side, but somehow surreal, distorted – like the crinkling of dry paper.

'Ah, it seems we have a good patient,' a satisfied voice sounded, a dark countenance in the corner of his vision. He could just make out, tilting his head slightly, *Magonde!* . . . looming over slowly, ominously, blocking out a large portion of the light.

'I am so pleased,' Magonde gloated with an ever-widening smile. 'How are we feeling now, Mr Steel?'

Steel became aware slowly. He remembered vaguely that he had awoken at some time earlier in the night, and Magonde had started his questioning then – his attitudes ranging from sympathy, through impatience, to at one time a complete loss of control – Steel remembered only a short, leather-thonged stick raised high above his face. The first question had been the diamonds' whereabouts, and at length Steel had answered that they were in a secure deposit and could be released only to him personally. It was the only factor that ensured his indispensability.

For a while the use of his own name had plagued his thoughts – there had been no identification of him earlier, he was sure; then he recalled the question of the 'inside' connection, and there was also a possibility of the large negro gaining the information while in the Ensors' taxi. Whatever the case, the extent of the information could pin-point its source; Steel had tried as much as possible to draw Magonde out, but to no avail. The memory of the Ensors and the large negro had brought up the question of Paul Ensor's welfare in his own mind, but Magonde had declined to comment, as if slyly reminding him that such information was reciprocal. The large negro and the one from the photograph were towards the side of the room, he could see, and he had tried to make out other objects in the room. But through it all his grip on consciousness had been weak. Movements and words occurred through a vague haze and he was aware only that he couldn't move, the upper half of his body being almost totally numb. Magonde had at all times referred to his two colleagues by their tribal names, but now he seemed more preoccupied with explaining the intricacies of his own situation.

'The names of my two colleagues will mean nothing to you – they are merely "brotherhood" names,' he emphasized. 'You see, once we are stripped of our "Westernization", we lose our identity in your world, we become dark, shadowy. But as for my own identity. . . . That, I'm afraid, is a completely different matter. Even a reasonably well-read man of the street would recognize me. As for you, Mr Steel, if I am correct in my supposition, not only would you most certainly recognize me, but you may also be in a position to attach various significances – significances, I might add, that would not only be awkward, but also, perhaps, highly dangerous.' Magonde lifted his head slightly. 'So now I hope you can see the dilemma of my situation. In a sense I am torn between two objectives.'

Steel was faintly detached. He could now move slightly, and could just make out a bit more of the side-wall: the slim negro to one side carried a rifle . . . the shape of the stock and magazine . . . Armalite AR-18. A fuller picture emerged: the shells from the vault siege, *the same calibre!*

'Am I to forego one for the other?' Magonde mused, moving to one side. 'Now let me see . . . the diamonds are a means to an end, and in serving that end, my identity must surely at some time become known. So, in that respect, we have no *ultimate* dangers.' Magonde seemed suddenly caught up in his own dramatics. 'As you look at me and talk to me now, Mr Steel, the "security forces", or whatever names you wish to attach to them, may have already discovered my involvement.'

Steel was aware that he couldn't move his arms or his legs, and now he struggled to look further down, but at that moment Magonde came in close, clutching tight under his chin with one hand.

411

'. . . But now, Mr Steel, we have the question of *your* identity.' Magonde glared faintly. 'Oh yes, we have a number of obvious assumptions: an agent for the CSO or Consortium, part of a "special security force" perhaps; or even more recognizable agencies: the CIA, MI6, SDECE. But you see, Mr Steel, in a way that too is unimportant, and not because you probably wouldn't answer me – or at least put me to great trouble to draw an answer from you – but because once the *sides* are established, the names mean very much the same thing.' Magonde released his grip and turned away. 'Black, white; good, evil; strong, weak; left, right. Once the basic beliefs have been clearly defined, it's very easy to categorize. It's very easy to follow the leader. If they are shouting loud enough and all saying the same thing, you can even do it blindfold – the *shout* will drown out everything else.'

The images flashed back through Steel's mind – Cleary, Wilson, Ugbaja's attack on him, Deborah Ensor by the klong the night before – and suddenly he felt a new hatred for Magonde well up inside. He looked down. The white bands fell into his vision first, cut thick and rough in cotton and pinning each hand down tight at the wrist, nailed hard each side on to the rough wood beneath. It was a work-bench, Steel could see clearly now; before he had only been able to view a part of it to one side, and the white sheet at his neck spread almost down to his upper thigh. But also at that point he could see something else – a clumsy grouping of four thin wires trailing out from one leg like cat's whiskers, and another deeper beyond, coming out from a point to-wards the ball-joint of the same ankle.

'What you should ask yourself, Mr Steel, is if you are a part of the South African security establishment, why have the implications been distorted in order to gain outside involvement? If you are not, ask the same question, but from the *outside* viewpoint.'

Steel tried not to let his surprise show; an indication either way could be an instant betrayal, but then he couldn't help thinking of his own suspicions during his meeting with

Ostermeir.

Magonde walked to the far side of the room and talked with Bature for a while; when he returned he asked again about the diamonds' whereabouts. Steel had considered that, in essence at least, Magonde had accepted his earlier answer, but now he realized that the lapses in time were purely a psychological ploy; the same questions, the same game to wear him down slowly.

'Of course, there is a more obvious answer – one which we're both aware of,' Steel said at length, knowing that Magonde would pick up on the inference. 'My value to you at present is dependent purely and simply on the information you require. Once we've crossed that hurdle. . . .'

'Once we've crossed it, Mr Steel, I will have the diamonds. And you have only my word that revenge, on you at least, does not interest me. You will be able to recover from your wounds. You have been badly hurt, and it might be fatal for you to suffer further injury. You were very lucky in many respects,' Magonde added. 'The tank in the boat was a small one, but nevertheless it exploded in quite a cruel and vicious manner. The shrapnel was embedded deeply here, in your upper thigh, and some more towards your ankle on the other leg.' Magonde pointed delicately with one hand. 'Some recent injuries could also have proved rather awkward, if they had re-opened. Luckily they didn't so I have merely cleaned them and renewed the bandages.' For a moment Steel was conscious of Magonde staring intently, but Steel turned away to one side, and after a while Magonde resumed, as though suddenly deciding to let the point pass. 'At first I was rather concerned – if concern is an appropriate word in this instance. I feared that the water of the klong would be that of a normal canal – in most cases, still and stagnant. If so, there would probably have been serious infection. But the water appeared to have a definite saltiness, and I can only assume that it is in some way refreshed by the tides.'

Steel looked on curiously. There were almost three sides of Magonde becoming apparent: at first forceful, direct, at other times paranoid, almost megalomaniacal, and now calm, understanding, showing a pride in his work – though still a certain *vanity*. It seemed that they were closely entwined, counterbalancing each other. Perhaps the balances could be used *against* each other – a reversal of psychological pressures.

Magonde leant further over, now with an expression of mock gravity. 'Unfortunately, Mr Steel, I must explore the other possibilities of that situation.' Magonde pointed to the main cluster of needles. 'The *Nei-Ching*, or acupuncture as you may know it better, has been used for years as a cure for ailments in Eastern lands. In this case, I have used it purely for anaesthetic purposes, but the principles are much the same. A simple series of needles positioned in strategic nerves. There is another, shorter needle in the side of your neck,' he gestured, 'which you can probably neither see nor feel. You should feel numb on the right-hand side of your body, and there should be very little feeling below your waist . . . am I correct?'

Steel nodded blankly, the same thoughts revolving slowly. A trait shown in Magonde's earlier impromptu loss of control was now returning in an unnecessary display of his own medical prowess . . . *Vanity!* If only he could play it up to advantage. *But how?*

'. . . Without the needles you would feel excruciating pain. Your wound is still hopelessly raw and there was no morphine or any other form of analgesic medicine administered.'

Vanity. . . . Before, the conversation had been guarded, Steel mused, but now Magonde had hinted at his own identity, and so in that region at least, there could be open battle.

'You do understand the implications, Mr Steel . . . I hope I have prepared you somewhat,' Magonde added, plucking out the first few needles.

Magonde's demeanour was almost apologetic, as if he looked upon his own actions as necessary, but yet didn't condone them.

'It is the one in your neck which controls the nerve,' Magonde stated, and he leant over and extracted a short needle from not far below Steel's earlobe.

Steel prepared himself for the sudden onslaught of pain; but it didn't come, the numbness was still there, he could sense, as he tried to grip one hand into a fist.

Magonde smiled wryly at Steel's bemused expression. 'You must forgive me, Mr Steel. It is in fact a common misconception – most likely instigated by the speed of the initial anaesthesia. The effects, under normal circumstances, take almost half an hour to wear off.'

It was apparent again: self-indulgence, pride, *vanity!*

'. . . The needle in your neck was stimulating the pituitary gland, which, in turn, produced a natural hormone within your body called endorphin. It has very much the same effect as morphine but without so many of the associated unpleasant post-operative symptoms. It seems ironic, Mr Steel, that for years acupuncture has been taboo in Western medicine and only recently have these particular properties been discovered. . . . I could have warned you, but then again, anticipation, in itself, serves a certain purpose.'

Curiously, it was the medical minutiae which sparked a portion of Steel's subconscious, previously vague . . . *the file report!*

Magonde turned to Bature. 'Please pass me my medical bag.' And then quickly back to Steel. . . . 'However, when a small dose of naloxone is administered, as with morphine, the anaesthetic effects subside within a matter of minutes.'

Steel tilted up slightly, watching the slim negro pass across a black leather bag; and something else, something that he hadn't noticed before, on top of the packing crates to one side – his own gun, cleaned and stripped! Why? A collector, a connoisseur perhaps?

Magonde had spread out a large rolled cloth to one side. Inside was a series of variously sized needles in concentric rows, following a systematic gradation of thickness and length – small Chinese calligraphic inscriptions marking off each section.

. . . The file! . . . thoughts returning slowly, a conscious distraction from Magonde's attentive preparations . . . . An outspoken alliance with the Ghanaian President, Kwame Nkrumah, he recalled, and then his subsequent exile from Amgawi by the country's military leader and President, Sabuyo Zilemba.

Magonde picked out a syringe and a small bottle from the black bag.

But it was the medical details. Steel spurred himself. . . . The campaigns against malaria and diphtheria – the clandestine forays across the Amgawi border to visit small bands of tribal guerillas on the pretext of medical missions.

Magonde half-filled the syringe, squirting a short glistening stream up towards the fluorescent light.

'Rike shi har yanzu!'

Karfi gripped Steel's arm tight at the elbow and Magonde pinched the skin just below, bringing up a radial artery and inserting the needle purposefully, intently. 'At some stage you will experience a strong phrenotropia. You will not be able to clearly discern fantasy from reality – or, for that matter, any conscious thoughts or speech.'

. . . *The file again*, pushing away outward consciousness. The later, even stronger alliance with Nkrumah's protégés, furthering the aims of the All African Committee for Political Co-ordination even after Nkrumah's death. And then his open defiance of Dr Koff Busia, Nkrumah's successor; his subsequent profound public statements supporting Nkrumah's 'Big Lie' theory. . . . The press releases. News conferences. . . . 'So this is what happened to the great Dr Magonde and his medical principles,' Steel spat, as the content of the syringe coursed through him. 'Whatever happened to the Hippocratic oath?'

Magonde appeared unruffled. 'It's amazing how the realization of my identity suddenly refreshes your memory, Mr Steel.' He pulled out the needle, dabbing a spirit-soaked wad of cotton-wool on quickly afterwards. 'It will only be a matter of minutes now,' he commented in a matter-of-fact tone.

'"Gold and diamonds are the white man's lure!"' Steel hissed between clenched teeth. '"They harbour the potential of Africa's destruction", if I remember the quotation well. Doesn't that strike a small hypocritical note?'

Magonde laughed faintly, selecting one of the shorter needles from the spread cloth. 'There are also other quotations: "From the ashes of destruction" . . . and "if you live by the sword". . . . The gold and diamonds of Africa symbolize power, Mr Steel – purely and simply. It is the use of that power that draws the line between good and evil.'

'And is *this* the good?'

Bature was on his feet quickly. 'He's testing you out – don't fall for it!'

Magonde glared back contemptuously, without answering. 'Take Bature here for instance, Mr Steel – he believes that killing a few "pigs" and government officials will solve the world's problems. A show of force by clumsy, fragmented terrorist activities.' Magonde's expression deepened, and it was obvious that some form of conflict was suddenly at work deep within him. 'When *he* first came to me, he believed in the Muslim ideology of spilling the white man's blood to cleanse the black man's soul. His other course, as with Baldwin, would have been to adapt the white man's heritage, because his own heritage had been taken from him. The white women in his world were portrayed as untouchable to him – through their glossy magazines, the glamour of their films and TV, the media. And *he* was portrayed at the bottom of the social strata. A menial workhorse captured in society's chains as surely as if they were made of iron. Yes, Mr Steel, that is how he saw it, but there are still forms of subjugation, perhaps some of them not so easily defined.' Magonde stopped suddenly; at times, when he talked about the subject at any length, the picture seemed so ridiculously clear: bands of soldiers marching upwards on clear golden sand, slaughtering all the blacks in sight, forging their way through, unflinching; not an ounce of the negroes' blood spilled on their own pristine white uniforms. There were many similar scenarios in his mind, all of them with the same two opposing groups of characters, but with different backgrounds. And it was almost the same image that he saw now, in the modern age, only money had replaced the weapons; subtle discrimination, replaced hatred; law and the 'system', the plain brutality. '. . . Now, as you may well know, Mr Steel, our chains are social, economic, political.'

Vague at first, but gradually taking form . . . part of a quotation of Nkrumah's. . . . 'South Africa is the biggest impediment to the liberation and unity of the African Continent.' . . . Re-stated strongly by Magonde prior to the forming of Amgawi's rebel army; an indicator of a much broader, *Pan African* freedom . . . *the proclamation!* 'And this is what's left of Amgawi's noble cause, is it? Down to chasing a few white man's dollars.'

Magonde stiffened. 'You still have the traits of the filthy imperialists who first invaded our land – patronizing, disdainful. The "cause", Mr Steel, will always be the same – always purposeful . . . always strong. I may die, but others will follow; and not only in Amgawi, but in many other African lands.' Magonde took out a short needle from the cloths and inserted it in the side of Steel's neck. 'Soon now . . . soon you will feel the pain.'

Steel watched him. The conflict was working its way deeper. . . . *If only.* . . . *Just a bit further!* 'So now you've decided to depose the white man and set yourself up as king,' Steel baited him. 'But nothing will really change for the people. Just that the black face acts as a placebo. . . . Hopefully they won't realize that the dictatorship's the same until it's too late.'

'Very often it is the black men that are the puppets of the white profiteers, you know that well,' Magonde said flatly. He turned absently back to his black leather bag and took out a bottle of surgical spirit. 'That is not the case with *our* brotherhood, Mr Steel. We have been the servants for too long. Now is the time for a direct reversal.'

It was the mention of 'brotherhood' that sent Steel's mind racing back to the finer details of the report. . . . *There was a brother,* he recalled, politically active at the time of the forming of the rebel army, but who disappeared mysteriously . . . and then the quiet lull. . . . 'What happened – did the path of the cause suddenly diminish with your brother's disappearance? Lose its direction? Become white man's fodder again?. . . . Were you too weak without him?'

Magonde's colour deepened. 'My brother's vow to the cause, as with mine, is undying!' he asserted, the faces of the Sarakunas returning in a brief, daunting vision. He poured a generous quantity of the clear white spirit directly on the spread of coagulated blood staining the cloth bound at Steel's thigh.

'You've been quiet for a long time,' Steel taunted. 'What is this – the first silent revolution in history?'

'The cause is stronger than ever!' Magonde glared at him. 'You will see! You will see. . . .' *The Sarakunas. And Joachim!*

'Beware the silent en . . .' Steel started, but at that moment, the wave of pain hit him in a rush, a jolting spasm spreading upwards from his neck, seeming to tear at the underside of his skull; and another, lower down, a deep searing of torn and ruptured ligaments. A sudden surge of vomit burned from his stomach to the back of his throat, and then the same darkness was returning, warm, familiar . . . but this time somehow welcome.

'Shafe bakirsa!' Magonde spat.

Karfi wiped Steel clean with a bandage and then jammed the bloodied cloth hard in his mouth to prevent him biting on his tongue in an involuntary spasm.

'Soon you will change your mind,' Magonde soothed, and he watched Steel's eyes glazing slowly, his head tilting sharply to one side. 'Soon, my friend . . . ' he repeated abstractedly, cradling Steel's head; although already he feared he had said too much.

It was February, 1965. The South-West African summer was at its height; consistently oppressive – long days of dry, harsh sunshine sapping the last life from the few shrubs remaining in the Namib Desert, pitiful spindles of brown and faded green clinging desperately to the shade of small rock-crevices.

Leon Magonde looked out across the barren landscape from the train window, wiping the sweat from his brow for what seemed the umpteenth time. The journey had been long and arduous, he reflected: by Land Rover and train to Lagos, the flight to Johannesburg, and now the second train journey from there with the change at Bloemfontein. There was no comprehensive rail system throughout western Africa, although southern Africa had compensated for this. 'As many miles of track as the rest of Africa combined', he recalled from the text books. . . . *White man's trappings!*

The train ended in Luderitz, and then there would be another journey by Land Rover. South this time, he reminded himself, once again plucking out the letter from the top pocket of his safari shirt – South to Port Nolloth for supplies and then on through the coastal desert to Honde-klip Bay; and there finally, he resolved, there might be a clue . . . just *something*.

It had been a month since they had received news of the accident. And almost three months since the letter had arrived. The last from Joachim! Now, he knew, all the responsibilities would be his and Amwre's – there would be no more dreams of Joachim joining the 'cause'. 'He was always the wayward one, unlike us, without education,' Amwre had consoled him at the time. 'He did not take advantage of the privileges our father's imperialistic position afforded. But that, in itself, going against our own father's wishes, was a show of strength. There would have been great hopes for him. Of that, there is no doubt.'

And, most of all, Leon recalled, it was Amwre who was deeply embittered and mistrusted the sparse information passed on to them by the Port Nolloth police. 'He is too experienced a prospector to suffer at the hand of fate in a simple accident like this.'

But Leon knew, although it had not been mentioned directly, that it had been the other factors of the brief police

420

report that had added to that initial doubt: that Joachim, of all the crew members, was the only one to have had a limb severed – and for that to be, of all things, his head. It was explained by Sergeant Selubwe of the Port Nolloth police in a subsequent telephone conversation as a 'highly feasible result of the explosion'. 'Many of the metal components, especially those in the engine room, were thrown outwards with great force.'

Joachim's body was also, it transpired, one of only two to remain trapped among the wreckage as it sank – all the others having been thrown clear, although still drowning; a point that Leon himself had found particularly unusual, though, once again, it was explained with ease by Sergeant Selubwe. 'The explosion would have caused serious concussion. In such a situation, it is not at all unlikely that all occupants would drown. We have no reason to suspect anything other than an accident.'

It was another two hundred and eighty miles to Luderitz, and Leon Magonde spent much of the journey in similar contemplation, the bare, monotonous landscape passing as a vague background. It was much the same on the slightly shorter two-hundred-and-ten-mile stretch to Port Nolloth, although the driver and guide he had hired to Luderitz interrupted his thoughts frequently with casual remarks. 'There isn't much in Port Nolloth – just a lot of sand, salt water and a few mining plants. What would you want in a place like that?'

Leon mentioned the dredger 'accident', neglecting the finer details. 'I understand that a certain Sergeant Selubwe conducted the enquiry. I would just like to clarify a few points with him.'

'I know all about that Selubwe,' the driver snapped disdainfully. 'He's about the only policeman that you'll find for miles around, and he acts as if he was Commissioner. If it's not in Selubwe's interests, forget it. The mining corporations and the government keep him employed, and he's too busy tracking down 'plant smugglers' to be bothered with anything else. Believe me, he's a hard man to deal with.'

Leon thanked him for the information and the driver introduced himself as Kigo, an ex-Ovambo tribesman whose ancestry in the Namib Desert regions went back through centuries. 'I know every inch of this desert and coastline, and every man who's worth knowing,' he boasted jovially. 'I'll help you in whatever matters I can.'

Leon had initially decided to take out his own transport for the last leg of the journey as a matter of discretion concerning any finer details he might discover by the dredger site, but he found Kigo's assistance invaluable and decided to keep him on.

Port Nolloth proved to be very close to Kigo's description, comprising two straggling industrial plants and groups of outlying Nissen huts and makeshift dwellings. And, as Kigo had indicated, Sergeant Selubwe was both belligerent and uninterested. 'I told you the results of my investigation on the phone, Mr Magonde, and that you would be wasting your time in coming out here. The matter is closed, and there will be no more enquiries by my department.'

Selubwe's 'department', Leon later discovered from Kigo, comprised another four Bantus and two Land Rovers. 'If you want some action, you'll have to investigate yourself and if you come up with some information, report it to the police at Luderitz or Keetsmanhoop,' Kigo suggested. 'There are decent sized forces at both places and if it's worthwhile, they'll override Selubwe's authority.'

Leon had resolved that he might have to conduct enquiries himself before setting out, and so this came as no surprise. They camped the night at Port Nolloth and set off for Hondeklip Bay early the next day.

In all respects, the journey proved to be a disappointment, falling below even Leon's low expectations. Sergeant Selubwe had mentioned that on his last inspection almost three weeks beforehand a small part of the dredger had been visible above the waterline, clinging to a part of the rocky outcrop, but now, he could see, nothing remained.

'The heavy currents could have pulled it under,' Kigo speculated, 'but hopefully, the tide's just a bit higher than when Selubwe was here – we should wait until later in the day.'

They set a camp on the shoreline close to the water's edge and began their surveillance through the mist of the turbulent salt spray. It was a long and tedious six hours, and the tide went out almost to its extremity, exposing a good quarter of a mile of sand before them. The rocky outcrop gradually appeared larger and more ominous, but there was still no sign of any wreckage. All hope was slowly dying, their idle conversation, too, diminishing in the fading light.

Leon suggested taking out a dinghy to investigate closer. 'Before the sun gets too low.'

'It's too risky,' Kigo warned. 'Any of those rocks could dash you to pieces and anyway the sand is constantly churning up from the bottom – there's no visibility in the water.'

To Leon, it was the fact that he had travelled so far that pushed him towards a decision he knew he would not have otherwise made – *the total futility of such a journey!* . . . 'It's my only hope – are you with me or not?'

Kigo had braved the waters before, and that had taught *him* their dangers and pitfalls. Reluctantly he agreed but suggested that it would be best if they prepared the equipment required that evening and set out at first light in the morning. 'The waters are normally calmer at that time.'

Leon quickly saw the sense of this, momentarily quelling his impatience to know what lay beneath the water's surface. 'Okay, whatever arrangements we have to make – but I must see it for myself.'

'There is only one man in this region who can provide the equipment we'll need,' Kigo offered thoughtfully – 'Rudi Deutzmyer.'

Rudi Deutzmyer was known by all who regularly visited the region as the 'old Dutchman of the desert'. Certainly, nobody else lived in the region, but there were a few hardy groups of prospectors who would return at intervals, and even though their absence had been at times for a number of years, Rudi would still greet them as close friends. They appreciated Rudi for this trait, although none of them had troubled to reason why. And Rudi would never admit, even to himself, that they were the nearest thing to friends that he could ever lay claim to.

It was in this manner that he greeted Kigo and 'the friend whom he believed he hadn't seen before'. 'Although my eyesight isn't so hot these days,' he admitted. 'The glitter of diamond stone is about all it's good for now.'

Deutzmyer's small general store stood at the crossroads of the coastal road and the rough dirt track which trailed deeper into the desert towards Springbok. It was rough, wooden and tumbledown, and crammed to the ceiling with a vast conglomeration of prospecting equipment and tinned food.

Each day, Deutzmyer would prospect for a few hours and then return and seat himself stolidly in a rocking chair on the front 'boardwalk' porch of the store. His daily prospecting had diminished over the past thirty years, and he had seen all the strikes worthy of note in the area. He would eagerly tell any passers-by as much, filling a clay pipe with shag and drawing deeply on it as his reminiscing gained momentum. The store kept him in the region with a 'grub stake', he would explain, but still he went on for the 'big find'. His skin was as dark and creased as dried leather and his eyes a bleary pale blue, but his mind was still sharp, especially in matters of prospecting and in recalling the few visitors to the region.

Kigo knew this, as did many of the 'regulars', and he explained the predicament of his 'friend' and what they had planned. 'We'll need the largest inflatable you've got, Rudi – especially if it's going to be rough tomorrow. And a powerful outboard with two oars as a standby. She could easily get jammed with the spray.'

Already, in many ways, the dinghy run was beginning to seem a futile exercise and Leon welcomed any additional information, when Rudi casually mentioned, as he was preparing the equipment, how it was such a 'coincidence' that he'd prepared 'almost exactly the same equipment just a week before the dredger went down for one of those fellas.'

Leon asked why and then it was Deutzmyer's turn to show surprise, looking anxiously between the two of them. 'You saw Selubwe – didn't he tell you? There was a few fellas out here looking at the dredger about the same time.'

Leon glared at Kigo. 'Damn that Selubwe.'

He probably didn't think it important,' Rudi added thoughtfully. 'It's the same damn thing he kept telling me when I told him about it first off. "It was an accident," he said. "Who the hell cares who was in the area – they could've been miles away at the time." But I told him there was something to it.'

'Do you remember who they were?' Leon enquired pointedly.

Deutzmyer went over to a drawer, rustling through a bunch of crumpled papers tied with string. 'If he was like everybody else, he'd have filled out a receipt for his equipment.' It took him another few minutes and then he passed across a small brown slip. 'There it is, if you can read it. He was a tall gentleman, dark hair, a thick European accent – from one of the Slav countries, I'd guess,' Deutzmyer mused, drawing heavily on his pipe.

To Leon, from the scrawled signature in the bottom corner, the first name was evident, but however hard he studied the surname, he could not draw a clear distinction between the two choices: *Joseph Matral or Matrai?* . . . 'Was there anybody else?' he quizzed.

'He had a partner – a German fella who was in about a week beforehand and I'd already seen him a few months before that, but I can't remember his name. He didn't take out any equipment – just food.'

Leon asked for a more detailed description of both men and Rudi drew vivid verbal pictures of the two men, adding, 'There was something else – the one thing that I thought most unusual, and I mentioned it to Sergeant Selubwe at the time. The dark-haired fella mentioned in passing that an American was coming out to look at the dredger. He didn't mention any names, but then the day of the accident I saw a Land Rover go by here, well-packed with supplies

425

and Bantu helpers. I've seen it around before, but it took me a while to remember, and the fella in question is an American, although he's been in these parts for a while now. His name's Bradley Vansen, a claims financier he is. Alway works with a big Xhosa tribesman and at least three Bantus. If you want to know a bit more about him, I suggest you ask in Kimberley. Word has it, he's a big man around there.'

Leon thanked Rudi for the information, and the next day they set out towards the rock outcrop, though Leon's interest in the exercise was less than it had been initially, and rapidly waning. As Kigo had predicted, the water was cloudy and nothing could be seen further than a few feet below the surface. They returned promptly, making plans to take Deutzmyer's advice, although Leon considered that one last call to Sergeant Selubwe would be prudent.

It was from a radio-phone forty miles north, and the line was weak. Sergeant Selubwe merely repeated the essence of his conversation with Deutzmyer. 'Until there is some concrete evidence of something other than an accident, my enquiries are closed. All you have there, Mr Magonde, is a collection of hearsay from an old Dutch prospector.'

Leon had felt an initial hopelessness regarding the enquiries, and now they had reached a blank wall.

Kigo made an effort to console him on the long drive to Kimberley. 'I know how you feel, and I don't like saying this, but believe me it's true – if they had been white men on board instead of Bantus, things would have been different.'

It was a curious feeling, but already Leon harboured an indefinable hatred towards the 'white prospectors and financiers' the 'old Dutchman' had detailed, without even fully knowing their involvement – for the simple fact that they were white, as much as anything else. . . . *Damned hypocrisy! Imperialism!*

It was with the same tenacity that he made his initial enquiries in Kimberley. Nobody there had heard of Joseph Matrai or Matral, but there many eager to impart information regarding Bradley Vansen. 'Yes – he had been out on a claim-financing expedition during that period,' one prospector recalled, mentally checking back through his own activities for the month in question.

Much of the information followed the same pattern: the enormous spread of Vansen's interests and the competence of his 'organization', the burly Xhosa always at his side and the chain of Bantu helpers, invariably well-versed in the claim area in question.

As the days went by, Leon gradually sank back into dejection, with no direct or tangible information regarding Vansen and the dredger, barring the fact that he was 'absent' at the time.

He had sat through many 'I remember when' stories and felt that he was about to be imparted another, as he sat down at the opposite end of a bar trestle table to a man know only as 'Rigas'. 'Short for Rodriguez,' the tousle-haired prospector told him.

Leon smiled with as much patience as he could muster. 'Go on.'

Rodriguez continued, explaining that it was a story told to him by a friend regarding Vansen, and could only be passed on in confidence. 'My life could depend on your discretion.'

'Okay,' Leon agreed, a small interest sparking at the prospector's unorthodox approach.

Rodriguez detailed the practice that he had heard Vansen implemented on many of his claim-financing expeditions. 'A mild poison tainting the whisky, enough to make the propectors unconscious – and then if anything turned out bad. . . .' Rodriguez drew an invisible line across his throat with one finger.

Leon immediately saw the significance of Rodriguez's story, and contacted Sergeant Selubwe the following day; but again Selubwe reiterated his doctrine on hearsay. Recalling Kigo's advice, Leon contacted the police at Luderitz but they said that they could not intervene in the case without some more tangible evidence, and 'until such time, the investigation would remain in the hands of Sergeant Selubwe'. Exasperated, Leon returned to his lone enquiries, finally sending a telegram to Amwre, short but to the point: *HAVE FOUND A THORN – INVESTIGATING FURTHER.*

Leon stayed another full week in Kimberley, finding out as much as he could about Vansen's operations, although he quickly realized that the vast detail was far surpassing his earlier expectancies. He travelled on to Johannesburg, cross-referencing a mass of company and claim titles, finally separating the numerous branches into a collection of clearly defined categories: *Three mining companies solely owned by Vansen, with claim interests in South Africa, Botswana, South-West Africa, Ghana, Sierra Leone and a number of the small enclaves on the West African coast, including Leon's homeland, Amgawi. Some fifty-five per cent had clear titles in Vansen's name, the remainder being shared with various named partners, mainly those working the individual claims, holding forty-nine per cent each.* However, as Leon had discovered while in Kimberley, that percentage was rapidly increasing in Vansen's favour as he 'starved the partners out', as one prospector bluntly put it.

Leon returned to Amgawi; it had been almost a full month since his departure. Amwre showed strong indignation at all the events surrounding the accident and, in particular, the police attitude – but his anger was mollified by the vast portfolio of information that Leon set before him. 'If we cannot gain retribution through the law, then we must seek other means,' he stated flatly.

It marked the start of a process that even Leon, at such early stages, could not have foreseen. Each step of Vansen's progress was followed carefully: the 'starvation' take-overs and the gradual addition of each new mining company. And when finally in April 1970, Vansen Consolidated Mines was declared a public corporation, Leon was once again in Johannesburg, searching through files and registers; all new features of the parent company and its now greatly expanded seven subsidiary companies were duly noted and interpreted. The facts, the figures, and in particular, *the man himself.*

'His activities will now be much easier to follow, due to the press coverage,' Leon commented enthusiastically, as their 'portfolio' gained new dimensions.

The culmination of their investigation came in November 1971, when Jansen signed an agreement with Amgawi's president, Sabuyo Zilemba, for a new mining plant to exploit the newly discovered diamond wealth of the country's northern regions. 'And so at last the capitalist bird comes home to roost,' Amwre Magonde announced smugly. 'Now he is that much nearer our grasp.'

Leon Magonde knew that he should have shared Amwre's enthusiasm, but as so often occurs with those of an active intellectual disposition, with the culmination of one project in sight, his thoughts turned to other matters: the name on the receipt from Deutzmyer's store – *Joseph Matral or Matrai?*

It made no difference, sources he had conferred with in both Kimberley and Johannesburg had heard of neither name. There had been a small lead provided by a Johannesburg diamond merchant shortly after the dredger incident, but nothing since. Somehow it seemed that the young prospector and his German partner had disappeared from the face of the earth.

Shadows were deeper along the narrow street, the clouds completey cleared away now, a mass of stars like scattered silver dust across the rich velvet of the sky.

Surak picked out the brightest stars, studying the apparent fluctuation of their light, enjoying the sudden feeling of *oneness* with them, as if the very intensity of his attention had spanned the great distance that lay between them, the depth of the night at last a close companion – calm, all-encompassing, all-seeing . . . feeling its awesome power course through his body. . . . *Pra jaw ny sa-wahn!*

It had been a fortuitous set of circumstances, he considered, opening his eyes slowly, once again scanning the length of the shadowed side-street: the green Datsun, as before, set close into the kerb on the far side, facing away from him. Beyond, the tail of the grey Toyota extended from the rear slipway of the warehouse across the street.

It had been a surprise, he recalled, when he had initially seen the blond-haired Westerner enter the green Datsun in the car park of the Dusit Thani across from the stadium. Then, turning his attention quickly to the English *farang*'s taxi, he had followed it cautiously to the Sheraton Hotel. Once again, he had followed the second taxi and the grey Toyota after the frantic shoot-out, but had lost them among a heavy stream of traffic approaching Lam Luang Road. And then his ultimate surprise while coasting thoughtfully through nearby streets, trying to pick up the tail once again, when he sighted the blond-haired Westerner's green Datsun travelling slowly but purposefully on a cross street, but still in the same general direction. He remembered, in particular, that his decision to follow had been through a lack of immediately apparent alternatives – an ambiguity increased by the Datsun's final arrival across the street from the small warehouse.

And then the long wait, the seeds of doubt growing stronger with each passing hour, but finally quelled by the arrival of the grey Toyota. The three negroes and the chauffeur alighted swiftly, and a body, bloodied and ghostly among the shadows, was hustled impatiently through the side door. There was a glimpse of royal-blue shirt caught momentarily in the beam from the car's interior light. . . .
The English farang!

A lesson in patience, Surak mused.

That had been almost four hours ago, he contemplated, although now, unlike before, he felt confident that such vigilance would be worthwhile, rewarded: the task of the *Bpratahn* consummated.

Surak took the short black rod from his side. He unscrewed the silver cap, pulling out the lead ball from its hollow basin, and ran his fingers gently up and down the sharp cheese-wire . . . . *Patience*, he chided himself – *a precious virtue!* The most essential quality for those wishing attainment of Grand Master, he reflected. Patience!

Sheaves of wheat climbed high, seeming to reach almost to the sky at points, thrusting upwards proudly, but somehow threatening – dark and then blinding light, breaking through the sporadic gaps, a wall of yellow swaying frantically back and forth with the gusting wind.

It was Edenbridge. . . . He could tell because of the barn on the ridge at the end of the broad field and the cluster of tumbledown farmhouses in the coomb to one side. And he was a boy again, and the wheat seemed so much taller. Then suddenly the wind was coming from behind him and he was running . . . *running* . . . trying to keep ahead of it, the tall sheaves lashing against his body, fighting his way through . . . *fighting*. . . . But somehow wasteful, futile – the wind coming down upon him, swirling around his body, enveloping him totally. . . . And he closed his eyes, surrendering peaceably to it, wishing it to finish.

When it finally did, almost as suddenly as it had started, the silence was empty, deathly. He opened his eyes again slowly: there was a lake there before him, although he could never remember a lake in those parts before, and so he looked on curiously, the water dark and murky. A heavy thrust came from behind without warning, catching his breath, throwing him forwards, and falling . . . *falling!*

But when he looked up, expecting to see the water all around him, he was running again, the sheaves of wheat much higher than before, taller even than himself.

And there were faces, breaking through at intervals, stark, *ghostly* . . . *Cleary! Haskell!*

They were pointing upwards, all trying to say something, but no words came out – all struggling to warn him, pleading soulfully, their eyes bleary and pale.

And then suddenly he realized, as if someone had played some dreadful trick on him. He was in the lake still, running downwards through its murky fathoms, the mud at its bottom clinging all around him, and turning now, clawing his way upwards through the darkness – seeing the light of the surface up above but never coming closer to it . . .

thrashing at the water all around – *clogging! . . . suffocating!* . . . feeling it flood into his mouth and through his body . . . sinking slowly back down again. . . .

And then the light from above was coming down to meet him, and another face, more prominent, less ghostly than the others was at its side, but at first indiscernible from the heavy glare – moving downwards slowly . . . closer . . . *closer!*

And then startlingly apparent.

A gradual dawning . . . *Magonde!* . . . a familiar grimace merging with the light itself, blocking a part of it out.

'Welcome back, Mr Steel,' the voice boomed, a dull echo seeming to reverberate from all around. 'You are with us again.'

There came a gradual awareness of what had gone before, of events taking shape. . . .

Aware that at some time in the night he had been turned over on the bench and the long needles inserted into the hollow of his back, searching out the sensitive nerves at either side of his spine . . . the accompanying explanation from Magonde, drawing him out, *taunting!*

And the questions – monotonous, consistent, returning time and time again to the same laboured points.

But most of all, the pain; searing, *excruciating*, holding out for the final blanket of warm darkness that could never come soon enough.

'Mr Steel.' Magonde tested him again. 'I trust you are sufficiently revived. I would like you to move the fingers of your right hand.'

There had been other awakenings during the long night, Steel recalled, frequent and sometimes abrupt, but clouded in heavy delirium. He focused more intently on Magonde. 'Yes?'

'Your right hand, Mr Steel,' Magonde prompted impatiently. 'Will you please move your fingers.'

It was a simple motion, but Steel concentrated his effort, unaware of whether he'd succeeded or not, a heavy numbness pervading his body.

'Yes, good,' Magonde affirmed, studying him pensively. 'And now the left.'

There was a pain even through the numbness, Steel could sense, but he was aware of movement from his thumb and small finger.

Magonde turned away. 'Your motor senses appear to have sufficiently recovered. Of course, at first your legs will be quite weak – especially your injured leg,' he mused, a smile playing slightly on his lips. 'Our conversations over the past hours have covered a broad range of subjects – I have found them most enlightening, and there are certain aspects which appear to have an immediate relevance to the matter at hand. For my own convenience I will for the moment accept these.'

Nkrumah! Salbuyo Zilemba! The 'cause'! . . . Surely already there was too much at stake.

'Bature will get you some clean clothes and for our *own* security, you'll be blindfolded till we reach the Democracy Monument. You can lead us from there.'

Steel lolled his head to one side, and he could just see a slat of light coming from underneath the large corrugated-iron door to one side. *It was morning* . . . his mind racing to take stock of time and what Magonde had just said; a question of safety, *security*. . . . 'Only one man,' he spluttered frantically. 'Only one man can come in with me to collect the deposit.'

'That is acceptable,' Magonde agreed, glancing briefly towards the far corner. 'That will also be Bature. Is there anything else?'

'No,' Steel said blankly, although he knew that there *was*, unable to immediately pin-point a relevance . . . *just one small detail!* His thoughts cleared slowly, finally, aware only of one ultimate contingency which clouded all else – whatever had been agreed, Magonde would still intend to kill him. Now, perhaps more than ever. This was only the first hurdle.

24

The early morning sounds of the klong village seemed to come from all around, and Paul Ensor awoke slowly: there were three women, backs bent, washing clothes among the shallows at the end of the muddy bank. The sun was a large orange disc, picking out the gentle rippling that they set up in the water with their flurried motions.

He was sheltered below a small bridge, the trelliswork of a side-support casting heavier shadows across his body as the sun rose higher. Behind him were the sounds of children playing, high-pitched and carefree, the brief distraught bawling of an infant breaking the harmony.

The bank of the klong he lay on rose gradually upwards, becoming progressively steeper, forming a small hill, and the main part of the village was set on its brow, a crooked extension at one side straggling awkwardly down to the waterside. The dwellings bordering the water itself were raised on wooden stilts, and the lapping water could be picked out by the darker shades on the grey wood a few inches above the waterline.

There were few trees, but the shrubbery was heavy midway up the bank, mostly mangrove and pandanus. The night before, after the rains, the ground had been awash – a thick, dark mire. But now even the early sun was intense, drying the earth a light powdery brown, matching the faded patch-boarding, straw and dried palm fronds of the shanty dwellings – mottled shades of brown and grey evoking a certain beauty from the haphazard squalor.

Paul Ensor crawled out from beneath the bridge, brushing off the dried mud from his clothing. One of the women at the waterside saw him emerge and she prompted the others, all of them looking at him briefly before turning their attention back to their wash; then again glancing over fleetingly as he walked up the slope and started his way across the rough wooden planks of the bridge. He trudged slowly towards the far side, as if in contemplation, staring blankly down into the water below.

The sunlight cast uneven silver dapples, but the water itself was dark green and brown, the brightly-painted railings reflected in murky hues of yellow and red, as if in some sickly, clownish contrast.

The events of the night before played over slowly in his mind: Deborah falling . . . the sound of footsteps in the distance behind, coming ever closer, then the two lone shots, ricocheting off the wall close by. But he was already behind the second gap, running deeper. . . .

And then it was the third gap; then the fourth . . . weaving quickly through the industrial maze, the footsteps becoming more distant, fading, indiscernible among the sound of the driving rain.

At some point, he had finally lost the sound of the footsteps completely, although he wasn't sure exactly *when* . . . resting for a moment against a warehouse wall, feeling his rapid breathing subsiding gradually, a burning deep in his chest, listening to the stillness of the night.

But still it didn't seem enough – he was still too close to the horror and he'd run on out of the industrial estate, across the broad flats of a rice field awash with the rain, keeping to the high ridges above the thick mire of the irrigation channels, and then through a short expanse of pandanus brush at its end – finally coming to the same small bridge, the lights of the klong village just visible the other side.

He remembered crossing the bridge and sitting on the muddy bank of the klong, looking down into the water below. For a long while he stayed there, losing track of time – aware only that the rain had eased slightly, the clouds moving fast across the sky as he looked up, a small portion of the moon just visible, casting a faint light on to the water;

small pockets of white foam a last vestige of the torrent.

And now he looked down into the same water, clenching one fist hard at his side. It had been only yesterday by the floating market that he'd done the same, *and Deborah had been alive!* Although now it all seemed in some past life. The same as he'd felt in the taxi coming back from the arena, he recalled – the gap between them, *obscure, indefinable!* As if what had happened had created a barrier, exaggerated even more by their lack of comprehension of all the events. He felt a profound grief well up from deep inside that Deborah had died in that way, *at that time.* When there was so much misunderstanding and heart-felt emptiness between them. . . . *And mistrust.*

They had never seemed so far apart, and now it could never be resolved. . . . *Never!*

The nightmarish events revolved slowly around again and despite the pain, he almost welcomed them, as if the suffering could expiate the guilt he felt. 'Oh God!' he screamed out loud, slamming his clenched fist against the wooden railing. . . .

The arena! The final moments!

He fought to wrench the last image from his mind. The large negro standing resolutely, raising his gun, firing once again . . . and Deborah slipping away from his grasp, falling to the ground, limp, *helpless.*

But it stayed there obstinately, and he shook his head furiously from side to side, the darkness of the vision seeming to cloud all else – the brightness outside, the water below him; as if for that brief moment he had returned to the incident and it was happening all over again, and that somehow he would return time and time again, until . . . until? No! . . . 'No!' he spat, crushing his fist harder against the railing, opening his eyes once again.

The brightness seemed to draw him out as his emotions ebbed and his tears fell freely as if in that moment he had sensed a more profound, universal unfairness and could wash away his own sorrows and those of the world, the swelling waters below his willing companion.

A young Thai boy had walked on to the bridge, intrigued by the strange visitor and then, startled by his sudden outburst, halted sharply in his tracks, looking on curiously, his rounded eyes wide and darkly inquisitive.

In that brief moment the small boy shared a part of the stranger's sorrow, although he knew he was far from understanding it; he had seen women cry, and young girls and boys in the village, but never a grown man. Let alone a white man. The *farangs* had always been the strong ones, the people from afar who they looked up to. But all he felt now was pity, his small mouth gaping slightly in awe as he edged closer.

Paul Ensor was aware of the boy as he came within a few yards, and at first he looked away, hiding his sorrow in embarrassment; but then he quickly gathered his composure, turning back to face the boy as directly as he felt his momentary control would allow.

It was a warm, innocent gaze, Paul sensed immediately, but there was a curiosity and sadness beneath it that, although he fought away the sudden realization, he knew in so many ways reflected his own frustration and hopelessness. As hopeless as he had felt the day before, he cursed inwardly – *a pawn!* But now with one difference. He was alone. *Deborah was gone.* He no longer had to think for both of them.

The small boy turned suddenly and ran off the bridge and back up the well-worn track of dried mud towards the first cluster of shanty dwellings.

Paul Ensor watched him thoughtfully, again taking in the full span of the village and the gently sloping hillside towards the canal itself. Deeper down the channel and on the opposite side to the village, he could just make out a small grove of tall coconut palms. The broad, undulating furrows of a rice field extended directly behind, merging into other flat fields, mostly of deep green, stretching lazily in tidy oblongs towards the haze of the horizon.

There couldn't be a more beautiful day, or more beautiful surroundings, he contemplated, although reality seemed dull to him, and he thought again of Manchester: urban sprawl, cloudy skies, factory chimneys . . . but most of all, Deborah! She had been there then, he remembered, and suddenly he wished he could swap the days – push it all back as it had been, blot it out completely as though it had never happened.

There had been so many plans and then in the end it had all been forgotten, so futile – Deborah lost. *Blot it out.*

'Out!' he goaded himself, and although he hadn't been conscious of it before, when he looked down he saw his hands clawing cruelly at the paint of the railing, drawing blood from beneath his fingernails. The emotion, suddenly rising above all else, took him by surprise. . . . Revenge!

However, he quickly found himself mentally ridiculing that compulsive instinct – what revenge was there for a manufacturing chemist? *Against knives and guns!* The painful reminder of his lack of choice returned – the monotony of his life so far, a chain of consistently easy options. Comfortable. Calculating. . . . *Predictable.* The things that he had always wanted to do but. . . .

But now; he stopped himself suddenly, *things were different.*

Before it had been a matter of responsibility. Of fear. Of indefinable duties and concerns for a loved one that no longer held any relevance.

There was no responsibility! And when he thought about it deeper, searching out an answer from the void of the water below, there was also no fear anymore.

There was nothing . . . *nothing!*

Only revenge.

But how?

There had been a number of turns since they had left the warehouse, Steel was aware through the darkness of the blindfold, though the repetitive swaying motions were numbing his senses. His thoughts revolved slowly. There wouldn't be much time. . . . *The hotel* . . . passing over the diamonds. . . . *And then?*

He was crouched low in the back of the car between the two negroes, and when his head bobbed up involuntarily from a sudden motion of the car, he could feel the firm press of cool metal against his neck. There had been quite a collection of noises from outside the car shortly after leaving the warehouse, and then it had been quiet again for a while. A rough rumbling interrupted rudely and suddenly as if they were crossing a bridge or a succession of railway tracks, and then once again, after a short while, the hustle and bustle outside returned, more pronounced than before, increasing in volume and intensity as they continued. Street noises: a conglomeration of engines revving and idling, filling the spectrum of tones – horns beeping sporadically, voices and other movements forming a vague background, too fused to be picked out individually.

Soon, he reminded himself. . . . *The hotel. Mr Tom.* . . . Some form of warning? *Just something!*

'Mr Steel, we are approaching the Democracy Monument,' Magonde's voice came sharply from the front. And to Karfi, 'Kawad da zane!'

Steel felt a tugging motion at the back of his head, the cloth falling away, and then the sudden light streaming in from all around, not as stark as the fluorescent strips of the warehouse, but somehow much fuller and more intense, seeming to sear deeply inwards; a dull, persistent ache began somewhere behind his eyes.

They were approaching from Ratchdamnoen Avenue, he became slowly aware, picking out the landmarks of the TOT building and the Majestic Hotel across the far side.

'Turn right out of the square,' he prompted.

They approached slowly and kept in to the kerb, skirting the heavy flow of traffic close to the central roundabout. As they made the turn into Din So Road, Steel sat back. 'Straight on for a while.' He was again conscious of the gun at his side. It was, as he'd thought earlier, his own gun, Bature seemingly fascinated by the 'Renaissance' styling.

It was quiet in the car, a forced uneasy silence. Steel

marked off the first cross-street, the golden expanse of the Wat Suthat looming up quickly afterwards and slipping into the frame of the driver's rear-view mirror as they coasted by.

'Turn left at the next main street,' Steel directed. 'There should be lights.'

The Chareon Krung was the busier of the two roads, the traffic banked in three lanes each way, but the lights had changed to green as they approached, and the chauffeur made the turn slowly and purposefully, as detached and intent as always. *He* had never spoken, Steel reflected, and during Magonde's questioning had stayed in the adjoining office.

Traffic was becoming progressively thicker towards the junction with the Chakrawat and Vorachak Roads and Steel focused his attention ahead. . . .

A moment! . . . If there were to be one, it would be during heavy traffic, Steel contemplated; Bature's concentration distracted momentarily – *the gun jolted free*. . . . And escape through the jostling crowds and the heavy mêlée of closely grouped vehicles.

'How much further?' Magonde snapped, staring icily towards the bottleneck ahead.

'About a mile.'

The tail-back eased slightly before they had drawn fully to a halt and Steel cursed to himself. . . . *Damn!*

A succession of side-streets passed swiftly by as they picked up speed, and Steel maintained an intent observation through the side-window for the cluster of foreign embassies on the right which he knew would signal the Silom Road turn-off.

It was longer in coming than Steel had thought. 'Just a few more, and then we take a left,' he offered, letting out his breath slowly.

'Okay,' Magonde said curtly. Steel felt the tension building in the following silence.

'Three more,' Steel confirmed after a second, picking out the Wat Tramit to their left.

There was still some slow-moving traffic, but they took the outer lane, travelling swiftly along the wide avenue which curved gradually, following the contour of the Chao Phraya River. The embassies appeared among an expanse of greenery backing on to the river itself: mostly colonial-style buildings in white, with Eastern architecture displayed in brightly coloured pagoda-style roofs at intervals.

'Here,' Steel prompted sharply. 'Left!'

Magonde scanned the width of the Silom Road as they completed the turn. 'Are we near yet?' he quizzed impatiently.

The hotel's slipway could just be picked out in the distance. The pains in Steel's hand and thigh were becoming gradually more insistent.

'Yes, a couple of hundred yards ahead, on the left – the Hotel Narao.' There was no longer any point in concealing the *exact* location. Already it appeared that Magonde had fully accepted the necessity of his presence in 'deposit claiming'. 'They're in the hotel safe,' he added, in response to Magonde's suddenly raised eyebrow.

Magonde drew a fresh breath after a moment, maintaining the same aloof posture. 'It goes without saying, Mr Steel, that you will act normally during this withdrawal. If there are any complications – Bature has strict instructions. And believe me, Mr Steel, he would not hesitate in killing you. . . .'

Magonde broke off momentarily as they came up to the hotel, and the chauffeur waited for some passing traffic, then swung sharply into the slip-road and pulled up towards its end.

'And so, Mr Steel, there should be no problems. We have already ascertained that you can walk, at least without a pronounced limp. Bature will be close at hand, watching and listening. There will be no exaggerated movements and you will say nothing out of the ordinary. Is that quite clear?'

Steel recalled his painful pacing up and down the length of the warehouse. At first, hopelessly stumbling, assisted by Karfi, and then, after a while, without assistance, his limp becoming gradually less noticeable, until he had satisfied Magonde's painstaking attention to detail. . . . 'Yes,' he complied but thought, *you bastard!* 'Shall we just say, we have an understanding,' he smiled faintly.

'Let's get it done,' Bature urged irritably, swinging the door wide. He held his gun under a folded jacket.

Steel didn't look back, but he could sense that his composure had, to some extent, rattled Magonde. As directed, he walked a few paces ahead, acknowledging the doorman with a brief, inconsequential nod.

The interior of the lobby was quiet, with only a few people among the seating partitions to one side, and an elderly couple just visible towards the far end of the elongated reception desk. Steel cursed inwardly; he had hoped there would be more people present. 'All elements offer a possible distraction to both a target and an assailant', he recalled from 'observance' training. There was a clock on the far wall behind the desk, he noted, glancing frantically around. . . . *Time?* 11:22 a.m. The tours would have left in the early morning and lunch was over an hour away.

A moment, he reminded himself, approaching the desk, conscious of Bature's movements a few steps behind, taking up a nonchalant stance at the edge of the seating enclosure, glancing back towards the entrance as if awaiting a friend. A professional. *It wouldn't be easy!*

The desk clerk lifted his head from some papers to one side. 'Yes sir?'

'My name's Steel – Jeffrey Steel. I have a deposit here I'd like to collect.' And Steel watched the clerk's face intently for any alteration in expression; just a small indication . . . a nuance.

'Yes, sir. One moment – I'll check for you,' the clerk said; he hardly even looked directly at Steel, turning away abruptly, accustomed to discretion. He flicked perfunctorily through some files at the back, stopping twice at intervals before picking out a small yellow card. He scanned the details briefly as he returned. 'Ah yes, I see. The deposit was countersigned by Mr Chareompond. If you will wait one moment sir, I'll call him from his office.'

'Yes, of course,' Steel smiled his accord, and for a split second he was sure he saw a flicker of apprehension on the clerk's face – a fleeting glimpse past him . . . *or was it a trick of the light from the upward beam of the desk-lamp?* Certainly no outward recognition or apprehension remained.

The clerk turned away. 'One moment,' he repeated cordially.

There were many types of deposit made at the Narao. But all, without exception, fell into two clearly defined categories: the small everyday deposits – cameras, costume jewellery and assorted items of trivia and little intrinsic value – all countersigned by the attending clerk at the time. And then there were those items where a substantially greater value was attached and the countersignature of the hotel manager was required. It was this latter, and more unusual, category which aroused the desk clerk's curiosity. It was then he recalled the significance of 'Mr Steel'. He opened the door to Chareompond's office, closing it firmly behind him.

Chareompond appeared bemused at the boldness of the intrusion – desk clerks invariably knocked first and made their announcements from a half-opened door. . . . 'Yes?'

'I'm sorry, Mr Chareompond,' the clerk gibbered hastily.'You asked to be informed immediately of Mr Steel's return.'

'And he's here now?'

The clerk nodded. 'Yes.'

'Is there anyone with him?'

'No, sir.'

Chareompond recalled the descriptions of the men at the Sheraton. 'There are two negro men that I'm thinking of in particular – one is slim and average height, and the other is very tall and heavily built. Is there anyone who might fit either of those descriptions in the lobby, that you can see?'

'Yes – there was a negro man who entered about the same time and is now standing by the lounge area.' The clerk pointed casually over one shoulder towards the closed door. 'He's quite thin, average height.'

Chareompond sat back deeper in his chair, putting the end of his pen thoughtfully to his bottom lip. 'I want you to go back out there and inform Mr Steel that I won't keep him long. And, above all, you must remain composed and give the impression that nothing is out of the ordinary – nothing!'

The desk clerk repeated his instructions, briefly nodding his understanding. 'Of course – yes, sir.'

Chareompond picked up the internal phone and waited for the door to close firmly again. He dialled Dinsengwayo's room and informed him of the essence of the conversation just past, adding, 'I believe he could be in some immediate danger.'

Dinsengwayo's response was abrupt and cold. 'I see.'

Chareompond remained in thought for a moment, breathing deeply. He put on his jacket and, before exiting, drew heavily on any inner reserves of calm that might remain.

Walking confidently out of his office, he forced a smile. 'Ah yes, Mr Steel – your deposit!'

And Steel knew immediately by the tone of Mr Tom's greeting that *everything* lay in the balance.

Mikeka Dinsengwayo came out of his room like an enraged bull, fumbling with a gun held in both hands. He moved his beefy frame down the extension of corridor towards the elevators with surprising agility, startling a room-maid half-way along.

Dinsengwayo, ignoring her exclamation, punched the elevator button frantically, resuming his fumbling in between sporadic upward glances. It was a large gun: a Smith and Wesson .44 magnum. Dinsengwayo slipped in the last few shells, swinging the magazine back in with an audible 'click'. He continued looking furtively towards the lighted indicator, punching the button twice more in quick succession.

'Come on,' he hissed under his breath.

The first elevator was on the ground floor and the other appeared to be stuck obstinately on the third floor.

'Damn you,' he cursed. 'Come on, come on. . . .'

He backed away hesitantly and took one last assessment from the top of the stairwell, then turned resolutely and headed down, taking the steps two and three at a time in an ever-widening and hasty stride, half-stumbling at intervals, clutching on to the balustrade for balance.

The sudden urgency and the blind, impulsive motions made his adrenalin rise sharply, his breath stunted to low, repeated gasps deep in his barrel chest. . . . *Damn! Four floors . . . three. . . .*

At the top of the second-floor stairwell he alarmed a group of dallying elderly tourists, pushing his way through brusquely. 'Please. . . .' he shouted desperately, a path clearing amidst muted screams and intakes of breath at the sight of his gun.

He slowed on reaching the first-floor vestibule. It was wider than the others, with two rows of shops on either side of a small lounge. The staircase, he recalled, widened out in open-plan style and wound down from the edge of the 'arcade' complex which formed a mezzanine to the main foyer. A perfect view of the reception area could be gained from the top of the stairwell or the mezzanine railings, he realized, covering the distance to the far end of the lounge area more cautiously, purposefully.

It was only a matter of a few yards to the railing's edge, but Dinsengwayo treated the approach with almost maniacal care: 5.56 mm, he reminded himself – the report detailing the brutal efficiency of the Consortium break-in, still painfully vivid. . . . Stealth would be vital! He edged closer, easing an insistent stickiness of his shirt from his back. Closely massed globules of sweat had broken out on his forehead, and his palm was damp as he tightened his gun-grip in anticipation.

The expanse of the foyer appeared as an oblong spread of Persian carpets broken by light-coloured marble and clusters of tropical plants, twenty feet below. From the high ceiling an extravagant chandelier descended in a profusion of bronze and glass tiers, coming to within ten feet of the central area from which the main foyer lounge extended.

At the far side, the reception desk formed a rich walnut-panelled border and Dinsengwayo scanned its length intently, picking out Chareompond at its furthest section which angled back towards the main entrance. Chareompond, he could see, was placing a small drawstring bag on top of the reception desk and swivelling around a register for the man opposite him to sign . . . . *Tall, light brown hair*, Dinsengwayo noted – the man fitted Chareompond's description of Steel, although he could not be sure; the man's back was turned almost completely towards him.

He could pick out the negro Chareompond had mentioned quite easily, standing towards the edge of the lounge area: slim, dressed casually, a jacket slung between his supposedly folded hands. At intervals he had glanced over during Steel's signing of the register, Dinsengwayo had noted, and there was no longer any doubt.

Position! Dinsengwayo shifted slightly to one side so that any people moving suddenly from the lounge area wouldn't block his vision. He braced his legs hard and raised his gun with both hands – the recoil would be heavy – looking around deliberately, measuredly, fixing the slim negro firmly in his sights. And he remembered *Rosenkrands. The guards from the vault. . . . Now!*

But something else, moving into his vision in that same instant, halted his action: a blond-haired man seated at the far end of the lounge partitions, half-concealed from the reception desk, glancing over at intervals with mild interest.

The recognition was instantaneous, but at first obscure, his thoughts racing frantically back through years and events, a blur of situations, faces and surroundings milling haphazardly in his mind. Then it came: Vansen's recurring premonition.

The young German! . . . But how? and most of all, *why?*

Bature had a vague sense from the corner of his eye of someone observing from the mezzanine and perhaps, if the figure hadn't remained in such a threatening position, he wouldn't have troubled to look up at it directly. And then, with full realization dawning, he was drawing his own gun out from beneath his jacket, swinging around and aiming.

Dinsengwayo's concentration returned sharply.

To Steel, the shots seemed almost simultaneous – two together, and then one shortly afterwards, the central chandelier exploding in cascades of showering glass and tangled metal; then a figure on the mezzanine was falling suddenly backwards and Bature was reeling away at a tangent, the side of his hip opening up in a rapidly spreading ragged oval.

Frantic screams arose from all around as groups of tourists and hotel staff took cover, mostly among the lounge partitions.

Steel covered the short distance swiftly, gripping Bature's gun-arm before he could swing back around. He clutched on desperately, fighting to shake the gun loose, but Bature's strength seemed to return as he regained his balance, and Steel could feel some of the persistent pains and weakness of the past hours flood back in to his body: dull, harrowing aches from his hand and thigh, a vague darkness always close. He forced it back.

The gun started turning irresistibly towards him, firing suddenly into the air, the single bullet whistling through foliage, burying itself into plaster on the far wall, prompting more screams from the huddled tourists.

Bature tensed his muscles hard, grabbing Steel with his free hand, clawing at his face and chin, his determination building as he sensed Steel's grip weakening.

It was a desperate action, but Steel felt his thoughts clouding rapidly. *Now*, he spurred himself, freeing one hand and swinging his elbow sharply back into Bature's throat.

Steel heard the windpipe snap and gripped Bature's arm, shaking it frantically, feeling it grow rapidly limp – the gun finally dropping and scudding quickly across the carpet and on to a strip of marble.

Bature fell, the constriction mottling his face and neck in hues of faint purple, a tortured gasping rising as his lungs expelled the last vestiges of breath in his body.

Steel picked up the gun and started his way up the

sweeping stairwell towards the prone figure on the mezzanine. Mr Tom emerged from his cowered position behind the reception desk and followed, coming to stand just behind Steel as he crouched over the body.

'He was asking for you, Jeff.' Mr Tom enlightened him soberly. 'His name's Dinsengwayo, from some diamond association or other.'

Steel nodded pensively. 'I see.' The connection dawned on him slowly. . . . *Identification. The CSO!*

The bullet had entered near the centre of Dinsengwayo's chest, Steel noted, and his breathing was shallow, subdued.

Dinsengwayo flickered his eyes open at the sound of voices, some scrambled thoughts flooding back again, but fading rapidly, *all so rapidly. The dredger! The young German!* He gripped Steel's hand fiercely, struggling to indicate the foyer. 'The blond man,' he spluttered, continuing almost in a whisper.

'Call an ambulance.' Steel swung around on Mr Tom, leaning still closer.

It formed nothing more than a garbled monotone, but he picked out the phrases, 'unexpected danger' and 'nineteen sixty-five', standing up finally and letting Dinsengwayo settle back again.

Steel looked thoughtfully towards the spread of the foyer below, but Franz Zeifert had already slipped discreetly back through the main entrance, losing himself among the midday bustle of trade further along the Silom Road.

Two thoughts were prevalent: *Karfi! And the automatic rifle on the back window-shelf!*

All else was rapidly diminishing as Steel made his way back down the spiral of steps, a confusion of images fighting his more immediate concerns.

Groups of tourists emerging cautiously from behind the lounge partitions stared at him as he passed, alarmed by his frighteningly intense expression.

Steel checked the magazine as he picked up speed across the foyer . . . *three shots!* He slammed it back home firmly, gritting his teeth against the ever-building pain in his thigh, his leg dragging obstinately with the increased length of each stride.

The doorman, startled by the shots, stepped aside as Steel swung the door wide, mumbling imprecations under his breath.

The grey Toyota was no more than twenty yards away from the main entrance and Steel set his aim swiftly and steadfastly on its back window, adjusting quickly in the starkly contrasting sunlight to the shadowed figures inside.

Magonde had fixed the main span of the Narao's entrance in the Toyota's wing-mirror, and as he'd anticipated, there had been few arrivals or departures; his increasingly anxious speculation, as the extra minutes passed, turned to panic as Steel appeared.

'Move away . . .' he directed frantically with his ebony stick. 'Move . . . quickly! . . .'

The chauffeur had left the engine running, and rammed into first swiftly, flooring the accelerator hard, joining the sporadic flow of two-lane traffic.

Magonde braced sharply against the abrupt jolt, watching the image of Steel rapidly diminish.

The first shot took out the back window, filling the interior with shards of swirling glass. The second was much quieter – a dull, muffled thud, seeming insignificant by comparison; except that Magonde was faintly surprised by the chauffeur lurching suddenly forwards. His surprise turned to a fast-consuming panic as he watched a sluice of blood spreading in spider strands across the windscreen and dashboard, the car veering wildly off at a tangent.

The oncoming traffic formed a blur, cars and bicycles swerving frantically away, and Magonde was already reaching for the wheel when the sudden futility of the action overwhelmed him; he pushed his feet hard against the floor, lifting himself upwards on the seat away from it, as if in some final, desperate escape, his eyes ever-widening.

The truck was long and split into two open steel trailer-sections and stacked high with teak logs from Lampang. The driver jammed his brakes and blasted his air-horns in a reflex reaction, although he knew instinctively that he would not stop in time.

To Magonde, the front of the truck appeared as a large, glistening steel grille, looming up swiftly like an apocalyptic wall, a solid collision bar protruding, split by bold white ox horns around which garlands of orchids were interlaced; a colourful adornment which hopefully, with the aid of Buddha, would protect the driver from the evil spirits of the road. He became aware of his own voice – distant, detached, indoctrinating the 'brothers' of Amgawi, talking of the inevitability of death, *of its acceptance* . . . a divine preparation for the 'cause', *and yet now*. . . .

The Toyota concertina-ed under the crushing impact, the forty-ton follow-through shunting it forwards like a toy, the mangled grey frame twisting to a side-angle and rolling over twice; although miraculously, as if in final defiance, landing upright. After a second, its petrol tank exploded, spewing a torch of flame high into the air.

The truck remained several yards away, clear of the spreading flames, but its rear trailer had started into a lazy jack-knife from the abrupt halt, the side stanchions splitting and a stack of logs rolling out and tumbling in a confused array on to the Silom Road.

Oncoming cars swerved violently, some seeking the apparent safety of the sidewalk, others braking too late, sliding inexorably into the wreckage of the truck.

Steel held his arm up, both in protection against the bewildering cataclysm and as a shield against the intense sunlight. After a moment, everything appeared to have settled, and Steel made his way swiftly through the confusion towards the Toyota. The flames had died a fraction, but were still blazing fiercely at the back of the car.

A distance of a good ten feet was the closest allowed by the fierce heat and the constant trail of toxic black vapours, but Steel could just make out the figures inside as the smoke was blown across the far side of the car: already heavily discoloured, distended, puffy red blisters covering the skin, mostly bereft of bodily hair – features only recognizable by the solid contours of bone structure beneath. . . . *Magonde!* And on the far side, straining his eyes still further through the billowing haze, *the chauffeur*. The back was still too heavily enveloped in flame, and Steel waited a moment longer before moving closer.

At intervals, there were gaps among the tongues of fire that leaped from behind, licking cruelly around the two heads in the front, but still there was no sign of a figure in the back . . . *Karfi?* The collision had opened up the side passenger door at a crooked angle, and as Steel edged still closer, a partial view of the front seat could be gained. There was a stunted ebony stick gripped tight in Magonde's hands, and the Basikasingo figure, he could see, had rolled out of the glove-compartment and on to the floor. Both were heavily charred, but their basic form was still discernible.

It was the first time that Steel had noticed a similarity . . . *the carved faces!* The same sharp jawline and closed, bulging eyelids – a fleeting, horrific image, accentuated even more by their fiery decomposition. *Demonic! Leering!* And then something else; small at first, but gradually becoming clearer, etched in darkness by the carbon, an inscription on the ebony stick. He could pick out a part of 'memory' and 'Joachim', but the last part, 'January 1965', was much clearer, as was the triangle directly below.

The persistent heat was now almost unbearable. Steel squinted his eyes through the stinging smoke, and the full extent of the back seat gradually became visible to him. . . . *It was empty!*

His mind began to race desperately, and he stepped sharply back from the tangled inferno, swinging wildly around and taking in the length and breadth of the road. *For God's sake . . . where was Karfi?*

Groups of people had amassed now, forming a semi-circle round the spectacle, and very little could be seen past them.

Steel stood in awe for a moment, his thoughts of the past hours gradually gelling. The main questions had been answered, he resolved, breaking abruptly out of his reverie, pushing his way brusquely back through the crowds; but now there were other diverse, more complex questions . . . *Karfi? Ensor? And the blond man that Dinsengwayo had mentioned?*

In the distance, an ambulance was weaving its way through the jumbled maze of traffic, the urgency of its flashing orange light and wailing siren marking its haphazard progress. But as Steel was soon to discover, it was already too late.

Mikeka Dinsengwayo was dead.

The market stalls were crammed into a small recess to one side of the Silom Road. People wandered excitedly among the stalls and Karfi had just paid a merchant for a slice of fresh watermelon, weaving his way swiftly back through the crowd, when the collision occurred: there was a loud buffeting and rending of metal, the explosion sounding only seconds afterwards.

Realization came slowly to Karfi – the colour of the car and the vague form of figures inside. A dull, confused anger began to build up from deep inside, the first sickly sweet juices trickling out copiously as he bit hard into the soft red fruit; Magonde was dead: the cause was dead in the blazing fire of the wreckage. . . . *The Sarakunas!* However, a suddenly renewed glimmer in his dark eyes mirrored a new purpose.

Two other men observed the incident with similar intent – each with their own clandestine interpretations.

Sadrudin Bhakra kept the old apothecary in much the same style that he had done for the past twenty-two years. It was a small wood-framed store set among the labyrinth of streets between Ratchdamneon Avenue and Bamron Ruang Road; it was not a place that you would find easily, unless you knew or had already been informed of its location. A large bay-window displayed an intricate array of herbs and medicinal plants and roots, and the glass itself was etched in gold, announcing the proprietor's name and some of the more notable commodities provided inside.

It was mid-morning and Bhakra looked up with barely concealed bewilderment at the *farang* who entered; a small brass bell above the door served both as an announcement and a distraction from his painstaking crucible-blending of dry powdered chemicals: a wide selection of variously-coloured glass bottles spread in a neat line on the counter-top before him.

'Dy pohm choo-ay koon?' he ventured, following the path of the *farang* deeper into the store with an indignant glance above his wire-frame spectacles. It was rare that *farangs* came in the store, but then there was something different about this particular one. His clothing, normally a point of pristine cleanliness among tourists, was soiled and bloodied, some spots marring even the white of his shoes, Bhakra noted, eyeing the figure closer with an ever-growing and obvious outward disdain. 'Yes?' he prompted again – it was one of the few *farang* words in his vocabulary.

Paul Ensor remained faintly detached, scanning the rows of dusty wooden shelves behind Bhakra, although the Thai inscriptions on the bottles and jars meant little to him. He knew instinctively that the English words would be misinterpreted and pointed to the pen in Bhakra's top pocket. 'If you please?' he forced a smile.

'Bpawk-gap?' Bhakra enquired.

'Yes,' Ensor complied, seeing Bhakra reach for the pen.

'Gra-daht doo-ay!' Bhakra added, passing over a small notepad from under the workbench at the same time.

Ensor wrote the equation down in block print: H_2SO_4. Bhakra was already looking over curiously before he had fully swivelled the pad back around.

'Koon dtawng gahn nee?' Bhakra raised an eyebrow with mounting trepidation at the *farang*'s unusual appearance and wild expression. 'Tahm-my . . . why want this?' he managed finally.

'Gold! . . .' Ensor explained graphically, pointing to his wrist-watch; making his way back from the klong village, he had finally recalled the quantities of the chemical he had supplied to a Mancunian factory producing gold and silver bracelets. 'To etch in gold,' he emphasized, drawing an imaginary pattern across the band with his finger.

'Tawng!' Bhakra exclaimed, picking up on the intimation; it was true – many local goldsmiths and jewellers regularly requested the chemical. His reluctance faded. 'Pohm mee bahng tee.' He pointed to a small back-room. 'One moment.'

Through a small gap in the door, Ensor watched the grey-haired chemist reach for one of the uppermost shelves, climbing down from his short ladder and turning back with the closest he had yet come to a smile. 'Nee bpen mahn!' he indicated the label proudly, setting the bottle down on the counter.

There was a cluster of Thai print that Ensor couldn't understand, but in the corner the symbols H2SO4 were stamped clearly in red ink. 'Yes, good,' he nodded. 'How much?'

'Yee-sip gow baht,' Bhakra said, busying himself with wrapping the bottle in brown wax paper, and then noting Ensor's blank expression he began to indicate with his fingers. A more satisfied smile emerged as Ensor counted out the right money. 'Krahp mahk dee!'

Ensor took his package with an abrupt acknowledgement. 'Thank you.' His attempts at pleasantry suddenly exhausted, he made his way swiftly out.

Within minutes, he had taken a taxi out of the bustling maze of small streets, heading towards the southern reaches of the city and the Hotel Narao.

It was early evening and Steel had booked a call to London over an hour beforehand. There was a gradual sense of everything winding down; the medication a local doctor had provided that afternoon was beginning to take effect, easing the insistent pains and soothing his jaded nerves. He rested back further on the hotel bed, the dull, subdued rays of a side-lamp mellowing the atmosphere. *Nine-twenty for the flight out*, he reminded himself, glancing briefly at his watch – *over three hours to go!* He would pick up the diplomatic pouch from Cullen on the way to the airport. It would be 10 a.m. in London, and Stannard would be completing his morning mail and dealing with any inter-departmental enquiries and memos carried over from the day before.

Rawsthorne had called earlier that morning and had left not only the photographs from the arena but also another file relayed on the wire from London. Steel had called back to determine its original time of arrival, and then, after some mumbled apologies from Rawsthorne regarding the unavoidable delay outside the arena, had confirmed that Rawsthorne would again accompany him after collection of the diplomatic pouch.

And now Steel leafed through the photographs for the third time: *Paul Ensor, Magonde, Deborah Ensor, Karfi.* The photographs appeared particularly clear, vibrant, and it somehow seemed unrealistic that the lives of the people in them could have been shattered so suddenly, so dramatically. For a moment the whirlwind events of the past twenty-four hours played over again in his mind, and then he was turning the last of the photographs, firmly pushing away the pictures in his mind.

As for the file, the details would help towards compilation of a final report, he considered, but nothing more. Steel glanced back briefly through the main points: *Nathan Tomlinson. Black Panthers Oakland Chapter, 1963. Eldridge Cleaver. Ghana. Nkrumah. Amwre Magonde.* Much of the information was what he'd already ascertained, and for a moment he cursed the timing of its arrival; but a small section began to intrigue him more and more – a related snippet of conversation that looked almost out of place with the rest of the report: '. . . Cut and dried months back. They're just going through the motions now.' He turned it over in his mind for a few moments more in silence, cross-referencing it mentally with the main factors of the case, and with more recent, intangible clues: *Joachim, 1965, the triangle*. But with no quickly apparent answer. Then again, whatever had been the full extent of Magonde's plan, the preparations would have been considerable, and perhaps he was making too much of it; the COUNTELPRO source couldn't possibly have known about the events at Heathrow, or for that matter, those since – only a matter of days had passed. After a moment he pushed the file away and turned his thoughts to other concerns.

One of the most harrowing was still that of Paul Ensor, he reminded himself, an earlier call to the Sheraton having confirmed his non-return. Steel began to wonder if Karfi *had* caught up with him during the chase by the klong the night before . . . *only time would tell!* He would inform Cullen of the situation and leave instructions that if nothing had transpired within a few days, a 'trace' should be initiated through the Central Bangkok Police Department. As yet, there had also been no official announcement of the recovery of Deborah Ensor's body, and Cullen had deployed a group of 'staffers' to look at the area in question, but to no avail. 'Either her body's been picked up by some locals, or by a nearby hospital, or by the police, and they're delaying notification for some reason,' Cullen had commented. It was a vexing situation; a premature request for a trace would add an awkward angle to the already complicated questions posed by the events of the past two days, and until an 'official release', he considered, it would be best if the police remained unaware of the full implications. Already they were too heavily involved, and as he'd explained earlier to Mr Tom prior to an intense bout of questioning from Lieutenant Dwaonong – 'The situation is verging dangerously close to diplomatic intervention by local government officials, and until there is some form of liaison with London, the full details should be guarded as much as possible. Till then, Mr Cullen at the British Embassy will vouch satisfactorily for my involvement in these affairs.'

All the same, the loose ends and the clumsy trail of

events would be difficult to explain to Stannard, he concluded, balling his fist hard at his side in concentration; *especially the Ensors.*

It was a pointless deliberation – he glanced back towards the muted light of the table-lamp. The original objectives of the assignment had, to a large extent, been fulfilled, the diamonds returned. The main answers were as apparent as they were ever likely to be: straightforward theft by a Pan-African Liberation group and an ultimate sale to a London-based diamond merchant with the probable intent of financial gain to assist in purchase of arms. The essential body of information could be cross-referenced from file reports on Amgawi and the activities of Dr Magonde.

However, one key factor remained, Steel mused anxiously – one which had been prevalent throughout – the question of 'inside' information. Whoever it was would probably still be there. Still informative. Still lethal. *And still there was Karfi!*

The urgent ringing of the telephone broke his reverie.

The three Thai women were huddled closely over the girl on the makeshift bed. The hut was small and the paraffin lamp at its centre cast insufficient light, so they had lit some candles to one side, the dappled rays somehow making the girl's features appear softer, more frail.

One of the women leant over closer, mopping gently at the girl's brow with a cloth. *Who could do something like this?* she thought concernedly; the girl seemed little more than a teenager. She wiped away the thick, almost constant perspiration with the cloth, then renewed some of the bandages as the doctor had suggested. Another of the women put the bloodied bandages in a pot of boiling water on a stove to one side.

The ambulance would arrive soon, the doctor had informed them; there was nothing more that *he* could do.

The first woman leant over again, mopping more intently at the girl's brow, looking deeply into her cold yet placid expression, feeling her shallow breath fall gently against

457

the back of her hand. Outside, the growing heaviness of the monsoon rains gave the Thai woman a sense of impending doom. It seemed unlikely that the girl would live through the night.

25

The sunlight was dying in the large frame window to one side and Surak could feel a trickle of sweat run down the ridge of his neck as he bowed deeper.

Mongkai looked on impassively. 'Dtawn rahp!' he gestured finally. . . . 'If you would like to take a seat, *ny pohn*.'

'*Kawp Koon*. Yes, thank you, *Bpratahn*.' Surak gave one final small bow, taking one of three indicated chairs arranged in a semi-circle opposite Mongkai's much larger and more ornate high-backed chair.

It was a tedious ritual, but Surak observed the old formalities as he had done through the years past, remaining silent until Mongkai had indicated that he could speak.

Mongkai relished Surak's composure for a moment, reflecting that so many of his other *ny pohns* and most certainly the *tahahns* would show some agitation at such a juncture. 'Mahk sa-by dee,' he said finally. 'So . . . what new arises to bring you here at this stage, *ny pohn?*'

Surak detected displeasure in Mongkai's tone – perhaps because he had not already completed the assignment, he reflected, hastening his reply. 'There is much to tell, *Bpratahn*.' And he sensed from Mongkai's short nod that it had been clearly understood that he would not request such a counsel unless it was absolutely necessary.

He resumed fluently, detailing the total course of events since the initial description of the *farang* Englishman by Pen: the exchange, the chase and the two gunfights. . . .

Mongkai stopped him at one point. '*Ah-ry*. And this Englishman is still alive?'

'Yes,' Surak complied, making it clear exactly who *had* died and the factors that remained. '*Gahp nahp-teu!* As you can see, there is much more involved than was first considered, *Bpratahn.*'

Mongkai stroked his chin thoughtfully. 'This Englishman – you believe he still has the diamonds?'

'Yes.'

'*Dahng nahn.* And the diamonds themselves – you believe them to be real?'

'Yes,' Surak nodded resolutely, his conviction formed by the sequence of events so far. 'It would be unfeasible for so many men to be involved in a mere ruse,' he added with equal certainty.

'It appears that our good friend Mr Pen was correct with his information.' Mongkai looked back towards Surak with obvious intrigue. '*Dee-oh nee!* What of this blond *farang* who, as you say, does no more than observe?'

For the first time, Surak displayed a distinct confidence, smiling faintly. 'There will be no problems in that respect, *Bpratahn.* I am aware of his movements at all times, as with the others. Conversely, *they* are totally unaware of *my* involvement. Such a position offers an obvious advantage, *ney?*'

Mongkai mildly bowed his gratification. 'Yes – an admirable situation.'

'You may also be assured, *Bpratahn*, that with the assistance of good *karma*, I shall maintain this advantage until the task is completed.' Surak looked down as if subduing his sudden enthusiasm. 'There is, however, one matter in which I would particularly value your couselling, *Bpratahn.*'

'Yes?' Mongkai quizzed abruptly, his countenance clouding faintly.

'In order to gain the diamonds, it will probably be necessary to kill the *farang* Englishman.'

Mongkai raised an eyebrow at the irregularity of the comment. 'Do you see a problem in this?'

'No,' Surak shook his head faintly, politely intimating misinterpretation. 'It is just that we know little of this *farang* – we do not know his purpose in this, or *who* he represents. With respect, *Bpratahn*, you yourself have previously cautioned against attack on an "unknown" enemy.'

Mongkai held one hand up in acceptance. 'Of course, you are right to mention this,' he said, quickly recalling the objective of his own dictate: 'Not only were the attributes of an "unknown enemy" likely to be underestimated, but in the case of reprisals, it would be wise to know from which direction they would be likely to come.' '*Peu-uh*. Yes, I see your point,' he added, sinking deeper into contemplation.

He remained in the same position for some moments, once again stroking his chin, his thoughts revolving slowly, painstakingly. *Pen's original visit – and now Surak's added, unusually involved breadth of information.* . . . An intricate web; it was difficult to discern any clear picture. However, one consideration was overriding, as it had been during Pen's initial detailing of the situation – *the possible reward.* . . . 'No,' he stated finally, fixing an intense glare on Surak. 'There is too much involved for us to be put off by such a matter now. You will proceed as agreed in our first meeting. If necessary, you will kill the English *farang*.'

'*Mahk sa-by dee!* Yes – I understand,' Surak said.

'However, as I say, you did well to bring this to my notice,' Mongkai emphasized, not wishing to slight Surak's efforts by implying that requesting counsel had been unnecessary. 'Is there anything else?'

'No, *Bpratahn* – all else is satisfactory.'

'Good. . . . Again I will wish you good fortune, *ny pohn*. Until our next counsel,' he affirmed, making a motion with one hand, 'Sa-wahn laa lohk!'

Surak bowed deeply, crossing his hands in front of him, 'Kawp koon, *Bpratahn*.'

'Koo dy bpy,' Mongkai nodded imperceptibly, and he watched Surak rise and walk away, his even pace echoing slightly among the cavernous extremities of the large room. The door shut quietly behind him.

Mongkai glanced abstractedly through the frame of the side-window, allowing his thoughts to mellow with the fading sunlight, picking out the furthest reaches of the lush tropical gardens which spread in a gentle slope away from the house – a final cluster of coconut palms and a large banyan tree forming a distant boundary. Already the shadows of the garden were heavy. The sky above was streaked with a pale pinky-red.

In another hour it would be dark.

Prime Minister John Vorster sat hunched over the report that General Van den Bergh had laid before him, leafing through the pages slowly, deliberately; occasionally flicking back suddenly, as if seeking some special, specific confirmation. At length, Vorster sat back.

'Quite complete, it would appear.'

'Yes,' Van den Bergh agreed. 'All over, bar the whooping and shouting, if you'll excuse the expression.'

Vorster looked back down the report, and for a moment the previous silence of the small office returned.

'Does this Ghelani fellow answer the internal security questions that arose?'

'Most of them,' Van den Bergh amended slightly. 'At least those that we could have fully expected an answer to on an investigation of this type.'

'And when exactly does Jeffrey Steel return?'

'Early tomorrow morning, London time.'

Vorster paused for a second, considering the information in relation to the report in total. 'So the only remaining questions are the Amgawi henchman and one of the Sowetans.'

'Both of them are only mildly significant,' Van den Bergh said discardingly.

'But wasn't it the Sowetans who diverted the riot to the city centre that day?'

'Yes, they most certainly were in league with the local black student body,' Van den Bergh said sharply, not wishing to be misunderstood. 'But without Magonde they will lack direction. Through this American, Tomlinson, he informed them not only *where*, but also *when* the riots

461

should be staged. With most of them dead. . . .' Van den Bergh paused markedly. 'And, well, likewise with this chap Karfi. Magonde appeared very much his mentor.'

Vorster was staring intently across the table, but Van den Bergh could sense some faint doubt still, and continued. 'You see, as far as we can ascertain, at every juncture – the riots, the assassin in Paris, the cargo-worker in London – Magonde used "outside" contacts in order to shield his true identity and purpose. In addition, in most cases he used Tomlinson to make the contact, thereby making the whole operation particularly faceless.'

'Quite clever, this Magonde,' Vorster commented blandly.

'Yes, but not quite clever enough,' Van den Bergh rejoined, waving his arm towards the report.

Vorster seemed to enjoy Van den Bergh's unexpected hint of acrimony, and for the first time a faint smile eased his heavy seriousness. 'I've never met one who was *that* clever,' he said, and he closed the report in an overtly deliberate motion.

The cover of the file bore the crest of the Republic of South Africa – a lion above the shield of the four provinces with flanking springbok and gemsbok, and underneath the motto, *Ex Unitate Vires* – 'Strength from Unity'. It reminded Prime Minister John Vorster of something from that bygone era – something he had contemplated at some length during the past weeks of uncertainty – a quote from Sir Richard Southey, Cape Colonial Secretary, upon discovery of the Star of South Africa: 'This is the rock upon which the future success of South Africa will be built'. Ironic, he had thought at the time, that diamonds might have also proved to be its downfall.

Franz Zeifert had waited almost three hours to get a call through to Inverness and when it had finally been relayed, he was both disappointed and mildly surprised to hear Jennifer's voice beyond the abrupt, garbled instructions of the operator.

'Yes, Franz, I'm afraid Joseph is in Antwerp – he left just last night.'

Zeifert was already scrambling for a pen and paper. 'I must get in touch with him, Jennifer, it's urgent. Do you know where he's staying?'

'Yes – it's always the same place with Joseph. You know what he's like.'

Zeifert took down the full address, recalling halfway through that it was usually the Plaza Hotel, although on one occasion he remembered him switching to the De Keyser. 'Thanks, Jennifer – I won't talk long, the line's so bad.'

They exchanged some niceties, compared the weather, and he rang off, looking at the phone as if it had caused him some personal injury. It would be too late to put a call through to Antwerp, he thought, considering the relaying procedure just past. He checked his watch: 6:44 p.m. There would be other more immediate matters to deal with, he concluded, deciding quickly on the only alternative which he knew would convey urgency – *a telegram*. He scribbled out a provisional wording below the Plaza's address: *The Africans are out of it. There are some other complications. However, I am still confident of dealing on one of the transfers.*

Joseph Matrai picked up the telegram on returning to the Plaza at lunchtime, a smile coming faintly to his lips as he scanned it, placing the slip of paper snugly in his inside pocket. He took a quick change of clothes and dined at a small restaurant on Frankrijklei, whose eight-course menu was enthusiastically recommended by Egon Ronay.

The meal and the accompanying wine gave him a sense of euphoric self-indulgence, and by mid-afternoon he had crossed the wide avenues of the city centre and was again back among the diamond cloisters of Pelikaanstraat, where for centuries the Hassidic Jews of the city had plied their trade. Matrai recalled his early days of buying in the district, when his efforts had been spurned due to both his ethnic background and unorthodox approach. Now times were different, he considered, the added comfort of the telegram in his pocket augmenting the obscure warmth he already felt deep inside – as if in that sublime moment of realization, the street had suddenly become *his*: the tightly cramped shop fronts, the vaults, the Jews with their homburgs and skull caps, the small black-leather pouches filled with diamonds . . . everything! He felt a sudden overwhelming confidence that the fulfilment of the long years of expectation was at last close at hand.

Things had turned full circle.

There was a pilgrimage to the southern city of Nakhon Sri Thammarat the next day, and Don Muang Airport was heavily crowded with Buddhists from throughout Bangkok and its outlying areas, a wide array of orange robes and orange-and-black umbrellas dotted among the evening's regular travellers.

Steel had checked in his main luggage and was ready to go through customs when the announcement came, barely audible above the massed confusion of voices and movement reverberating from the high ceiling. 'Mr Steel to information desk. . . . Mr Jeffrey Steel, booked on British Airways Flight AJ274 to London, to the information desk, please.'

It took a moment for the full realization to evolve, and then Steel started jostling his way back through the crowds; from midway he could discern the information desk light close to the ticket counters he had just come from, across the far side. He felt someone brush against him, and clutched the diplomatic pouch tighter under his arm. The call couldn't be from Cullen, he thought – their meeting had been too recent, and Cullen was a meticulous planner. All the details would have been covered at the time. He scanned quickly back over the preparations: *The diplomatic pouch – an accompanying gun-permit for protection of the same, on the flight out.* . . . And, of course, an escort. He could still see Rawsthorne standing where he had left him just a few moments beforehand, now looking anxiously above the crowds, following Steel's path, his two-piece black suit and dark tie curiously conspicuous among the

464

colourful milieu. It had also been Cullen's suggestion to issue Rawsthorne with a gun, Steel recalled. A 'better to play it safe' reaction to his explanation of the possible danger remaining – Karfi having gone unaccounted for in the earlier affray.

Rawsthorne, weaving his way hastily through the crowd, caught up with Steel just before the desk. 'What is it?'

'I don't know. I was hoping you might be able to provide the answers. Is your Mr Cullen in the habit of putting through last minute send-offs?'

Rawsthorne's frown deepened. 'I certainly wouldn't think so.'

They reached the desk; on their enquiry, the first clerk directed them further along. The clerk in question appeared mildly preoccupied, but he put his papers aside before Steel had fully completed his introduction and reference to the 'announcement a moment ago'.

'Ah yes, Mr Steel, I have something here for you.' The clerk went to one side and rustled in a drawer, pulling out a key. 'Apparently an item was left for you here in one of our safety deposit boxes,' he added, noting Steel's faintly bemused expression.

'When was this?'

'Only an hour or so ago, sir.'

Karfi? . . . 'Do you remember what he looked like?'

The clerk appeared blank.

Steel leant forwards with obvious outward consternation. 'I mean – was he tall? fat? small? black? white? . . .'

The clerk retained a quizzical countenance. 'He was just a normal Thai, sir. Perhaps, if anything, slightly smaller than the average.'

'I see.' Karfi could have employed a messenger, but then there was the question of communication . . . language? 'Thank you,' he acknowledged the clerk finally, taking the key.

'You'll find the safety deposit area on the far side of the lounge, sir,' the clerk prompted. 'It's just along from the first pay-phones near the main entrance.'

'Yes – thank you.'

'What do you think it might be?' Rawsthorne interjected as they walked away from the desk.

'I don't know yet, I'm still trying to work it out.' And Steel thought again of a *messenger*, but this time from Ensor . . . *a possibility!* Perhaps it was Mr Tom, although again *their* last meeting had been too recent, he considered finally. 'Tell me,' he turned back to Rawsthorne, momentarily dodging a *Pra sohng*'s orange bamboo-frame umbrella perched on the ground, 'I contacted a "liaison operative" in Singapore recently – supposedly the closest we have out here right now. If he wanted to get a message back to me, is it likely he would by-pass the embassy?'

'Depends on the classification,' Rawsthorne suggested casually. 'It's been known to happen before.'

'Yes,' Steel agreed, recalling his own file data on the topic.

A memory of the incident at the Cat Club played fleetingly at the back of his mind, although this, of all the assumptions, he considered the weakest. As Cullen had initially informed him, 'if it was a *tahahn*, there would probably be no repercussions'.

Ahead, there was a small group of *Pra sohngs* by the telephone kiosks, and Steel picked his way through impatiently, Rawsthorne keeping directly behind; there was a wide corridor to their right.

'It's just past the washrooms, on the opposite side,' Rawsthorne pointed out, as Steel came to a halt, reading the Thai inscriptions on a plaque to one side.

The safety deposit room was a small annexe less than ten yards from the main foyer, but that short distance seemed to provide it with a curious insulation, the hubbub behind fading quickly as they approached.

'Do you think it might be this negro chap you're concerned about?' Rawsthorne ventured.

'I don't think so,' Steel responded firmly, and he noticed Rawsthorne reassuringly test the outline of the gun in his jacket. There was something else nagging at Steel's mind;

he pushed it away sharply. 'Still, best to be safe,' he agreed. 'You stay here and keep watch – I'll go inside.'

The annexe was a good forty feet long and thirty wide; its oblong shape was accentuated by three rows of seven-foot-high sectioned-steel units which spread towards the small skylight windows at its far end. The entrance was open, but the interior of the room was obscured from the main lounge, its confines only visible from a section of the corridor just past the washrooms, where Rawsthorne had now positioned himself. Opposite the elongated steel units were three cubicles for 'private inspection', and the units themselves were split into a number of small boxes no more than eight inches square, some larger sections making up the three bottom rows.

Steel started counting his way along, referring from time to time to the plastic tab of the key in his hand: *191*. The numbers at the end were in three digits, he could just make out, and he moved up further, picking them out as he got closer, *156 . . . 163 . . . .*

At that moment a small Thai man dressed in black trousers and a white shirt walked in, making his way swiftly towards the back of the room, seemingly preoccupied with his own purpose, totally ignoring Steel's presence. Steel tensed momentarily, but there was something about the small man's nonchalant, distracted attitude that induced a quick return to his previous thoughts . . . *191*, was all but a few sections from the end, he could see now.

Rawsthorne appeared fleetingly in the entrance, shrugging. 'Probably maintenance or just one of the local labourers,' he muttered.

Steel stood still for a moment, looking back thoughtfully. He heard the man's footsteps shuffling about for a while, and then a door closing at the back of the room. 'Okay,' he nodded.

Rawsthorne took back his position outside.

It was one of the upper deposit boxes and Steel put the diplomatic pouch at his feet, raising himself up slightly and turning the key in the lock.

Suddenly there was darkness.

Steel's heart froze. He'd only had a glimpse of the inside of the safety deposit box. A small envelope lay there.

Instinctively, he found himself looking up at the ceiling – all of the strip-lights had gone out at the same time, he noted, clutching impulsively at his gun, but for the moment leaving it in its holster.

There was some light coming in from the streetlamps of the airport slip-road outside, split into three triangular bars by the skylight windows. It merged faintly with the light coming in from the main entrance, mostly picking out the area between the three cubicles and the first units, the recesses behind merging rapidly into deeper darkness.

Rawsthorne was back in the entrance. 'What happened?'

'I don't know,' Steel snapped. 'Try the switches.'

There was a panel of four to one side of the door, and Rawsthorne flicked them back and forth impatiently.

'Probably a fuse,' Steel commented, glancing up again.

'Yes,' Rawsthorne agreed nervously.

A soft whistling came from somewhere behind them.

The motion was so fast that initially Steel disbelieved what he was seeing, squinting his eyes in the shallow light; but then apparent, *horrifyingly apparent* . . . a thin wire, glistening faintly in loops, trailing around Rawsthorne's neck, drawing sharply back.

Steel drew out his gun.

Rawsthorne's figure stayed frozen for an instant, then lurched backwards in a clumsy motion, his hands flailing upwards desperately, clawing at his own neck.

Sickeningly spellbound . . . motionless. . . .

And then a sharpening of senses, adjusting more to the darkness – the shadows and recesses of the room where Rawsthorne had been only a moment before.

Steel started edging his way down cautiously, and there was a muted gargling and then a faint, insignificant snapping from the depths of the partitioned-off area. Steel felt the small hairs bristle at the back of his neck, but on impulse he picked up pace, suddenly conscious of his growing proximity to the sounds.

Shadows were deeper towards the end, and the sounds died suddenly, giving way to a dark, fathomless silence.

Rawsthorne's legs appeared first, straggling out at an awkward angle, and Steel moved into the space quickly, covering the area behind with his gun. The light was dull, but forms and outlines gradually became discernible. There were two protrusions from the safety deposit units beyond and the pale opalescence of the emulsioned wall at the side, but nothing else – no other shadows . . . *nothing!* Steel kept his position, catching his breath, straining at every sound: the background bustle of the airport lounge, a truck idling its way through a nearby slip-road, a horn beeping somewhere in the distance; but no sounds from within the annexe, no movement . . . *nothing!*

Steel cast his eyes down slowly . . . Rawsthorne's body was split in two at the neck, his head at the far corner of the room, pools of darkness spread unevenly between. Steel felt a nausea rising swiftly from inside, a chain of vomit splattering freely to the marble floor . . . *Haskell!*

Damn, he cursed himself, wiping the last spittle from his mouth, stepping back frenziedly, haphazardly . . . *Karfi?* A vague prior connection with Magonde and Haskell played at the back of his mind; but then he had always assumed that Haskell's death was connected with his drug investigations.

The faint outline of a reflection flickered across the smooth metal units to one side, and Steel was already turning, halting in his retreat towards the entrance.

The sound came from behind this time; scything . . . *whistling.*

At first, it was a tight, constricting sensation, the thin wire looping swiftly around his arm, pulling it away and down. Steel could see his assailant now, highlighted in the ghostly beam from the windows above – small, greased-back hair, black trousers and a white shirt. . . . *The Thai from the back of the room! Why?*

Steel tried desperately to raise his gun and swing it around, but the wire clamped tighter, tugging to one side, cutting quickly through the thick cloth of his jacket, a pencil-line of red emerging lazily and radiating outwards. Pain came in a jolting spasm, and then there was numbness, spreading slowly upwards, the main muscle control collapsing as the wire cut deeper.

Steel's gun clattered to the floor.

In a sharp motion, Steel lurched forwards to ease the tautness, but the wire took up the slack; then, without warning, the small Thai ran forwards, twirling the short black rod in his hand, the wire spinning haphazardly in his path.

Steel put up his other arm to parry the attack, but the small Thai leapt into the air, the blur of a foot hurtling suddenly towards him, striking him solidly in the chest.

The hard metal units formed a solid backstop, but Steel felt all the breath leave his body as he connected – sliding awkwardly to the ground, scrambling . . . *focusing*. It was a few yards to one side, he could just make out in the dull light . . . *his gun*.

The wire was loose, the last length trailing back to the rod, and Steel reached out to the side, rolling his body into the motion. . . .

It came down quickly again, whistling ominously through the air, and it was the first time that Steel could clearly see the object – *a lead ball* – striking the frame of the gun sharply, spinning it further away.

And then reeling swiftly back. . . .

Steel scrambled further along, and the ball whistled down again, smashing into the cabinets behind.

Jesus! A sense of hopelessness gripped him, his pain returning suddenly, dull confusion the only anaesthetic . . . *still further*. . . . If he didn't get away quickly; *if?* He was firmly on his feet and lurching towards the far end of the room and the skylight windows, when it came back again . . . a soft whistling and a clattering of metal from somewhere in the darkness.

The small Thai was silhouetted in the light from the entrance he could see now, and he suddenly realized that *he* formed a similar outline with the backlight of the skylight windows. He couldn't make out the black rod or the wire anymore.

But his own silhouette!

He lunged frantically away from the stark beams of light, but the wire seemed to whistle more urgently than before, and suddenly he could feel something light around his neck, trailing rapidly and then pulling taut, constricting . . . *cutting!* There was a cloud in his mind and a heavy palpitation from deep inside. The wire reeled inwards swiftly, taking up the slack, but still a loop appeared, the tension easing slightly. Steel fought to spin his head out, clawing desperately at the loose trailings.

The small Thai spun into the air again, and his foot came from a different angle this time; a solid impact, catching Steel to one side, throwing him suddenly back. . . .

Steel felt something give way behind him, and then flap sharply back – an oblong of darkness, five-foot high . . . *a cubicle door!* Then he slammed into the rear wall, jolting the last fight from his body, and suddenly he was sliding slowly and clumsily to the marble floor. The wire became taut again, scything cruelly into the flesh of his neck.

Everything was clouding. . . .

There was a small gap beneath the door, the faint light from outside spilling in widening bands in front of it, back towards the entrance. Two suddenly brighter flashes came from the side; dull, muffled thuds coinciding, breaking the silence.

At first, Steel attached little significance to the sounds, his thoughts clouding still further. He was aware of the weakness of his own body, a trail of blood running rapidly from his neck, warm and moist beneath him. For a moment, he was back in the klong, among its muddy depths, clawing upwards. . . .

The wire slackened suddenly and Steel could see the small Thai's body slump awkwardly to one side, a dull hole opened up like a ragged plum in one side of his face. A curious silence returned and Steel became aware of footsteps to one side. . . .

They moved out from the thicker band of light, across to the far side of the room . . . *the diplomatic pouch!*

The darkness was thick, enveloping, and for a moment Steel was unsure of the colour of the hand reaching out among the shadows, picking up the pouch. The figure straightened and walked closer, crouching low over the body of the Thai, and in that same instant a fawn-coloured trilby hat fell deftly and silently to the floor . . . *Karfi!* In a minute, it would all be over, the door would open. . . .

The figure straightened.

But then there was something else, at first indiscernible among the heavy shadows: the shoes. *The shoes were white!* And he remembered the boat at the floating market. The few brief, flurried motions underneath the taxi by the klong. *But the hat?*

The figure was moving still closer, now highlighted more distinctly by the beam of light from outside.

The conflict of thoughts momentarily confused Steel, and when he finally did attempt to make a sound, the constriction in his throat dragged it back down, a weak groan finally emanating.

The white shoes stopped in their path for a moment, as though a decision were forming, and then turned resolutely and walked away. . . .

Back towards the square of light.

Paul Ensor felt that everyone was looking at him – but suddenly it didn't matter anymore . . . *Deborah! Karfi!* It was all finished and a black emptiness replaced the burning purpose that for the last hours had driven him onwards . . . *onwards!*

He pushed his way back through the crowds of the airport, people turning . . . *staring!* The orange robes were a blur to his vision, becoming a background. . . . *And voices – strange, empty.* . . . All merging together in a deafening clamour.

He could just pick out the entrance ahead, and he moved quickly towards it, clutching the leather pouch tighter under his arm; but suddenly there was another man among the crowds, fighting his way purposefully towards him, his eyes fixed on *him*, unlike the others, unflinching . . . *determined!*

At intervals, he could see the man above the others, peering over, weaving through the mass more frantically, coming to cut across his path. He veered to one side, but the man only increased his pace, and then suddenly, as with everything else, it didn't matter anymore. . . . *It was unimportant.* He stopped.

The man slowed the last few steps, advancing his hand warmly in greeting. 'Good evening – my name's Franz Zeifert.'

Epilogue

Leon Magonde sat in a chair before his dressing-table, which for the last long months had been his desk and, to a large extent, his own private world. A bookcase to one side was stacked with magazines and popular paperbacks; but here and there, interspersed discreetly, were books relating to Ghana and Amgawi, *The Teachings of Karl Marx, Cuba Since the Revolution*. Even more discreet was the false bottom to one of the drawers, under which were duplicate keys to the main safe of the large house.

Leon started opening the letter. Amwre was dead! . . . He had feared as much when he had first seen the postmark. It seemed that his whole life revolved around letters. The last to arrive in such a manner had been the start of eleven years of work; of scheming, *planning!*

Oh God! Why? . . .

'If you are reading this, then you will know . . .' the first line started. Leon read on, absorbing each word as if it were in an ancient script, viewed for the first time, his eyes becoming increasingly heavy as the words gained breadth and meaning. 'It is now too late for us to supply arms to our brothers in the same way', he read from the second paragraph. 'We have been cheated most cruelly, but the fight must go on. . . .'

Leon had thought as much himself, on their first dealings with Matrai. 'He will go only where the money and power lead him,' he had warned Amwre at the time.

'And it is that and that alone which will make him so vulnerable,' Amwre had responded elatedly. 'He will become a victim of his own capitalist instincts.'

Leon remembered, in particular, the unusual way in which they had finally discovered the whereabouts of Joseph Matrai – an article in London's *Sunday Times*, which Amwre, since Oxford, had continued subscribing to with some regularity: an appendage to the main 'Home News' section, detailing the inheritance of one of Scotland's largest land estates.

It was even more fortuitous in its timing, Leon mused, coming just after they had succeeded in getting closer to Vansen, the first outline details of Consortium activities beginning to filter through. Amwre had gone to investigate, commenting early on, 'Our friend Mr Matrai and his German colleague still appear to be involved with diamonds.' And then after months of longer, more detailed enquiries: 'Joseph Matrai, it seems, is one of Europe's leading private diamond merchants. On occasions, he hoards large quantities of gems for both personal control and financial gain.'

It was another three years before the final parts of the plan began to knit together, and Amwre was eager to point out the significance of Joseph Matrai's 'hoarding' practice. 'It is ideal. He would not be able to resist the tremendous power and control that the Consortium diamonds would give him. That alone will ensure us of a ready outlet and a good price to support our arms-purchasing. Then we will implement our final action – the emergent nations of Africa, like Amgawi, will be freed. In the process, our two capitalists, Vansen and Matrai, will be thwarted.'

It was thoughts of that final action that brought Leon to the last paragraph. 'It was instructed that this letter would be sent to you from Ghana upon my death. At the same time, another letter would be sent by our good colleague, Diallo Telli – one which we have spoken of many times through the years past. A copy is enclosed. . . .'

Leon flicked over to the page beneath. It was addressed to *Viktor G Afanasyev – PRAVDA – Moskva – UI Pravdy 24 – USSR*.

He read the body of print furiously, his nerves tensing with every word, clutching the paper even tighter. The culmination of their years of tedious investigation – a lucid documentation of background activities and minutiae related to 'an illegal South African Consortium formed as a false protection to "free world" diamond trade and openly condoned by the CSO and Western governments'.

Leon held the page down, his eyes fixed towards some distant inanimate object. In a few days forty million people in Russia would read the story. The news agency, TASS, would promptly spread the story out of the Eastern Bloc, and by the end of the week it would be read over coffee and bread rolls in every major city throughout the world. Matrai's attempt to blackmail the Consortium would be rendered futile. He would be ruined. The first part of Magonde's revenge would be complete. *Stock-marketeers would go running! Diamond prices would tumble!* The South African economy would be jeopardised. Mines would close down. There would be industrial unrest, even mass violence, a situation ripe for exploitation. The emergent diamond nations of Africa would either become independent or would form an alliance with Soviet trade. . . . *The 'cause' was nearing an end!*

Leon Magonde looked back to the first page of the letter, reading the last line with a final, reverent intent. . . .

'As you know, Leon, there is only one detail remaining . . . .'

It was as if all the events were being played back. At first they were the same as in the hospital a week before: of Christine, of Edenbridge. But somehow *Edenbridge* merged into the nightmare with Magonde, and it was then that everything else recurred – the past week seeming to take up large, disproportionate segments of his life.

Steel remembered awaking at some time in the darkness, glancing over at some faint pencils of light coming in at the far end of the room, straining to identify the sounds from outside: a car passing, a railway, a dog barking somewhere in the distance. They were *London* noises, he realized, the other points of reality flooding back, the first hospital in Bangkok, Cullen, the flight over. When he was conscious, he could remember all the other times he had awoken, but then when he slipped back again, the dreams seemed to cloud all else.

At some time during the following day Kenton called, mentioning something about Deborah Ensor and 'the large negro that Cullen had described'. There was a file and a photograph that Kenton had passed across, but Steel didn't look at them till later, till the cloud in his mind had faded sufficiently for him to concentrate; then studying intently, drinking in every word . . . *Deborah Ensor was still alive. . . . Based on available evidence, Paul Ensor killed the large negro. . . .* It didn't make sense! And then he remembered Deborah's small movement by the klong that night. He looked hastily at the photograph, which according to the file had been taken at the back of one of Don Muang Airport's loading bays. It was most certainly the large negro, he could make out, even though the features were grossly distorted, reminding him somehow of a hallowe'en mask he had seen melting on a bonfire as a child. The hat had obviously been a deliberate signal by Ensor – and the gun he used had been Karfi's. The file answered some of the questions: *Acid! Revenge!* The cloud returned, the same dream merging slowly with the image in the photograph.

Then it was the next day, the events in between hazy, distorted, and Kenton was there again, trying to fill in the gaps. . . . Deborah Ensor had been found without any identification by some locals, thus the delay. . . . There had been serious internal bleeding and for a few days she'd been on the danger list, but she'd pulled through. . . .

It was another two days before he saw Kenton again, *or was it three?* He only remembered the main points of the conversation. . . . The CSO had received a ransom demand . . . Paul Ensor had been apprehended in Jakarta, en route to Sydney, after having passed on the diamonds. He'd taken them because they had been used as a ransom for his wife, and when he thought she was dead he seized them in revenge. . . . As for the Thai in the annexe, Ensor wasn't sure exactly what would confront him at the time – whether Magonde or Bature were still alive. It was shock more than anything else. . . . 'If we can come to some form of agreement with the diamond merchant, we won't be pressing charges . . . and Ensor will receive the equivalent of a recovery fee.'

It took a while for all the details to sink in. Afterwards, Steel couldn't help wondering whether the explanation of motive had come from Ensor himself, or as a result of circumstancial deduction by Kenton and whatever psychoanalysts the SIS had deemed necessary to call in. It didn't matter. To them the case would seem so neatly packaged – the London diamond merchant traced, the Ensors' silence guaranteed under threat of proceedings, all members of the 'African liberation group' either dead or in custody. That was all that was important now, he cursed inwardly, a neat file; something that would look good in the records, the annals, 'cut and dried and taped and packaged. . . .' 'Complete and, in the light of the circumstances, satisfactory,' Stannard would no doubt remark. But for the Ensors it could be neither. Steel wondered how they could rebuild their lives. For Deborah, there would be those lingering memories of betrayal and abandonment; the only salve would be the realization of how much Paul had been manipulated, and of how when he thought her dead, his obsessive love for her had temporarily unhinged him. They were both back in Manchester, Steel saw from the file: Deborah in hospital and Paul at home – presumably alone with his thoughts. He wondered if Stannard or Kenton would offer them any official explanation. If they didn't he knew now that he would send his own, personal note.

Something began to nag at the back of his mind in the passing hours: the report from the first London boardroom meeting had stated that the Russians would only supply *organized* rebel forces with arms, and while it was true that a large injection of capital would make Amgawi's rebel force appear more organized, Magonde had mentioned South Africa exaggerating the *implications*. . . . If he was aware of those much deeper implications, why would he satisfy himself purely with a supply of arms?

And it was then, at some time in the depth of the night, that other parts of the conversation and the events following recurred . . . *'the brotherhood'*, *1965*, *Joachim*, *the triangle*. *Joachim*, he recalled, was the name of Magonde's brother who had died before the height of the first Amgawi revolution. *1965*, if he remembered well, was the year of his death . . . and then at length he found himself contemplating *the triangle*. His first thought was its depiction of Bangkok's 'Golden Triangle' but then, he reminded himself, Magonde couldn't possibly have been aware of that. Perhaps it represented the nations of the three rebel contingents: Amgawi and Ghana as the first African nations to gain independence; America as the country, which in media terms, had most expounded the theories of 'Black Consciousness'; and South Africa, the last bastion of white minority rule.

If that was the case, he thought, Magonde had over-estimated the implications equally as much as the South African hierarchy had, but ironically, for almost totally opposed reasons. As for the 'outside agencies', they had played 'piggy-in-the-middle', split between their commitment to Third World advancement, their opposition to the apartheid system, and their maintenance of South Africa's natural resources under the Western Free Trade umbrella. But then somehow *all* the ironies were complete: Magonde based his strategy on meticulous planning and yet had overlooked those very contingencies which could not be controlled. South Africa had inveigled the help of 'outside agencies' by exaggerating the circumstances, and yet would now have to bear the brunt of those very same *circumstances*. And the agencies themselves had looked upon Magonde as just another black African megalomaniac, intent on a highly predictable armed struggle, ignoring whatever more complex motives might exist.

Steel remembered the thoughts coming slowly, but in a

clear, logical sequence, as if the long hours in the hospital bed had allowed them to fall suddenly into place; but then at some point he stopped . . . a memory from his sub-conscious surfacing . . . *1965?* Dinsengwayo had mentioned the same year in his dying breath! And he could have kicked himself – the implications and motives had suddenly been so clear that he knew *why*, but not *how* or *where*, and it was then that other segments of Magonde's conversation came flooding back. . . . 'My brother's vow to the cause, as with mine, is undying' . . . . Of course, that was what was wrong, what had seemed so terribly out of place – *it was in the present tense!* And yet Joachim Magonde had been dead for over ten years. He could vaguely recall the mention of another brother from one of the files, but *he* had never been considered politically active in quite the same way.

It seemed hours that he lay there in the darkness, staring blankly at the faint slats of light on the far side of the room, and he fell asleep almost without realizing it, the same thoughts jumbling haphazardly with the dreams of earlier nights. Then suddenly he was wide awake again, some more of Magonde's words playing starkly through his mind. . . . 'That is not the case with our "brotherhood". We have been the servants for too long. Now is the time for a direct, ironic reversal. . . .'

Who else would be virtually beyond suspicion, Steel mused, especially with so little file data available? . . . 'All the Consortium employees have been checked – they're clean. The President keeps a duplicate batch of "finger-print" transparencies in a private safe as an added protection against an internal fraud,' he remembered from Ostermeir's initial briefing. *Yet another irony!*

Steel called for a nurse to bring a telephone to his bedside. It was five or six in the morning, he judged from the depth of light now coming in through the window, and he awoke Kenton at home, explaining his thoughts as quickly and concisely as possible.

'I can only notify Ostermeir – he's our only point of direct contact,' Kenton commented, and in the following minutes he tried to put a call through to Johannesburg.

But the line was engaged.

Bradley Vansen secured himself in the small office at the end of the regency-style vestibule. He set up a tape-recorder to one side, and once again began leafing through the file spread out at the centre of his desk. . . . *It made no sense!* Now, even more than with the first report, he thought, picking his way through anxiously, scanning details at random . . . *Mikeka dead!* A British agent seriously injured, and a British tourist . . . *a tourist!* finally taking the diamonds. Its reading appeared as ridiculous as it had done first thing that morning, he considered, but still it lay there, looking back at him as if in some final defiant glory.

Damn! he cursed, smashing his fist hard into the desk-top. . . . *And where the hell was Amgawi?* He glanced indignantly at a map of Africa on the side-wall, picking out the irregular spread of blue pins. . . . *Oh yes*, he had a plant there, he recalled finally. Amgawi had been the new name since independence. He turned back a page, again studying the reference: 'An initial theft engineered and executed by members of the "People's Liberation Army of Amgawi" and aided by local Sowetan rebels; the combined forces headed by Dr Amwre Magonde, a prominent North-West African revolutionary figure. A prime motive appeared to be the intended sale of the goods to a London diamond merchant in order to finance arms, although our information does not fully expound this particular connection or its possible implications. . . .'

Vansen looked up . . . *Magonde? Dr Amwre Magonde?* The name meant nothing to him. Still, it was the only part of the report to hold any substance, he contemplated – there were so many other small details which seemed to have little or no immediate relevance: *The possible involvement of a local "bandit"? . . . A blond man that Mikeka had appeared concerned about in his dying moments? . . . The murder of a CIA agent, Gene Haskell?*

And on a more pertinent note, there was still the daunting

question of 'inside information', the report aptly pointed out, *perhaps now more than ever!*

Vansen tore himself away, his thoughts spiralling once more into confusion. . . . *And now this*, he reminded himself, tentatively reaching for the cassette to one side. . . . *A ransom!*

'The original, of course, is still being held at the CSO headquarters in London,' Jan Ostermeir had informed him. A clear indication that if he didn't approve the conditions, the CSO *would*. 'They're very concerned about preserving present relationships,' Ostermeir had added unnecessarily. . . . *At all costs, business must go on!* Vansen goaded himself, slotting the cassette into the recorder mouth, flapping it down and pressing 'Play'. . . .

He had put off playing the tape earlier. The main details of the ransom were contained in the report: two thousand, six hundred million Swiss francs was the amount involved – payment to be made to a Zürich bank. If the requirements were not met, offloading of selected gems would begin in key markets. . . . *What else was there to know?*

The voice on the tape droned on.

Vansen leant back into the rich leather of his swivel chair, staring abstractedly towards the map of Africa on the wall, some thoughts of Mikeka revolving as an ethereal background to his listening. . . . *The early days. . . . The spread of his acquisitions!*

It all seemed so distant now. . . .

At first it was only a small sign – a change in intonation. Vansen leant forwards, stopping the tape abruptly, winding it back . . . pressing 'Play' again.

It came clearer this time: a rounding of vowels – an edge to the consonants, a certain European 'thickness' among the undertones, becoming more distinct as he listened closer, his thoughts panning frantically back through the years. . . .

Where? . . . When?

He stopped the tape again and played it back with increasing absorption, listening closer on the same group of words, picking out the individual syllables; the phrase 'hopefully the arrangement' nagging persistently at the back of his mind. . . . And then suddenly a picture began to emerge, although he knew immediately that if it hadn't been for his premonition of the past years, he would never have recognized the significance . . . *1965! . . . The dredger!* The young Hungarian had used the same words on that first day in his Kimberley office.

In that same frenetic instant, a much larger significance overwhelmed him: *the blond man that Mikeka had seen in Bangkok. . . . The full meaning of his premonition! Now here. . . . Here!*

Vansen clutched at the telephone to one side, punching out the numbers fiercely.

The dialling signal was long and monotonous, seeming to defy his increasing urgency.

A female voice tinkled finally at the other end. 'State Security, Section Four.'

'Colonel Ostermeir, please.'

'And who should I say is calling?'

'Bradley Vansen.'

'One moment, please.'

There was a short pause and then a curt, familiar voice came through, 'Yes?'

'Colonel Ostermeir – Bradley Vansen here. . . .'

A faint cough. 'Yes, Mr Vansen – obviously you received the file?'

'Yes.'

'It was sent by courier last night,' Ostermeir commented, as though confirming that already-accepted efficiency.

'Yes, yes, it's not that,' Vansen muttered impatiently, casting his eyes down. 'It's something on the tape – the voice itself. . . . I've played it over and over again and there's no longer any possible mistake. . . .'

At that moment, the door to the office opened and Vansen's servant stood in the entrance, formal and pristine in his starched white uniform.

'One moment.' Vansen broke off, and he covered the

mouthpiece with one hand, lifting an inquisitive eyebrow. 'Yes. . . ? I am busy, you know.'

The servant stayed in the doorway, unmoving. Then slowly he began to smile, and for the first time Vansen noticed the object in his right hand – *a gun*, raised swiftly, pointing . . . *aiming*.

Vansen held up an arm in a weak, futile defence, and he felt a warmth exploding in his chest – and then a second, although he was on the floor now, and the room was spinning slowly around, *around*. . . . But gradually, with each revolution, it became darker, and then finally all that he could see clearly were the faces of the two prospectors . . . *the Hungarian, the young German*; though, somehow, their haunting expressions seemed to share his surprise.

Leon Magonde turned from the doorway and walked back along the lonely recesses of the hallway. By midnight, he would have boarded a plane to Lagos. All the details were complete. The 'cause' would take its path.

In Johannesburg's Pritchard Street, above the clattering of typewriters from an adjoining office, Jan Ostermeir had heard the muffled conglomeration of sounds, but now everything was silent.

'Mr Vansen,' he called urgently after a second.

There was no answer.

A faint sound alerted him momentarily, but just as quickly it was gone. The only sound was some interference on the line.

'Vansen!' he spat again, but the silence returned, quickly enveloping him.

Ostermeir was about to place the receiver back, when he became slowly aware of something beyond the faint 'seashell' noises on the line, and he controlled his breathing, trying frantically to dampen the whispers of his body, straining his hearing past the background noises and shallow echoes.

Finally he recognized it – faint and barely discernible.

It was the sound of somebody breathing.

Other Arrow Books of interest:

ENEMIES

Richard Harris

'It starts out like a Hitchcock story . . .' *Newsday*

'. . . it grips like a fist . . .' *Cosmopolitan*

'. . . and the ending is a real shocker' *Chicago Tribune*

Until the morning that he woke up in the gutter beside the corpse of a woman he didn't know, John Flood's greatest enemy had always been himself. Then suddenly he was the only friend he had. Overnight, he had become a fugitive, a man hunted on all sides, with no one left to trust. For John Flood had stumbled upon the most horrific secret in history – a conspiracy too appalling to be believed, and too frightening not to be believed. For John Flood, what begins as a nightmare will end as a soft, apocalyptic scream.

£1.60

THE SECOND LADY

Irving Wallace

From the author of such world bestsellers as *The Word*, *The Prize* and *The Fan Club* comes a searing novel of the most intimate duplicity – and of the deadliest deception.

Billie Bradford is beautiful, intelligent, enchanting and the First Lady of the United States. In Russia there exists a woman who is her exact double, down to the most secret detail. They call her the Second Lady.

It is the Second Lady who will share the Presidential spotlight, who will be privy to state secrets and who will sleep in the President's bed . . . just long enough to tip the balance of power away from the West. While the real Billie Bradford must fight her ruthless jailers in a foreign land – with the only weapon she has . . .

£1.75

THE BETTER ANGELS

Charles McCarry

Women have always wanted and adored Julian. Men have always feared and envied him. He is the second most powerful man in the United States and nations turn on his decisions. No one knows better than Julian Hubbard the realities of America towards the end of the twentieth century: ruthless politics, corrupted causes and deadly ideals.

But on the eve of a Presidential election, America faces a threat that could destroy democracy. As terrorism, violence and viciousness erupt on the campaign trail, Julian Hubbard becomes the focus of a desperate moral dilemma.

Thought-provoking and superbly written, *The Better Angels* is an unforgettable novel of ideas, character and shattering suspense.

'Taut and exciting'   *Daily Mail*

'Ruthless and sophisticated . . . sharply readable'   *Guardian*

£1·50

DEATH OF A POLITICIAN

Richard Condon

Walter Bodmor Slurrie was ex-Vice President, ex-Senator, ex-Congressman – and he was going to be the next President. Until he became the ex-Walter Bodmor Slurrie.

His death could have been ordered by a number of organizations – from the KGB to the CIA, from the Mafia to the Secret Police. He could have been killed by one of his many enemies, or one of his rather fewer friends.

A suspense thriller in the highest Condon tradition, *Death of a Politician* is a novel about America – about those who own it, run it and occasionally rent it out to their fellow citizen.

'There are few funnier Americans than Condon' *Observer*

'Condon writes wildly funny, exuberant yet elegantly controlled and devastatingly accurate satires' *Tribune*

£1.50

THE VALHALLA EXCHANGE

Harry Patterson

Fact!
Dawn April 30th 1945. Russian radar reports a light aircraft
leaving one of the last strongholds in besieged Berlin –
passengers and destination unknown.

Fiction?
In a concret bunker beneath the burning city, Reichsleiter
Martin Bormann assembles a crack team to fly him out of a
tightening Soviet ring around the capital. Objective – the
medieval fortress of Arlberg where a group of VIP prisoners
are to be used as bargaining counters in the epic struggle to
come.

'Patterson is in his element here, with lots of fast, fierce
fighting, subterfuge and inside betrayals.'
Publishers Weekly

£1.50

TO CATCH A KING

Harry Patterson

His previous bestsellers include *The Eagle has Landed*, *The Valhalla Exchange* and *Storm Warning*. Now Harry Patterson (alias Jack Higgins) has transformed the facts of history into his most compelling thriller to date.

July 1940. While the world awaits the invasion of England, a plot unfolds in Lisbon that could change the course of the war. Its instigator: Adolf Hitler. Its target: the Duke of Windsor. Its aim: to catch a king. Only one man could have conceived of so daring, so deadly a plot. Only the maddest moments of history could have made it possible.

£1·10

TWILIGHT STRIKE

Michael Stewart

The perfect assassination. He is the last dictator in Europe –
a man both revered and reviled. It will be a simple act of
political passion, an unextraordinary murder by extremists . . .

But what if the ageing leader has been planning an alliance
that could cause World War III? What if both super powers
need him dead? And what if the twilight strike itself conceals a
mission that is even more sinister?

Caught up in a global nightmare of betrayal and conspiracy is
one man with a desperate personal stake in the outcome.

£1.25

THE D'ARTAGNAN SIGNATURE

Robert Rostand

A dying man whispers a name to his torturers and the hunt begins for the D'Artagnan signature – the power of attorney that will authorize the release of a fortune from a Swiss bank.

It is money tainted by violence, money extorted by the OAS to fund its reign of terror in Algeria; and now the scent of death is strong once more as old hatreds flare and blood-feuds are revived.

Again, the innocent are to be entangled along with the guilty, as the hunters – and those who hunt the hunters – draw close to their goal.

£1.50

BESTSELLERS FROM ARROW

All these books are available from your bookshop or newsagent or you can order them direct. Just tick the titles you want and complete the form below.

A CHOICE OF CATASTROPHIES	Isaac Asimov	£1.95
BRUACH BLEND	Lillian Beckwith	95p
THE HISTORY MAN	Malcolm Bradbury	£1.60
A LITTLE ZIT ON THE SIDE	Jasper Carrott	£1.25
EENY MEENY MINEY MOLE	Marcel A'Agneau	£1.50
HERO	Leslie Deane	£1.75
TRAVELS WITH FORTUNE	Christine Dodwell	£1.50
11th ARROW BOOK OF CROSSWORDS	Frank Henchard	95p
THE LOW CALORIE MENU BOOK	Joyce Hughes	90p
THE PALMISTRY OF LOVE	David Brandon-Jones	£1.50
DEATH DREAMS	William Katz	£1.25
PASSAGE TO MUTINY	Alexander Kent	£1.50
HEARTSOUNDS	Marth Weinman Lear	£1.75
LOOSELY ENGAGED	Christopher Matthew	£1.25
HARLOT	Margaret Pemberton	£1.60
TALES FROM A LONG ROOM	Peter Tinniswood	£1.50
INCIDENT ON ATH	E. C. Tubb	£1.15
THE SECOND LADY	Irving Wallace	£1.75
STAND BY YOUR MAN	Tammy Wynette	£1.75
DEATH ON ACCOUNT	Margaret Yorke	£1.00

Postage

Total

ARROW BOOKS, BOOKSERVICE BY POST, PO BOX 29, DOUGLAS, ISLE OF MAN, BRITISH ISLES

Please enclose a cheque or postal order made out to Arrow Books Limited for the amount due including 10p per book for postage and packing for orders within the UK and 12p for overseas orders.

Please print clearly

NAME ....

ADDRESS..

....

Whilst every effort is made to keep prices down and to keep popular books in print, Arrow Books cannot guarantee that prices will be the same as those advertised here or that the books will be available.